About the Author

Ivana Christman decisively opened up her computer just after her fortieth birthday and wrote a story she considered for twenty years. Her goal was to author a book that was suspenseful, exhilarating and emotionally gripping. Ivana is an owner and the President of a management company in the mid-Atlantic where she can be creative, but with limitation. Writing *Under the Elm* was the first chance for her to focus on a passion project without dictation from the outside world; allowing imagination without limitation. After many moves, Ivana now lives with her husband and children back in Indiana, enjoying life's journey.

Under the Elm

Ivana Christman

Under the Elm

Olympia Publishers
London

www.olympiapublishers.com

OLYMPIA PAPERBACK EDITION

A CIP catalogue record for this
title is available from the British
Library.

ISBN: 978-1-80439-462-5

First Published in 2024

Olympia Publishers
Tallis House
2 Tallis Street
London
EC4Y 0AB

Printed in Great Britain

Dedication

I dedicate this book to anyone who hasn't quite found their place yet in this world. Don't compare yourself to anyone; be kind, be happy, be yourself.

Acknowledgements

Thank you to my husband, Adam. You love all my weirdness and continue to support me through every new adventure. You are my favorite, forever and always.

Chapter One

The Elm Tree

"You have three choices here; I shoot you dead where you sit and I make a shallow grave for you, you turn your sick and perverted ass into the police to rot in jail, or you fucking run and you run fast; you run far… you get the hell out of this place and never show your face again."

I could hear the words clearly, but the voices were distorted. As I was hidden behind the stack of firewood, my body trembled. What was I looking at? Who was I looking at? I didn't recognize the silhouettes, but my vantagepoint was limited. I could see the man in the center held a shotgun over his shoulder, but I couldn't see if the other two men were armed. The cornstalks were tall and obstructed my view. The men stood on the large embankment by the overgrown elm tree that the farmer who leased the land used as his area to rest when tending to the crops. This small section of the field was too steep, and the soil puddled and deteriorated during rainstorms, so, the crop was planted all around this small half-acre that offered nothing more than a picturesque scene. The tree was large, and the branches sprawled outwards to offer considerable shade. I had never seen anyone there but Jack the farmer. These men didn't belong there, and my gut was telling me something very bad was going on.

We bought the over three-hundred-acre estate about eighteen

years ago, when my oldest brother was just a toddler, and my parents were getting ready to have another baby. My dad said that my mom wanted land in this precise area of town and even knocked on doors asking if anyone was looking to sell. She did this for over two years; adamant that this was where she was going to raise her kids. They didn't have a big budget, so when she knocked on the door to the house we live in now, and the family said they owned all the three hundred acres along with the house, my mom was disheartened because that was too much for them to afford, let alone take care of. But, as they talked more, the previous owner explained that the land in the back was managed by another farmer and his lease agreement was actually profitable to him and it might still be an option for them to buy. My mom used their phone to call my dad and they made an offer that day. My dad said my mom cried the day they moved in, because it was the exact area of town she had wanted, but never dreamed she could live there. She always said it was the pregnancy hormones that made her so emotional over it, my dad says otherwise.

My parents were from a much larger town north of here and were total city dwellers before moving. Dad said from the day they got engaged, my mom said she wanted to move to this town to raise her family. Neither of them ever explained what drew her here, but Dad loved her so much he didn't care where they lived. As long as she was happy.

The land has been maintained since before we moved here, all by the same family who live just down the street. Jack was there long before we bought it and even though he is much slower and needs more help these days, he is active and involved in the crops. He is old and surely past a reasonable retirement age, but he is consistently in the fields doing the work of a man half his age.

Jack and his wife lived opposite side of FM250, the main road to access our house and his, where he grew up. He lived a few miles away after he returned from military service when he was first married Edna, but still worked the land with his dad. His parents both died at relatively young ages, so he moved back into their house and became a farmer full time shortly after.

Jack and Edna have four grown children, who I don't believe have much to do with the farm any more. Their house sits on around two hundred acres where they have corn on most of it, but have carved out a section for a few cattle, chickens, and a small garden his wife tends to. He doesn't sell his cows too often, but when crop production is down, my dad and some of his friends will buy a half cow or more for the deep freeze to help him get by. Jack is a genuinely lovely man that I remember being around most of my life. His wife always pays us children compliments when we see her, which I know makes my parents proud.

Jack has been farming his farm and our land for a little over thirty years now, with no plan to stop any time soon. Jack and Edna are like family to us.

Growing up, Jack would stop when he would see us in the wooded part of the field and tell us stories of tire swings he made for his kids on this tree, or a tree fort his oldest built out of old metal and wood scraps over in another corner. It seemed he knew everything that had ever happened in those fields and everyone who stepped foot on that soil. It was his land as much as ours. We loved his stories; he had a raspy voice, searing blue eyes and when he told stories you just couldn't look away. They always ended with a hook leaving us on the edge of our seats but then he would tell us he would finish it next time we saw him. He always kept his promise.

When my parents first met with him about his lease and the crops, he mentioned this place under the elm tree. He discussed everything about his farming methods in a businesslike manner, but when he spoke about the elm tree, he lit up and it became more personal. He said that he looked forward to his lunch under that tree every day, but he most valued the days when his wife would meet him there for a picnic together. He wanted to be sure that his lease contract could continue under our ownership, but he was just as concerned that we would leave this little spot for him to continue to enjoy. Which we did.

He was a simple man, and this small spot was plain, but it was part of his life; it was part of him. Jack told us that he packed the same lunch every day and would sit on the large log he strategically placed under the beautiful elm tree so he could enjoy his hot black coffee, ham, mustard, and pickle on white and his wife would pack him some delicious dessert she made the night prior. He said she made the best pies in town, but his favorite by far was her apple pie. Whenever that was packed in his lunch, he said he was able to work a little harder that day. You could find Jack sitting under the elm tree around the same time, nearly every day. This was his spot and my family never touched it. My dad told all the kids to not mess with it and in my lifetime, we never have.

I take my four-wheeler up and down the dirt drive that divides the crops, or I ride it along the fence line even though I am told to stop doing that, as one wrong bounce could throw me into the neighbor's electric fence. But I love being alone and riding up to find a great area to sit and read or daydream. It is what I looked forward to all summer long. I appreciate these rides, and I love being alone in the fields. I have a few spots where I like to sit and read, but none are as good as the shade under the elm tree. I never sat there or bothered it at all, but I do stare at it all the time. I resonate with that area in the field; it feels like another place all together.

I admire the farmer's spot, as I think it is so lovely. It is the largest tree out in the fields, and it stands alone with nothing else around it. It feels like the sun shines down on the elm leaves, even when everything around it is overcast and gray. I always stop and look at the tree whenever I pass it; it just makes me smile. I feel a connection with Jack in my own way, because I think I am an old soul that appreciates the small things in life, like him. I relish the small things; I notice every detail and my brain doesn't forget a thing. I think there is so much chaos in the world, so the small things that can be written off as insignificant are sometimes the total opposite. They can be the most significant to remember. I like those details. The things that no one else remembers or maybe even notices. I remember those things and can offer precise details that others don't even notice.

That is why today I stopped during my walk home just to look at the tree like I always do. Just this time, it's not the same. The picturesque tree no longer felt light and welcoming, it felt dark, harrowing, and strange, as armed men stood there.

I rode my four-wheeler into the field hours earlier to relax and finish a book. When I went to start it back up, no luck; the gas tank must have been coasting on fumes on my way up, because it was completely empty. I have done this too many times to count, and my parents were constantly reminding me to check the fuel level before I went for a ride, but I always forget. As I was walking back to our house, which was at least a mile away, the intense August heat made it hard to breathe. I was tired and drenched in sweat while freaking out over what my parents would say about me running out of gas *again*. I knew my dad

15

would probably be home when I got there, so my stomach was in knots, and I started biting my nails while thinking of any way to explain this without getting into trouble. As I walked on the folded grass where my four-wheeler tire marks were, just along the tree line, I looked up just in time to see the elm tree in the distance. I paused to see the top of the tree, and then slowly focused my eyes on the entire landscape around it. I was in a daze, trying not to think about my upcoming punishment.

Along the path I was walking that sided with the electric fence, there were several trees we have recently cut down, as the roots were causing an issue with the crops. My dad left the logs nicely stacked and would pull his truck back into the field to pick them up whenever needed. My mom kept saying to bring the entire stack home so they can properly dry and be used, but my dad didn't give that notion much thought. He liked doing it the way he wanted; I did, too. I loved where the stack was positioned, as I would climb up to the top, sit and stare off at that elm tree with a perfect view. I would just sit on top of the pile of wood and stare but in my years of exploring the field alone, I never sat under the elm tree. Not once. I don't even know why my dad's words telling us to leave it alone resonated, but they did. So, I admired it from afar as Jack's spot.

Today, as I worried about how much trouble I was going to be in when I got home, so I stopped to delay the inevitable. The large tree was mesmerizing to me. I went to place my foot into the small pocket within the stack of wood which I had done twenty times before to climb up and as I lifted my body slightly, I saw the men by the tree. I kept my foot in the pocket but ducked down as my gut said something was wrong. The air was stale and sweat covered my body; I started to breathe erratically and felt like I was about to have a panic attack. I moved slowly to the corner of the stack, laying my stomach on top of it, and peered back over to see if I really just saw what I hoped I'd only imagined.

My hands were wet with sweat so as I tried holding myself on the stack, my grip gave away and I lost my balance, almost falling to the ground with a thud. I caught myself while in a bent position, and scooted my stomach more forward, now with my feet sort of dangling beneath me. I had to stay low to avoid being seen, but with the cornstalks' height, it was hard to peer over without sitting on top of the logs completely. The heat was beating down on my head and part of my back was exposed as my shirt was caught on the bark of the wood. It felt like my face was going to burst, it was so hot. My eyes were on fire, and fingertips were white as I held onto the edge of stack.

It was so hot in August that the ground seemed to sizzle. Sweat was dripping down my forehead into my eyes. As I tried to wipe it away without making any real movement, I spread dirt from the firewood across my face. It burned and irritated my skin, which made laying on top of the stack even more challenging. But I was frozen. I could feel the blood coursing through me. My heartbeat was all I could focus on. I could hear it as I tried to take small, short breaths, assuring I didn't make a sound. But my breathing was so short and unsteady that I started to feel lightheaded like I was going to pass out. Between the heat, my nerves and not breathing, I was seconds away from falling over.

I shook my head and tried to get myself together. I focused on taking full breaths and tried to steady my mind. I looked at the tree that always gave me calm to try to bring my body back to normal. I steadied my eyes on the leaves, then the branches, then the trunk and then down to the men.

The three men were talking, more quietly now. I couldn't

17

make out the words as clearly, but I could see as they moved their bodies toward each other, that there was a fourth person sitting in an old wooden dining room chair. The stain was aged off, there were water spots all over it like it had sat in the rain and the spindles were dated and ornate. Something you would see at your grandmother's house or at an old antique store. The chair looked familiar, but I couldn't think from where. I couldn't think at all. How did it get out in the middle of a three-hundred-acre cornfield? Why was a man sitting in it? Who was the man?

The man in the chair didn't look bound, but all I could see was a portion of the side of face and his left arm, which was exposed as he wasn't wearing a shirt. The hair on his arm was light, but his skin was sun kissed and red. The side of this face looked youthful. No facial hair that I could see, but I couldn't see his eyes, just his part of his cheek and ear. The sun was setting directly behind him, and the auburn of the sunset glared so strongly that his hair color could have been blonde, red, or even light brown. I couldn't make out much more than the shadow the sun was casting around him. His hair looked wet; it was shaggy, and untamed. I tried to change my position to get a better look but was stopped abruptly.

Suddenly, a sharp sting roused me. I almost squealed in pain, so I lifted my knee close to my face to see what was going on. As I gained focus on what I was looking at, I felt another sharp sting near the same spot. I was near tears now and holding back any sound, as I attempted to see what it was. As I tilted my head slightly to look down, I saw wasps all around my leg. There was a mud dauber's nest somewhere in the stack and I must have moved the logs around just enough to piss them off. They were swarming around my dangling legs, stinging me repeatedly.

I had nowhere to go. Nowhere to move. As I tried to kick

18

them away, they kept clinging to the sticky sweat on my leg. I tried to scoot my body a few inches away, but my other leg was asleep from dangling lifeless for so long. One leg was burning from the wasp stings that persisted and the other was numb and unable to move with the feeling of pins and needles. I climbed off the stack and tried to move back away slightly, while crouched down. I could see through one empty line of the crops, directly to where the men were standing. I was better hidden here, but the wasps were amping up even more. I looked around for anything to fill the hole where they were swarming out of.

There were a few loose logs on the ground that had fallen off the stack, so I tried to reach for them and drag them over to block in most of the wasps. I gently pulled over two logs and started to make a barricade around the hole where I saw most of the wasps coming out of. But as I reached for a third log which was heavier and a little further away, I fell over and made a loud rustle sound in the grass with a thud.

That's it, I thought. I was not paying attention to the men the last minute or two while I was trying to deal with the wasps, and I was sure they had seen me or heard me by now. Something about this situation felt like a scene in a horror movie right before someone dies. I just felt like they were going to walk over to me and kill me.

I lay there, lifeless, awaiting my fate. I have an active imagination and read thrillers, so my mind went dark, and it went there right away. I didn't imagine any positive scenario where I lived. I began to panic. My eyes squinted shut, my hands in full fists, and my body still. *Here I am, fifteen and preparing for death*, was all I could think. I started thinking of whether they would shoot me, or slit my throat, or grab me and take me to be tortured. Every second I laid there, my thoughts got worse, and I imagined some gruesome way they were going to dismember me or beat me to death. *Then*, I thought, *what if they just shoot me; will I ever be found?*

No, really, who would find me if they killed me and just left me there? Would it be the farmer? One of my brothers or sisters? My parents?

My always-reeling imagination upset me even more. Tears filled my eyes as I ran through horrific scenario after horrific scenario in my mind. I began to quietly sob. I was losing all realistic perspective when I heard something.

Suddenly, there was a loud cry to, "Stop!" that startled my rambling thoughts of fear and turned them into curiosity. After the scream, I could hear some sort of muffled arguing followed by two shots, something hitting the ground and someone saying, "What the fuck? Fuck! God dammit, what are we going to do now? I never told you to shoot!" It sounded like fighting in the distance, and men were yelling at each other to go this way or grab that. It sounded like chaos. As I pulled myself up and realized no one was standing over me with a shotgun, I crawled back over to look.

Tears began to roll down my cheeks as I saw one man's shirt with blood on it, so I covered my mouth as I choked back crying loudly. Something bad just happened and it looks like someone had been shot. I could see the chair was still there, knocked over, and now it was empty. There was a white and blue truck about thirty feet from where the men were standing that I had not noticed when I first saw the men. It was sitting on the edge of the dirt road that goes up between the crops from our house all the way to the back of the farm. I could see someone in the driver's seat and the three men were still standing by the tree looking for something on the ground by where the chair was.

The truck looked like it was from the late 1970s, blue and white and covered in rust. One of the doors was replaced with one that didn't match, as it had a green hue, was completely discolored from oxidation, and didn't fit the vintage of the truck. The tires didn't match, as one looked like a temporary spare, and the windshield had a large crack across it. The truck bed had no closure, and it was filled with trash and debris. There were no plates, but there was a trailer hitch with some metal decorative item hanging below it. I could make it out, because it was a very distinctive shape I had grown up knowing; an Ichthys. We just call them 'Jesus fish,' but we had them on shirts, on bumper stickers and several of my brothers and cousins had them on a long black necklace they received from church camp last summer. When living in a small Midwest town, it was as common to see as an American flag in a yard or a cross on a necklace.

A truck in this disrepair was something commonly seen on a farm like ours, but it was not one I recognized. As the man drove forward to pick up the others, I could see that there was a total of four men.

The man in the driver's seat was wearing a shirt and the back of his head didn't look like the man that was sitting in the chair, as his hair was cut short from the back with a small military-style cut on top. He was noticeably short in stature as it looked as if he could barely see over the steering wheel. He had dark facial hair and very dark, tanned skin. The truck pulled forward, stopped and the tall man with the shotgun told the other two to 'hurry the fuck up' as they kept looking on the ground. Finally, the men took the chair and threw it in the back of the truck bed and two of the men jumped in there as well. The man that was wielding the shotgun got into the passenger side of the truck, slamming the door three separate times, attempting to get it to close. As the men

21

in the truck bed settled down to drive away, they turned their bodies backwards, facing me straight on.

My eyes opened as if I had seen a ghost. I could feel the knot in my throat enlarge. I couldn't swallow, and my eyes burned as I couldn't blink. My entire body began to quiver as I watched them look noticeably perplexed. One of them had a handgun in his left hand as he propped it up on the ledge of the truck bed. The other had nothing in his hands, but there was blood all over his shirt, splatters on his face and some on his hands. They looked shocked and like they were there against their will. I couldn't breathe. I couldn't move. I couldn't believe what I was looking at.

The truck turned around and drove the opposite direction than the main access road, which didn't make sense. The only thing in the direction they were going was an old, vacant farmhouse where the owners had died years ago, a cow barn that had not been occupied in twenty years, some equipment the farmer kept stored, and one neighbor with their electric fence that surrounded the fields. There were only two gates that direction, but one was the driveway out of the farmhouse that was overgrown, and part of the bridge that crossed the creek was missing, and the other was always chained and locked. That one only gave access to our neighbor's backfield and eventually their home, but we never used it, even when it was open. These neighbors were not friendly, and we had been at odds with them for years. After they shot one of our dogs they said had wandered onto their land years ago, we had extraordinarily little to no contact with them.

The opposite direction they were headed was our house and before you got there, you could turn off and get onto the main FM250 road. The same road our house, the old farmhouse and the neighbor's house, exited onto, and really the easiest way out of the field. There were no fences or gates and the only other thing on it for miles, besides these three houses, was a small church and cemetery on the opposite side of road, and the farmer's house which was a ways down his dirt drive. As I watched them drive off, I knew they were not our neighbors, but I was too far back to watch which way they exited once they headed that way.

I watched for as long as I could before I got up and began to walk through the corn, over to the tree. The truck was long gone now, and for the first time I stood under the tree that I had gazed at for so many years. I looked around and saw their fresh tire marks but also saw other marks that looked older, but the same tread shape. There were these tiny, clipped pieces of what looked like polaroid pictures and one large footprint in a puddle near the tree. As I walked around, it was almost completely dark, and I needed to head home, fast. I had less than fifteen minutes of any sort of daylight left and unless I ran, I was not going to make it before it was pitch black out. But right before I turned to walk the dirt road back, I saw a splattering of blood on the ground where the chair sat. It wasn't a lot of blood, like something I guessed would be associated with a dead body, but I wasn't really sure what that would even look like. I looked around, no drag marks, no other markings I could see, but it was getting dark, and I couldn't see much. As I started to walk toward the road back to my house, I saw on the ground a black, braided, leather necklace, with a broken clasp. It looked like it used to have a charm but was no longer there. I picked it up and placed it in my pocket. I recognized this necklace, like I had seen it before.

I looked up the dirt road to where the truck went one last time, and tears began to stream down my face again. The shock was now taking over my body and I felt immobile. I wondered where they went and why they went that way. They were not the neighbors, and they were not friends of the neighbors because I knew the two men in the back of the truck…

Chapter Two

Family

I made it back home, but don't remember a minute of the walk, as my mind was in a fog the entire time. By the time I arrived, the sun had been gone for some time, and all I could see was the shadows made as the moonlight pushed through the trees. These fields are overwhelming in the day, but at night, they feel like they come alive. As I got closer to home, my fast-paced walk turned into a jog and eventually I was sprinting as I didn't want to spend another minute out there. When I saw the floodlights on the house, I finally felt that I could breathe again. I paused for a minute before going up to the house, thinking of what to say if my dad was sitting there waiting for me. I couldn't face him. I don't think I would be able to talk to him without breaking down if he was there when I walked in the front door. I tried to muster together my thoughts before going in, but I don't think I was really ready to face my fate.

I walked in the front door to find my mom on the phone, sitting at the end of the sofa. She glared at me and shouted, "Where have you been?" I asked her first if Dad was home and she said he was on his way when the office paged him about an issue at a jobsite, so he had to turn around and go back. He is a custom home builder who works in neighborhoods normally around thirty to forty-five minutes away. He owned the business and could normally push off issues to his site manager or partner, but bigger issues he always handled himself. Mom said that the new custom home he was building for the orthopedic surgeon had been broken into and vandalized. The HVAC unit was stolen along with some appliances that were just delivered and some other smaller items. He called her from a payphone not too far from home to let her know it would be late and to eat without him. I am sure he squeezed in some profanities about how the world is fucked up and you can't trust anyone these days as he says that a lot recently. There have been several jobsites with missing materials over the last year, and recently it seems to only have gotten more frequent, and with more expensive items. She said she would save him some dinner and handle it however he needed to.

She hung up the phone with who seemed to be her friend Janet, and again asked me where I had been. I explained to her that I ran out of gas in the back of the field and had to walk home. I begged her not to tell Dad when he got home; I really did not want him to know. She agreed but said that I had to get it back to the house tomorrow, and I wasn't allowed to ask my siblings to help me.

Don't *let my siblings* help me? Please. This entire house was filled with too many people already and no one helped anyone. I think my parents only breed narcissists. We were raised to be 'God-fearing' and to always do the right thing, but that was the farthest from the truth. My parents even gave us these ridiculously religious names and always said it would be a way to help guide us in life. My parents were good people and very selfless for us kids, but I am not sure how much *God* would approve of how we all acted.

My dad drank every night when he came home. He didn't have a drink of choice, but said gin tasted like sweat from an old man's ass, and vodka was only for women and pussies. He loved to gamble, but only in Las Vegas. My parents tried to go out there a few times a year, but my dad would never buy a lottery ticket or gamble in any way in our home. His friends play poker for money, but he never joins. He loves playing card games and will play for quarters sometimes, but that's the extent of it. His parents passed away when he was young, so he has been self-sufficient for a long time. He knows that some indulgences in life carry too much risk, so he is good about setting boundaries for himself. He doesn't think one or two drinks a night can ruin him, but his temptation when gambling is far too great. He can lose control easily, so he always has my mom by his side to help him stay in line.

My mom, on other hand, isn't a big drinker, but she was a closet smoker. Everyone knew she smoked, but they thought only a few a week. The trash can and man that worked at the gas station would tell you otherwise. She smokes practically a pack a day, always Virginia Slims because they were classy, in her words. Mom will sit on the phone and gossip nonstop. She always comes off as if she genuinely cares but really, she just wants the dirt to spread to anyone who will listen. That whole 'thou shalt not covet' is my favorite one for her to break. She will sit every night telling my dad of the new boats, cars, and jewelry her friends are getting, asking him what *we* could do to make more money so we could have the same. They curse and fabricate truths and only go to church during the holidays or when my dad is looking for new clients these days. We used to be very strict in our religion, but it has waned significantly in recent years. I am not sure if my parent's faith changed, or they didn't like our church or some other reason, but there was a seismic shift in the last decade or so.

27

They like to use us kids as an excuse to miss church service. Like we have a game or are sick or something else completely untrue, when the reality is that they like to sleep in, read the paper and not speak until noon on Sunday. They make sure we were reminded to be 'God's children' each day and send us to church without them to save face, regularly. It is such a joke, but no one minds it as much as I do. Zach even volunteers to go to represent the family without being asked.

My oldest brother, Zach, short for Zachariah, a modern version of Zechariah, is the best out of all of us. He still attends church, even when no one else goes, is enrolled in college, makes good grades, and volunteers at the church summer camps every year. He is the voice of reason for most of us and always stops us the minute we got a little unruly, which happens quite often. He had one girlfriend, I remember, in high school, but no one else he has brought around since then. He is with my cousins a lot, who are around the same age and went to our high school, but he does not have a lot of friends other than them. After he went off to college last year, he still comes home every weekend to hang with them but never brings any new college friends around. His school is less than an hour away, he only has classes three days a week, and he is always around town up to who knows what. It's like he avoids college and still lives in the past, within our small-minded little town.

We tease Zach a lot because he is very tall, handsome, and incredibly smart, but he is not so great at sports. He is the clumsy one of the family and finished high school without ever being on any team sport. Which says a lot when you live in a small town like this. With two hundred kids in your graduating class, a man who is 6'2 and lean with muscles would seem appealing, well, not so much with Zach. He is simply put, horrible at any sport he has ever tried. He is very artistic and loves photography, so he spends a lot of time alone with these hobbies. He has a large, quarter-sized birthmark on his neck, below his right ear that he is embarrassed by, so he always wears his hair long. He said it doesn't bother him, but we all know it does. He is the only one of the six children that I try to be kind to, because he is always good to me.

Below Zach is Adam, and he is the opposite in every way. He always steals Dad's beer, smokes like a chimney and is willing to do anything that will press our parents' nerves. He says that there is a whole big world out there for us to see and this cult-like home our parents created is oppressive and filled with lies. He is always getting into trouble, but because he is a phenomenal athlete, like an all-star at every sport, the school and my parents let him get away with it. A day doesn't go by where he is without a girlfriend, and they are perpetually the prettiest girls around. He treats them dreadfully, but they always come back for more. He is never rude or mean to them, but he sort of drags them around until he is bored and moves onto the next without a second thought. He is model-good-looking, and my mom brags about his looks to anyone who will listen, while my dad brags on his talents like they are his own. Adam's arrogance fills a room, but it is also what draws people to him. I think he is super cool, but I also know he is a complete dick to everyone around. He gets away with everything, and as much as it pisses me off, I admire his blatant confidence. I also love that he doesn't put up with our parents' hypocritical religious ways. Whenever they force it on him, he will cite scripture to them, explain the areas of the bible they breach, and sort of mic drop and walk away. He is such an ass, but I love how he knows who he is, and he never backs down.

My older sister, Eve, yes, just like in the garden with Adam, so incredibly crass of my parents, is perfect in every way. Well, that is how my parents see her at least. She is never in trouble, is the most popular girl in school, even with the older kids, she makes good grades, is a part of every after-school anything, is of course head cheerleader and has a body of a twenty-year-old stripper, which started when she was thirteen. She is about 5'9, weighs nothing, and during my last turn at laundry, I was lucky enough to see that she is now a 32-D cup size. She does have some acne from time to time, which I enjoy too much, but Jesus, how many upper hands can one girl be given? She is fake nice to everyone's face, but I hear her in her room on the phone with her best friend Olivia spreading the most insensitive rumors about everyone. She is evil to me, and I can't stand to be around her. Kids at school tell me how cool it is that Eve is my sister, but it couldn't be further from the truth. She is a complete bitch, in my opinion, and her fakeness makes my skin crawl. But pretty girls get away with it, and high school perpetuates popularity based on nothing really more than looks, so, for Eve, she is the most popular. She is a ghastly human, but there is no denying she is beautiful. Of course, Mom adores her and gives her anything she asks for, and it makes my blood boil. She is the epitome of the golden child and abuses it in every way she can.

Next in the lineup is me. Now, the funniest part of it all was that my parents were dedicated to giving us these religious names, so one would think that I would get one too. My parents said that I was going to be Rachel, Sarah, and even thought about Ruth. But when I was born, I was the most beautiful baby they had ever seen, *their words, not mine*, so I needed a unique name. They sat at the hospital with a baby book in hand, sifting through the names, being pressured by the hospital administrator to pick so we could be released. They said nothing was right. So, my mom closed her eyes and thought about the most beautiful places she had ever been. And my dad said her eyes shot open and she blurted out, "Montana!" My dad and her went there camping back in the late 1970s and stayed by a lake that my mom said was the most breathtaking place she had ever been. There was nothing around them for miles, so they just lived off the random snacks and water they packed, and planned their future together. They were just married and totally in love. She said that Montana was the place she loved the most and so, here I am, Montana, but everyone calls me Monty.

I don't fit into my family at all. The beauty of my newborn life faded, and I have become this awkward teen. I am shorter than my sister at about 5'7, I don't think an A-cup bra is filled out when I wear it. I am lanky and very thin, I like to wear my hair long, but it's always in a ponytail, and I am certainly not popular. I have nice skin, which my mom always tells me to take care of, and my hair is the lightest out of all the kids, light blonde, which she is constantly telling me is something women pay for. Everyone else in the family is brunette, so I look adopted. I have blue eyes, and everyone else has green, and I just got my braces off after three and half years of misery. No one else in my family needed braces and have perfect smiles, of course. Nothing about me looks or acts like the others, and the more I try to fit in, the more I am confident that I do not belong.

From looks, to lifestyle, to God, we are different in every way. I don't even know if I believe in God, but I know I don't believe in the indoctrination that has been prevalent my entire life. My family brings up God in every scenario. If I get a good grade, I am to thank God for allowing me the opportunity to go to school, have books and a brain that works. I was thinking that's

31

more because of the taxes we pay for the school, that the law requires me to go and the genetics I was given, but I digress.

I am athletic like Adam, but I am not really interested in team sports. I am a self-proclaimed weirdo. I like to be alone with my thoughts as much as possible. I read all the time and I just walk places, with no destination in mind. I feel much more comfortable around adults, as almost anyone my age is caddy, ignorant and downright boring as all hell. I like two people my age and they are the only good friends at school, but of course, my mom doesn't care for either of them. I don't try to fit into this family, but it sometimes feels like I am being pushed out of the family for being different. My two friends, Mandy, and Hunter, are the only people I feel totally accept me.

The ever-changing hair color on Mandy makes my mom think she is promiscuous, but the truth is she has never even kissed anyone. She has the most stunning face, and her eyes are large and doe-like. She has very tan skin naturally and her body is something that I would die to have. She dresses like she is an old man, though, with polyester everything, all three sizes too big, and you would think she was fifty pounds heavier than she was. She doesn't have any piercings, but she swears the minute she is eighteen that will all change, as she cuts out magazines of weird body piercings and tattoos and puts them in a scrapbook saying she is getting all of them one day. I don't believe her, but who knows. Her grades are low, but I don't think she really tries. She only loves music, and you will never see her without her Walkman and headphones. She knows every cool band and can already play four instruments very well. She has a gorgeous singing voice too, but you will never hear it. She is too shy to make a peep in front of anyone, but I've heard her sing once and it brought tears to my eyes. She doesn't fit the cutesy, popular mold like the wax figures Eve is friends with, so my mom doesn't give her a chance. But she is truly a good person and I trust her, and I don't really trust anyone. Maybe Hunter, but not like I trust Mandy.

Hunter is weird, like me, but with crazy good looks. He had a stutter when he was younger that kids to this day tease him about, even though it has been gone for several years. He is good at any sport he tries and hasn't gone through any of the weird ugly teen stuff like the rest of us. Mandy is in love with him, but tells me she only wants to be friends, which I find suspect. I am always curious to why he is friends with us, but the reality is, I think we are the only ones that never made fun of him growing up. He and I were in church summer camp together in middle school and became friends when we kept running into each other after sneaking away from some ridiculous trust exercises that were hosted by some nerdy man that had no business telling us how to fit in and make friends.

Hunter is sharp-witted and always has a cunning and clever response to anyone who has something nasty to say. He knows so much it blows my mind. I read all the time and I am confident I know much more than other kids my age, but whenever I share some interesting facts I've learned, Hunter will take it and extrapolate into more specific and intriguing details. He made the varsity baseball team as a freshman and the soccer, and track and field coaches kiss his ass to be on their teams too. He is a solid B student which is unimaginable because I do not know anyone as smart as him. He is a walking encyclopedia, but I think not trying is his own version of rebellion. My mom thinks being friends with a sixteen-year-old boy is inappropriate, and he must have ill-intention for hanging out with me. The misinterpretation my mom has of our friendship is sadly what defines her as a mom.

She is always off-base and trusts bad people and blows off the good ones. She thinks she can relate to me because she is a young mom, but that makes me feel even more unlike her.

My mom was immensely popular, attractive, and well-liked, just like Eve. She cannot understand my viewpoint because it is so different than her own. She had my brother when she was only twenty-two, and by the time she was thirty, she had six children. I don't plan to even start until I am in my thirties, if I have kids at all. An intimate relationship is completely not on my radar any time soon. I can't stand looking at myself naked in the mirror, so I am certainly not ready for someone else to feel up on me, let alone see me that way.

She told me once after she drunkenly came home after a fundraiser that she has been with more men than just my father and I screamed and covered my ears. She kept telling me it was okay to share yourself with another if you are safe, you love each other and are honest. I tried running out of the room, just to have her shout, "Men loved me, so it was only fair to share myself a little!" Gag. Her arrogance in that moment proved she is Eve's mom, and made me feel so distant from her.

Mom misses her youth and sometimes she wishes she would have had done more living before being married with children so young. She loves my dad and is incredibly happy, but sometimes I think when she looks at Eve, she is jealous. But when she looks at me, she simply doesn't know what to talk about. I am painfully aware of my unlike-ness to my family. I have been uninvited to family functions, as my parents say my attitude is negative and brings everyone down. I don't think it is negative, I just don't want to praise mundane accomplishments like my family does. My eye-rolling is a little bit much from time to time, but if I must hear of how proud we are of someone having a baby, or graduating eighth grade or getting their driver's license, I might lose it. So, I am no one's favorite in the family. But with six of us, my troubles can blend in and never take center-stage as there is always some other kid that takes all the focus.

The last two kids who just turned eleven are the twins Simon and Delilah. They were a complete surprise to the family as my dad had a vasectomy, performed by a urologist whose home he had built, but apparently never went back in for his sperm check. I sadly know these gruesome details a child should never know about her father, as my parents re-tell their 'miracle' conception story every holiday. I don't see what the miracle was; they were supposed to go back to assure he was all set, he didn't, and in turn found out his soldiers were still marching. *But God is great and works in mysterious ways,* according to them. Another one of those mundane accomplishments that we are so proud of. Now, don't get me wrong, I love the twins and they are the funniest kids around, but my parents sort of checked out of raising them, so they are assholes, too.

Simon plays pranks on everyone, and he doesn't care if it causes physical harm. If he finds it funny, he is going to do it. He is smaller than Delilah and seems to have a complex about his height. So, he makes fun of you before you have a chance to make fun of him. He is constantly reading joke books and talking back to our parents, using clever hyperbole, but still totally disrespectful. When they go to chastise him, he always says it is part of his act and he needs to practice and gets away with it. The twins still share a room, as we are out of space in the house. Once Zach went off to school, I finally moved out of sharing a room with Eve, and I am not about to move back with Satan because my parents think the twins are getting too old to share, being the opposite sex. Delilah doesn't mind, and that is all that should matter.

Delilah is incredibly timid, and she hates her height. She towers over other kids in her grade and is always slouched over, trying to shrink. Her and Eve must have the same genetics because her chest is already bigger than mine, and I found Dad's duct tape recently in the bathroom. She tapes down her chest to try to hide them, as she might look like Eve, but she does not want to flaunt it like her. She comes off as boring and doesn't have many interests other than mimicking her friends. There is no way to tell who she is, as she is a chameleon who changes based on who she is around.

At one point, she convinced my parents to pay for riding lessons at a stable an hour away, because she wanted to be an equestrian. My mom moved her schedule around and scrounged up money to cover the first three months of lessons, which were not cheap. After three weeks, Delilah had lost interest and refused to go back. The reality was the girl at school she was mimicking had said she didn't want to be friends any more, so that was that. Delilah is wildly clever though, and she hits you with one- liners all the time. You don't expect it from her slouched and quiet demeanor, but she will shoot in with something so witty that the entire room will burst into laughter. She is incredibly close to my dad, and they have a special bond. He relates to her based on their lack of knowing who they are. She doesn't know who she is and struggles to find her place. He never got to figure that out either having to grow up so fast. He just had to be responsible and take care of his siblings when his parents died, so, he never got to really think about who he wanted to be.

He tells us how he had planned to go to medical school to specialize in pediatrics, but it just wasn't on the cards. It makes sense as his closest friends are all doctors, and he will study medical journals for fun. He doesn't push medicine on any of us, but he has pushed all of us to take harder science and math classes, and likes to test us on silly things like basic anatomy and how to handle someone who is choking or having a seizure. Delilah plays this up with him the most, and it makes them very close.

Being a builder was not his dream, but he started something from nothing, and he has been incredibly successful at it. He says he looks at a house like the human body, and all he is doing is putting it together the way it is supposed to be. His work is spectacular, and I love looking at the photos when he is done, but I mostly love hearing when some spouse comes in and makes ludicrous changes last minute that ruins my dad's vision. If you want to piss him off, add a fireplace or change a tile a week before completion. He says if it was an innovative idea or they had taste, he wouldn't mind, but it's always the ones without vision who fuck it all up. His name is the business, so it makes sense that he wants to be sure it represents him properly, but sometimes hearing of the trivial things that bother him is funny. However, he should take some responsibility when things fall to shit, as some things that seem to damage the company reputation come directly from him. As he likes to give jobs to family, which is *always* the worst idea, and even after he is burned, he does it again.

My uncle Ted has worked for my dad for as long as I have been alive, and they have a seemingly great working relationship. They seem to balance like weights on a scale. The family drama in the business is never Uncle Ted, it's always other family members. My dad hired Ted's son Ryan a few summers ago, which ended horribly. He never showed up to work, would break into the houses mid construction to host parties for his friends, and at the height of his employment he came to work drunk, fell off a scaffold, filed for workman's comp, and got it. Ryan didn't return after that summer but is still at our house all the time. Ryan has apologized endlessly, which seemed to work as my dad simply brushed it off and moved on. But I think my mom is still more pissed than him. Funny thing is, my dad didn't learn from this, and, last summer, hired two of my cousins on my mom's side who live near us.

Their dad is in the army as a high-ranking commander who gets placed overseas a lot. To avoid the kids moving around schools, both of the boys stay with Uncle Ted and Aunt Lisa when their parents are gone. They are actually not related, but it is a small town, and we are all super close, so we have been raised together. My parents would offer, but we really just don't have the room, plus I think my mom finds them a little annoying, as well.

Their dad is strict and militant on just about everything, down to how he cuts his food, so you would think some of it would rub off on them, but it doesn't… at all. They are complete messes, and you would think had no discipline whatsoever. They are rude, talk back, and it feels like Uncle Jim and Aunt Loni just let everything slide. I am a kid and know they are wasted space, but apparently my dad likes a good challenge.

They were hired to do basic jobsite cleanup, run errands and be grunt labor for a few months. It was sort of a favor to Uncle Ted, just to get them out of the house, but it did not go well. The problem was, they are not bright and even basic projects confused them. The oldest, Daniel, flunked eighth grade and barely graduated high school. He is Zach's age and closest friend, which I don't get. Zach even helped him cheat in school just to finish up with a like 1.25 GPA. Daniel's younger brother

Harrison, who we all call Sunny, also not all there, but he is conniving and untrustworthy, too. I imagine him ending up in prison one day. I feel like every bad idea any of the guys has, he is always the one behind it. He started school a year late, due to not being ready for kindergarten. Which I don't get, either; like, if you go to learn letters, colors, and numbers, what is it you *don't* know to get in when five to be held back from starting kindergarten? He is going to be a senior this year with Adam, but Adam doesn't hang out with him much. Zach does, which seems strange since he is in college now, but maybe being around idiots makes Zach feel better. I just avoid him and Daniel altogether. They are a bunch of dullards who think it is clever to make fun of my flat chest and how I don't look like the rest of the family. They always told me as a kid that I was adopted, and my parents just felt sorry for me at the orphanage. Which is why I look different and have a weird name. It used to really bother me, but now I know life in high school does not tell a story of what real life is going to be, and they are both idiots whose opinions mean nothing to me.

They are so incredibly embarrassing to be around. My mom wants to like them, since they are her sister's kids, but she really doesn't. She might have less tolerance for them than me, and that says a lot. When they worked for my dad, it was sort of the last attempt at my parents trying to excuse their behavior.

While they worked for my dad, they didn't do anything too crazy. They showed up, which was already one better than Ryan, seemed to always be sober and they would hang around for the entire day and not really complain. Sad that these are the highlights of their time at the company. But basic jobsite cleanup like 'throw the debris into the dumpster' was not clear to them. So, my dad would send them to a house that was getting ready for the turnkey inspection and say to clean up and throw away all trash to prepare for the cleaners. They would throw some large cuts of sheetrock away or some appliance packaging and stop for the day. There would still be garbage everywhere, from fast food trash from the crew, tile cuts all in the yard and loose boards all over but they would say it was all done and ready for the landscapers and cleaners. After my dad dealt with their deficient skills for a few weeks, he was fed up. He had them go to the corporate office and work in the shop organizing and making inventory of materials instead. They fucked that up too. Miscounting and mislabeling items, losing items and even breaking items when they were moving them. One night they left the shop door unlocked and my dad had thousands of dollars of supplies stolen. The next day was their last day. My Aunt Loni called my dad begging for another chance, but when he explained what had in fact happened, she said she understood and left it alone. But I don't think she believes what my dad told her and some part of her is holding a grudge. My dad never heard a word from Uncle Jim because I think he knows that they are complete as clowns.

We all go to the same church and usually sit together, but it feels odd now. My parents attend less and less but my cousins and their parents, when in town, always sit with us kids and behave as if nothing is wrong. But my Aunt Loni will now make snide remarks about my dad's business under her breath or make sure to have some gossipy rumor to bring up about one of us kids messing something up that she says loud enough for someone in the congregation hear. She has not let it all go, no matter what she told my parents. The rumors and gossip are awful in our town already, and when Aunt Loni is around, she makes it even worse. The rumor mill for our town is in full swing after Sunday sermons, even though it is supposed to be the *Lord's Day,* in my parent's words. Don't get me wrong, my mom fully engages when she is there, but she would lose it if she knew what her sister was saying about us. The only recent distraction from our family has been the previous youth minister taking over more full time as the primary minister in charge. His good looks have taken more the center stage of town chatter, trumping any of the other frivolous nonsense.

There have been a lot of changes in the church in the most recent few years, and with the youth minister who used to be way more behind the scenes taking over, has made the women in town to swoon whenever he was around. He is easy on the eyes for sure, but he is also very mysterious. He simply showed up in our small town one day to take over the youth minister position. This was always done by someone local as a part time gig and when it wasn't filled, some high school or college extreme evangelical would fill in. Not usually something that was advertised in the paper or shared with the other chapter of the church. Our church was so small that it felt like the larger chapter the next town up sort of gave us the remnants they no longer needed. But he didn't come from there, either.

We are not a town on the map for anything noteworthy and our church has no money, so I am not even sure how they were able to pay him. But from what I understood, this was his full-time job, and once he took over the youth portion, he really amped up the camps and programs and all the changes were appreciated and well received. When our minister was in talks about moving to the larger chapter north of us, I don't think anyone thought Tate, the youth minister, would be taking over. But here he is, filling in more and more and keeping the town ladies in a frenzy.

Tate seemingly showed up out of nowhere and didn't know a soul in town. But he jumped right in, like he was versed in our people, our town, and our ways of doing things. He never felt like a stranger at all, which was a bit mysterious. He doesn't talk much about anything before moving here, so it is hard to get a real read on him. But he is very nice, and I know all the teens love having him around, and it seems like the adults do too.

The first time I met Tate, he made eye-contact with me, and it felt like he was ready to say my name before I introduced myself. My parents could have already spoken to him, but it felt like he knew me. Like he really knew me in detail. I am not uncomfortable around him at all, but something about him seems off. I can't put my finger on it, but I feel like there is so much more there that needs uncovered.

Chapter Three

Church

The church we went to was on FM 250 just down the road from our house. There were two locations for the church and the minister would alternate between the small run-down location by us and the beautiful new building the next town up about thirty minutes away. The location by us was ridiculously small and the building was falling apart. We were constantly doing fundraisers to raise money to build a new, larger building, but with a little congregation, and not a lot of people in the town, the attempts seemed futile. Our family made a good living, I think, as we always had what we needed, and I don't ever remember my parents arguing over money, but we didn't have a lot of extra each month according to my mom. My dad was not able to do his antiquated ten percent tithing each week, so he found other ways to help. The way our parents assisted was by volunteering us kids for work at the church. They never volunteered themselves, which was pretty shitty, but they pimped us out as their penance. My parents must have had a lot that needed forgiven, because at least one of us was doing something for the church every week.

Zach was always at the church even when our parents had not asked. He even got my moron cousins Daniel and Sunny to help him whenever he was there. They would host youth group sessions, put together picnics, help repair leaks on the roof and were always a part of the summer camps. Ryan used to help and one day a few months ago, he just stopped showing up, and he stopped coming around our house too.

Ryan had gotten really into partying and hanging with a new crowd last year, but he still visited Zach and talked to him regularly. Zach said there was nothing to worry about, but Zach was consistently seeing the good in people, even the worst kinds of people. Randomly, a few months ago, my uncle said Ryan took some savings he had and decided to travel abroad and see the world. That was not like him at all, and when we asked Zach, he corroborated the story, but something didn't make sense. Ryan was very co-dependent, so to travel alone just wasn't him. He was also a creature of habit, so staying somewhere new every night just didn't make any sense at all. I didn't buy the whole story, but also don't really care that much about Ryan's whereabouts.

We all just assumed he was off on a bender of drugs and booze somewhere. Ryan was not afraid to try just about anything, and other than showing up to work drunk, he normally held it together well, which was scary to think about. He didn't fear the hard stuff and could function when on anything. He even got Adam to try things way outside of his comfort zone, and Adam is not easily convinced to do anything he doesn't want to do.

Adam told me that the first and only heavy drug he ever did was with Ryan, and it was super sketchy and kept him away from anything but beer and weed. He said Ryan ran around with some strange characters that he didn't trust, and one night with him was enough. He said he thinks what he did was laced with something even stronger and he felt like he was being set up. He called my dad to pick him up he was so worried. Adam didn't fear much, so for him to be spooked like that was concerning. Ryan is timid and pushed around by people. He has the tendency to never want to say no to anything or anyone, no matter how bad he knows it will be. Adam is the complete opposite. He doesn't feel pressure, ever. He does what he wants and if he doesn't want to, he will simply tell you that. He gets away with just about anything around our house and when Mom and Dad ask him to help with anything, if he doesn't want to, he probably won't do it. Including when they ask him to help at the church.

He hardly helps at church, but that is more due to his extracurricular activities and the fact that I am pretty sure he is an atheist. But that is an entirely different part of Adam. Adam always says he has some function or practice or something to do, and my parents never actually look into it to see if he is telling the truth. If they did, they would know that many times he was really off making out with his girlfriend and getting drunk on my dad's beer. It is strange to see the discomfort on my parent's face to discipline Adam. If I didn't know better, I would think he had dirt on them, just because he literally gets away with everything. No one else gets it like that... well, Eve is a close second, but my parents reel her in from time to time without hesitation.

Eve volunteers to help out and is actually busy with activities. She helps at the church on the weekends but never during the week because of the plethora of other things she is a part of. Even during summer break, she has a million things for school to do, it is crazy to see her color-coded calendar, filling in every spare minute the entire summer. Whenever she has a section of free time, she will even mark to pray, or volunteer at the church or something else conservative and not what a seventeen-year-old should be doing.

Eve is the most devout out of all of us, but I guess I would thank God too for giving me the easiest life possible. She is constantly praying; she never leaves home without her cross necklace on, bible in her backpack and stick up her ass. She never curses in front of an adult, but put her on the phone with Olivia and she is a sailor. She must have learned it from my parents; do what you need to, just say you're sorry and ask for God's forgiveness and all is good. I find all of it to be unbearable. She is so fake, but no one seems to see it or think it but me. I don't have as many activities, so I get stuck with the most chores just because I am always home. So, I look for ways to leave the house, no matter how little interest I have in whatever it is.

I often go to church and volunteer almost every week, even though it makes me anxious. But I just need to get out of my house, and without being old enough to drive while living in the middle of nowhere, it leaves me very few options. I don't mind helping at the church usually because I am put on a task I can do alone, so I don't have to socialize… which I find to be the worst part of church. If loving thy neighbor means to talk to them about the most awfully boring things, I decline to do that one.

Lots of times I just show up at church and hide in the basement with a book and Cheetos, not doing anything really at all. If there is any group work, I get anxious and have to find alternatives to working with the old church ladies. I have flat-out faked cramps to go home. I am *that* antisocial.

I connivingly persuade Mandy and Hunter to help often, which makes it manageable and stops me from talking to anyone new. The minister is coming to our location less and less, so the youth minister, Tate, is preaching more often, while also really trying to improve the church. He has projects for volunteers any day of the week, so there is always a sign-up sheet with open slots for things to take on. His ideas are good, but him leading the church is weird to me. He is so young and incredibly nervous when up there preaching his sermons. He is great at tasks and projects and talking with the teens, but on stage he is not so great. His voice cracks, and he doesn't have the enthusiasm our regular minister has. Tate is in his mid-twenties to late-twenties and is not from our town. He is from a Chicago suburb, which made him interesting to the people of Blakesville, Indiana. Chicago is the 'big city' that everyone talks about while sharing their one, tragically boring Windy City tale. Normally centered around visiting Navy Pier. Not interesting at all.

Tate smiles and acts genuinely interested in their stories, which is very nice of him, but there is no way he is actually interested. He is just really good at making everyone feel important, which is a great quality of his.

Tate is universally attractive; tall, light hair, nice smile and searing blue eyes. He isn't married but he is raising a young boy, Sam. No one has many details on their relationship, but the rumor is he is keeping Sam while both parents are in the military and have been moving around while on active duty. They are supposedly family friends of Tate's, and he is helping them out so Sam can be in a stable environment. There seems like a lot more to that story, mostly why no one in town has ever met his parents nor does Sam ever talk about them, but no one in the town really brings any of that up. I remember asking my parents once about Sam and Tate's relationship, and my mom said it was all just so sad and what Tate was doing was the best for Sam but would never extrapolate any more than that.

Our town loves to gossip but the Tate and Sam relationship is never really the topic of conversation. I am just a kid, so I just assume there are details I am not privy to, and I am not that invested in finding out. They both live in our town, but Tate drove Sam to another school the next town over during the school year. I am not sure why he had to go to another school, as our schools were small, but good academically. Maybe it had something to do with his parents and something they want, who knows.

Sam is very soft-spoken and always answers with a 'yes, ma'am... no, ma'am,' so to speak, but doesn't talk much overall. He constantly wears the same long-sleeved, light blue t-shirt under his church clothes, even in the dead heat of summer. He seems a tad peculiar, but for our town, that doesn't say too much. Tate on the other hand, is less peculiar and more just eye candy for the women. I have not gotten those hormones yet that make me swoon for boys, but even I can see how attractive he is. Although quiet and reserved, he has a presence about him that is enticing. Men were always trying to impress him, telling him of some ten-point point buck they shot, or large-mouth bass they caught; just an embarrassing way for them to swing their dicks around with each other. While the women nurture him and play the 'damsel in distress' whenever they can. Some offer him desserts, casseroles, or a dreadful, knitted monstrosity while the more aggressive divorcees and widows request some manual labor at their homes for some cash. It appears that he continuously takes them up on their offers because during the summer you can find a shirtless Tate in some lady's front yard pulling, yanking, or digging something up. Tate is best described as gentle and kind by most who know him; but bring up one of his hot button topics and be prepared to watch him go off the deep end.

We live in a very conversative town, where if you want to rock the boat, you get the hell out. Its anti-change, pro-Christian, and pro-ultra-conservative. I am vehemently aware that my anti-organized religious views will never be accepted, and if they knew I was liberal, pro-choice, and supported gay rights, I might as well hand them the stones to throw at me. The town, and my parents, would say I was young, uneducated and the devil needed to rid things from my life. When in reality, I am the most well-read person I know, and do follow one bible verse in the bible, and quote it whenever my parents say I am not mature or educated. *Do not judge, or you too will be judged. For in the same way you judge others, you will be judged, and with the measure you use, it will be measured to you. Why do you look at the speck of sawdust in your brother's eye and pay no attention to the plank in your own eye? – Mathew 7:1*

They always say I take the verse out of context and need to read all of the bible. But the funny thing is, I have. I have read all of it, because I am an avid reader and want to know what the big fuss is about. I think it is filled with hypocritical nonsense and between daughters sleeping with dads, people turning to salt, clean and unclean animals, floods, and frogs, I just cannot possibly take it at face-value. They normally tell me to shut up whenever I have a strong, supported argument, so I have learned to just shut up. I am not going to change the world from Blakesville, Indiana, so why waste my breath? But I do like to cite verses to them where their only response is to tell me to shut up, never to offer an arguable real rebuttal.

I instead entrust my feelings to my closest friends, but otherwise, I follow the righteous path that I was given, no matter how much I hate smiling at the town's racist, prejudiced, and fascist ways of life. I am not about to fight this town in a battle I don't have an actual chance of winning. Instead, I sit back and wait until I can get the hell out of here; three more years and counting.

Tate seemingly fit right into town with expressing close-minded views on the world, but it feels more like a way to be liked and not truly how he feels. Sermons were very on point with bible verses with extraordinarily little extrapolation or interpretation, but occasionally he will sprinkle in a little bigoted remark to reel in the crowd. He will say we were all God's children, but he knew the town wanted him to mean that only for people who looked and believed like them. It feels forced to get a congregational approval, but he makes sure the town accepts him. His acceptance and mixing in with everyone are things Tate tends to focus on. If he ever rocks the proverbial boat and doesn't get an accepting response, he changes opinion, focuses, and redirects to get others back on board with him. But deep down, I feel he is pretty liberal, but stays in his lane like I do.

My parents are a tad more liberal than others in this town too, and have had Tate and Sam over for dinner frequently. But one dinner I remember more than the others. My dad offered Tate a beer, which turned into several, and he sort of loosened up. Tate's opinions seemed more open-minded than he let on. He talked about the change the world needed and how to better the economy, moral and ethical lacking in politics and the church, better education and so on. He would go off on a little tangent and then pause to make sure my parents were still on board and not ready to stone him, but I think they thought his outlook was refreshing.

During the dinner, Tate would bring up the crime in Chicago and how so many criminals get away with their crimes for so long, as they are not relevant to whatever political agenda was the current hot point. He really focused on bettering the judicial system, improving education for the youth, and pushing for harsher punishment for criminals. He had a passion for change, which might be why he got into ministry, but coming to our small town seemed like a lost cause. It is 1996 in the world, but in Blakesville, it's more like 1976. We are very behind in the times, and change is the town's least favorite six-letter word.

Tate's open-minded world views seem to narrow when it comes to homosexuality, though. He doesn't want to really talk about it, and if it is being discussed at church or anyone had questions, he will cite Genesis, Leviticus, and Corinthians to support God's outlook and apparent hate for homosexuals, and his demeanor would change whenever anyone talked about it. He didn't want to touch any conversations on the topic, he never chose a side, but something about it really upset him. My parents were neutral on the gay conversation, and accepted that with so many children, it might be something they have to come to grips with one day. So, they did not voice their opinions one way or another, and assertively changed the subject with Tate when it was brought up.

Now, I am not aware of anyone in Blakesville coming out, but I am confident in assuming that our town has a few people who were not on the path to a *conventional lifestyle*. The town made it clear that the Army's motto of *don't ask, don't tell,* was something to adopt and follow. Everyone is noticeably clear on their contempt for homosexuals, so even if you knew who you were and that you were gay, everyone here made it clear you don't tell anyone. And you definitely don't act on it.

Tate made sure not to express his modern worldly thoughts in his sermons, but homosexual abominations were a sprinkled in topic every now and then. I just assumed he was new to all of this and that was just an area of the bible he knew well. But after a year of him performing more and more sermons, the topic feels very personal to him. He is timid in his preaching, and he mumbles at times where you must look at his mouth to try to figure out his words. But, when speaking of the detriment to society gay people were, men especially, he would become

51

flushed, his voice would raise, and you would see spittle come from his mouth as he shouted out to condemn them. He would pace back and forth and gesticulate wildly. He would go overboard at times, then catch himself and pause mid-thought, then stammer away his last words on the topic. It did not appear to phase any of the congregation, as I would just look around to meet eyes with someone to see their shock like mine. But no eyes were there. No one seemed bothered. Many times, they would applaud him and yell, "Amen!"

The people in this town would yell 'Amen' to just about anything that was said with vigor and confidence. They are such meek people. Everyone might look different, but it seems like one brain is leading them all. To not have an opinion on anything or be willing to condemn someone else knowing the skeletons hanging in your closet is so fucked up. I am a kid, so I know my place, but the adults are supposed to do better and be better, but it seemed that being hateful to a big percentage of the population is the only acceptable choice for them.

I like Tate, but I don't know if he has enough in him to lead this town to anything better. I actually don't think he is sold on homosexuals being abominations either; it feels like someone close to him might have come out and hurt him with their secret, or it was such a shock. His opinion doesn't seem to be one that comes from religious indoctrination. It seems to come from a sad place that hurts him. His passion really shines when he speaks of changing the world and making it a better place. But his views were socially liberal, so he knew that was not going to get the town to accept him. Unfortunately, acceptance is all people tend to care about. But it was obvious that he enjoyed talking to my mom, as she has similar views to him.

My mom is more liberal and agrees with his views on

Chicago as she marveled at the vibrant city, but she never speaks on her opinions of homosexuals. In my heart, I think if one of us kids came out, she would support and love us the same way. She vehemently did not want to talk about homosexuality with Tate when he was over, and she always changed the subject swiftly. She seems very close to him, like they really understand each other, and it seems like Tate is very comfortable around her. She is nearly old enough to be his mother, so it felt like a very maternal relationship that allowed her to check him and put him in his place when he overstepped; but it also allowed her to be maternal and care for him when he needed it. She and him discuss many topics while my dad tops off their drinks or lights her cigarette, but mostly they talked about Chicago. She always loves to talk to him about when she lived in Chicago, as all of us were so tired of hearing about it, but Tate would listen intently.

My mom talks about her youth and some of the wild things she did while retelling the same stories over and over again. Mom stayed in Chicago the summer after she graduated high school and still avidly talks about the food, museums, shopping, and style people had. She came home at the end of that summer and swore to move there one day to live this glamorous life, but instead met my dad and became a small-town housewife with a lot of kids. She keeps in touch with many people she met that summer, and she still gets together with a few of them for weekends in the city. She writes them long letters that talk about our family, the farm and she will sometimes enclose polaroid pictures of houses my dad has finished. She is proud of her life but enjoys when she can sneak away for a little glamour in the city. One of her friends there, Janet, visits our home often and we even call her Aunt Janet, even though we are not actually related.

Aunt Janet thinks our farm is stunning and she always takes

a mason jar of soil back with her after a visit to put into her potted house plants. She is completely wild with blue-colored sunglasses, never wears a bra, her only make up is Vaseline on her lips and she thinks shaving is optional. She is so different than my mom, but they mesh incredibly well. My mom really lets loose when Janet is around and it's the only time I find my mom interesting. I will sit near them and just listen to the stories they tell because so many of them are fascinating. Janet tells stories with so much detail you feel like you lived it with her. She loves gossip, like my mom, so when she visits, it's normally several days of coffee, wine, and cigarettes mixed with a hundred juicy stories. I have even gotten good at reading lips from her visits, because some parts of the crazier stories they whisper as they are just too crazy to say out loud.

Janet's husband died a few years ago after having a massive stroke at age thirty-seven. It was a complete shock that no one was prepared for. They lived a very modest life, as he was an underpaid professor at the University of Chicago, and she worked part time at a salon as a receptionist. She didn't make any money, but my mom said she did it just to hear the gossip in her neighborhood. True Janet awesomeness.

When her husband died, she found out that he had a family trust that he had never told her about, and she was paid out nearly four million dollars. She now spends her days traveling, visiting us, and buying the best potted soil on the market. She hardly spends any of it, though. She even lives in the same tiny house she once shared with her husband, and still works part time in the salon. She has more time on her hands now, and tends to visit us more, which I personally enjoy. Her beliefs better align with mine, so it makes me feel less of an outcast when she is around. Janet is not religious at all and every time she visits, she gives my family an earful of about how organized religion will be the true end to society. In the past, any weekend she was with us, we ask her to go to Sunday service, to which she laughs and offers some muttering of how it is going to fuck us all up and we need to avoid it like the plague. She doesn't even like stepping foot on the grounds of the church. One visit last year, my mom had a large desk she was donating to the church office, and she asked Janet to ride with her and dad to drop it off and she refused. She said that if she stepped foot in that building, she might burst into flames and the risk was simply too much. Her melodrama for anything religious is great and somehow the wildly made-up assumptions she makes actually seem to get my mom to relax. It doesn't make any sense, but I think we all appreciated seeing Mom chill out.

Janet's ability to loosen my mom up is incredible. Even during visits now my mom doesn't push church on us as much, and she never asks Janet to go with us any more. She hasn't invited her to go since Tate has been taking over, which might just be her trying not to be even more embarrassed by our church these days. Even though she would never go, that chance of her saying yes might just be too great of a risk for my mom. Tate is green, timid, and not a great representation of a well-ran church, and the jokes Janet could make might be a little too much to take. My mom still loved Janet being around and she seemed to be visiting more and more in the past few months.

Fortuitously, Janet is coming into town today, and after last night, I welcome some wild Aunt Janet time. I need to listen to the troubles in other people's lives with their nonsense gossip to escape. I need to clear my head and try to stop thinking of those men, the chair and the shots fired last night. I need to figure out who they all are and why they were there, but right now, I will enjoy some relaxing, Aunt Janet time.

Chapter Four

Minister Bailey

Janet stormed through the front door and immediately yelled for Adam to get her bags from the car. She knows he steals some of her weed each visit, so she started to pack a little extra in a baggie with his name on it. My parents would freak out if they knew, but it is a little thing between the two of them, and it is special. Adam ran out the door while Janet plopped down on the sofa, yelling at one of the twins to crank down the AC. The house is never cool enough for Janet; she would tell my dad that she 'will get enough time in hell one day,' so until then, she wants it sixty-eight degrees with a cold drink in her hand. I ran over to her to hand her an iced tea and she squeezed me so hard I nearly dropped it to the floor. She looked me up and down and told me that the runway awaits, and my looks are wasted in a town like this. I was immediately uneasy and brushed my hair ineptly behind my ears and slouched down.

Adam laughed at the notion and said, "Only if flat-chested girls who look like dudes are the new *it* thing."

To which Janet replied, "Honey, it's not the new thing, it is the thing, the only thing. And when she is making millions walking the runway and you are a bald, has-been, quarterback who must retell stories of your high school days to stay relevant, remember this moment… because today doesn't matter, but tomorrow sure as hell does!" Adam recoiled and ran his hands over his hair to ensure it was still thick and luscious. She then walked over to him, hugged him tight and whispered, "You know you have it all, don't ruin it by making others who have less know they have less or feel they have less." He smiled and carried her bags down to the basement where we had a hide-away bed that was only ever used by her or my brother, Zach.

Janet has a way of making all of us feel special. She knows I am insecure in my looks, especially since I don't look like anyone in the family. She always brings fashion magazines to glance through while sitting on the back porch with a drink in hand. She points out the new hot models, and who they were modeling for, always big names. Then she will try to be sly about it too, but I know she only points out girls with similar features to me. She never gets my attention specifically, but would rather open the magazine wide, pull it far it front of her and is in awe over the beauty of these girls. She always mentions Kate Moss and how she is only 5'7 and the hottest thing now, just to bring a small smile to my face. She knows what she is doing and even though it is vaguely pandering, I welcome it.

My mom didn't waste a moment after Janet's arrival, immediately telling her about the latest divorce in town and that rumor is that they haven't had sex in years. This was my cue to get a snack and get settled in, as it was going to be a long night. Janet chimed in and made comments about the people Mom told her about, and the best part is that these are people that she doesn't even know, but she has strong opinions about the people they *should* be. I constantly catch myself smirking and chuckling at her calling people in this town small-minded, ignorant, and every asshole man my mom talks about is sure to be referenced as a man with a tiny dick by Aunt Janet. My mom gets flush and tells her to stop, but at the same time, I know my mom is thinking the same thing. Her goody-goody, Christian housewife facade fades when Aunt Janet is here. My dad doesn't seem to mind this vaguely wild version of my mom either, and sometimes I think he enjoys hearing her curse or get a little tipsy.

My dad only got upset once that I can remember, and it wasn't about my mom but rather the time Aunt Janet brought lube and condoms for Zach when he turned sixteen. I didn't know what lube was back then, but I had heard the term condom. After that visit and the fight that erupted, I learned that both were bad and not morally approved for a teen boy. I now know that is complete ignorance, but my dad I guess had his reasons for feeling that way. Aunt Janet brushed it off and now is just more hush when giving us gifts that are fine for kids our age, just maybe not fine for kids our age in a town like *this*.

Aunt Janet knows to never tell my dad to calm down or chill out, but she also knows when to whisper and when to deny. If my dad ever found the weed in Adam's room, Aunt Janet would act horrified and shocked with my parents and would even help think of a punishment. She doesn't want to get banned from the house, as how else would we get all our confidence-boosting compliments and paraphernalia? She knows her ultra-liberal ways are needed here; she just has to be careful how they are conveyed. But we know deep down that even if it seems like she is on their side, she is really on ours.

Even more reason why all of us kids trust her. We just know she can play the game and she is here as much for us as she is for my mom. She even found ways to bond with Eve, but it is different. Eve already gets everything she wants, so Janet just brings her something from a trendy boutique in Chicago that no one else in our town could have. Eve will brag about it in school with her friends to no end. She always thanks Aunt Janet but tries to play it cool like it is not big deal... even though Aunt Janet always finds something that is out-of-this-world cool for her.

On the other hand, I know my relationship with Janet is more real and honest, but I admire how she finds a connection to everyone. That's why Aunt Janet is so special.

The twins are still young, so anything with sugar makes them happy. Janet always brings bags of candy for them, and they love it. She brought them candy cigarettes last visit and my mom immediately took them away and threw them in the trash, chastising Janet for the gift. Janet laughed and then handed them like twenty more things of candy before the twins ran off and nearly puked after eating it all in one sitting. The irony; as my mom questioned Janet for the tawdry gift of candy cigarettes given to young, impressionable kids as the gift could teach them immoral behavior, she was smoking a *real cigarette* in our kitchen where all of us kids could see. She never saw the absurdity, which makes it even funnier.

Aunt Janet would smile and nod along with whatever crazy thing my mom and dad would be upset about, and she made sure to not repeat the same action again, well, at least not in front of them. But she always opens herself up to questions from us, offers varying world views and is just a real ally to all of us. My mom is better around Aunt Janet, too, and so every time she is around, we can handle Mom a little more. Mom is liberal for our town, but she can be really uptight and strict. So, a little Aunt Janet goes a long way.

This visit is no different so far. They smoke and drink wine and gossip until the wee hours the first night, which I love to listen to. Unfortunately, there wasn't really anything juicy or worthwhile to stay for that night. The last topic they covered was how leathered some lady in town's skin is now that she has an at-home tanning bed. Funny, but not one of the crazy-good stories I am used to.

I was about to put myself to bed, when Aunt Janet asked my mom if she read the news clipping she sent in the last letter, to which my mom responds, "Oh Janet, I did, and I don't even know what to say. I know you are not a religious person, but that is not something that happens in most churches... not in our church. Minister Bailey is a disturbed man, but maybe he has paid his dues for what he has done. We need to be forgiving and move on. Maybe he shouldn't be blasted in newspapers again, so we all have to relive what happened years ago. I just don't want to revisit any of it again. I feel sick just thinking about everything that went down and I just don't want to do it again. We are just now *finally* able to put it behind us and I want to do that; not read any more about it. Janet, you know why I don't want to do this again. You know what we went through..."

I didn't know what they were referring to, but my mom's voice trembled, and she sounded extremely upset. They were sitting at the dining room table, and I was on the edge of the sofa around the corner. I was only a few feet away, but not within their view. I don't think they knew I was there, as there was no way they would have discussed this so openly if they did.

Aunt Janet stuttered as she tried to respond without fully exploding in anger. "You think he *has paid,* for what he has done? A few years behind bars and because he is a man of God, it is enough? The church and his wife covered it up for years and let it continue. I cannot believe he is out of jail after a few years. That's enough, you think? What about the girl, Rebecca; she is dead, and you know good and well he did that? She doesn't get another chance like him, is that fair? What if it was Adam? Or Monty? You think a few years is okay?"

"Stop, all right, stop it. I don't want to think about my children and that whole situation. I understand it shook your town, but the judge decided and it's over now. What will us arguing over it help? There are people who were a part of it who just want it to be in the past. They want to move on with their lives and with it being in the papers repeatedly, they must relive it, and some just can't. Some are not strong enough to live through what happened, the court case and the verdict again. He is out on parole and will be kept under a watchful eye, and I don't want to live in fear again being close to it all," Mom said.

Janet muttered to herself, something along the lines of, *Goddammit, Rebecca.*

I sat there, leaning closer to the edge of the wall as I was trying to figure out what they were talking about. Who was dead and how did they know her?

Janet stood up and scooted her chair out from the table. She walked to the edge of the dining room, where she saw me sitting there to her right and my mom to her left. She looked down and back up and wiped her eyes and said, "Rebecca, I love you, I do. And I want us to be in each other's lives forever. But you don't understand the world. You don't understand loss. You don't understand tragedy. You are oblivious to this subject matter. You are blinded by your faith and are willing to excuse behavior that is truly appalling because it was performed by someone who has since repented for his sins and asked for forgiveness. There is no coming back for those victims. There is no way to move forward and just be normal. You are worried about minister Bailey being slandered on the pages of a newspaper, while a girl is dead because of him. Kids dropped out of school and have ruined lives because of him. Kids refused to testify out of fear he would kill them just like her. Kids refused to come forward because they are

61

shells of who they once were. So many lives ruined. So many we don't even know about. My town was shaken because of him, and you say he paid his dues after some time in jail. Not just my town, me. I am personally shaken, and you know how close this was to me. Please, you know she won't even leave me alone, which is why I am here for this long, to hide from her!

"The only way he pays his dues is when he is dead. He doesn't deserve a life now, those kids did. That girl did. He took their lives away from them and no request for forgiveness from God will ever give them back what they lost. You need to wake the fuck up. If he would have done this to one of your children, who are not even my own, I would kill him dead. I would make him suffer a thousand deaths. I would torture and maim him, and I would not ask God for forgiveness. As God should know that he deserved every minute I spent destroying him… you need to wake the fuck up, as your take on this is completely fucked."

Janet sauntered past me, she looked me straight in the eyes, reached out her hand and met mine. She folded it into hers, smiled, while tears streamed down her face. Then she walked away to her room downstairs.

I could hear my mom crying softly in the kitchen, I didn't want her to know I was sitting within earshot. So, I quietly moved myself off the sofa and scrambled into my room. I heard her put their glasses into the sink and then sob as she walked past my door to go to hers.

I am not ready for this.

I sat on my bed and just stared off for a few minutes. I just kept thinking about the last twenty-four hours and how it had been surrounded by a dark, ominous cloud. I expected fun gossip and storytelling, not hearing about some dead girl and a disturbed man getting out of jail who supposedly killed her. These were not things that happened in my town or to people we know. These were things I saw in movies and thought were so fake. Our town talked about bad produce at the market, some kid getting into a good college or rumors of some family being in financial trouble. Not about prisons, murders, and anything illegal.

I wrote down the name *Minister Bailey* on the inside of my notebook and the town Janet was from, Oak City, IL. Something was telling me I needed to look into this. I had never heard my mom like that, and it seemed personal to her in some way, so it was not just random gossip.

Right then, I needed to get some rest as my mind was spinning. The next day, I was to find this news clipping and figure out who minister Bailey is.

The next morning, I was supposed to help at the church as there was a picnic on Sunday and I oversee getting games together for the kids, but I wanted to look into this Bailey guy. I called Mandy and asked her to cover for me, as I needed to go to the library and wanted to talk with Aunt Janet. Mandy agreed to fill in for me, so I called the church to let them know she was going to be me for the day. I didn't tell my mom I was switching with Mandy, as I needed to be able to still get out of the house without the million questions she always imposes on me.

As I walked into the kitchen, my mom and Aunt Janet seemed good. They were laughing over coffee and appeared to either have made up or decided to move past it. Either way, there didn't appear to be any tension.

As I sat down, I gave my mom the doe-eyes and then begged her to make my favorite 'eggs in a hole,' since it was the weekend and I joked I was her favorite. She giggled and agreed. While I waited for my favorite breakfast that I cannot make as good as my mom, I sat next to Aunt Janet and asked about her next trip she has planned. Since her husband passed, she takes these amazing adventures from African safaris to cruises around Norway and most recently trekked through Switzerland. But to my surprise, she said that she had nothing on the books and was planning on just spending more time with us. I looked over to my mom who reluctantly paused for a minute, then smiled. I was elated but said why anyone would ever choose here over Paris, Rome, or London was beyond me.

Janet laughed. "Oh, honey, I have already seen those cities and they are true wonders. But being with you all is what brings me the most joy. I am alone these days, and drinking tea in London, having pasta in Rome, or eating croissants in Paris is empty. I'd rather have iced tea on this porch here, with spaghetti your mom has overcooked, and I am just as happy with a McDonald's apple pie as I am with some French pastry." Janet always had a way to make the parts of my life I thought were awful feel magical and enough. I still wanted to go to those cities and would have loved to leave right then, but I understood what she meant.

As my mom placed my delicious breakfast in front of me, she reminded me to chew before I swallowed. I am incredibly thin, but I'm a good eater. I am not too picky but there are a few things I just love: Cheetos, eggs in a hole, tacos, and ice cream, any flavor but strawberry. I don't know what my mom did differently than me when I try to make this breakfast, but somehow, she made white bread, eggs with salt and pepper taste like a gourmet meal. When I was younger, I put ketchup on it, and now I sometimes add some tabasco, but no matter how I eat it, I normally choke from eating too fast and not properly chewing. So, each time my mom makes it, she reminds me to chew, like I am still a child.

I ate quickly while thinking about where my mom would keep her letters from friends, but my thoughts were quickly disturbed as mom yelled for all the kids to come into the kitchen. Everyone staggered in, while my dad didn't move from the couch where he sat and drank coffee until he finished the newspaper, front to back. Normally, Zach is here over the weekends too, but called yesterday and said he was too busy moving to his new dorm before school starts, so he couldn't come this weekend. I was bummed because I like when he is around, but it is also so cool he is at college doing adult stuff. I cannot wait to grow up. As I daydreamed about living with my own rules, I snapped back to reality as the kitchen filled up with everyone.

Mom got everyone's attention and said that Aunt Janet was going to stay a few weeks and she would like everyone's help around the house while she was here visiting. School was starting next month, and we needed to get out of our lazy summer routines, to which Eve and Adam laughed and mumbled under their breaths. Most would hardly call their summer lazy due to all their sports and activities, so it felt more like a dig at me and the twins.

Mom said that today was filled with running errands, so we were to fend for ourselves for lunch and were going to order pizzas for dinner, which was immediately curious to all of us. We never ordered pizza unless we had guests over or mom was sick. Aunt Janet we don't treat like a guest, so it was odd that mom was ordering out. I took it though because pizza is another food I love. Hell, I love all food!

Right before we all broke from the kitchen huddle, mom said they might invite some family over tonight, then asked if one of us would get the cooler out of the garage so we could put some

65

sodas on ice for dinner. That's it. That's why we were getting pizza. The term 'some family' over is always our cousins Sunny and Daniel and their parents when in town, but their dad is deployed right now, and Uncle Ted, Aunt Lisa, and Ryan. Since Ryan was supposedly off in Europe, I didn't expect him either.

Mom was not about ready to cook for an army of people like that, so pizza was always our go-to. I don't care for my cousins at all, so I was already dreading that night. Maybe I could have some friends over to soften the blows from my cousin's presence. The twins interjected in the middle of mom talking and asked to be dropped off at their friend's house for the day, to which my dad shouted from the other room, "Sure, I will take you there when I am all done with the paper." Eve said Olivia was picking her up to go to the mall and get supplies for school. Adam didn't say where he was going for the day, just snuck out of the kitchen mid conversation, true to Adam form. I was shocked that no one asked me what I was up to for the day, but this gave me a chance to look for the letters and to ride my bike to the library to look at news clippings there.

I went to go shower and clean up for the day, when I heard everyone disperse and leave. By the time I came out of my room, the house was empty, and our house was never empty. I double checked the garage to make sure all the cars were gone, and I looked at the front and back porch before I went into my parents' room. I started looking in their dresser, closet, shoe boxes until I realized my mom's letters were not in there. My parents had minimal items in their room, and not a lot of hiding spots. I began to walk down the hallway wondering if my mom didn't keep them at all, when I stopped where I stood and yelled, "Fuuuuccckk!" My four-wheeler was still in the field! I never got it the day before, shit. I was so distracted and got busy on who

66

knows what, I never went back to the field. My dad never said a word either, so he must not have noticed it wasn't parked in the open carport behind the house. I wanted to find those letters, but I did not want to deal with my dad or my mom coming home to notice it missing. So, change of plans. Collecting my four-wheeler was top priority now.

I thought about riding my bike back there, but then how would my bike get back? So, my only option was to walk, and I didn't want to walk that path again. I was numb even thinking about it. Plus, it was another blisteringly hot day, and a mile walk carrying a gas can is the definition of a terrible day. My mom said I couldn't ask any siblings for help, and I wouldn't ask *them* for help, so my next idea was technically following the rules.

I rode my bike down to farmer Jack's house and knocked on his door. His wife Edna opened it and smiled from ear to ear. "Oh, Monty, how are you dear? Is anything wrong?"

"No ma'am, I was just wondering if Jack was going to be heading into the field today at all. I ran out of gas and need to bring a gas can up there to fill up my four-wheeler to get it home." Edna is the sweetest woman around and hurried me into the house to get out of the heat. She shouted for Jack while she poured lemonade from a pitcher on the able. Jack walked into the kitchen, smiling like Edna did when she opened the door. "Well, Monty, it's good to see you. What brings you to our kitchen today?" I explained to him my dilemma and he immediately instructed me to throw my bike in the back of his truck and to hop in. He had some gas cans already in there and said he would take me back to the field and then drop my bike back at my house when done. He had just saved me tons of time and I could not have been more thankful.

While driving back on the dirt road through the cornfields, I pointed to the far corner of the tree line, where my four-wheeler was. As I was pointing, Jack stopped right next to the elm tree. He pointed over to it and asked, "Do you know the story of this tree?" I stared at where the chair sat just a day ago and looked at the ground where the blood was. My entire body quivered, while I squinted my eyes tight trying to unsee it. You could still see some markings on the ground. As I tried not to think about it, flashes of Thursday night filled my head before I answered him. I had to shake my entire body to rid myself of the images.

"No, sir, my dad just said it was your special spot, and we were never to bother it."

He smiled so sweetly at that and continued, "My father planted that tree when he was around your age. This land was never his, but he was a farmhand here when he was young, and he just loved this spot. He would run over and sit on that little hill whenever on a break, but it didn't help on those hot days. So, one summer while working, he saw a small elm tree in the tree line and dug it up. He dug a big hole right there on the tiny hill and replanted the elm tree. He didn't have any reason to, but just thought the field needed an elm tree right there and as it grew, it would offer the shade needed on a hot summer day. As he grew up and eventually bought the farm across the way that I have now, he told me about that tree. When I was ready, I walked myself over to the man who owned this land and asked if he would allow me to take over these fields to grow corn, when he was ready to retire. It was just good timing I guess, as he retired from farming that year and I started leasing this land right away.

"I didn't know as much about farming as my father, but I learned, and I dedicated my life to it. Before my father passed away, he just said to take care of that elm tree, and whenever I see it, to think of him. So, when your daddy bought up this land,

I was so grateful he let me still farm here and he let me keep this spot. But, darling, you don't need to leave my spot alone, as my father would want you to enjoy the shade. That log over there is as much mine as it is yours, and you are welcome to enjoy this spot anytime you want. And if you ever find me here over my lunch break, stop by, as I can promise you that Edna packed me some of her delicious pie that I am happy share."

His words brought tears to my eyes. I thanked him and told him that I would bend my dad's rules and enjoy the elm tree. He smiled again and drove on until he got to the end, where my four-wheeler was. He helped me put some gas in it and made sure it started before he turned around to head back. As I turned to take the dirt road back, I saw Jack stopped with his head turned toward the old cow barn. It was on our part of the land, but we never used it. I don't even remember ever even peering inside of it. As I looked the same direction as Jack, I saw the old structure with weeds around it, a small dirt path to the doors and old rusty farm equipment laying on each side. It had a double door enclosure on the front that had a chain and padlock. We didn't keep anything inside, so I was unsure why it was locked up. I assume my dad locked it to keep all of us out of there, as it looked like it could collapse at any moment. But as I looked at Jack stopped in front of me, I wondered what he was looking at. After a minute or two, he continued driving and I stayed behind him.

When we got to the end of the dirt road to turn onto FM 250 to get to the front of my house or to continue the narrowing road to come up the back of our house, he stopped and smiled at me, waved, and said to 'stop by anytime!' I knew it was simply a pleasant thing to say, but I also felt like he meant it and I wanted to take him up on it. I had questions about these fields that maybe he could answer one day.

As I pulled my four-wheeler back under the carport, Jack dropped my bike in the front yard, and I waved one more time. I went in the house for a drink of water, some snacks, and my backpack when my dad walked in the front door. He looked pissed about something, and I wondered if he had found out about me running out of gas.

I grabbed a banana and walked over to him and timidly asked if everything was okay, but before I could finish my question, he slammed his keys down on the console table and shouted, "Why the fuck is everyone so goddam incompetent?" My dad cursed, but normally not the 'f' word, and not often when talking directly to us kids. I didn't really know what to say; I was so caught off-guard. Before I could answer, he told me to tell Mom that he had to head back out to a jobsite again as there was more shit that was missing, and he must get to the bottom of it. I didn't dare ask what jobsite, as if my mom needed to know, she could page him and find out. He went back into his room and came out changed into his dirty work gear. Not stuff he wore often any more, normally what he wore when completing projects around the house, so I wasn't sure what he was up to. He grabbed his pager, his keys and stormed out the front door. I followed him out and just asked about the twins. 'Dad, how do you want the twins to get home?" to which he replied to leave a note for Mom inside to pick them up by four p.m. if he was not back by then. I complied and left the note under the fruit bowl and headed out to the library.

I love the library in our town. It smells old inside, but a smell that I want to bottle up. Every time I open a book to read it, I have to press my nose inside the pages and get a big whiff. It is one of my favorite smells in this world. The best part of the library other than the smell is that no one bothers me there. I can sit quietly for hours reading about anything. I will get so lost in stories that I won't realize hours have passed and I think it's been only minutes. No one else in my family loves books like me.

Eve is an exceptionally good student, but she would never read for fun unless it was a Seventeen Magazine or directions on her new facial cleanser. I, on the other hand, know everyone that works at the library, and we have such a good rapport that when I am not there for a few days, they will begin to worry and even call my house to check on me. One of the librarians, Cliff, always pulls books he thinks I will love, and he is usually spot on.

Cliff is one of the people in town I assume lives a very *unconventional lifestyle*. I would never ask if anyone was gay, but if I were to guess, I would guess Cliff was. He is so kind and creative, and he has these amazing stories to share. He dresses very edgy and has this passion for plays and musicals. He saves money to take trips to Chicago to see *Cats*, *Phantom of the Opera* or whatever is the new and hot show and after will glide through the stacks telling me about how wonderful the shows were.

He has a roommate, Bruce, who works in the town thirty minutes away as a financial advisor at a bank. I have never met Bruce, but the way Cliff describes him, I just sort of imagine a balding, muscular man, who lays in tanning beds and drives a BMW. Bruce travels with Cliff to shows and they splurge on fancy dinners and cocktails. Things that a librarian cannot afford, so I assume Bruce pays. Even the house Cliff lives in is genuinely nicer than something I would assume he can afford, even with a roommate.

I never asked if he owned it or if Bruce did or what, but it was right in town across from the post office, with gorgeous landscaping, a little picket fence around it and the most idyllic design. It is the most beautiful house in the downtown area, and before I knew Cliff lived there, my mom would always say how adorable it was and how she loved the Victorian style. She appreciated the stunning light blue paint and canary yellow front door and how when the flower boxes were blooming, it looked like a picture in a magazine. I completely agree and was so pleased to find out I knew who lived inside.

I picture the way it is decorated, but I would never dare to ask Cliff to show me, even though I am sure he would without hesitation. I preferred using my imagination instead. I picture large pieces of art on the wall and sleek furniture with large throw pillows. Mismatched drinking glasses that each had a story behind where they came from. An eccentric dining room table and four chairs that sat at it, but two extra in the corners when they were hosting. I imagine it smells like honeysuckle, for no other reason than that was my favorite smell, other than the inside of old books. Every time I pass the house, I imagine a new detail inside. I have been doing it for so long, I would be crushed to see it for real and it be nothing like my vision. I also just enjoy my library relationship with Cliff so much, between listening to his stories and sharing good reads that I don't want to taint that in any way. Like, what if the house was a total mess inside, smelled like old shoes and didn't have a tasteful piece of art in sight? I would feel completely broken.

I walked into the library and was immediately greeted with Cliff's familiar face. He walked out from the behind the counter to give me a light hug and point to a stack of books he pulled for me. He immediately began telling me how he was so disappointed because he was supposed to be Chicago seeing Les Misérables that night, but Bruce was home sick, so they had to cancel the trip. He went onto tell me that the church picnic tomorrow was going to be so fun, and he couldn't wait to see what drama unfolded.

We always banter about the craziness that happens at these town and church functions. I listen to the kid tales, and he listens to the adult ones; then we convene during my next library visit to share the juicy details. I guess I am more like my mom than I thought, as I do enjoy gossip exceedingly more than I should.

Cliff went on for a few minutes about his change of plans and how he has been on the phone for hours moving his ticket, hotel, and dinner reservations around before asking me what brought me in for the day.

Cliff sort of realized he was going on and on when he finally grabbed my hands and asked how I had been and what he could help me with. I explained that I needed to look for some newspaper archives but had never done that before – if he could help. He immediately obliged and walked me over to the archives and asked what we were looking for. "I am not completely sure what I am looking for, but I overheard some story between mom and Aunt Janet that happened in Oak City, IL. Something about a minister with the last name Bailey and getting out of…"

Before I could finish, Cliff yelled, "Jail!"

The entire library turned to him as he looked down and dragged me over to a desk where the microfiche reader was, then sat me down. "Monty, why are you looking into minister Bailey? This is a bad man, and I don't think you need to go snooping into anything to do with him," Cliff said. I insisted that I was simply curious because it seemed like a truly relevant topic for my mom and Aunt Janet, and I wanted to know why. I explained that Janet was from Oak City, so she was awfully familiar with the situation, but in no way was she going to fill me in. Cliff's face appeared poignantly. His normally happy and inviting face was completely downtrodden. He looked me straight in the eyes and sighed. "Monty, I will tell you what happened, but you need to be ready, as it is truly tragic. Are you mentally prepared to hear something extremely horrifying?" I nodded as I swallowed the knot in my throat, and my entire body felt weak and nervous. I second guessed my decision immediately.

Cliff walked me past the checkout desk and told the other person working that he was going to take an early lunch break and be back in a bit. He walked me outside and sat me down on the picnic benches behind the library. He looked at me, even more distraught than before and began.

"Monty, first, I trust you and I think you are wise beyond your years. I know you *know* that I am different, and that Bruce is not just my roommate. He is my boyfriend and has been for over two years. Because of where we live, it is not something we can be open about, so we keep it very under wraps and if we ever want to hold hands or have a romantic dinner, we go to Chicago. We can be ourselves there and it feels good. But hatred exists everywhere. And there is a lot of hatred toward gay people and bad people take something that is natural and make it into something that it is not. Bad people exist everywhere. Minister Bailey is one of those bad people. He is the worst kind of the bad. His actions affected people like me and Bruce, and it reiterated these false and fucked up notions that all gay men were bad men. When this story came out, it was horrifying for more than just those involved. Monty, if at any time you are uncomfortable, please tell me to stop. This is just a lot, and it makes me sick even thinking about it again."

I nodded again that I was ready, but I was now really unsure. I think I am mature and can handle just about anything, but the way Cliff was describing this, I hoped I was right. I hoped I didn't crumble or run away in tears halfway through the story. I took a deep breath and muttered, "Go ahead, I'm ready."

"Come with me to my house; instead of just telling you everything, let me show you. My house is just down the street, I have a lot of what you are looking for saved there," Cliff said.

Great. Just as I ruminated about how much I love imagining what his house looked and smelled like but was so glad I didn't really know; it was all going to be ruined. I was now on my way to his house to get documents about a case that apparently was so huge that not only were Aunt Janet and mom involved, so was my librarian? This week just kept getting weirder.

I wanted to know now more than ever, so I followed Cliff to his car, and we got in.

During the quick drive, Cliff continued, "Several years ago, a young girl in minister Bailey's congregation found out she was pregnant. The girl, Grace Stewart, told her parents that it was a boy she had been seeing, but the boy adamantly denied ever doing anything more than kissing her. When they prodded the young girl more after his denial, she closed up completely and didn't want to talk about it. The boy's family pleaded with her to tell the truth, but she wouldn't say anything. She stopped saying he was the father, but she never denied it either. The boy and his family were living in hell, as the town was conservative, and they mistook her shutting everyone out as the boy acted against her will. He was being ridiculed and teased and threats were coming to him and his family.

"It was such a scandal for Oak City, that the boy and his family eventually uprooted their lives and moved out of town. They were starting to get death threats and no matter how much they pleaded with Grace to tell the truth to make it stop, she wouldn't say anything.

"During the beginning of her pregnancy, Grace's mother passed away from breast cancer. It was a battle she had been struggling with for several years and her body finally gave out. At a time when a girl truly needs her mother the most, she was gone, and Grace was very alone. It was just her and her father, and he was distant and hard to talk to. He was not dealing with the loss of his wife well and fell into a deep depression. He didn't know what to do with her, so he started sending her off to church more often, to be out of the house while he mourned. She was very reluctant to be around anyone, let alone be at the church, so it might have helped him out, but poor Grace was struggling immensely."

We pulled up behind the house and walked to the back door. I was just as nervous to see the house as I was to hear this story. We walked in and I smiled. Cliff looked at me like I was nuts, as he is here telling me this tragic story, but I was smiling from ear to ear.

His house was just as I pictured. Ornate and modern décor at every turn. Beautiful vintage glassware in a modern hutch. Throw pillows and colorful blankets adorned the couch and there were exactly four chairs around the kitchen table, all different and unique with two extras off to the side. There was limited art on the wall, but the rugs, pillows, chairs, and décor made up for it. It did not smell of honeysuckle, but it was filled with warm vanilla with a hint of cinnamon.

"Hmm, no honeysuckle," I blurted out without thinking. Cliff turned to me. "What about honeysuckle?"

"Oh, umm, sorry, it's so silly. I just always imagine what people's houses smell like and I guessed yours would be honeysuckle. Totally weird, I know," I responded while feeling about three inches tall.

"Oh, ha, not to worry. I do that too. We don't do a lot of floral in here, we love sandalwood, pine, vanilla, cinnamon, and

Jasmine," Cliff said, while making me feel normal and not like a complete weirdo.

Cliff walked back into a room that looked like an office and came out with a filing box. He motioned for me to have a seat next to him at the table and started to pull stacks of paper out.

"Okay, as I was saying… people who were interviewed after the tragedy, and I will get to that, said they saw Grace at church often, always in the back, always standoffish and as the months progressed during her pregnancy, she became a shell of who she used to be. They said that she looked ill, with dark circles under her eyes, pale skin and tattered hair and clothing. She would shudder if someone touched her arm or hand, and she would not make eye-contact with anyone. Many assumed it was not just the pregnancy, but the scandal with the boy that left town combined with her mother's death all hitting her at once. But others, well, others thought it was something more, which later they found out to be right."

Cliff laid out different stacks of papers. Some news clippings, some looked like sworn affidavits, others were notes, and random photocopies and photos. This case was personal to him too for some reason, as he had a treasure-trove of information.

"A woman from the choir was interviewed after the arrest…"
"Okay, when you say tragedy and arrest, do you mean minister
Bailey?" I asked.

"Yes, let me get to that – this is all about his story, sorry it's long. As I was saying, a woman from the choir was interviewed after the arrest and said at one time, she tried to talk to Grace, just to be a shoulder for her. She believed everything this girl was going through as simply too much for anyone to go at alone, but she was completely shut out by Grace. The women interviewed thought with losing her mother and getting ready to become one herself, that another woman, a mother, could be helpful, but Grace didn't see it that way. Grace by this time had completely shut down. She was no longer speaking to anyone, and it appeared that was not eating or caring for herself. It became a topic at the church on how to get her help. She needed it.

"By this time, many people in town reached out to her father to offer assistance and support, but her father was completely broken hearted and was not able to be a good father to her. The church sort of took it upon themselves to try to help Grace, if for no one else than the baby. The baby deserved support, whether Grace or her father could give it to him.

"Grace was having a boy and before she stopped talking to everyone, she had talked about potentially naming him Sebastian. So, the church started collecting slightly used baby clothes, a bed, highchair, and other supplies to help her get on her feet when he arrived. Near the end of her pregnancy, the church had a sort of baby shower to give her everything they collected that had been stored in the basement of the church.

"One of the men in the congregation arrived at the church before service to start setting up the hall downstairs to prepare for Grace's baby shower. He was setting out tables and chairs, had balloons and the goal was to make it a really nice gathering for Grace to know she was loved, the baby was loved, and everyone was there to help her in any way they could.

"As he was finishing up, he decided to pull all the baby items out and put them on display. They were kept in the basement, through a storage room, in a back area that looked to be an old bedroom like one a janitor or someone would stay in. The storage area was damp, and no one wanted the items to get damaged, which is why they moved them further back into the private room…

"Monty, are you okay? It gets really fucked up now and I just want to make sure you are okay," Cliff asked.

I responded confidently that I was, but the truth was that I was terrified. "Yes, Cliff, I am big girl, I can handle it."

"Okay, so as he opened the door to where the baby items were kept, he walked in on minister Bailey half dressed, with a blindfolded teen boy, whose hands were bound, laying on a bed, and he was performing oral sex on the boy while the boy wept. As the man saw the horror, he picked up a chair that was next to the bed and hit the minister over the head, knocking him to the ground. Immediately he began to untie the boy, remove his blindfold, and reached into the bins to find a baby blanket to cover him with. He helped the boy up the stairs to where they called the police from the phone in the office. The man was so distraught with what he had just witnessed that he didn't check to see if minister Bailey followed them, how hurt he was and never even looked at the face of the boy to see who he was. The man was in complete shock. As he explained to the 911 operator what was going on, he took off his jacket to wrap around the boy when he finally saw his face. The man began to sob while on the phone and could hardly keep any composure to give the address. As the operator asked if he knew who the victim was, he hesitantly said, 'The minister's stepson, Trent Bailey; he is here with me now.'

"The boy was no longer crying at this point, he just asked the man to barricade the basement door to make sure minister Bailey did not come up until the police arrived. He was calm and more collected than the man who found him, who was shaking and crying violently. As they sat there and waited, they heard sirens in the distance. As the man looked over to Trent, a small stream of tears ran down Trent's face, but his face otherwise sat cold and detached.

"As the police arrived, so did the congregation, as it was a spectacle within minutes. The police broke through the crowd and rushed the front of the church. Once inside, Trent and the man pointed to the basement door, so the police could find minister Bailey. Two police officers tended to Trent, but he refused to leave in an ambulance. He refused to leave the spot he was sitting in at all. He just stared at the basement door, impassive. As he watched it open, he saw his stepfather in handcuffs, still half-dressed, wrapped in a blanket. They made eye contact and Trent just said, 'Enjoy your penance.' Then, he stood up with the police officers and said he was ready to go to the hospital.

"The crowd had grown to what seemed like a wild mob of screaming and crying, while they watched the man that led their church, get led out in handcuffs and not much more than a blanket. He held his head low as the police walked him out and glanced up just as they placed him into the police car, where he made eye-contact with the young pregnant girl, Grace Stewart. As the police car drove away, Grace fell to the ground crying hysterically. One of the female police offices walked over to make sure she was okay, Grace whispered, 'Me too,' under her breath. The first words anyone had heard from her in months. The police asked what she meant, and she just looked down at her pregnant belly and once again said, 'Me too.'

"Grace locked eyes with the police officer, and she just broke down crying and said she was ready to talk. The police drove Grace to the police station and sat her down with two officers to take her statement. Since she was not eighteen yet, they called her father to come down, but he refused to come. He was in complete disbelief and said he would try to get himself together to pick her up. He gave verbal consent over the phone for her to give her statement, and then they got her permission to record her and told her she could take all the time she needed.

"Grace nervously gave gruesome details of what went down in that basement over the years, and several times the police officers taking her statement had to walk away to take a moment. She offered explicit details of the first time she was raped by minister Bailey, which led to the several month-long torture she was still living.

"Her statement was leaked to the press, so this is why I have copies of it. Also, I have a few connections, so I was able to get the entire statement, which you can read. But I have to warn you, I was in complete shock when I read it. I feel like it all has just stuck in my mind over the years, and it makes me sick when I think about her statement and the statements of the others."

"So, it wasn't just her, and the stepson Trent? There were others?" I asked.

"Unfortunately, yes. Many others. Some care forward, but most didn't. Look at this stack, start with her statement and then you can read more about the case. I will make us some snacks and check on Bruce. I don't want to read this right now; I just can't handle looking at it again. But take all the time you need," Cliff said.

I started with the statement, and as I picked up the papers, my hands were shaking, and my stomach felt like a pit. I was trying to act like I was okay in front of Cliff, but I wasn't. In the statement, Grace said that she had met with minister Bailey after school one day to discuss how she was struggling with her mother's illness. She said that she was angry at God for letting her mom get sick and knew she would eventually die, leaving her to grow up on her own. As her anger grew over her mother's illness, she confessed to minister Bailey that she had been taking some of her mom's prescription drugs that were very strong to dull the pain. She also confessed that she had been promiscuous with a few boys from school, resulting in her committing oral sex on them. She told him that she was doing things to just not be in her current mind, as her life was miserable and imagining her mother being gone was unbearable.

As minister Bailey listened during the first few visits, he gained her trust and told her that she would have to carry out dutiful acts for God in order for him to forgive her. She asked what that meant, and minister Bailey said it would take time and he could show her, so he set a day and time for them to meet each week to allow him to show her. After a few weeks, he eventually led her to the basement and said she looked tired and should lie down. He had her lie on the bed in the small room through the storage area and told her to close her eyes and he was going to lay hands on her and pray. After he was done praying, he moved his hands from the top of her head, down to her collar bone, down her arm and over to her stomach. He asked her if she wanted to devote herself to God, and if she was willing to truly work toward earning His forgiveness, to which she agreed.

Grace said the smell she could never forget. He always met with her after lunch, where he ate pizza before her meetings and the toppings nearly made her sick. It was a weird combination of anchovy, pineapple, sausage, and mushroom that his office smelled of, as well as his breath. It was an innate detail but was only mentioned because he was a creature of habit, down to what he ate each day of the week. She still cannot eat pizza.

Minister Bailey then moved his hand down from her stomach, and slid it underneath her underwear, to which she squealed and opened her eyes. He said if she was going to act like a whore for boys at school and steal from her parents while taking drugs illegally, he had to make her understand what she was doing to herself and how she was shaming God. He told her he had to make her feel that same shame in order not to repeat it any more. He told her their sessions were private and she was not to share them with anyone else, and if she did, he would be forced to tell her parents what she has been doing and she would be dammed to an eternal life in hell. As tears ran down her face, she agreed to do what he said was necessary to earn her way back to God, and she allowed him to push his fingers inside of her. He rubbed his hand in and out of her, then turning her onto her side. He then pulled her pants and underwear down, just below her cheeks. He took his hand and separated her cheeks, caressing her anus. He continued to spit onto his hand and force his fingers insider of her again.

She began to cry out in pain, and he told her it was pain she deserved, and she did this to herself. As she lay there, he continued to enter her vagina and anus with his fingers, as she squeezed her eyes closed. He made heavy breathing noises and kept telling her she was a sinner, and he was purging her of her sins. He became winded and caressed her faster and harder. As she begged him to stop, he told her it was the only way to save her. He screamed out to Jesus and said to forgive Grace for her sins and exhaled dramatically. He then extracted his hands from inside of her and told her to pull her pants up.

She sat up on the bed, with tears down her face. He asked her if she felt shame, to which she agreed, she did. He said that is what you should feel. If you feel shame, you are salvageable. If you did not, your soul is lost. She uttered that she felt shame and she didn't want to burn in hell and would do whatever necessary to save her soul. Minister Bailey reminded her that this was only between the two of them, and how he cared for people who have lost their way as much as she had, and that it was delicate and unique to them. She asked him if he would have to do that again and he admitted that he might, but each week it would be whatever God wanted in order to prove that she still loves him and was devoted to him. He would follow whatever God asked him to do.

The following week, she arrived at their meeting day and time, and he walked her down to the basement room again. This time, he immediately blindfolded her. He stood her against the wall and removed her pants. He then unbuttoned her shirt and exposed her breasts from her bra. He turned her around, spread her feet open and she felt something cold, like metal, between her legs. He slid it up her legs and stopped just outside of her vagina. He leaned forward and told her that her only way back to Him was through pain and showing her dedication. He took the object, to which she believes now was a narrow, metal pipe, and entered it into her. As she felt it enter her, she quivered and nearly fell to the ground. He grabbed the back of her hair and continued thrusting it inside of her. He asked if she was a virgin, to which she said she was. She could feel that he was aroused as he pressed against her. She asked what she was feeling against her back to which he didn't answer. This time was much quicker and within one or two minutes, he stopped. He turned her around, pulled her pants up and told her to cover herself. As she finished dressing, she removed her blindfold and asked again what she felt against her back.

He answered that a man has needs and Grace was a distraction from God and creating physical pain for him. He said that she should feel more shameful now than before and her body making him feel aroused was her fault and that he was sickened by how evil she was. He told her that he didn't think she was salvageable any more. She wept in response and told him she wanted to be saved and she would do whatever it took. He told her to come at the same time and day next week and he was going to try something different.

As Grace arrived the next week, she was hesitant to go inside the church. She wanted to be saved but part of her thought what he was doing was wrong. But he was an elder, he was the minister, he knew what God wanted and was there to do God's work, so she had to trust him. When she walked into the church, he immediately led her to the basement. When she entered the room, he shoved her down onto the bed. He yelled to remove all her clothes in an aggressive tone. She began to cry, as this didn't feel the same. This felt violent and his attitude scared her. As she undressed, she wept. He told her to wipe her eyes and put the blindfold on. She placed it over her eyes, and he pushed her down onto the bed, flat on her back. He asked her again if she was a virgin, to which she said yes. He said that to show true sacrifice to God, she must shed blood to honor him. As she laid there, unbale to see, she heard his belt buckle jostle, an unzipping and then the pressure of his body on top of hers.

He said he didn't want to do it, but she was so lost he didn't have an option, and in order to grow close to God, she had to offer true sacrament. He was aroused and took the tip of his penis and tried to enter her, but she was dry and not aroused, so she shrieked in pain. He continued to spit on her vagina, telling her he was disgusted he had to do this, but she had left him no choice. He took the tip of his penis and again tried to enter her. He was partially inside of her, and she cried, asking if he was taking her virginity. He responded that she was not really a virgin since she

85

had other boys' penises in her mouth, so her virginity was not even hers any more. It was God's and he was taking it to give to him, as penance. Her body wasn't ready for him to enter her, but he aggressively pushed until he was in. He thrust only a few times while she hysterically cried. He pulled his penis out and ejaculated all over her. He threw a cloth on top of her and told her to wipe it off. He then informed her that there was blood on the bed, so it had worked, but she needed to clean her vagina before she got dressed.

The next few months were more meetings of the same distinction, where he repeatedly raped her, with one of the times resulting in her pregnancy. During the visits, she was seeing other teens coming in and leaving the church looking troubled; but none of them ever spoke to one another. She remembered hearing the sound of a camera on several instances and footsteps around her when minister Bailey was on top of her.

She said that each time after the first two, he always blindfolded her, so she couldn't see. But she believed that there were other kids present and watching several times. She would hear murmurs and movement in and out of the room, but she was not sure until one of her last times there. Her last time with him, her blindfold was not secured tightly and left part of her eye uncovered. She turned her head to the side, she saw a boy there, around the same age or a little younger. He sat in a chair with his arms bound, trembling; he was not blindfolded. He had bruises on him, and he looked malnourished. She didn't recognize him from church or school and wondered who he could have been.

After months of the same, during her last visit with minister Bailey, Grace said she sat up after he was done and told him that she was pregnant. He screamed and threw items at her. He told her that she had ruined everything he was trying to do for her and

86

that now everyone would know she was truly a whore. He told her that she was to tell her family it was from being with another boy from school who liked her, and she was never to mention his name. He threatened her, blackmailed her and as she stood up crying, he kicked her from behind while she was half-dressed, so she fell to the ground. The boy that was sitting in the chair yelled to stop, and minister Bailey told him to shut his mouth, then struck him across the face. Grace pulled herself from the ground, grabbed her remaining clothes and ran out of the church.

She said she was never taken to the basement again. She attended church but if he passed her, he would spit on her, call her a whore, and tell her to enjoy her afterlife in hell, where she belonged.

It was at that time that she realized he never did this to save her. He never wanted to help her. He was a pedophile who preyed on disturbed youth, and he was pure evil. He abused his power and what he did to her was pure torture and now she had to live with it for the rest of her life. She explained that she never told anyone because she truly feared him. Her reputation was already destroyed being a pregnant teenager, so her only motivation to stay quiet was for her safety and her child's.

As she went on with her pregnancy, she would sit across the street sometimes and just watch teenagers going in and out of the church. She took polaroid pictures of several of them. Over her pregnancy, she saw ten different teens coming and going, all appearing to have the same relationship with minister Bailey as she did. But something she told the police was that she never saw that boy come and go into the church. She only saw him that one day and never again. She didn't know who he was, where he came from or how minister Bailey knew him. She told police that she recognized everyone she took pictures of, and she told them that Trent Bailey was one of them. She offered to share the photos with the police of Trent, but she said she would not share the others, as it was not her place; it was their decision. She had the pictures saved in a safe place and if others came forward, she would share them. The police said that could be tampering with evidence, but since the photos did not show minister Bailey doing anything, she stood her ground that she was not sharing them.

Grace stated that it was obvious that minister Bailey had elicited teens for his own sexual disfunction, and he knew which type of kids to target. They all had something personal in their lives he held as blackmail if they ever said anything. They were troubled outcasts who were losing their way to drugs, alcohol, sexual promiscuity or were enduring abuse at home.

Every teen she saw going in and out of the church were kids who were struggling in their life. She knew these kids; she knew some of them very personally. She had shared her personal struggles with some of them. She knew the hardships that many of them were going through. They sought help and guidance and he abused that. He destroyed them. Minister Bailey always said it was private, to never discuss it, as repentance for their sins. He lured them in by offering salvation and in turn mentally, physically, and sexually abused each of them. As Grace was finishing her first statement, her water broke, and she went into labor. They anticipated getting more specifics on every experience she had, as well as dates and times, but before they could schedule another meeting, they had to call for an ambulance. They called her father to let her know and even though she was in active labor, she promised to meet them again to offer more information that would help get minister Bailey locked up.

While Grace rode off to the hospital, they passed the church, where hundreds of people stood, surrounded by news vans. People were shouting at each other and there were already signs held by some touting his innocence. The situation became a spectacle for the town immediately, and this was before anyone knew of there being other children. It was before anyone knew Grace's story.

"Hey, are you feeling, okay? I see you are done with her statement. It's a lot, I know," Cliff asked.

"Yeah, I think so. I just feel sick. I cannot even imagine going through that," I replied.

Cliff went on to explain a little more. "If you look at the newspaper articles or any snippets from local news, only Trent Bailey was listed as a victim. Since he was a minor, his name was not mentioned, but it was insinuated that it was him. His mother kept silent the entire time, avoiding speaking to any news outlets, offered limited testimony to police and became reclusive; not being seen out hardly at all.

"No other children came forward right away, but the police received several anonymous calls asking about the case. They asked if their names had to be used, what proof did they need to come forward and what protection did they offer them from minister Bailey coming after them. A few parents came forward on the defense of minister Bailey, stating their child sought time with him to recover from depression, personal struggles, addiction, and other issues, and he, a devout Christian man, saved them. They called anyone who said otherwise liars, and said they deserved to burn in hell while minister Bailey deserved to be vindicated of these lies.

"Before the trial began, one boy and two females who were all over eighteen by this time, said minister Bailey had done this to them too. They didn't have many details to share but said they had moved on and done all they could to forget it. They offered timelines, offered the same details about him using blindfolds, which was not publicly known, they offered details about the room, and how he said it was their way to prove to God they were worthy of Him. That they were worthy of his love. Their stories mirrored that of Grace's, with less detail.

"The two females had very similar stories and were from around the same timeline. They each said that he never penetrated them with his penis, but he only used his fingers. They said that he used a paddle to spank them and after meeting with him only a few times, they knew something was wrong. They knew what he was doing was not right and they stopped seeing him. One of the girls told her parents she was still meeting with him to help guide her, but she would wander around the park nearby instead of going inside when they dropped her off. The other girl told her parents she felt 'fixed,' and she loved God and was on the right path, expressing that minister Bailey saved her just to avoid ever going back. But they didn't speak up because they were terrified of him.

"The boy on the other hand said that he believed minister Bailey was drugging him from the start. He would go to meet with him and would sit in his office and talk about what was bothering him. Minister Bailey would offer him a soda to drink, and he would become tired soon after. He had memories of lying in a bed without his pants on, being fondled. He would wake up clothed on the bed and minister Bailey would say he fell asleep in his office, so he laid him down there to rest up. After a few visits like this, minister Bailey started telling him to go down there with him. He coerced him to perform sexual acts and whenever he would refuse, he would threaten him. He used blackmail and said that he was a homosexual and was an abomination and if word got out, he would be shunned for life. The boy said that he was not the only one there at times, there was another boy he would see in the storage area. He always looked ill and had bruises on him.

"One of the last times minster Bailey touched him was around the time the town heard about Grace being pregnant. He said that he had seen Grace leaving in front of him one day and she was crying, disheveled and extremely upset. He went in and minister Bailey scolded him for being early and struck him across the face. He said he was a lost soul and there was no saving him. He said he should tell the whole town he was a faggot and that he wasn't learning anything from their lessons, he was only enjoying the sexual acts and becoming a perverted young man. At that point he turned to leave, and minster Bailey grabbed him from behind and choked him until he fell to the ground. He blacked out for a moment and came to, to minster Bailey masturbating over him. He stood up, startled, and ran out of the office. Minister Bailey screamed after him that if he said a word, he would kill him. He left and never returned.

"During his statement, he mentioned a boy, just like Grace did. Someone he didn't know from school or church, and it seemed like he was maybe being held against his will. He said that he heard the shutter of a camera in his dreams, when he thinks he was being drugged and he didn't know for sure, but his gut told him that there were pictures out there of what minister Bailey was doing. Like the boy was helping him photograph these horrific sex acts. By the looks of the boy, he believed he was being abused too, but he looked far worse. He told the police to find this boy and they would have the proof they needed. He swore that this boy was the key to getting minister Bailey for good.

"The police searched to find any kids that were missing at the time, at around that age and with that description. They posted a sketch at one point based on Grace and the other boy's description, and they even questioned Trent, but Trent refused to talk about any of it. It was of no benefit, as no one else ever formally came forward. There were calls to police with people sobbing and breathing on the other end of the phone, but this case was so personal, it seemed like many couldn't come forward. They feared the outcome for them. Minister Bailey had power and secrets on them, and he was able to keep them in hiding that way.

"The really fucked up part was that Minister Bailey was released on bail almost right away. He was able to get the ones that thought him to be innocent to raise his bail money and money to get one of the best lawyers in Chicago. Someone a minister could not afford on his own. Minister Bailey had a following that supported him blindly, and he became more of a celebrity during the trial than a villain. His case hinged on the witness statement from the man that found Trent Bailey in the basement of the church with minister Bailey. He was being threatened and intimidated and at one point he and his family were placed on police surveillance as he feared for his life. People picketed his home and work and called him a liar, pervert, and sexual predator. Some argued that he was the one sexually assaulting kids and minister Bailey was the one that found him, and he beat him and staged the entire scene before the police arrived. They even said he had bribed the parties that came forward to say it was minister Bailey and not him. The town was completely divided by this case.

"The kicker was, Grace did not file a lawsuit against minister Bailey for anything other than statutory rape. She did not want the skepticism that surrounded the abuse and just wanted to move on and raise her child. Police had her statement, she had photos, she had dates, times, and details that no one else could have known. But she changed her version of the truth and said she was a willing participant, but a minor and therefore her and her father wanted the charge of statutory rape. In addition, her attorneys wanted a DNA test to prove that Sebastian was minister Bailey's. Grace denied wanting this request, as she wanted to move on. But during the end of his trial, before conviction, she agreed to petition for DNA, she just needed to file the paperwork."

"That is so fucked up! Why would she change her story? I don't understand," I asked.

"Because she knew that even behind bars, he was a danger to her and her son, and she just had to protect the two of them. This trial was long and arduous and took over two years before minister Bailey was convicted of any crimes. When convicted, he was to serve twelve years in prison, but while out on bail, was given forty-eight hours to get his affairs in order before he turned himself in. They literally acted like it was a white-collar crime and it was no big deal. The day minster Bailey was to report to prison, the news broke that Grace Steward had killed herself. The news was that she had taken shattered glass from a windowpane and slit her wrists, while her son was at the home with her. She was found by her father in the middle of the day, after a neighbor called him at work about Sebastian crying hysterically for hours. "It appeared to her father and first responders that there was a struggle, and no one could explain how the window had glass inside the home, like someone came in from someone breaking it from the outside, and why she would have chosen that method. Grace was lying on the living room floor, next to a knocked over chair, blood everywhere and her son screaming on the floor next to her. The toddler had a large cut and was bleeding, while lying on his mother hysterically crying. The scene was gruesome and didn't add up. Grace's father swears that there is no way that she would ever take her own life and if she did, never with her son by her side. She loved him and would never cause him such pain. "The theory of many was that minister Bailey went to her house and killed her before he went off to prison. To make sure her story never changed again. Trent Bailey, on the other hand, disappeared. He never pressed charges at all, and his mother says she lost all contact with him before the trial began. Weird, right? He was seventeen when everything happened, and many thought it was simply too much for him to take. People in town that supported minister Bailey called his son a liar, a faggot and said that he was twisted and was just another abomination out there to ruin someone's life. The charges against minister Bailey were all from the three people that came forward, and Grace. He was formally charged with three counts of first-degree sexual abuse, two counts of child enticement and four counts of unlawful sexual conduct with a minor.

"There were more severe charges on the table, but without Trent or Grace wanting anything more than statutory rape, they were all dismissed. Grace's son was placed into foster care, as her dad said that after losing his wife and daughter, he was not mentally fit to raise the child. He wanted what was best for him, and growing up with this tragedy around him would never offer him an opportunity at life. He collaborated with a social worker who swore to find him the best home possible. So, I am guessing what your mom and Aunt Janet were talking about is, last month, after serving only seven years in prison, minister Bailey got out on parole. There have been mixed reviews, and many think it was enough time, some thought too much as they assumed his innocence and others thought he should have died in prison. The wife's side was never really discussed, and she was never interviewed or spoke on the story. She just sort of disappeared too. So that is where we are today…"

I sat stunned. I didn't know what to even say. But as I looked at Cliff's face, stricken with sadness, I felt like there was more to the story. "Is that the whole story? Is there anything else regarding the families or the minister or anything else?" I asked.

"Is that it? Is that not enough?" answered Cliff.

"No, no, I am not saying it is not enough. It is completely heartbreaking, and I am speechless. It just feels *more* personal to you, or you are holding something back. Is it because I am so young, you don't think I can handle any more?"

"No, it's because I know what happened to Trent after the story broke, and I know one of the victims who did not go forward. This case is very close to me to this day and his early release is painful. I have not been able to talk to anyone about it, but I am worried about victims who didn't come forward before that he will intimidate or potentially hurt to assure he never has to go back to prison. He is a sick man and there is so much more that he did that was not covered in the trial or on the news. So much worse… I just don't want to talk about it any more, I feel sick," Cliff said while motioning me to walk back outside to the car with him.

Chapter Five

The Letters

I wanted to ask more questions. I wanted to console Cliff, but I knew he was done with the conversation, and I needed to give him space. I trusted him and I felt so grateful that he could entrust his own personal story with me. I was thankful he was willing to tell me about minister Bailey as I didn't think I could have discovered any of that on my own. I want to share with him what happened under the elm tree two nights ago, but now was not the time. I knew I could trust him and when the time was right, when I learned what I needed to, I could go to him if needed.

Once back at the library, I rode my bike home, but not before stopping at the local mart. I wanted to stay on my dad's good side, because the last time I saw him, he was pissed, and I didn't want to add anything to what was already on his shoulders. I went into the mart and bought a bag of ice for the cooler to put the drinks in when I got home. I precariously placed it on the small bicycle saddle and tried to tie it down with an extra shoelace from my backpack. It didn't look great, but I just wanted it to hold until I got home.

I pulled up next to the garage and the cars were all there. As I lugged the bag of ice through the garage, none of my siblings had gotten the cooler like Mom asked, so I went to grab it. I climbed up the shelving to scoot it to the edge, when a smaller individual cooler with a small handle fell to the ground. The sound was loud, and I saw a piece of plastic shoot across the garage floor. Dammit, here was another thing to piss my parents off about. I never saw them use this small one before, so I thought that maybe if I put it back on the shelf, they may never notice it was broken now.

I moved the large cooler down, then dumped the ice inside before picking up the smaller one and cleaning up the piece that fell off. As I picked up the smaller cooler, I saw inside were stacks of mail. As I reached in, I pulled out envelope after envelope, all addressed to Rebecca Patterson. I couldn't believe it; by complete accident I found my mom's letters and within the envelopes were photos, handwritten letters, and several news clippings. I could now dig into why this case was so personal to my mom and Aunt Janet. But first I needed to get through the night, as our house was full, and I didn't want to get caught going through my mom's stuff. She had it all hidden for a reason. I just needed to figure out why.

I carried the cooler with ice inside and set it next to the table. I started to open the cases of soda and drop them into the ice when my mom asked me where I had been. "Umm, I went to get ice in town, didn't want to add more to yours or Dad's list today. Just chilling the soda now," I said. Her response was strange; my mom hugged me tight and stared at me like I had just given her a kidney. She was an emotional person, but this was different. Something was off with her, but I couldn't figure out what it was. Right when I was looking at Mom bewildered with her unjustified response to me getting ice, my cousin Daniel walked by and smacked the back of head while yelling, "Hey, nerd, what's new in flat chest land?" My mom told him to cut it out but didn't do anything more. I just looked at him and smiled. Daniel was super troubled, in my opinion, and I just wanted to avoid any additional interaction with him. I had more important things on my mind than how to cleverly respond to his childish remarks.

As the family members started pouring into the room, my anxiety increased. I don't fit in with my immediate family, so add aunts, uncles and cousins into the mix and I am just a loner with nowhere to go. I walked over to my mom and asked if Mandy and Hunter could come over to hang out with me and help protect me again Daniel and Sunny. She knew they always picked on me and without Zach here, I had no real hope of survival. She agreed but said they had to go by nine. I ran into my room to call them up and within fifteen minutes Hunter's mom was dropping them both off at the door. They lived on the same street a few houses apart, so their moms took turns driving them around. I was the only one that lived so far out in the county, super annoying. Finally, familiar faces that I trusted and who wouldn't smack the back of my head or call me names.

Mandy twirled through the front door and hugged me while Hunter knocked, even though the door was already open, before coming in. He greeted me with a 'hey' but then walked over to my mom and dad and did the whole, *Mr. and Mrs. Patterson, thank you for having me over tonight, if you need help with anything, please let me know!* I would say he was a total kiss ass, but he wasn't. He means what he says, and he is just a genuinely nice guy.

The twins saw Hunter and ran over to him; they adore Hunter. He picked up Delilah, gave her a spin, and then did this bizarre handshake with Simon only the two of them knew. Before we could all sneak away from the chaos and chill in my room, Hunter said hey to Adam and they gave a very 'bro-worthy' half hug and talked football season and cross country. Mandy and I kept making yawning motions while checking our imaginary watches until he got the hint and bowed out from the chaos. I grabbed a couple sodas and Mandy grabbed a box of cheese pizza and we escaped to my room. There were so many people in the house that even with my door closed, it sounded like my parents were hosting a raging party outside my room. I immediately shoved two slices of pizza in my mouth, not properly chewing, and washed it down with my favorite Big Red soda. We never had soda in the house unless it was pizza night, and I could drink Big Red forever. I was in heaven at that moment.

Mandy and Hunter immediately teased me on how fast I was eating, but I didn't care. It was a crazy day, and I never had my lunch since I was busy learning about the ominous story from Oak City. I wanted to fill them in about everything that had happened over the past few days, but before I shared about the men under the elm, I thought the minister Bailey story was more pertinent as the letters that were waiting. As I filled them in on everything Cliff told me, other than his personal story about him and Bruce, every few minutes someone was at my door needing something or just bothering us for no reason. It took an hour to get the whole story out, and Mandy and Hunter didn't say a word the entire time. When I was done, Hunter was speechless, while Mandy looked visibly upset. "Can you imagine what Grace was going through? Do you think she took her life, or do you think minister Bailey killed her? I wonder what happened to the boy, Sebastian, I sure hope he was adopted into a good family," Mandy said.

"Grace? What about Trent? Being raped is horrible no matter who you are, but being raped by your stepfather! Does that make the minister gay? Was he gay or straight since he was married and raping girls too? There is so much to unpack here but I am also confused on where his wife was during all of this. Did she

99

know anything was going on? Are there any stories from her take on things?" Hunter asked.

I didn't have the answers, but we kept going back and forth on details I got from Cliff before I remembered the cooler. "Wait, I forgot to mention one hugely important part of the story. When my mom and Aunt Janet were talking about this last night, they mentioned letters and news clippings on the case and something about it is personal to them, but I don't know why. I looked for the letters in my parents' room earlier, but nothing. But when I was getting a cooler from the garage before you got here, I knocked over a smaller cooler and found the letters in it! I wanted to grab them so we could look at them now, but everyone was already here, and it was too risky. I plan on getting them later once everyone is gone."

Hunter and Mandy were both on the edge of their seats, wondering how in the world I was sitting in here with the letters out there. They kept trying to convince me to let them create a diversion while I go and grab them, but with one mistake my mom would move them somewhere and I would never find again. My plan was better; once everyone went to bed, I would get them so we could go through them the next day.

No sooner than I finished my thought, my mom came to the door and told us to stop being antisocial and to join the group. I rolled my eyes and begged to be allowed to stay in my room, but she was adamite that was not an option. I stood up and dragged my feet to the door and followed my mom into the mayhem, while Mandy and Hunter followed. As I began to sit on the floor next to the sofa, Sunny bumped me with his ass so hard that I fell to the ground.

"Seriously, are you a child? Is something wrong with you and your brother? Keep your goddamn hands to yourself or I will kick your ass!" I screamed.

Oh, fuck. I'm dead. My parents will lose their shit for me cussing in front of them and the rest of the family. I squinted my eyes shut and when I opened them, I was ready for my dad to go nuts, but he didn't.

"Daniel and Sunny, I am sick of your shit. She is right and she *should* kick your asses. Leave all the kids alone and grow up. I will not repeat myself," Dad asserted.

I don't know what just happened, but I was stunned. I didn't get questioned on where I was all day, my mom got emotional for me getting ice and now my dad defended me cussing and threatening someone. When I came back from the field, did I go through a wormhole and enter another dimension? None of this made any sense, but I took it while it lasted.

Sunny mumbled an apology under his breath, and I wanted to think he really felt bad, but I think he was just embarrassed for my dad calling him out. He was a bigger ass than Daniel for sure and I don't think he has a semblance of a conscience. Maybe there was hope for Daniel, but not Sunny.

The room was tense and not just from my outburst. I felt like the adults were all not saying something, I just didn't know what. Aunt Janet was always the life of the party, but even she seemed subdued. I didn't know what to do, but thought maybe I could lift the tension in some way. I asked my mom what errands she and Aunt Janet ran and then went on to ask the twins how their playdate was. My mom started listing everything she accomplished and as she went through each item, and she seemed to light up when she realized how much she accomplished today. Aunt Janet started to chime in and laugh at our small-town stores and lack of available men. She said that when she was ready to date again, she knew the first place not to go: Blakesville,

Indiana. The room laughed and it started to lighten up.

Holy shit. My awkward ass was just social and created an ice breaker. Not a big moment for most, but for me, this was huge. I need to mark the date: Saturday, August 3rd, 1996, I was not completely and embarrassingly awkward!

Simon and Delilah said that they had an awesome time at their friend's for one reason: their pool. They swam all day and were sun kissed and still smelled like chlorine. I love that smell. My dad was sitting next to Delilah when she blurted out, "So what does a girl have to do to get a pool of her own?"

My dad chuckled and said, "Save up about twenty-five thousand dollars and I will help you build one." Delilah rolled her eyes and gave a 'whatever' and then pranced off into the kitchen. I stared at my dad, and he was just looking at the floor, absolutely distracted.

"Dad were you able to take care of the work issue today?" I asked with a nice bubbly tone.

He looked up from the ground and turned his head straight onto Uncle Ted, and stated, "No, actually, I didn't. Shit is showing up missing at every job site, and all varied materials, like almost enough to build entirely different home or to renovate one. It all smells fishy, and I will get to the bottom of this and whoever is behind it will pay!"

The room went silent, and that thick tension filled back into the room. Uncle Ted defensively responded, "Why are you looking at me, do you think I have something to do with it, or I know who does? I can assure you that this is as much of an issue for me as it is for you, so don't go around making comments that are absurd!"

My dad did not like that response at all. "If you were doing *your* job, doing your site visits, and setting up security like you are supposed to, this wouldn't be happening. You say it's as much on you as on me, so do I get to take the loss out of your paycheck? Oh wait, I don't. I have to eat the costs and I have to find a way to handle the customers, all while you get to clock out at five and go home. You are not heading back to jobsites on the weekends or after hours and you are not the one paying to investigate what is going on. So don't give me your partnership bullshit. Do your fucking job and get a handle on this or else I won't be able to keep paying you, and you can find another company to do a half-ass job at," Dad yelled.

"What do you mean paying to investigate?" Uncle Ted asked with a look of worry.

"Well, when I am losing thousands a week, and you are no help, I have had to hire people who can. It's interesting what private investigators, security cameras and security guards can find out," Dad said with a menacing look.

"You are being ridiculous, Mike, and wasting more money… I think it's only fair of you to the let employees know they are being watched. This is wrong," Uncle Ted said while brushing imaginary things off of his pants.

"Oh, I am not watching employees, so not to worry. But lots of good leads to follow up on," Dad said while staring Uncle Ted straight in the eyes.

The entire room went silent, my Aunt Lisa smacked her lap and stood up, then motioned Uncle Ted to follow. "I think this night is over and we are going to head home. Thank you, Rebecca, and Mike, for having us, but we must get going," Lisa said. As they walked toward the front door, Sunny and Daniel said they were heading home too. Daniel said to tell Zach to call him if he needed any help moving. Sunny made a stunned face at that notion and ran out to the car without saying a word to anyone. My dad got up and walked behind them all to shut the door. He meandered over to the cooler and pulled out a beer. As he cracked it open, he looked at Aunt Janet and said, "You are not about to let me drink this alone – let's go sit on the porch; I need to get out of this room!" Aunt Janet smiled and followed him to the cooler and then outside.

My mom told the twins to get ready for bed and told me that my friends needed to get going soon. I smiled and agreed and then my mom grabbed a beer, which she never drank, her pack of Virginia Slims, and she went out back to the porch. I don't know what was going on tonight, but nothing was making any sense.

As the room emptied, Hunter looked at me and motioned his head toward the garage door. Mandy said she was going to go into the kitchen and clean up the pizza boxes, so that she could make sure the three of them stayed on the porch and didn't catch us. I didn't want to get the letters yet, but the plan wasn't awful, so I agreed. First, I went into my room and emptied my backpack; it was embarrassing to do in front of Hunter, because along with a few books and pencils, there were about twenty empty snack wrappers. As he smirked at the pile of garbage on my floor, I picked the bag up and headed toward the garage. I looked at Mandy and she nodded that it was all clear. Hunter stood outside the garage door as I ran in. As fast as I could, I emptied the contents of the small cooler into my backpack and as I zipped it closed, before I stood up, I was startled by Adam saying, "What the hell are you three getting into?"

I was frozen for a moment, then turned around to see him smoking one of Mom's cigarettes next to the garage door that was still open. I responded with, "Shouldn't I ask you the same? Where the hell were you hiding out during the fucking shit-show inside earlier? And smoking when Mom and Dad are both here, God it must feel good to have no rules and get away with anything!"

"Listen, Monty, there is shit going on in this family that you have no clue about, so pardon me if I stay away from the insanity that our family creates. I was wondering when you would learn about Mom's letters – there is some juicy stuff in there, just be ready to learn a whole lot of shit that you might not be ready for," Adam said.

"Wait, you know about the letters? How do you know about the letters? I just overheard Mom and Aunt Janet talking last night and I wanted to know what they were talking about, and I accidentally knocked this over and saw them earlier."

"Monty, I don't know anything new in the cooler, but found the same hiding spot of Mom's a while ago and read a lot of the stuff in there. What I learned completely change my life. I don't look at our parents, our family, God, or this fucking town the same. And I hated it all before, but now I just want to get the hell out. Just be in the right head space before you look at them, as they really fucked me up," Adam said.

I stared at Adam for a few seconds while he took a big drag of his cigarette before going back into the house. Mandy and Hunter followed me into my room, and I locked the door. I was strictly forbidden from locking it when friends were over, but I would take that risk over getting caught with the letters. There were only a few minutes left before Hunter's mom would be here to pick them both up, so I emptied the contents of the bag on the floor, on the other side of my bed, where if you opened the door to my room, you couldn't see them. There were at least one hundred letters saved. As we looked at the postage marks, these spanned over years and there were several different senders they came from. I made three stacks and wrapped a hair-tie around each, then slid them under my bed. I walked Hunter and Mandy to my bedroom door, and we agreed to meet after the church picnic tomorrow. As they walked to my front door, Hunter's mom drove up the driveway and they both looked back at me and gave a small smirk. There was a lot to unpack right now, and I was so glad I had two friends I could trust.

I walked over to the kitchen to make a bowl of ice cream before bed, and the sliding door to the back porch was open, with just the screen door closed. As I put the container back in the freezer, I heard my Aunt Janet sobbing. I took my bowl and moved over to the corner of the kitchen floor next to the door and sat down to try to hear what was going on. There was only the hood vent light on over the stove so I don't think they could see me, but I wasn't sure. As I sat, I leaned in to make out their words. "But *it's her* and I don't want to talk to her. She has been to my house everyday begging for me to help her, and I just can't. I can't be in my house because she is either outside waiting or calling me thirty times a day; and I am so thankful to be here, but when will this end? When can I stop hiding from her? Before I left yesterday, she waited in a car out front of my house for three hours, just glaring at my front door. How can I live like that? I sent my neighbor to her car to ask for directions so I could sneak past to get to my own car to come here. This is my nightmare and I know I must do something, but what?" Aunt Janet questioned.

My mom, now matching her tears, blew her nose and answered with, "Oh Janet, I don't know how to help you with this. I want to say to just give her what she wants, so she will leave you alone, but I don't know if she really will leave you alone. There is no right answer, but please know you can stay here forever. I have not told you yet, but she has been writing me

106

too; I have gotten four letters in the past few months. I haven't responded but she is looking for answers that I don't have for her and wouldn't share even if I did. She is lost and confused, and she wants help, but she is looking down the wrong paths for those answers."

I sat there befuddled. Were there more pieces to this puzzle? As I took a spoonful of ice cream, I heard my dad get up. I moved my body just a little to try to see what was going on out of the corner of my eye, and he just stood up, placed his elbows on the railing, placed his face in his hands and began to cry. I had never seen my dad cry; I started to tear up just hearing him.

He turned around and grabbed one of Aunt Janet's hands and one of my mom's hands and said, "We did the right thing, I know we did. I know that if we had the chance to do it over again, we would do it the same way. We have been through harder times than this, so we can get past this. She is not going to affect our family or you, Janet. We need to think about what she is really looking for and what we can actually give her. We are not telling her where he has been and we are not telling her who helped, but we can tell her that he is alive, and we can push her in a completely different direction. He wants nothing to do with her and he swears she knew *everything* that was going on. I don't know what to believe, but I do know our loyalty is not with her and we have chosen our side and we will stick to that. Should I just call her and tell her to back the fuck off you two, or what, you tell me?" Dad said.

Aunt Janet responded with, "The letters, what did she say in the letters?"

Oh shit, I have the letters, what if they go to get them and they are gone? I knew I should have waited until everyone was in bed. God, why didn't I go with my gut?

107

"Janet, the letters from her are complete nonsense. She rants on for pages that she didn't know and that he was lying the entire time. She says if she just sees him again, she can explain it all and she can fix it. But I really don't believe her. There are holes in what she says and part of me thinks she helped. That she engaged in some way. And I know, that is not a very Christian thing to think, but dammit, I do. I have known her for so long and there was always something that seemed off, something that was hidden. I don't want to offer one bit of help to her. I say fuck her; we are not calling her, and we just stay put here and come up with something else. We don't owe her anything and we are being harassed. For God's sake, we should go to the police and file a restraining order!"

"We cannot do that, Rebecca, are you insane? We are not innocent here, so we are not about to involve the police. Plus, you know who they side with, and I am not about to have my name plastered out there and what we did exploited as something that was wrong, because it wasn't! But I know that is not how the law looks at it," Dad said.

Aunt Janet responded with, "Okay, no one call her or write her. I am going to stay here, and we will think of a way to get her to go away, without the police. In the meantime, we need to make sure he knows what is going on with her. Rebecca, do you still have his number; can we call him tomorrow? I never kept track because I thought it could harm him. When he left, I let him go and didn't even keep his number written anywhere. I don't trust her and wouldn't put it past her to break into my house. When I cut ties, I meant it. His safety was my only priority!"

"I do... I know how to contact him, and I will take care of this tomorrow," Mom said pensively.

I peered out of the screen door. As my mom muttered those

words, my dad gave her a look like I had never seen. It was anger, it was hurt, it was honestly cold-hearted. He looked scared underneath the grimaced face. I don't think he wanted her to contact whoever they were talking about.

I didn't know what I was missing, but I was sure the letters had some answers. I wanted to start looking at them that night, but I thought I needed my friends support if I saw something in there that I was not ready for. I placed my bowl in the sink and as I turned around, the three of them stood in the doorway.

"Oh, Monty, I didn't know you were in here... umm, what are you doing," Mom hesitantly asked.

Realizing my presence was not wanted, I simply responded with, "Oh, I wasn't, just putting this old dish in the sink before I head to bed, love you guys, night!"

I put my head down and just short of ran to my room. My heart was racing as I thought they knew I had heard something I wasn't supposed to. Shit. One more thing to worry about.

I got ready for bed and turned on my clock radio to listen to music to distract my mind. Last I remember was going over the previous forty-eight hours and trying to make any sense of it all. I must have dozed off quickly mid-thought, as I barely remember closing my eyes or falling asleep.

The next morning, I woke up to the usual Patterson chaos, as everyone was practically screaming in the house. Everyone was getting ready for church since my parents were asking us all to attend before the picnic. It was not common that we all went as a family, so I think this added to the usual morning nonsense.

As I went into the kitchen, I saw Aunt Janet sitting on the back porch with a cup of coffee. I walked over to her and sat down next to her and cheerfully said, "Good morning, Aunt

Janet!"

As she turned to me, she smiled and gasped, "Oh, Monty, it is so good to see you. It is such a stunning morning; I even watched the sunrise. Feels like we have a little break in the god-awful heat this summer, as right now there is a small breeze coming in and it feels wonderful. Just feels like it is going to a really good day."

It was good to see her in better spirits today, but I couldn't shake the conversation from last night. I needed to get to the letters so I could get answers.

I gave Aunt Janet a squeeze and went back into the house. My mom made a pile of Eggo waffles, and some orange slices scattered across the table. I was making a plate, when Dad walked in, already in his church clothes with the paper folded in his hand. I smiled at him and mumbled a 'good morning' through a large bite of waffle, and he just smiled and poured himself some more coffee. He seemed normal, but him choosing to join us for church was not normal. So, I still felt confused.

I got myself ready for church and met the family on the front porch. We were all there, except Aunt Janet. "Mom, is Aunt Janet not coming with us today?" I asked.

To which she gave a chuckle and said, "Oh, honey, if she steps inside a church she is worried it will burst into flames, you know that, so no, she won't be joining us. But she will be here after the picnic, so don't you worry." We all piled into the van and drove the two minutes to church.

It was so strange being there with the entire family. If the past few days had not been bizarre enough, getting the seven of us to attend together, when it wasn't a holiday, was maybe even stranger. When I got out of the car, Mandy and Hunter were there and we immediately ran and got seats in the very back. My parents, the twins and Eve sat with my cousins and Aunt and Uncle, acting like nothing happened last night, while Adam found some people from school and chose a spot far away from all of us.

As Tate walked up to begin his sermon, he said that today's sermon was going to be about forgiveness. He asked all of us if there was ever a time we needed to be forgiven. He continued to ask if there was ever a time when we had to forgive. The sermon was the best he had ever had, and I even enjoyed it. He referenced bible verses, but very few. He seemed driven emotionally by it and he spoke up; we could actually hear him. I didn't have to read his lips once because he didn't mumble.

When he was done, he reminded everyone of the picnic out back and to make sure to thank all the volunteers that made it all possible. As he began listing names, he said mine, and my mom looked so proud and applauded, when no one else was applauded for; super embarrassing. The thing was, I didn't help, but rather Mandy did my work for me, so I had this surge of guilt that she wasn't recognized like she should have been. I whispered I was sorry, and she gave me such a stern look and responded with, "Are you serious? I do *not* need anyone here thinking I support this nonsense; I am good if they don't even learn my name!" The three of us laughed and got up to walk out to the picnic.

As we walked out back, I saw Edna and Jack near the dessert table. I went over to say hello, but before words could leave my mouth, they both shouted, "Monty, oh, how are you dear?" Jack went on about how the congregation was in for such a treat, as Edna made ten pies, all assorted flavors. He said if his wild and unruly past kept him out of heaven, he didn't mind one bit, because he has been tasting it every day with Edna's pies. She just blushed and told him to be quiet. The two of them were truly adorable. I smiled at them both, grabbed a piece of peach with a big pile of whipped cream on top and went to sit under some trees with Mandy and Hunter.

Hunter sat next to me and immediately asked if I had brought the letters. "No way, I can't be carrying those around. I think we should head back after the picnic; I will grab them and let's go meet in my field by the old cow barn. No one is ever back there, and I am sure my mom won't catch us there." Mandy and Hunter agreed it was a good plan and they went off and said 'hi' to other kids from school. I sat there devouring the pie, as Jack was right; this was the best pie I had ever had. I had my eye on the dessert table planning my next slice when I saw a short man, small amount of scruff on his face and a military-style fade haircut talking to Jack. My heart sank into my stomach... the man driving the truck!

I didn't know who he was, I had never seen him before, but Jack and him looked like they knew each other well. I kept staring at them, completely stunned. I had to do something. I had to figure out who he was.

I stood up, walked over to the table, my knees quivering, my stomach in knots and my hands shaking just trying to hold the empty plate. I muttered, "Oh, Jack, you are right, this is the best pie I have ever tasted. I can't imagine anything being better than that peach!"

He laughed, and said, "Monty, the peach is good, but the apple is worth breaking the law for!" The joke was funny, but given the situation, I didn't laugh, I just froze. As I reached for the apple and tried to keep with the small talk, Jack said, "Where are my manners? Greg, this is Monty, her family owns the land we lease. And Monty, this is Greg, he is my new farmhand that is helping me get ready for harvest. I am not the young man I used to be, so we use my brain and Greg's brute strength!"

"Nice to meet you, Monty... so you're a Patterson?" Greg asked.

"Hi, Greg, yes, I am, but don't hold that against me," then I laughed. But Greg didn't. He gave me a strange look and just quietly said something to Jack and walked away.

Greg was him. Greg was the person driving the truck on Thursday night. He worked for Jack, but how did he know the other guys? I didn't understand the connection between him and the other men. I had never seen him around, so he must have been new. So, who was in the chair and who had the shotgun, and how do they have a connection to Jack's farmhand, Greg?

I felt like I needed to talk through this with Mandy and Hunter, but one thing at a time. I needed to get through this picnic and work on the letters. I knew there was information in them I needed to know. As I sort of stared off, thinking about everything going on, I saw my mom in the distance.

My mom looked annoyed, made eye contact with me, and then walked over. She leaned in and whispered, "These people are total dullards. I don't think I ever noticed it until Janet pointed it out. I sure hope you don't turn out like any of them!"

I laughed and said, "Mom, are you seriously just realizing this? This town is stuck in the wrong part of history and the people are about as interesting as watching paint dry." She laughed and told me to gather up the twins and get loaded into the van.

The picnic had just started, but my mom made her appearance and quickly decided it was not for her, which was totally fine with me. I yelled for the twins and then told Mandy and Hunter to meet me in one hour. While we gathered everyone up, I saw Mom talking to Tate, then she gave him a long hug before walking over to the van. It was a good sermon, so I was sure she was letting him know. Maybe he had it in him after all.

As we all piled back in the van, Adam said he was going out with some friends and stayed behind. Of course, my parents agreed without asking any questions of who and where, but I guess that is how it goes with Adam. Eve sat next to me and was trying to get my attention in the van. As my eyes turned to where she was pointing, I saw her holding a folded-up letter. I shrugged, insinuating I didn't know what I was looking at, as she whispered, "Jason gave this to me, and wants to meet up!"

I didn't know what to say, but Jason was *not* a good guy. He was friends with our idiot cousins, wildly good looking, but not a good guy. Rumor was that he took another girl from school out for a few weeks, convinced her to sleep with him and then completely blew her off before spreading a rumor that she was a whore. He had also been known to do a lot of drugs, and Zach said he did some really terrible things to people. I didn't know everything that Zach knew, but I trusted his opinion on Jason, and he would not approve of Eve going out with him.

I did not like Jason, and other than his looks, I didn't know why any girl would go for him. As we pulled into the driveway, I looked at Eve with a worrisome look and when we got out of the car, I grabbed her hand. "Eve, I worry that Jason is going to take advantage of you. He seems to collect women, use them, and then throw them away," I said.

"Monty, just because no one wants to be with you, doesn't mean you need to ruin this for me. I am not going to marry him; he just wants to meet up later for a party some local kids are throwing. I am not going to drink and would never touch drugs, so there is no harm in just showing up," Eve shouted.

I simply nodded and walked into the house. I didn't know

whose party it was, but I didn't know of a time Eve had gone to a party, so it was already out of character for her to go. Jason was bad, he was very bad, and I was worried Eve was going to find that out the very hard way. But I said my piece, and she was going to do whatever she wanted anyway. I had other things to worry about and couldn't spend time on her right now.

I scurried into my room, grabbed my backpack, loaded it up with some snacks and the letters and headed outside. But as I stepped one foot off the porch, my dad shouted and asked where I was going. Of course, at our house, I get questioned, while Adam doesn't have to explain anything to them, and Eve prepares for some raging party. Such a double standard.

"Dad, I am taking my four-wheeler out for a ride, that's it," I shouted back at him.

"Well, make sure you check the gas before you go, you always forget," he shouted back.

He was right, I do always forget. There was a little in there from when Jack helped me, but I needed to add more. As I reached for the big gas can, I picked it up and the lid was not on all the way, so it spilled all over my shirt, arms, and hands. I wreaked of gasoline, fuck.

I cleaned up best I could, then filled up the tank and took off. I could smell myself the entire ride, but it seemed to fade by time I got to the field – well, that, or I was just getting used to the smell. When I pulled up close to the cow barn, I parked the four-wheeler just to the side of the dirt road at the end of the crops. There were a lot of weeds past the crops on the way to barn, but they were pushed down, and the path was somewhat cleared. It looked like the area had been bush hogged recently, but overgrowth was already coming back. I never really came this close to it, so nothing seemed out of the ordinary.

115

I was about fifteen minutes earlier than I had told Mandy and Hunter to meet. So, I plopped down and started organizing the letters by sender and date. While I was sitting, I heard a movement in the cow barn. I jumped up thinking at first it was collapsing, or some wild animals were inside; I was sitting against the side wall, ready to be crushed or attacked. But then I heard talking inside. I walked around the side of the barn to the front where the double doors were. The chain and padlock were gone, there was a small crack in the door and as I walked closer, I could hear distinct voices.

I didn't want to make any noise or create a shadow peering through the door, so I got down on my hands and knees and crawled over. As I peered in, I saw the white and blue truck and Greg. That's where they went Thursday night, to the barn! That must have been why Jack was looking at the barn yesterday, maybe be noticed tracks or noticed the chain and padlock. I couldn't see who Greg was talking to, as the other man was on the side of the barn completely out of my vision. But I knew the voice; it gave me goosebumps just to hear it. Ryan.

"Listen, we can't do this, we need a new plan. What happened the other night can't happen again and now he is just out there and can say or do anything. I don't think you have a handle on what the hell is going on. This is not the plan, and if you don't figure this shit out, I am walking away, and you can clean up this mess. You need to know that I am not covering for you with the police, you are on your own," Greg yelled.

"I know him, and he is not going to go to the police. The other night was out of hand, but you know that wasn't my call. I didn't want to scare him like that; he is reasonable, and we just need to talk to him. Let me go to his place and try to catch him when he is not expecting it; I think I can reason with him," Ryan

116

said.

"Are you mental? You can't reason with him; he has pictures, knows who we are and what we are doing! He knows too much! We need to get rid of him, there is no other way," Greg screamed.

"Listen, I am not going to *get rid* of anyone, that was never the plan. I can explain to him what is going on and I can get the pictures, I know I can. It is his word against ours, so he is not going to go to the police. You know who the real problem is, and we need to focus on him and the task at hand," Ryan said.

"Ryan, do you forget that he is still in there? It is not just his word, he could lead the police there right now," Greg said.

"No, no, he is not there. I moved him Thursday night after the incident. I wasn't taking any chances. Only I know where he is now; we are fine. You need to chill the fuck out while I figure out what to do next. I am first going to find him and try to reason with him, if that doesn't work, we can discuss more extreme measures. But stay close to the others and make sure they trust you. I am far more worried about what is going on there than this issue," Ryan said.

"In the meantime, you need to stay out of sight, and I need to stay away from your family. Your cousin gave me a look today at the picnic like she knows something. It was super creepy. But I don't know how she would know me," Greg said.

"Who, Monty? Are you serious? She is just a kid; she is weird and just odd; she is no one to be worried about. I assure you; she didn't give you any look, she is just unusual around everyone. Now, let's get this truck working, I only have a few hours before I need to get out of sight, unlatch the hood," Ryan said.

All I could think was *Shit, Mandy and Hunter were going to be there any minute and this is not safe. I need to get back on my four-wheeler and stop them before they ride back here. But if I start my four-wheeler back up, they might hear it.* Just as the thought crossed my mind, I heard, "Do you smell gas?"

Oh, fuck.

"Dude, we are literally in a barn with an old-as-fuck truck, yeah, I smell gas, and oil and all kinds of shit," Ryan said.

But the gas smell was me; they could smell me. I slid my body away from the door and ran back to my four-wheeler. I was just going to risk them hearing it start up because I had to get the hell out of there when the music started up in the barn. I have never been so happy to hear *Journey* in my life. As the music blasted, I knew it was my chance to start my four-wheeler back up.

I started it up and drove out of there as fast as I could. I got to the end of the dirt road to stop Mandy and Hunter as they turned off FM 250. No sooner did I arrive; they rode up on their bikes. I told them the farmer was out in the field and it was noisy and impossible to go through the letters. I convinced Hunter to let me ride on the back of his bike and for us to head over to the cemetery, just down the way. I left my four-wheeler at the end of the dirt road, parked off to the side and hopped on with Hunter. Hunter made sure to tell me I smelled like shit no less than ten times on the sixty-second bike ride. God, I did smell bad.

We went to the back of the cemetery near the mausoleums, which was creepy enough, but the only place to sit was under a tree next to a freshly filled burial spot for a lady who died a few days prior. She was ninety-four and a crotchety old lady, but her funeral had quite the turnout. There were flowers all over the fresh dirt. Eerie.

But eerie did not quite describe where we were and what we were about to get into. I opened the backpack and pulled out the envelopes. We each took a stack and organized by date and sender. The minute we got started, Mandy gasped, drawing our attention. "Umm, Monty, your mom knows Trent Bailey. This entire stack is from Trent, going back about seven or eight years," Mandy acclaimed.

"How would my mom know him? That doesn't make any sense at all. Okay, let's keep organizing and we can start reading once we get everything put together," I directed.

The piles were divided into five new stacks of senders: Janet Bridges (Aunt Janet), Trent Bailey, Tracy Lilliam, Angie Sauer, and John Doe.

I stared at the stacks. I knew Janet. I knew Tracy was one of the friends Mom made the summer she lived in Chicago. They kept in touch, and I believe she met up with her when in Chicago, but we had never met her. I knew the name Angie Sauer, but I couldn't remember where. Trent Bailey was the largest surprise; we knew who he was, but no idea the connection between him and my mom. Then John Doe. Why would there be someone writing to my mom using an alias name? His stack was small, and so was Angie's. Trent and Aunt Janet's stacks were the largest and there were at least twenty-five or so from Tracy.

I knew there was information from Janet because of what I overheard them talking about, so I started with her letters. Mandy went to Angie's and Hunter started with John Doe. We saved Trent's to look at together. Tracy's, I assumed would not be as important, but at this point, I didn't rule anything out. So, we were not going to skip over them, but wanted to go through the rest first.

As we started to dig in, we kept finding tidbits of information at every turn. It was overwhelming. Mandy started making notes of what the pertinent information was, who it was from, the date and kept it all logged in her tablet. Her OCD for organization came in handy often, and I appreciated her keeping us all on task. Having chronological notes was necessary because there was so much information there.

The letters from Aunt Janet were regular; very light and playful. Around the time her husband passed away, her letters were infrequent and very short. She was utterly heartbroken and said she did not have the energy to call or write, she just wanted to sit and be alone. As time passed, she would engage in questions about all of us kids, arguments between my parents and then started talking about her travels. She would go into details about where she had been, what she saw, the incredible food and wine and just how much she wished she could be experiencing those trips with her late husband.

The more I perused her letters, she never mentioned anything about the minister Bailey case. The entire stack was personal and appeared to be a friend writing a friend, nothing more. However, as I skimmed the last few letters, I saw the news clippings she brought up the other night folded inside the envelopes. She didn't write anything pertaining to them in her letters, she only said things like, *"p.s. Look who is out... p.s. Fuck justice... p.s. Prayers my ass, sick and fucked up lawyers and people made this happen..."*at the close of her letters. It was obviously a topic they talked about, and both knew about, which is why there was no backstory or dialogue in the letters about him. But still nothing on why they even talked about him.

The news clippings made my stomach twinge, as they included photos of minister Bailey active during a sermon or helping at a charity function right next to his mugshot. The headlines read, Bring *Justice for Bailey,* and *Prayers Answered, Bailey Released,* but the one that made me truly feel sick was, *God's Will Finally Done.*

How could the newspaper be so incredibly close-minded and one-sided? The articles went on to re-tell his story, but they were opinion pieces and they made it out to sound like the kids were lying and he was unjustly imprisoned. Nowhere in them did they offer a neutral take or consider how the kids, now grown, would handle it. It was completely fucked up. I could totally see why Aunt Janet was so upset.

Mandy and Hunter were so engrossed in what they were reading, I could barely get their attention to tell them there wasn't really much I could find. As I tried to ask if they found anything, they both looked up at me unnervingly at the same time, both looking horrified.

"What?" I screamed. "What did you find?" I asked. "Monty, Angie is minister Bailey's wife. Trent is her son and minister Bailey adopted him when he was young. She knows your mom well," Mandy said with a creak in her voice.

"But how? How would my mom know minister Bailey's wife? And why does that name sound familiar?" I said.

Mandy continued to read through the letters from Angie; each one was demanding answers and information about where Trent had gone. In each correspondence, she mentioned that she called Janet, stopped by her home and even by her work, but Janet refused to speak with her. She begged my mom in each letter to help get answers from Janet on where Trent went and if he was okay. The tone in the letters did not feel like a desperate mother looking for her son to make sure he was safe or to see how she could help him. The tone was more of a desperate woman who feared someone learning something they shouldn't if he spoke up. She never said she just hoped he was healthy and well, or if he had gotten help for what had occurred. It was all about who helped him hide from her, how he had vanished without a trace, and he should come forward and be with her.

Angie was distressed and her letters were manic. In each letter she became more obsessed with getting my mom to find answers for her and for her to use her friendship with Janet to get her to talk. In the last letter she said,

Rebecca, I plead with you to talk to my sister, she must know something. I know she helped him hide and she is probably giving him money to live. IT HAS TO STOP NOW. Janet needs to stop helping him and make him come home. He needs to talk to me, his mother, and no one else. She is my family, but what she is doing is not right. Please talk with her and get her to tell me the truth. Get Trent out of hiding and home with me, where he belongs.

"Sauer sounds familiar because it is Janet's maiden name; Angie is her sister," Mandy and I said it together in perfect sync. Angie is pushing my mom to talk to Janet, because she knew Janet and my mom are very close, and my mom might be the only person who could help Janet to speak up.

The letters were to my mom, but it looked like she never wrote Angie back. They were just plea after plea to get Janet to respond and tell her where her son was. The letters came back-to-back, starting just a few weeks ago, right around the time minister Bailey was released early from prison. So why now? If Angie cared about her son, why did she never invoke my mom to help her before? His release from prison spooked Angie for some reason and made her hysterical. I wonder if she worried about her safety with minister Bailey, or if she was worried Trent would say something that would hurt her in some way. The last letter was just over a week prior, so I wondered if she would keep writing. In the middle of my wandering thought, Hunter found something else.

Hunter shot his head up and said, "Well, are you ready for another twist? As I am reading these letters from John Doe, they are aggressive, threatening and it is all directed at your mom, Monty. There was no signature on the first few, but this last one is signed 'Bailey.' He was writing to your mom from prison, but this last letter must be sent from somewhere else, look at the postmark on the envelop, it's from a different city. It appears he is out now, and he is not happy. Look at some of the things he says."

As I looked over the pages, he underlined particular words three and four times that say things like, *not a monster... revenge... I will find him... keep your mouth shut... I know what you did...*

"What does he mean by he knows what she did?" I asked Mandy and Hunter.

They both shrugged their shoulders and looked back down at the letters.

As I tried to wrap my head around this, I couldn't stop thinking about what my dad said the other night on the porch... *We are not telling her where he has been and we are not telling her who helped, but we can tell her that he is alive, and we can push her in a completely different direction.*

My parents and Janet must have helped Trent hide and stay in hiding. I am not sure how minister Bailey and Angie found out, or made the connection, but it seemed like they might be in danger in some way if they don't speak up. These letters were threats, and if the story of minister Bailey was true, he was willing to do whatever it takes for what he wants.

My family was in danger, and I was not sure my mom had told Janet or even my dad how bad it was. I just looked at Mandy and Hunter, and we shared a look of despair.

This was not just a story of interest; it was a story about my family.

Chapter Six

Trent Bailey

We were running out of daylight, so we packed everything up and headed back to drop me at my four-wheeler. I planned to put all the letters we had gone through back into the cooler, so if my mom was to check, she might not realize any were missing. The three of us agreed to look over the Trent Bailey and Tracey Lilliam letters tomorrow. The plan was to meet at the library this time. That way, if we had any questions, maybe Cliff could help. When I got back home, I walked onto the back porch where Aunt Janet, Mom, Dad, and the twins were. The twins were working on this remote-control car that used to be Zach's, while my dad laughed at their inept skills. Mom and Aunt Janet were talking quietly, so I stood close while pretending to watch the twins work to hear what they were talking about. But no sooner did I stand there, they both stopped their conversation abruptly.

"Well, Monty, you have been a busy bee today, what new trouble did you get yourself into?" Mom asked.

"You know, Mom, the usual, just did some hard drugs, then sacrificed an animal, followed up with satanic worship, you know, the usual Sunday afternoon shenanigans," I snickered.

"Oh Monty, not funny! You can just be so crude… Anyway, I am not in the mood to make dinner tonight, so I have convinced your Aunt Janet to go into town and pick up Chinese food for the troops. I am going to try to get through some of the laundry and dishes. Do you want to help me?" Mom asked.

As I began to begrudgingly answer that I would help, Aunt Janet interrupted.

"Oh, bull shit! You don't want to fold your dad's underwear, why don't you ride with me and help me navigate through your enormous, metropolitan town?" she sarcastically requested.

"Umm, Mom, if that's okay with you, I would love to get out of the house with Aunt Janet," I said.

Within minutes I had the food order in hand and was getting into Aunt Janet's super cute Bronco. It was her late husband's when he was in college and once he died, she had it fully restored. It was a 1976 Ford Bronco that was painted a deep gold, almost brown, with a white hard top and white around the tires, with light tan interior and chrome finishes. It was not practical at all, and was always in the shop, but it was totally her style. She also had a small SUV she kept for the obscenely snowy and icy Chicago winters, but the Bronco was always what she drove to visit us. She told me that when I turn sixteen, she would gift it to me, as she didn't know anyone else in this world that would love it and take care of it like I would. She was right, and even though I hardly thought she would really give it to me one day, I loved to think about driving it around as my very own.

We started toward town, but as we turned onto the main road just past our house, she pulled off to the side. As I looked at her inquisitively, she asked, "Did you see Ryan?"

I was inherently confused and did not know where this was coming from, but I could tell she knew more than she was letting on, so I decided to be honest with her.

"I did, earlier today. He was in the cow barn with Jack's farmhand Greg. I thought he was out of the country, so I was very confused to see him. I didn't know what to do, so I hid from him

125

and didn't let him see me. It seems bizarre to say out loud, but something felt off, so I hid," I told Janet.

"Listen, honey, I don't know how much you know, but Zach and Adam know some, and I think it's time to let you in on a few things. It is not my place to fill you in on everything, but I want to make sure you stay safe. I am staying here for a while, not just because I love you kids, but because it is not safe for me right now back home. My sister is on a mission to find information I really don't have, but even if I did, I wouldn't tell her. She only wants it for bad, bad reasons. There are some terrible people out there and they feel that they were wronged and now want to get back at the people they allege wronged them. My sister, Angie, is one of those people, and I know you are a Christian and are supposed to forgive, but hell, these people do not deserve forgiveness. Your cousin Ryan is somehow involved, and I don't know what side he is on or even how he got involved, but this is becoming more complex by the day.

"I wasn't completely sure, which is why I am asking you, as I swear I saw him in the field today when I was out walking while you all were at church. I also think I saw him with your uncle Ted the other day driving in town, but I am not sure. Someone was with your uncle, and I assumed it was Ryan; I just wasn't sure as I passed them. However, when I saw him today, I knew it was him. I just don't know why they would lie about where Ryan is, and I don't think your parents know your Aunt and Uncle are lying about his whereabouts. I am not a conspiracy theorist, but I think Ryan is up to something, and I don't know what. And there is a chance Ted could be involved, or just covering for him, but it just doesn't make any sense to say he is out of the country when he is in this damn town...sorry I am blabbering on.

"Just, listen, honey, I need you to stay away from Ryan if

126

you see him again. Hiding was the right thing to do. I know he is family, but until I can figure this all out, please stay away, okay? If he is saying he is somewhere else and is actually here, my gut tells me it's because of something categorically bad," she asked. "Aunt Janet, first, I wouldn't say I am a Christian, so I don't make decisions based on what the church would say. I am forced to do this organized religion stuff, because of my parents. But it is not what I believe. So, let's not make that assumption again. I don't know everything you are referring to, but do you think this has anything to do with minister Bailey, or your nephew Trent?" I asked.

"How do you know about them?" she demanded as her tone turned from concerned to angry.

"I have not told anyone this, and I am worried about who to even trust. But I overheard you and Mom the other night, and I accidentally found an entire container filled with letters. I did some digging and asked a few people some questions. I haven't gone through all the letters, but in them, I realized that your sister is Angie and Trent is your nephew. I think I am piecing a lot of it together, but still can't figure out what your sister wants and where your nephew went. Also, why didn't he testify?"

"Monty, I don't know where he is, honest. But that is what my sister thinks she can get from me. I don't think it is to reconnect with him, either, part of me thinks she wants to harm him or make sure he keeps his mouth shut. She is still in love with Minister Bailey or in some way under his power and influence, and last we spoke, she swore he was innocent. I don't know where Trent is, I really don't, but even if I did, I would never tell her. She is pathological and as much as she swears her husband is innocent, in my gut, I swear she knew what he was doing and maybe even helped him orchestrate it… I don't know.

Something just doesn't add up. I haven't spoken to her since he went to prison.

"I know, that is a horrific thing to accuse someone of, but there are so many pieces to the story that don't add up and so much the media and the courts did not share. I know more and part of me thinks she wants to get to me to scare me as well... I just don't know, but I am worried, and I cannot shake this ongoing fear I have," Janet said while wiping tears from her eyes. "Aunt Janet, what about the boy that was talked about from the kids that came forward? Do you know who he is? Or where he is?" I asked.

"I believe I do know who he is, but I don't know what happened to him. I remember a young boy at their home often when I visited. At first, they would tell me it was one of Trent's friends, but they were never even in the same room together. Then, they told me he was living in an abusive home, and they were helping him out while they worked with law enforcement and child protective services to get temporary custody of him, for his safety, but that is not the truth. I don't know how Angie and minister Bailey first connected with the boy at all, that is still very unclear, but I think he was severely abused in that home and in that room in the church. I think he was living in the church basement, held against his will. Maybe it's why Angie is trying to connect with me, because I am the only person that is not part of this case that saw that boy outside of the church and I can testify that he existed. As no one else interviewed knew who he was... not one person.

"He was not registered at school and no one at church had any clue of a boy they were helping. Even local police and CPS said there was no case that they were involved in when I asked. As soon as I heard that, I severed all ties with my sister. I knew at that moment that they were guilty of more than anyone was saying," she answered.

"Sorry, with all of the questions, but I feel like things are coming together, just with several areas that are still unknown. If I can get answers, maybe I could help."

"No, Monty! You need to stay clear of all of this. I am happy to talk to you and I can answer your questions, but only for you to be inquisitive, not for you to play detective. These are real crimes committed by really bad people and you do not want to get involved in any way. I am going to do some digging into finding out why Ryan is here, and I promise I will let you know what I find out. But you need to stay out of this and stay safe. I want to get Ted alone and see if he tells me the truth. If he doesn't, I worry that he is covering up something for Ryan. And maybe I am wrong, maybe it has nothing to do with the shit with my family, but the timing is too coincidental, and the letters, calls and threats all seem driven by more than just minister Bailey being let out. I don't know what I am looking to uncover, but something more is there," she said.

I trusted her and I thought I could help her, but I needed to be upfront about everything I knew.

"Aunt Janet, I agree with you, and I will stay safe, I promise. But I think there is something you need to know. I have not told anyone yet, as I didn't even know what there was to tell or who to trust, but I do trust you. You treat me like an equal and you are the only one who tells me anything. This is super messed up, sorry to just drop it on you...

"The other night, the night before you got here, I ran out of gas in the field, and I had to walk all the way through the field home. It was around sunset, and I was dragging my feet a bit, because I was scared to let my dad know I ran out of gas, again.

129

I went to stop for a quick moment to look at this elm tree I always stare at, and I saw three men, one with a shotgun standing and facing another man, shirtless in a chair. They were threatening him and said that he could turn himself into police, run and never come back, or let them kill him right there and bury him. I slipped and fell at one point, so I was unable to see what was going on for a minute, when all of a sudden, I heard two shots fired. I don't know if they meant to shoot the gun or not, but the men argued and were irate afterwards. When I was able to see again, I saw that the man in the chair was gone, the chair was knocked over, and there was blood on the ground... but no body. They were looking all over the ground and picking something small up and they seemed to be looking for something they didn't find.

"When they were done searching, I saw there was another man driving this old truck, he pulled over to them and they got inside of the truck and took off. Today, when I saw Ryan in the cow barn, the truck was in there too. So was the man who was driving the truck. I knew it was him because I met him earlier in the day at the picnic. It's our neighbor Jack's new farmhand, Greg. I don't know how Ryan and Greg know each other, but they were discussing what went down on Thursday. Ryan was saying he knew the guy, I think the guy that was in the chair, and that he was going to talk to him. He said he wouldn't go to the police. But Greg kept saying they needed to keep him quiet because he knew too much already.

"Look, I don't know who the man was in the chair, I could only see like five percent of his face, but I think he was shot before he ran into the cornstalks. I mean, he could still be there. He could be dead in there. I have no idea. And I know, I should have gone to the police, but Aunt Janet, I don't know who to trust. I didn't even tell my best friends about this because none of it makes any sense to me, at all." As I finished my sentence, I began to cry. It felt good to say out loud, but knowing I didn't look for who ran off, or tell anyone, made me feel sick. Like, *if he is dead now, is it my fault?*

"Monty, how do you know that none of them were Ryan, if you didn't see all of their faces?" Janet asked.

"Aunt Janet, the man in the chair had longer hair, so it was not him. Plus, he and Greg were talking about what happened while in the cow barn. Greg was sort of filling him in, so there was no way Ryan was there. The man with the shotgun was much taller than Ryan, and even without seeing his face, how he was dressed and his silhouette in the distance, just seemed to be someone older. Greg was the one driving the truck and the other two men, I saw some of their faces and they were not him. Different heights, hair, and weight. But I agree, Ryan is involved in something very bad. They were talking about killing someone if he didn't clear things up," I said.

"Oh dear, killing someone? How is it this out of hand? I just don't know who Greg is to Ryan and what they are involved in. It could have something to do with my sister, but that just doesn't track. Honey, I need you to stay safe and if something happens or you see something, come to me. I hate telling you to not talk to your parents about this, but on this topic, I really want you to come to me first. I trust your parents, but with Ryan being involved, I just want to make sure they can stay neutral and see everything clearly. I need to figure this out, shit, I just don't even know where to start. I need to talk to Ted, without saying too much, but after the explosion in your living room last night, I don't know if Ted wants to talk to any of us right now," Janet said.

I nodded and agreed to share everything with her, and to stay out of sight. I trusted her, just not enough to tell her I knew two of the men… yet. I will, but I had a few ideas that might help this all make sense and I needed to trust myself on this. I will inform her, although not until the time was right.

Aunt Janet pulled back onto the road, and we drove into town. We picked up the Chinese food and then stopped at the minimart for a bottle of wine for her and some sodas for the rest of us. When we pulled back into the house, Adam was leaving in a complete huff.

"Adam, we got dinner. I ordered you your favorite cashew chicken, aren't you staying for dinner?" I asked.

"Thanks, Monty. I am not really hungry, but could you save it for me for later?" Adam asked.

"Of course," I agreed.

Something bad had just happened, because when we walked back into the house, you could hear a pin drop, it was so quiet, and the tension was thick. None of the dishes or laundry were done and my mom was off in her room. My dad greeted us and told us to let Eve and the twins know the food was here and go ahead and get started before he walked back into their room and shut the door.

I did not know what was going on, but it felt extremely uncomfortable.

Aunt Janet, Eve, the twins, and I sat at the table and ate while we tried to lighten the mood with Simon telling us some of his latest jokes. Delilah offered a few smart-witted comments about his jokes being dated and predictable, which just made us laugh even harder. As everyone was finishing up, Eve looked at Aunt Janet and asked, "Do you know why Mom and Dad were yelling at Adam?"

"Eve, we were gone getting dinner and looks like we came

at the tail end of something that created some thick tension. But no, I don't know what it was about," Aunt Janet responded.

"Oh, I know," shouted Delilah. "You do?" I asked inquisitively.

"Yep! Mom caught Adam smoking one of her cigarettes while in the garage and while she was scolding him, he asked why she was secretively talking to Tate while at the picnic. He said something about Mom acting super sketchy and that whatever she was doing it needed to stop before he told Dad," Delilah said.

"Delilah, sweetie, I am not sure what Adam was insinuating, but he is the minister, she is allowed to speak to him. Also, a lot of times, things you talk to your minister about are private, so I am sure it was nothing more than that. He was probably just deflecting from getting in trouble from smoking, that's all," Aunt Janet said.

Delilah nodded and sort of skipped off into the living room to finish one of her shows before Mom made her go to bed. I don't even think Simon was paying any attention; he was shoveling the remaining crab rangoon and egg rolls into his face, paying no mind to the use of napkins or properly chewing. With a mouth full, he dropped his plate in the sink and joined Delilah in the living room. Eve seemed like she wanted to say something but was holding back.

"Hey, Eve, are you still planning on going with your *friend* tonight?" I asked without mentioning it was a boy who was completely horrible.

"Monty, not that it is any of your business, but tonight is off and I am not sure I wanted to go anyway. So, I will probably stay in and have Olivia over," Eve said.

Now that didn't make any sense. Eve is obsessed with Jason,

133

so, what had changed in the few hours since I saw her last?

Aunt Janet was cleaning up the kitchen with a large, overpoured glass of wine and told us to get out of there and go relax. We got up and we both walked out to the porch to avoid watching the twins' annoying Nickelodeon show. I wanted to ask Eve what had changed, but she never told me anything. So, I was not expecting her to open up about any of it, when she looked at me and her eyes widened, and she asked, "Can you keep a secret?"

Now, my entire last few days had been nothing but secrets, and I knew I could, but why would she confide in me? We literally had nothing in common and she went out of her way to avoid me, so whatever she had to say had to be urgent, or she wouldn't be asking me.

"Of course, Eve, are you okay?" I asked.

"Okay, so, I called Jason to get details of the party and to make sure Oliva and a few other girls could come. He was super sketchy on the phone and just sort of said that the party was only for a small group, and I couldn't bring anyone with me. When I told him I wasn't comfortable with that, he berated me and said if I couldn't be chill, then I should just fuck off as well. I tried to play it cool and told him that I was just going to bring some friends so I could get a ride and have a cover for my alibi with my parents, but he said I didn't need to get a ride with my friends and didn't need to tell any of them what was going on. I explained that Mom wouldn't be okay with me riding with a boy before they properly met him and he just laughed at me," Eve said.

"Okay, so that's why you are not going, he was rude to you? That makes sense, you don't deserve that," I said.

"No Monty, there is more. I said sorry I have protective parents, but maybe I could lie and say Olivia was taking me and

I could ride with him, but he cut me off. He said I didn't need to lie to get a ride, because I didn't need a ride to my own backyard… so at this point I was so confused trying to figure out what he meant without sounding dumb; I just sort of laughed and asked what he meant. He said that the party was in the back of our field at the old, abandoned farmhouse, but he said the party wasn't going to be tonight any more, because some people got wind of it happening, so it was going to now be Friday."

"Okay, so that is trespassing, and you could get in some real trouble. Plus, I thought the place was like in bad shape and not safe to be inside of?" I said.

"I know, I don't want to break into a house, let alone do it with people I don't know and not sure I trust. But I don't want Jason to think I am a loser, or, like, not cool. What should I do? Like I haven't even talked to Olivia because she will just show up to the party whether I go or not and then Jason will be pissed. I like Jason and thought going to my first real party with him would be awesome, it's just, I have a bad feeling about this," Eve said.

"Eve, if it was me, I wouldn't go, but I know you are not me. I don't know what it is like to be popular, so the pressure you have is not something I understand. I also want to make sure you know, I do not trust Jason and I do not want you to date him, but that is on you. If you really want to go, what if I go with you, not to the party, but just sort of hang outside and watch for cops or just sort of be a lookout for you? If you feel unsafe, just lie, and say you want to smoke a cigarette and go outside. I can be outside and get out of there with you," I offered.

"Gross, like I would ever smoke. But I like that plan, is there any other reason I would want to go outside?" she asked.

"Well, do you plan on drinking?" I asked.

"I will like, hold a beer like I am drinking, but I hate the way it tastes, so I am not going to get drunk or anything. If there is, like, Zima or something, I might have one, but I really don't like to drink," Eve said.

"Okay, that works. Just say you are feeling a little dizzy and might get sick, so you go outside for some fresh air," I said.

"Okay, so are you sure you don't mind? Is this something I will have to pay for in some weird way, or you will extort me with later?" Eve asked.

"No. I don't want anything. I do want you to be safe and I am not changing any plans to be there with you. Plus, part of me is a little nosy wanting to know who is going to be there and just how these sort of parties go down anyway, so it's a win-win," I said.

"Monty, there is one more thing. I shouldn't even be telling you this, but you will probably see it when we go, so I am just giving you a heads-up, okay?" Eve said.

"Okay Eve, you are freaking me out, what is it?" I asked. "So, like, the house is not run-down any more. I heard some kid who graduated a few years ago has been fixing it up, and word got out it is the perfect party spot now. He covered all the windows so no one could see in, is somehow pulling electricity from the neighbors back there and even got the plumbing up and running. Like it is a for-real place now. So only a few people in school heard about it, which is what sparked this party. They don't want any of this getting out, so it is super-secret. Like rules on where to park and specific times to go, so no crowds heading in at the same time. Everyone who goes must make a crazy promise not to say a word and I even heard someone will be there with a camcorder to video who comes in and to get them drinking or doing whatever on camera, to keep them quiet about talking

136

about it," Eve confessed.

"Okay, Eve, shit. So, you want to go so badly, you will let someone pretty much blackmail you just to go? You have the best grades and are in all sorts of activities, what if this hurts you getting into college or getting scholarships? Aren't you worried about all of that?" I asked.

"Well, I am not really going to drink..." but I cut her off before she could finish.

"Not really drinking doesn't mean anything if they get you on video holding alcohol in a house you are trespassing in. This is not a little school slap on the wrist if you get caught. This is potential jail time, fines and not even graduating high school, let alone getting into college," I said, much louder than I should have.

"Monty, keep your voice down. And don't you think I get all of that? Don't you think I know the risk? I never break the rules. I never go to parties, I don't do anything bad, ever. I literally am the golden child, which you make fun of me for, because I do fucking everything that is expected of me. I am so tired of trying to be perfect. And for once, if I want to let loose, and go to a party and maybe make out with someone, I should do that! I am a teenager doing none of the teenager stuff you are supposed to do," she said.

"Okay, I get it. If you go, wear a hat, wear something cute and fun, but something you can sort of cover your face with. If you hold a drink, hold it in a koozie or a solo cup, don't hold anything that is labeled alcohol. If you see the camcorder, go into a different room, and always keep your back to it. If they video you when you walk in or make you say your name on camera, make a joke, and say someone from history in a silly way, then just walk in. Don't say your real name. If this is that important to you, you must be really smart about going. Don't drink anything someone gives you, with how secretive it is, I just worry they will be drugging drinks to get people to pass out and not even remember going," I said.

"Oh my God, no one will be drugging people, it's not that serious. Jesus, you always have to be so dark," Eve said.

She said that, but she has no idea how dark and dangerous Jason is. It took all of me not to say a word at that moment. But she trusted me, and I didn't want that to turn into a huge fight. What Jason might do is not relevant at this moment, to Eve anyway.

This might be the first time we had ever bonded over anything, and although the circumstances were awful, I appreciate having this with her.

I went back into the house, and even though we just ate dinner, ice cream was calling my name. I pulled out the mint chocolate chip and started to scoop it out when my mom walked into the kitchen. Her eyes were puffy and swollen; she had obviously been crying. She didn't even greet me, she just walked over to the sink and asked who already did the dishes. I simply shrugged my shoulders; I didn't want to engage as she was in a mood. I didn't get the vibe that she wanted to talk to anyone, let alone me, so I took my ice cream to my room.

I put on my pajamas, settled into my bed, and ate my ice cream. But with each bite, I couldn't stop looking over to my backpack. I know I said I would wait to go through more of these letters with Mandy and Hunter, but after my talk with Aunt Janet, I needed to dig in more, tonight. There was no way I could wait until tomorrow. I finished my last spoonful of ice cream, then I pulled my backpack onto the bed, taking out the stack from Trent, and starting with the oldest letters first.

The first letter was very formal; Trent knew my mother or knew of my mother, but it read like an introduction more than anything else. He was responding to a letter she sent him first, which was peculiar. Mom knows Janet, Angie is Janet's sister, so it can be assumed they had met, but how close was she to Trent? The letter didn't explain why she would be reaching out to him to begin with, but it was curious what she would have said to him in that letter. He simply answered with that he was doing okay, and that he would keep in touch. He mentioned that he was not speaking with anyone about what had happened and refused to speak with his mother. He told her that if she wanted to continue any correspondence, to send letters to his friend's house and gave the address.

The letters continued almost monthly for a few years. With each one, they got more familiar, and Trent opened up more about his father, but no details about his history of abuse. After the first year, he turned eighteen and decided to move out of Oak City. He gave my mother a new address in Illinois and said to contact him there. He still had no contact with either of his parents, even though they had both been looking for him, as well as his stepfather's attorneys, various news outlets and just about anyone that was aware of the case. He always thanked my mom for her keeping his whereabouts secret. He ended each letter after the first year with how much he appreciated their friendship.

What my mother wrote to Trent was never clear, but he was answering questions a lot in what he wrote back to her in the first part of each letter. Then he would end a letter with a paragraph about what he had been up to. The letters were cordial, and they were just an outlet for him with someone he could trust, and knowing how nosy my mom was, I am sure she enjoyed staying in the know and having something that was just hers.

Just before his dad's trial, Trent wrote to my mom and told her that he believed he had been followed that day and that he thought it was his stepdad or that one of his attorneys hired someone. He was very worried about their intention, and he said he had to get out of sight completely. He asked if she could call him and help him navigate his next steps and gave a number, date, and time.

After that request, there was no written correspondence between the two of them; well, nothing from him I could find. So, it was hard to decipher if she did call him and what happened. But, finally, six months after minister Bailey's conviction, Trent wrote to my mom again. In this letter, the tone was much different. He went from being cordial and friendly, to fearful and panicked.

His first letter after the long break was very direct, and it stated that he was sure that Grace was murdered by his stepfather, and he was next. Minister Bailey still had a following of people who believed him to be innocent. Trent was being followed and no matter where he went, they found him.

In the letters, Trent said he was sure that the way Grace was killed was a message to him directly, and his stepdad might have had help. In his letters, he explained that when he was a young teenager, he was at home playing with a baseball and bat in the house. His stepdad stormed in and told him to take it outside immediately, before he broke something. A few days later, Trent was in his house with just the baseball, tossing it up in the air and catching it while on the couch. His stepdad walked into the room, caught the ball mid toss, and screamed at him. He said he had already been warned, and then he threw the ball through the living room window, shattering it. He then picked up a large shard of glass and held it with his right hand while he gripped both of Trent's wrists with his left. He held the pointed edge of the glass against his wrist, breaking the skin slightly, making one of them bleed. Minister Bailey said that if he wanted to disobey him again, he would feel the wrath and he would end him. Trent was so frightened during the interaction, that he wet himself while sobbing. His stepfather called him a useless, pathetic boy while he said to clean up the mess. His mother was one room over during the interaction and never said a word or interjected.

The letter ended with him stating that hiding out the way he was, was not working any more, and he needed to do something more drastic, as minister Bailey behind bars was not keeping him safe in any way. The next several months of letters went back and forth on how to get his name changed, areas he could go that were off the radar and always set date, time, and phone numbers to call each other. I had gotten through most of the stack, but my eyes were getting heavy, and I really needed to get some sleep. I thought I would read one more, from years ago and leave the five or so more recent ones for tomorrow. As I opened the envelope, I immediately shot up out of my bed. I had to re-read the first paragraph twice, because I didn't believe it. As it read:

Dear Rebecca,

Your support has meant everything to me, without it, I wouldn't have known what to do. Your help with changing my name and finding a new, safe, and permanent home makes me finally feel at ease. I will start going by my new name once I am all moved, as I want a completely clean slate. But I am most thankful for you working with the social worker regarding Sebastian's case. His foster family has been wonderful, but they were clear that adoption was not in their plan. If your idea works and you can help place him with me, I can rebuild a family. We are not blood, but we are brothers and I want him to escape this

141

life. I should be able to write a few more times before the move, thank you again for all you have done. Until we see each other again...

All I could think about was how in the world was my mom, this person? Helping someone change their name, helping them find a safe place to live, and helping them adopt someone? None of it made any sense. I wanted to finish the letters, but my head was already reeling, and I couldn't keep my eyes open any more. I closed my eyes and all I could think was that I needed another chat with Aunt Janet tomorrow. I needed to know if Janet knew my mom did all of this, or if this was my mom acting alone.

Chapter Seven

In Plain Sight

The next morning, I woke up to thunderstorms and hard rainfall. The sky was dark blue and overcast and you could hear the rain hitting the roof and windows. It looked dreadful outside, and even the temperature had dropped fifteen degrees since yesterday. As I walked into the kitchen, I saw Mom, the twins and Adam all sitting around the table eating. Mom and Adam were not acknowledging each other at all, and the twins were arguing over which video game they were going to play when they were done. The room felt uneasy, and it was all because of this weird tension between Adam and my mom.

"Hey, Mom, where's Dad?" I asked.

"He already left for work; he was paged out earlier for the rain causing some leaks at one of his projects. Your sister said she isn't feeling well and is staying in bed. But I have a ton to do today, so if you could help keep an eye on the twins, that would be very helpful," Mom said.

I looked at Adam, who still had not glanced up from his bowl of cereal. I didn't know what fully went down between the two of them, but they normally did not fight this long. "So, I am guessing Adam doesn't have to help at all, or Eve, just me," I asked in a snarky tone.

"Yes, just you. You are fifteen and you will help me out when I ask! Don't mind Adam or Eve, which is none of your business and I am tired of explaining myself to my kids. You will do what I ask, end of conversation," Mom shouted at me.

"Okay, okay, I was joking. You don't need to yell. I don't have anything going on today, so I am happy to stay at home with them. Am I allowed to have Mandy and Hunter over?" I asked.

"Monty, you don't need your friends here twenty-four, seven. Today, just focus on the twins and complete the chores I have for you, and we can discuss your friends when I get back," Mom said while acting completely perplexed by something.

I went to pour a bowl of cereal when Aunt Janet strolled in. "Good morning, my lovelies! The day is bleak, but I love thunderstorms! Perfect day for hot coffee, a good book and a blanket to cozy up with… there is coffee made, isn't there?" she asked.

My mom poured her a cup and started to outline everything she needed to do today. Aunt Janet just smiled and nodded to the never-ending task list and at one point stopped my mom and just asked when she needed to be ready. Mom insisted that she didn't need to help with all of it but had a few things she wanted Aunt Janet to handle.

"Janet, you don't need to do the first few things with me, so take your time. I need to run by the church and drop off some old clothes and furniture, then Mike asked me to drop off his deposit bag at the bank and then I need to swing over to the hardware store for a few things. Why don't I do all that first, so you can get ready, then I can come and pick you up?" she asked.

"Rebecca, whatever you want. Just tell me where to be and when and I will have my ass ready," Janet said with a giggle.

Adam finished eating and just walked out of the kitchen. As he walked around the corner, my mom looked in his direction, and her face was sorrowful and puzzled.

I knew my mom would not want any of us to smoke, but this was not the face of a mother who was mad she caught her son smoking. Something much bigger was going on. I inhaled my food, as per usual, threw my dishes into the dishwasher and went down to Adam's room. I knocked, and to my surprise he said I could come in.

"Hey, it's none of my business, but what is going on between you and Mom? She seems super weird today and I just want to make sure you are okay. I heard about the smoking, but she seems way more upset than just catching you smoke. I figured she knew you did by now anyway," I said.

"I am okay, and you are right, it is a lot more than just the smoking. I know you have some of the letters, but Mom thinks I took them. Don't worry, I didn't rat you out. She is terrified that I am going to show them to Aunt Janet. I told her I don't have the letters, but she thinks I am lying. I don't give two shits why you have them and what you have read, but I am sure you have figured out a lot by now," Adam said.

"I put back most of them, I only have the ones from Trent and Tracey. I have a few left to read from Trent and haven't read the Tracey ones yet. I didn't figure they were important, so I can go put them back," I said.

"The Tracey ones aren't important? Monty, you need to read the last letters from Trent, and you will *want* to read the ones from Tracey. The shit about minister Bailey's wife being Angie, Aunt Janet's sister is fucked up. But the Tracey letters are why Mom is so upset. Those letters show that Mom and Dad broke the law and that's why Mom is so worried they are missing. Tracey is the missing puzzle piece; I am surprised you haven't figured that out yet," Adam said.

"I don't understand. Tracey is Mom's friend from a million

years ago, and they have weekends away with the other women they know there to drink and have dinners. How is she a part of this?" I asked.

"Monty, Mom does not just go drink and have dinner with her. Aunt Janet doesn't even really know her. Dad knows what him and Mom have done, of course, but he has no idea the extent or the role Tracey played in this. There are missing letters I never found, and I think Mom is hiding more information from Dad, not really anyone else. You will see. Read the letters then put them back on the ground, shoved to the back behind the shelves. Make it look like they fell out in some way and then stay far away from this. It's all super fucked up, Monty, it's monumentally fucked up," Adam said.

"Adam, I need to tell you something. I haven't told anyone but Aunt Janet. Last Thursday I was in the field, and I saw three men standing, one with a shotgun and another man in a chair. They threatened to kill him. I couldn't see who the man in the chair was, and I didn't see the men's faces at first, but when they turned around, I recognized two of them. One had a gun and one had blood on them. There were shots fired, but I never saw what happened to the man in the chair. The tallest man with the shotgun, I didn't see his face at all. As they were driving off in this old blue and white truck, I realized there was a fourth man with them driving and I didn't see his face, but he was distinctive; like I could pick him out of a crowd.

"On Sunday at the picnic, the guy that drove them away I found out is Greg, the new farmhand for Jack. They didn't see me, but I am freaking out. I was trying to investigate that when all of this minister Bailey shit came up. I feel like I am in the middle of a horror movie; nothing adds up," I said.

"Monty, who were the two men you know?" Adam asked.

146

"Adam, I forgot! Also, on Sunday after the picnic, I was by the cow barn and Greg was inside with the old truck, and he was talking to someone. I peered in and could see Greg but not the other man, but I could hear him, and I knew that voice immediately. It was Ryan! He wasn't there on Thursday, but he is involved, and he is definitely not in Europe. They were discussing what went down and that Ryan had to take care of it, or they needed to potentially kill someone to cover their tracks," I said.

"Monty! Who were the two men?" Adam demanded. "Sunny and Jason from school. Sunny was the one holding a handgun and Jason had blood on him. Eve is supposed to go out with Jason Friday, and I tried telling her he was a bad guy who used girls, but she doesn't care. She sure as hell wouldn't believe that he might be involved in a murder! I don't understand how this is all tied in. Janet saw Ryan in the field Sunday when we were at church and she asked me if I saw him too, which is why she knows some of this. She says she thinks he is mixed with something bad as well, but how would Aunt Janet know? She barely knows Ryan, but she is sure he is up to something bad. Adam, nothing is adding up and I am getting more freaked out by the day. I didn't tell Aunt Janet it was Sunny and Jason, that part I just need to understand better first. But I still don't know who the tall man in the middle with the shotgun was and who was in the chair and what happened to him. Adam, like, what if he is dead in the cornfield somewhere? I think they shot him, and he ran off. What if he bled out lost in the field? I am freaking out," I said to Adam with tears welling up in my eyes.

"Fuck. This is worse than I thought. I know Ryan is not in Europe, and I have known the entire time. Ryan got involved in some crazy stuff a while back, but this sounds a lot worse. Stay out of the field and away from our cousins and Jason. This is bigger than you think it is," Adam said.

"Adam, Eve is supposed to go to a party on Friday with Jason. She is scared because it is supposed to be at the abandoned farmhouse in the back of the field. I told her I would go sit out back and be there if anything goes down or the cops show up. I think it is so stupid she would go in the first place, but you can't talk her out of anything. She said someone fixed it up and some kids in school want to have a party there. The windows are blacked out, and they have power and plumbing and a whole system of when to come and where to park. Oh, and she said that there is supposed to be someone there with a camcorder to record everyone who comes in, as a sort of blackmail if they tell anyone," I said.

"The farmhouse! They can't go in there. Shit… Monty, have you been in it before? Do you know the story about it?" Adam asked.

"No, why would I trespass into an old run-down house?" I asked.

"Read the letters, then you will know why. Eve cannot go to that party. She cannot go into that house. There is bad shit that goes down there, and the history of the place is even more fucked up. Every party there is filled with drugs and not fun ones. That's where I was when Ryan gave me hard shit for the first time. Kids from our town have partied there for years. It's been inactive for at least a year now, as the last party there the cops showed up and arrested some college kids for trespassing and contributing to minors. I was at that party with Ryan, Zach, and Daniel. We snuck out the back and ran over to the cow barn and hid out. I haven't been back there since. I thought that whole scene shut down after that. I don't know who would have fixed it up since

148

then, but I have my thoughts. Cops patrol around it and our neighbor back there keeps an eye on it, or at least that is what I thought. You know Zach and how he never breaks the rules, and you couldn't drag him to a party, ever? So, it was really fucked up that the first time he ever goes to a party with us, the cops were out, and a ton of people got into trouble. Everyone swore he narked everyone out, but I think we were just too loud, and the neighbors heard us, or it was someone else trying to get us into trouble. But it is weird when I look back on that night and how it all played out," Adam said.

"But Tracey; what does Tracey have to do with an old farmhouse?" I asked.

"Read the letters. I need to make some calls, let's catch up tonight. In the meantime, don't say anything to Eve to not go to the party, she will do the complete opposite. I will see if I can figure out who is throwing it and see if I can get it shut down first. Just trust me, and do what I ask right now," Adam said.

Every. Fucking. Day. New and crazier shit came to light. I felt so much better talking to Adam; I felt safer. I was so glad not to be alone in this, it felt like I could breathe again. But all of this was weighing heavy on me, and I felt like I was drowning.

I went out to the living room to check on the twins and they asked if they could call their friends on the phone. I was in charge and didn't mind, so I told them to have at it, but said to keep the house clean and not make any messes today. Mom was in a mood and let's not add to it. They nodded and ran into the basement to call their friends.

I went down the hall and knocked on Eve's door and opened it a crack. "Hey, do you want any juice or hot tea or anything?" I asked.

"Thanks Monty, but I am okay. My head is pounding, do you

know if there is any aspirin in Mom and Dad's room?" she asked. "I am not sure but let me go look. Hold tight," I answered.

I walked to the end of the hall and my parent's bedroom door was closed all the way. Sort of odd, as normally it was open like the rest of ours unless they were in there. I walked in and went straight over to their bathroom. I found the aspirin in the medicine cabinet, and I poured two aspirin into my hand and filled a tiny dixie cup with water. As I went to walk down to give both to Eve, I noticed some papers on the bed. Probably just bills, but something made me want to look. Like when I saw them, I felt a pit in my stomach. Could just be everything else going on around me, but my curiosity was full-fledged.

I decided to take care of Eve first and then go back to their room, unsure of what was drawing me to the papers.

Eve took the pills and water, thanked me, then curled back under her blankets.

I walked back into their room with my heart pounding. I was shaking a bit and felt extremely nervous. I looked at the top of the stack of papers and the first few things were mortgage statements, old credit card bills and some LLC agreement with my dad's company name on it. Okay, precisely what I thought, boring bills. My heart rate started to slow, and I realized I was getting worked up for nothing. But then, as I went to put the stack back down, I dropped one piece of paper from the back of the pile. When I picked it up, it read:

Foster Agreement Name of Foster Parent(s) *Michael Patterson Rebecca Patterson*

I read through the entire page, and it was all of our information, address, phone number, number of children in the house, and so on. It did not list any children in foster care that were being placed out of the home, this looked like more of an approval letter to receive placement of a child. It wasn't completely clear, so I went back to the stack and kept sifting through the papers to see if there was anything else to make it make sense. Near the bottom, I found an Indiana Adoption Resources letter with a placement notification for a child named Sebastian Stewart. The letter was dated from a little over three years ago. Grace Stewart's son.

I collapsed to the ground. What had my parents done? I had never seen this kid and I knew he didn't live here. I felt sick and needed to get out of the room. I needed air. This must have been what Adam was talking about with them breaking the law. They falsified that they were fostering this child, but he was not here, so they were covering for someone, but who?

I ran out of the room, slamming the door. I went into the kitchen to get water and Aunt Janet was sitting at the table.

"Monty, what is it, what is going on?" she asked as the look on my face was complete shock.

"Aunt Janet, tell me the truth. What happened to Grace Stewart and her son? Really, what happened, don't lie to me," I demanded.

"Honey, that's what I don't know. People think minister Bailey killed her, but my sister swears there was no way. Grace's death was determined to be suicide. Her son was around two at the time and he was placed in foster care, with a great family. I don't believe they adopted him, but I really cannot say for sure. But last I heard, he was still in foster care in Illinois, but I am not sure if it was with the first family or not," she said.

"Bullshit. That is total bullshit, he is not in foster care in Illinois! My parents are his foster parents as of three years ago, but how? How did they foster him when he has never been here? We have never met him. And why would they fake that? Why are they involved with any of this?" I demanded.

"Monty, what are you talking about? Your parents know about the case because it was with my brother-in-law, but they don't know Grace or Sebastian. There is just no way," Janet remarked.

I ran down the hallway, grabbed the papers, and brought them to her. My mom should be back any minute, so I explained we had to have them back on the bed quickly.

Janet looked at the papers and just started to cry. I tried grabbing them from her to try to put them back, but she had a grip on them and was not letting go.

"Monty, I will not involve you. I will let your mom know I was borrowing something and got nosy. But you need to get out of here. I need to talk to your mom when she gets here. I am in complete shock, and I don't even know what to say. I am speechless, but I think this might answer some of my questions with Angie regarding Trent. I need to talk to your mom, but she won't open up and be honest if you kids are around. Go to the basement with the twins and just stay there for now," Janet said.

I went to the basement and the phone was free as the twins had shifted their attention to Willy Wonka on T.V. while snuggled under blankets. The weather looked and sounded even worse than before, as thunder was sounding every few seconds. There was active lightning in the distance and the rain was pouring into the window wells. It was dark and eerie in the basement; it gave me chills.

I walked over to the phone and called Mandy. I told her we couldn't meet up today because I had to watch the twins and definitely couldn't ride my bike in this weather. I filled her in on the letters I had read and where I left off. I let her know that I would ask my parents if I could go over to her house once everyone was home for the day, but my mom was in a mood, so who knew what she would say. I told her I was going to read the rest of the letters so I could put them back, and I would call and update her later on that day. She agreed to the plan and told me that if I couldn't get a ride to her, her mom would definitely bring her to my house tonight if needed.

I then called Hunter, but his mom said he wasn't home. Odd, because he got everywhere by bike, and no one was riding in this weather. But he also has lots of friends who drive, so he was probably with one of them. So, I left a message with her for him to call me later and I went and sat with the twins.

I heard the garage door opening, so I knew my mom was home. Within a few moments, I could hear muffled, loud, voices, coming from upstairs, but nothing I could make out. At one point the twins asked what was going on, but I just turned the T.V. up and told them not to worry about it. I wish I could have taken my own advice. I was worried about it. I couldn't imagine what Aunt Janet was saying or what my mom's reasoning could be. The yelling did not dissipate for some time, but all of a sudden it just stopped. I could hear some footsteps, but no one was talking. I stood up to start to go up the stairs and into my room when I was stopped mid-step by my mom.

"Monty, Aunt Janet, and me are leaving. Slight change of plans for the rest of the day, can you make lunch for the twins? Peanut butter and jelly are fine, just please make them eat a vegetable with it," she asked.

"Sure," I said. She then turned around and went back up the stairs. She didn't appear upset. She looked relieved in some way. Maybe she had been bottling that up for so long, that she felt good finally telling Aunt Janet the truth. I was more worried about Aunt Janet. I hope she didn't feel betrayed in any way. Maybe

Mom could shed some light on some of the holes that she couldn't piece together. I was trying to be optimistic; I needed something to get better and not just pile onto the shit that seemed to be getting worse by the day.

I went upstairs, and as I turned into the living room, I heard the garage door again. They were pulling out of the driveway. As I looked through the window, I could hardly see a thing due to the rain. But I could tell it was them in the van together, and it didn't look like they were yelling any more. I went back into my room because I didn't need to make lunch for at least an hour, so it was the perfect time to finish the letters. I left my bedroom door open slightly to hear the twins if they needed anything. I went to my last few letters from Trent first. I needed to finish them before moving onto Tracey.

I grabbed the five remaining letters from Trent. They were all older dates, the last being May of 1993; three years ago. The first four letters were personal updates. They were short, friendly, and vague. He never used his new name but mentioned his excitement for his classes he was finishing and how anxious he was for this next opportunity. He never mentioned what the training was in or the new job, but the letters to my mom felt like she already knew everything he was referring to. In the final letter, he wrote it as a goodbye.

Rebecca May 13, 1993

This friendship has meant everything to me. Having someone who knows the whole story as an ally and friend has been wonderful. The risks you have taken for me are beyond anything I could imagine, and I am forever in your debt. This is the last time I will write to you as Trent, as my new life starts tomorrow, all thanks to you. My life begins again tomorrow, and you did that for me. Until we meet again, or, until you meet the new me...

T. L.

I sat on my bed and all I could think about were the initials T. L. I looked at those initials and just stared. Then I looked at the date; May 1993, the same month and year my parents were awarded placement for Sebastian Stewart in the papers I found earlier. The same month our new youth minister Tate Lawson started at the church... T. L.

It was like a lightbulb. I gasped, then rubbed my hands over my face and head, shaking it in disbelief. My ears started to ring, and I felt disorientated. I fell back against the pillow on my bed and closed my eyes piecing it all together. The ringing in my ears was deafening, I could hardly think. I was just trying to focus on lining it all up.

My parents helped change Trent's name, falsified records to get Sebastian for him and helped move Trent to our town. Trent Bailey was our minister and the boy he took care of, Sam, was really Sebastian Stewart. Trent is Tate.

They had been hiding in plain sight for three years.

When Tate arrived here, there were always questions about who Sam was to him. He explained he was helping Sam's parents out, and since uncle Ted and Aunt Lisa do the same for Sunny and Daniel while their parents were stationed elsewhere, the story didn't seem too odd. But that story now sounds like it came from my mom. She was not that creative and making a small deviation to something familiar to her makes sense. No one in our town ever asked questions about Sunny and Daniel's parents being away for months at a time, so this was a perfect cover. The other part that was always unclear was why Sam went to a different school. No one ever talked about it, and some kids go to different schools to attend a private or Christian school, so this wasn't crazy either. But Sam just went to another public school, and it

155

bugged me. Now knowing my parents were his actual foster parents, I am sure they couldn't use their address at a school where all their kids have gone or go, without blowing their cover. But their address at a different school and using some way to get it approved based on his trauma, made perfect sense now.

Looking back at the letters, the only part I just didn't get was, why would Trent go into ministry? After all that happened to him with his stepdad and with the church, it seemed like such a crazy choice. Maybe that was pressure from my mom, or maybe it was just the safest cover; like it was the last place minister Bailey would look for him.

Aunt Janet now knew about Sebastian being technically in Mom and Dad's care, but did she know he was here in Blakesville? She told me she didn't know where Trent was, so was she lying to me, or was my mom lying to her?

Trent Bailey was here in our town hiding in plain sight, and now with minister Bailey out of jail, the whole plan might have been unraveling. I still didn't know how this tied to what happened in the field or with Ryan being here, and maybe none of it did, but there was only one way to find out.

Chapter Eight

The Farmhouse

I sat in my room without moving. I felt like I was in a trance. I held the last letter in my hand and squeezed it until it crinkled. The sound shocked me back to life; I shook my head, took a deep breath, and opened my eyes wide. I needed to put the Trent letters back, just hold onto the Tracey ones until I finished them. The less missing, the better. I scooped the Trent letters back into a pile and walked them back into the garage. I got down on the floor and shoved them under the shelving in the back and then pushed a sleeping bag and some rope coils in front of them. I planned on adding the last few once I finished them today.

I walked back into the house with my mind just piecing it all together. Trying to figure out if Mom told Aunt Janet all of this before they left, or if she was still hiding some of it. Aunt Janet didn't seem to realize where Trent was and acted like Sebastian was still in foster care just earlier today, so during their fight, did Mom tell her the truth? I stood at the kitchen counter in a daze. Simon came up to me and pushed my knees in, making me half collapse at the counter. I barked at him in response and told him to keep his hands off me. He cowered away and apologized. I apologized too; he was just playing around; I was just on edge and shouldn't take it out on him.

I pulled out the ingredients to make lunch and the twins asked if they could have some of the leftover soda from Saturday night. I felt bad for yelling at Simon, so I agreed, but told them not to tell Mom. She hated us having too much sugar during the day, and Simon was the worst if he had too much; he would literally bounce off the walls. But I was in charge right now, and I thought the twins should have a treat after being left here with just me while everyone else did whatever they wanted.

I plated their food and asked if they needed anything else. Delilah just asked, "So where did Adam go?" I had not realized the storm had cleared, and although still very overcast the rain had stopped. Adam must have left soon after.

"Oh, I didn't know he left. I am not sure where he went. Is Eve still here?" I asked. They both nodded 'yes' while they took bites of their sandwiches. I wondered where Adam went, but my gut told me he was going to try to figure out what the hell was going on in the field the other night.

While spooning peanut butter out to eat straight from the jar, the phone rang. Delilah beat us all to the phone and immediately was ecstatic to hear the person on the other end. "Oh, hi! I miss you so much, are you coming to visit this weekend? Aunt Janet is staying for a few weeks and Dad has been working like crazy. I just miss you and want to see you soon," Delilah spewed out in what felt like one breath. After a minute or two of chitchat, she walked over to me and said it was Zach and he wanted to talk to me.

"Hey, bro! Long time no talk. You know you can't just abandon me like last weekend. Family fun time is more like family trauma time without you here," I said.

"Hey, Monty, miss you too. Sorry I couldn't be there over the weekend, but I had a lot to get done. Umm, I have a strange question for you, totally no big deal if you don't know," he said. "Sure, but you know that no one tells me anything around here, so don't think I will know anything," I giggled.

"No, nothing major. Just curious if anyone knows when Ryan is supposed to get back from Europe," Zach asked.

"Oh, umm, no one has really talked about it. Umm, Uncle Ted and Aunt Lisa didn't mention anything over the weekend. Sunny and Daniel are still staying with them while their dad is stationed overseas and Aunt Loni is visiting him, so I am sure its chaotic over at their house right now," I responded.

"Okay, no worries. Just haven't talked to him in a while and we have been playing phone tag. Just trying to get his whereabouts," Zach responded.

Zach and Ryan are close, so it was weird that Zach would ask me. Normally he was more in the know than any of us. But after seeing Ryan yesterday, maybe he was dodging Zach, so no one found out he was actually here and not backpacking in Europe. He was up to something suspicious, so I was sure he didn't want to involve goody-goody Zach in any of it.

"Hey, well, tell everyone I say hi and I am going to try to come back this weekend. Just depends on everything I get done this week and how I am feeling," Zach responded.

"Oh, have you been sick?" I asked.

"Oh, umm, no. I just mean, like with being exhausted from moving and getting ready for classes. No, haven't been sick. Well, I need to get off here, talk soon. Love you." Then Zach ended the phone call abruptly. Not unlike him at all. He is not a phone guy and never even checks his answering machine messages at the dorm. He sounded a little homesick; hopefully, that made him drive down this weekend. I love having him around; he just makes me feel safe.

The twins finished eating and the sun was slowly starting to come out. Outside was humid and sopped, but the twins asked to

159

go outside and play. I said to go ahead and then brought a banana and some saltines to Eve, since she was still in bed. When I knocked on the door, I saw Eve fully dressed, putting her shoes on.

"Oh, hey, I brought you some snacks since you weren't feeling well," I said.

"Oh, thanks Monty, but the aspirin really did the trick. I think it's just PMS and I needed some sleep but now I am feeling much better, thanks. Is Mom here?" she asked.

"No, she left a while ago with Aunt Janet to run errands. Adam just left too, so it's just me and the twins the rest of the afternoon," I responded.

"Hmm, I'll leave her a note. But I was going to go by the church and help put things away from the picnic yesterday and then go over to Olivia's to hang out. Are all those clothes and that junk still here that Mom wanted to take to the church? I can take them if they are," she asked.

"No, actually Mom already went to the church this morning and dropped them off," I responded.

"Okay, well, if you are okay, I am heading out, but I will take that banana if you don't mind." And just like that, she grabbed the banana, her purse and headed out front to where Olivia was already waiting. I peered into the backyard and saw the twins on the deck, working on the remote-controlled car again. They brought out tons of beach towels to sit on and the weather was clearing and making it a seemingly decent afternoon. I realized now was the time to finish the letters and see what Tracey had to do with the farmhouse or just any of this.

I went into my room and left the door open again, so I could hear if the twins needed me. I opened my blinds, too, to watch the driveway for when mom pulled back in. I pulled out the envelopes while sitting at my desk and opened the oldest one first. It was dated a little over six years ago and when reading through it, it was a response to another letter. It looked like there was ongoing correspondence between Tracey and Mom from well before this letter, but I didn't see those anywhere in the stack with the others. The letter jumped right in, like in the middle of a conversation:

Rebecca,

With the trial over, it's a good time to really start making some moves. Sebastian is with a good family for now, and they have no interest in adoption, so that is good. I have been meeting with Grace's dad, and he is completely heartbroken without his wife and daughter, but he agrees this is best for his grandson. I hinted at our original idea of him taking legal guardianship of him and then just letting Trent care for him, but he doesn't want to do something that is not legal. He doesn't care what we do, if it is best for Sebastian, but he wants to be distanced from it. I also talked with the agency, and they would not award Sebastian to Trent. Given his history, no real home base, being single and his income not being sufficient to care for himself, let alone a toddler, it is just a no-go. Sorry. I say we go with option two.

I looked at the family estate with Gary Stewart, and he says that his wife did leave everything to Grace. She knew she would never move there or live in it but wanted her to be able to sell it and have some cash when she was done with school. But now with Grace gone, I am just battling with the attorneys on how to handle all of it. Gary won't go see the house and just said he must move on. He gave me full power to handle everything to do with the estate, so I will keep working on a solution.

I will keep on with the social worker and attorneys and update you when I know more.

Have to run, I have a plane to catch, but I will reach out once I get all settled. Stay positive. We will get this all straightened out.

Tracey

I didn't want to jump to conclusions, but based on what Adam said and this letter, it sounded like the old farmhouse was deeded to Grace Stewart. I always heard it was an old couple that both passed away and their kids didn't do anything with it, and let it sort of fall apart. So, if Grace's mom was left the farmhouse, I don't understand the connection with how Tracey, Mom's old friend, knew about it and the connection with Grace. I was missing something here. I felt like I was reading a suspense novel and couldn't put it down.

The next letter was a few weeks later, same tone as the first.

Rebecca,

Really great news, so glad we got to talk last week. The family that Sebastian is placed with has scheduled visits with Trent each week, and their relationship is really blossoming. Sebastian loves his time with Trent, and I hear the connection is strong. Sebastian is settling in well, but he cries out for his mom often at night. It is truly heartbreaking, so getting him with a sort of normalcy is the goal. Trent has been staying with friends and moving around to keep out of sight. I let him stay at my place for the last two weeks while I am away. I don't think he loves my city loft; he thinks everyone is watching him all the time, but I think he does enjoy my satellite dish, and that pizza can be delivered within minutes to my place.

He has been doing construction work and getting paid under the table to avoid any paper trails. I know as an attorney I should not support anything illegal, but I still don't trust those crazies who think minister Bailey is innocent. Such dumb fucks.

I spoke some more with the estate attorneys, and they said that the natural heir is Sebastian, but being a toddler, leaves it all sort of moot at the moment and it should be placed into a trust. They are working on a way to convince Gary to be power of attorney over Sebastian so he can make decisions on the estate while he is in foster care. But he still doesn't want to, so we are sort of at an impasse. But knowing that you and Mike can oversee the house for the most part and keep up with some of it offers some solace. If I could convince Gary, he could just sell it, take the money, and put that into a trust for Sebastian, but he is deeply depressed right now and seeking treatment in a facility. He said he is not in the right state of mind to do anything at all.

I have some powerhouse attorney friends who have some creative ideas, so I am still very optimistic. Part of me remains hopeful that Trent can pull through and maybe we can get him prepped for adoption in a few years. We just need all the smoke to settle. Trent wants it, he just must get his own life together first.

By the way, Angie keeps calling me, but I am avoiding her like the plague. I truly think she is mentally unwell. She acts like nothing has happened at all. She calls and leaves me messages about recipes and weather. I am like, 'hello, don't you remember your husband is in prison for molesting children, one being your son, who will not speak to you and is hiding from you?'

I don't believe I was ever friends with her. I don't believe I used to eat at their house with that sick son of bitch. She is trying to be friendly with me because she knows what I know, and she knows the power I have. She fears me, and she should. I will do all I can to help Trent and Sebastian and if I can prove it, I would make sure she rotted in jail with him. I know in my heart there is more to her story that is not being told, I just do. But I am not going to waste my energy on her now. However, once I make sure

Trent and Sebastian are safe, she is on my list!

I will call you once I am back home. This case is taking longer than usual. My partners are trying to push through, just a lot of discovery and this judge just doesn't seem to be in any sort of rush. Hoping to be home soon, maybe you could come up and see Trent with me once I am back. I think he would enjoy that.

Talk soon. Tracey

As I tried to figure out who Tracey really was to my mom, I kept thinking about her being friends with Angie. If Tracey and Aunt Janet didn't really know each other, how did Tracey know Angie and my mom? Just as I started to open the next letter, I saw my mom's van pulling back up the drive. I shuffled all the letters together and shoved them inside my pillowcase and ran out of my room. I plopped myself down on the couch, opened my book and waited for them to come in. Mom scurried past me, dropping bags and her purse, and running into the bathroom. Aunt Janet screamed down the hallway that maybe if she only had a few children, she would have some remnants of bladder control and then just laughed. I looked over to her and said, "You seem in good spirits, I take it your talk and running errands went well?"

In a whispered tone, Aunt Janet said, "Monty, I uncovered something big, I will fill you in the minute there are no listening ears."

This was huge! I could barely wait to hear what she found out, but she and my mom seemed good, so hopefully Mom filled her totally in and now we can piece more of the puzzle together. Mom whirled past me and started rambling off a hundred questions about where everyone was, who ate, if anyone called and so on. I told her I didn't know where Adam went, that Eve had just left with Olivia, and the twins ate lunch and were on the porch. I told her Zach called and said he would try to visit this weekend, but just depends on if he is feeling up to it after moving and getting ready for classes. Mom smiled and then looked at me straight on.

"Monty, look, I am sorry I was harsh on you earlier. You are right, I do make you do more than Adam and Eve, and it's not fair. I forget that you are almost sixteen and probably have a life too and would like to have options like your brother and sister, and you should. I had a long talk with Aunt Janet today, and she made a good point that you have never broken my trust, so I am not sure why I worry so much that you will. I love you and I honestly just worry about you. I worry about all my kids," Mom said.

I didn't know where this was coming from, but I was in shock. I just smiled at her and then walked over and gave her a hug. I didn't really know what to say but it felt good to not feel crazy for once. I really did feel like I was getting stuck with more chores and things to do than anyone else, so to have someone substantiate those theories made me feel good.

"Okay, I am making dinner tonight, and your dad wants steak, mashed potatoes, asparagus and is begging Aunt Janet to make dessert, since apparently she is a better baker than me. I got everything I needed from the store, but I forgot to get steak sauce and you know that the twins and your dad cannot eat steak, no matter how perfect I make it, without steak sauce. Monty, I don't need it for a few hours, would you mind riding your bike into town to grab some from the minimart? You can go to the library or to Hunter or Mandy's, or just whatever *you want* to do, if you are back by six-thirty... with the steak sauce," Mom said.

"Thanks, Mom! I have a stack of books I wanted to pick up from the library, so I'll probably just do that. But the bigger question I have is... what dessert is Aunt Janet making?" I jokingly asked.

"You know that it's going to be my infamous German chocolate cake with fresh coconut and dark chocolate shavings. Your mom has a bottle of Cabernet she has been holding hostage that I am taking as payment for my baking skills," Aunt Janet said whilst eyeballing the wine rack in the corner of the dining room that only held nice bottles that my dad got from clients. They were all very expensive and not wine to drink with pizza or Chinese, but apparently steak and chocolate cake call for a celebratory bottle.

I ran into my room to pack up my backpack and I called and told Mandy that I was off to the library and to meet me there. I asked her to call Hunter again, as when I called, he was still not home. I shoved the remaining envelopes into my backpack, ran into the kitchen to grab snacks, of course, then ran out to my bike. I just wanted to leave before my mom changed her mind. She was being overly nice, and I was not sure how long it was going to last. Before I stopped at the library, I ran into the minimart to get the steak sauce. I wanted to do it then, so I didn't forget on my way home. As I walked down the aisle, I heard a familiar voice saying my name. As I turned to look, I saw Thomas holding a bag of chips and some hostess snowballs. Thomas had worked for my dad for years and was referred to as Mr. Fix-it. He was a whiz with everything, and had helped around our house with cars, tractors, four-wheelers, appliances and who knows what else through the years. He was my dad's right hand in many ways, so we knew him like family.

"Hey, Thomas," I said. "What brings you to the minimart mid-afternoon and with my favorite hostess snowballs in hand no less?"

"Oh, Monty, I have been running around job sites all day and it has been one thing after another. Now your dad wants to check out an old company truck and see if I can get it working, so we can give it to two new guys to haul materials back and forth, even though I have told him it is a lost cause. I used to drive that truck around when I first started working with him and I am sure it has two-hundred and fifty thousand miles on it by now and I don't think a magician could get it running. But your dad seems to think *I can*. He swears we can get another season out of it if I give it my touch. I am flattered, but I also think your dad is delusional! So, I am just getting some snacks on my way out to work on it and then hopefully home for a long shower and some Wheel of Fortune on the couch," he said.

"Oh, cool, but where is the truck? Isn't it at the shop with the others?" I asked.

"No, your dad said he left it for the church to use some years ago, but when it really started to give them trouble, your dad picked it up and left it in that old cow barn in your field. I thought your dad scrapped it a while ago, until your dad brought it up today. So, I am heading over there now," he said.

The blue and white truck from the other night! Um, it definitely ran, and I just didn't know what he was going to find in that barn along with it.

"Oh, did he give you a key for the padlock on the door to the barn?" I asked.

"Umm, no, he didn't mention a padlock. I was in the field helping work on the bush hog a few months ago and I didn't notice it was locked up, but I wasn't really paying attention to the barn. Is it a key or combination lock?" he asked.

"A key I am pretty sure, and I don't know when the lock was put on, but I was riding back there last week and saw a chain and padlock on the door. I figured Dad didn't want any of us going in

167

there because it was old and falling apart. The lock looks new, and I am out there all of the time and had never noticed it before," I said.

"Well, shit. Hopefully, he took the lock off before sending me all the way down here. He is at a jobsite up north, and there is no way he will get back any time before six. I'll page him and ask if maybe he has the key at your house. Or maybe I will just have to cut the lock and chain off. I have bolt cutters in my truck, for worst case," he said.

"Okay, sorry to be the bearer of bad news. But maybe he left it unlocked for you, I don't know. I haven't been out there for a few days. Good luck," I shouted, and smiled.

He walked toward checkout ahead of me and grabbed the steak sauce from me and placed it on the belt and grabbed another package of snowballs, then paid for all of it. Thomas is one of the nicest people I know. I just hoped he didn't run into any trouble out of the field. I was hoping Ryan and Greg weren't out there, or whoever the other guy was. When he paged Dad, if Dad didn't put the lock on there, was it going to set off an alarm with how it got on there, which was an entirely new worry now packed into my chaotic brain. All I knew was that I was glad I was not out there right now, and I was going to steer clear.

"Hey, thanks for the heads up, Monty, hoping this was not a pointless trip down this way. But if I can't get in tonight, I don't mind heading home a little earlier than normal one bit. My wife would be happy to have me awake past eight o clock... take care, hun," he shouted as he walked toward his truck.

I was worried about what he might find, but I was not going to add any more stress to the pile of shit I was already digging through. I put the steak sauce and snowball into my backpack and headed over to the library. There was a traffic light out, maybe from the storm earlier, so I took a different road and passed Cliff's house. I stopped for a minute to look, as it truly was a beautiful house. As I looked to the window right of the front door, it looked like Bruce was in there with another man, arguing. It wasn't Cliff and I had only seen one picture of Bruce before, and it was on the beach with sunglasses, a hat and floating in the water, so I didn't have a good image to reference, but it was his house and it did resemble him, so it made sense.

Bruce was sitting facing the street while the other man was on the couch, with his side facing the street. They were both gesticulating, and it appeared they were shouting. I didn't want them to see me spying inside, so I placed my foot on the peddle to keep going when the man on the couch stood up. I only saw the back of him, but my heart sank into my stomach. That silhouette. The height. The style of clothing. It looked just like the man in the field that was holding the shotgun. His clothes were nearly identical. They were Wrangler-style jeans, with a brown belt, and they were very stained and dirty. The shirt was a plaid button down, but with the sleeves folded from the elbow down. It was partially tucked and looked like it was on over a t-shirt. This time he had a baseball cap on, as he didn't before, but it was the same figure.

I wanted to see if he left out of the front door, but I also didn't want him to see me. I peddled past the house and stopped at the neighbors. I scooted my bike onto their front yard and sat against Cliff and Bruce's fence. There was a large rose bush on the corner that concealed me, and I just sat and waited to see if I could get a better view of his face.

I waited for about five minutes, when I heard a vehicle start up. The way these houses were set up, there was an alleyway behind the houses where there were driveways, and some had detached garages. I totally forgot that. I was at the front of the house; the man must have left out of the back and was probably parked back there as well. I stood up and tried to look to the back alley, where I had a tiny view.

As I heard the vehicle get closer to the next house I was in the front of, I saw it. The blue and white truck that Thomas was heading back to our field to work on. He was not going to find it when he got there, because someone was already driving it in town.

It must have been someone who knew it was kept there by my dad after the church stopped using it, and someone who knew my dad wouldn't be in town right now to be blatant enough to drive it in plain sight. But the real question was, who?

I hopped onto my bike and peddled fast down the street to try to see which way he was turning. As I got to the end of the street, where you turn right toward the library or left to go back toward my house and the fields, he was turning left. We stopped at the same time, waiting for a car to pass, when I looked over and realized he must have seen me. His hat, which was a blue Chicago Cubs hat that had a very soiled brim, was pulled down very low, his right hand was against his face to sort of block it and he had his head tilted toward the floorboard.

This man knew me. I knew he did. Whoever this was, he knew where the truck was, he knew my family, and he might have been dumb enough to drive this truck in plain sight, but he didn't expect to see me. He didn't expect to see anyone in my family, I assume. He also must not have known my dad was sending Thomas down to work on the truck, or else he wouldn't have taken it out. The car passed and he peeled out onto the road. There were still no plates on the truck, which was another issue. Wasn't he worried about getting pulled over for driving an unregistered vehicle? As I turned into the library, I saw Hunter and Mandy waiting out front already. I smiled as I peddled closer to them, but my brain was now wondering who Bruce was to this person? Their connection could be related to the incident or maybe just a friendship. But I needed to find out.

"Hey, where have you been?" Mandy and Hunter asked. "Sorry, had to stop at the minimart first and then had a little run-in with someone, no big deal. I am here now and ready to dig into the rest of this," I explained. "I have the remaining letters I haven't finished reading yet, but let's make sure to be discreet in the library. I just don't trust anyone right now and I don't want anyone seeing what we are doing."

Mandy and Hunter agreed, and we walked in together. As we bee-lined straight to the back of the library where there were long skinny tables and chairs to sit and read at, I noticed Cliff out of the corner of my eye. I whispered to Mandy and Hunter, "Hey, take my backpack and get setup over there on that last table. The letters are inside, there are just a few left from Tracey, and I have big news about Trent. Like super big. But I need to go say 'hi' to Cliff first."

I walked toward Cliff, and he looked very upset. He was normally so happy and energetic, but his body language and facial expressions were solemn.

"Hey, Cliff, I just wanted to say hi and see how you are doing… Umm, you seem upset, so I don't want to bother you, but I am here if you need anything," I said.

"Hey, Monty, I am fine, just adulthood rearing its ugly head again. I will be fine, just need to get out of my own funk," Cliff responded.

"Okay, got it. Well, my friends and I are just doing some research and I wanted to also pick up those books you set aside for me, because I forgot them Saturday. And hey, I am here if you need anything," I said.

"Thank you. You get all settled in with your friends and I will get those books checked out and will bring them over to you. And thanks for asking about me, that means a lot. Just been fighting with Bruce the past few days and it just bums me out. I don't like a lot of his friends and he is very sensitive if I say anything disparaging about them. A lot of the people he hangs out with don't know he is gay, and he wants to keep it that way. You know how it can be, so I get it. But he also lets them say very disturbing things about homosexuals and it is offensive, well, I think to anyone. It is just not language I am used to hearing anywhere, but he lets it slide. There is one friend I just don't like at all, and he has been the topic lately. He is older, married, kids and seems like a very nice man on the outside. He is a client of Bruce's, and they became friends because of that. But as he got to know him, some weird shit came to light. I don't even engage when he is around, but I overheard them talking yesterday and the things he was saying were just awful. He was talking about some kid he knows mixed up in some bad shit and how he must be some faggot and he will do whatever he needs to do to assure his actions are addressed… with whatever means. I overheard that and stormed out of my room and told him to not talk like that in our home, and Bruce became mad at me… like is he serious? He asked him to leave, but it wouldn't change anything. He will stay friends with him and let him say such derogatory comments with a total pass. Just pisses me off," Cliff said.

All I could think was the man he was referring to could be the man that was just there with Bruce… which was the same man from the field. I needed to get his name, but not make it a big deal.

172

"Well, that is awful, I am so sorry. I don't get how anyone feels okay talking like that. Honestly, I don't get how anyone can feel that way. I mean, who is this guy and why is Bruce friends with him at all?" I asked.

"Well, he is a small client, but he is very well connected, so he has sent tons of work his way. And like I said, he is just a normal guy on the outside, so they will grab a drink or play pool or just hang out after work. I don't think they get deep in conversation too often, but sometimes when he has too much to drink, the claws come out and he can just be very offensive. They both work up north but live down here, such a small world, I guess, which they bond over," he responded.

Still no name. How the hell do I ask again without sounding ridiculous?

"Super strange. Do you think his family knows he is like this?" I asked.

"Oh, God, I don't know. One of his kids I think is in rehab, or was supposed to go to rehab, so I don't know if his parenting skills are that great either. I don't know anything about his wife at all, just some issues with his kid, but he doesn't want to ever talk about it," Cliff said.

"I sound so nosy, but it's a small town, I wonder if I know this man," I said, hoping he would respond with his name and a laugh.

"Girl, I would tell you if it was my place. I just don't want to make it a bigger issue than it already is. It's a small town, and I trust you, but I don't want to be spreading anyone else's dirty laundry around town. This is a me and Bruce issue and I need to keep it reeled into that. But Monty, I am sure you do know him. Your family knows everyone and if you looked hard enough, I am sure you could figure it out," Cliff said with a smile and a wink, and then he turned and walked over to get my books at the checkout.

The wink threw me off. It made me think I did know the person, and he knew I knew them. But I didn't know anyone who had a kid in rehab. I walked over to Mandy and Hunter where they were engrossed in a letter.

"Hey, anything good?" I asked.

"Okay, so we read the first two letters, we are caught up with you on Tracey. So crazy about the farmhouse being Grace Stewarts! I am waiting to find out your mom is like CIA or something with all this secretive stuff. But Monty, letter three, I think is what Adam was talking about. It answers so much, look," Mandy said.

"Okay, but before we move onto the next letter, I need to drop a bomb on you. Like grab onto the table and be prepared to freak out," I said. "Trent Bailey is Tate Lawson and Sebastian Stewart is Sam. My parents are Sebastian's legal foster parents and they falsified documents to get custody, but we have never had custody. My mom moved Trent here and got him that job, so it could work with Sebastian, since he is supposed to live with us. I mean, there have been people here meeting with my parents when Sam was over for a play date with the twins a few times, but now I am pretty sure they were social workers checking in. Like, my head has been spinning. But our town is so fucking sleepy, no one would notice and without any complaints; I am sure the social workers just let it all go without doing much checking.

"I don't think Aunt Janet knows that part, that they are here, but she knows my parents helped Trent significantly and she knows they keep in touch. Angie has been pestering Aunt Janet for months, which is why she is staying with us to hide from

Angie. Aunt Janet said Angie is looking for Trent and thinks she knows where to find him because she misses him and wants to help. But Aunt Janet thinks that is total bullshit. She said it's to find Trent and potentially harm him. Now that minister Bailey is out, she thinks Angie wants to make sure he never comes forward with any information, and that might mean by any means necessary," I said.

"Okay, what the actual fuck? Are you joking, Monty, like is this for real? This entire time, the kid that endured such horrible shit, is our minister? How can this even be?" Mandy questioned.

"I know, but it makes so much more sense. There is still lots to piece together, but we are getting there, I can feel it. But I will say, the minute I put it together with Tate and Sam, it answered every question I had about them when they arrived. From whom Sam was to Tate, why he goes to a different school, why my mom does so much for Tate and the church now that he is running it and why lots of my mom's meetings with Tate are secretive. So now we need to figure out who Tracey is to my mom and how my mom knew Grace's mom and about the farmhouse. Because now I know my mom wanted to move here specifically to do with something with Grace's mother, just I don't know what," I said.

"Well, I think we can get some answers to who Tracey is in the next letter; it all starts coming together, take a look," Mandy said.

Rebecca,

Sorry it has been a while; it has been a shitshow over here. Trent took off but he is keeping in touch. He has this entire plan now on how to get Sebastian, and it's not awful to be honest. He wants to get ordained, and he wants to right minister Bailey's wrongs. He even said he would get married to someone he doesn't even love if that makes it easier to get Sebastian. I told him that is not necessary, and he doesn't need to do what his mom did. I got the ball rolling in that direction since that is really what he wants to do.

I talked to some people about getting his name changed and I think that won't be that hard, but let's wait. I am enrolling him in a private Christian college, I am going to use his first and middle name and drop the Bailey. I talked with the school, and I know several people on the board there as well. They know the minister Bailey debacle and they said that won't be a problem keeping his enrollment confidential. They also said they don't share any of the student rosters with anyone and they will help keep him safe. After what he went through, they have been wonderful to work with.

I told Trent to change his hair up, think of a different backstory to tell other kids and avoid any deep questions. If he wants this to work, he must be careful.

He won't live on campus, so I am getting him an apartment, in my name. It is total shit, and I wouldn't be caught dead there, but it's what he wants. He feels safer, totally off the grid. He said he left my place in a rush because there was a green car circling around daily and he knew it was Angie. She was looking for me, I think, but he said he can't take any chances.

He is safe right now staying at an old client's guest house and he is still working construction. I did tell him we have to get a bank account opened so I can deposit money, but he is refusing. I just don't want to be meeting up and exchanging money like I am completing a drug deal every few weeks. But I will figure that out later.

Oh, and Angie... this woman knows no boundaries. I have not been close to her in years, and you and I both know that minister Bailey was dark and sinister for some time. He made my skin crawl before all this came forward. But Angie and my cousin had Trent, so she is family, but God, I don't like her. Why my cousin had to go out and die in a car accident and leave me to clean up the Angie and Trent shit is maddening enough, but her new level of crazy is just too much. Thank God I really love Trent and want to help him, so I am not going to worry about her dumb ass.

Whenever I want to go nuts on her, I just have to remember our summer together and the good times we have had, because she wasn't always this way. When Angie and you stayed with me the summer after my first year in law school was one of the best times of my life. Angie and my cousin were hot and heavy and honestly, if he was still around, I think she would be a different person. She wasn't always nuts; you remember normal Angie, don't you? I think I do.

I remember my newspaper post for summer roommates in that tiny apartment. It was blatantly exaggerated as a three bedroom, when really it was a one bedroom, with a nook and a dining room. But we made it work and it was incredible.

My cousin pushed Angie on me so she could stay in the city and not vacation with her parents in Michigan, and you called me out of nowhere. I thought you were going to be this country bumpkin, but you were actually the total opposite. That was one of the best summers of my life and I really am thankful that we have stayed friends through all of this. You have been such a blessing and Trent is so lucky to have you.

I really need to talk to Janet, too; she has been so helpful as well. We just never really knew each other, and I don't even know what to say. Maybe you can reintroduce us again, it's been twenty years, so hopefully we can have a fresh start and my friendship

177

with Angie back in the day won't taint her feelings of me.

Okay, maybe soon we can relive that summer of fun and put this mess behind us... soon. Bye for now, I have a trial coming up again and I am so not prepared. I am never going to make partner at this rate. Good thing after a few martinis I forget all about my lawyer ambitions!

Talk soon.

Tracey

"See, Monty, so Tracey is related to Trent, too – well, sort of. Your mom lived with Angie and Tracey that summer, so it now makes sense how they all know each other," Mandy said.

"Yeah, this all makes so much more sense. I am sort of remembering some of my mom's stories from that summer. Aunt Janet did not live with them, as she lived at home and looked over her parent's house. I remember her making snarky comments about how the summer they met she had to work and be a grown up while my mom partied and got a tan. I just always thought she was being snarky to be funny.

"Janet and Angie's parents had a lake house in Michigan, and they always stayed there for the summers, and this was one of the first summers neither of them joined their parents. Aunt Janet stayed back to make money before starting college and I don't really know Angie's story. She is older, but not by a lot. Maybe she was just in love and didn't want to leave him behind. I don't know.

"My mom has been there a few times for girl's trips, and I even think my dad and Zach went up there when he was little. I don't know if they have it any more, but I remember them talking about it often while I was growing up. If I remember correctly, my mom met Aunt Janet at a restaurant she worked at that summer. Angie would go there to get free food from her sister and brought my mom in, so that is how they met. They hit it off right away and my mom spent most of the summer with her and some of Janet's friends. Angie had a boyfriend, which I guess was Trent's dad or Tracey's cousin and Mom would say her roommate was gone a lot with her boyfriend, which is how her and Aunt Janet got so close. I still don't get how Janet and Tracey don't really know each other. It sounds like they have met, but she was closer to Angie. I am going to ask Aunt Janet about this tonight. She also told me she found out something big she wants to tell me. I cannot wait to find out what it is," I explained, quietly.

We had two more letters to look at and as I went to open the next one, I noticed Hunter had not said a thing this entire time. Not like him at all, as he loved this sort of drama, and he was normally asking questions and trying to culminate the backstory. How did he have nothing to say after the Trent/Tate bomb? Just not like him.

"Hey Hunter, are you feeling okay? You are being really quiet and if you have stuff you need to do, you can totally go. I wasn't trying to drag you here, sorry, I know you are busy," I said.

"No Monty, it's not you and it not all of this. I need to tell you both something and I just don't know how to say it without you freaking out. So, you have to promise to stay calm," he replied.

"Well, shit Hunter. Never tell women they need to stay calm before big news, as that is the last thing they are going to do. What is it, you have me very worried." Mandy exclaimed.

Three people in the stacks responded with a *Shhhhhhing* after Mandy was very loud in her response. We all looked around and when eyes were off us, we huddled closer together, and pushed our heads, until they were almost touching.

"Okay, I have been gone all day because I had a doctor appointment this morning to get my physical for school and my doctor is north in the city. When I was all done, I asked my mom if she would drop me at the mall for a little bit. I told her I would get a ride home, so she left me there to do some shopping. I needed to get shoes, so I went into the store and was trying them on when Jason, Sunny and some random guy came over to me. Jason and I are in shit together for school and even though he is an asshole, I am always nice to him and keep it cordial. But I don't have a clue why he is hanging out with your cousin, because I have never seen them together. Sunny is not really in *that* crowd," Hunter said.

"I know, Sunny is a loser, you can say that, you are not going to offend me. But who was the third person?" I asked.

"I couldn't figure it out at first; I didn't recognize him because he had a baseball hat on pulled far down, was wearing an oversized flannel shirt and really baggy pants and he was looking down at the ground. Again, not trying to sound like a dick, but not the normal look for dudes in Jason's entourage.

"Jason asked me what I have been up to and was just making small talk while Sunny and the other guy were over by the register talking to some girl that worked at the store. Jason quietly mentions there is a party this Friday and it is invite only and very small. He was only inviting a few people and even the guys with him didn't know about it. He said I could come, but I couldn't bring anyone, but he promised there would be entertainment. I said I didn't really know what that meant, and he just smirked and said I would not be disappointed. So, I asked him where it was, and he leaned in even closer and whispered 'the old farmhouse.' He said someone he knows has been fixing it up and it is primed and ready for a party. He said I had to go at exactly

9.15 p.m. if I was going to go and I had to park over at the cemetery and walk. He said he didn't want there to be any chance of the cops showing up. He said there will be drinks, party favors and entertainment and again reminded me to come alone and not tell anyone… but here is the weird part. Are you ready?" he asked.

"Yes, what, what is it!" I demanded.

"Jason sort gave me this weird handshake and pat on the back and when I looked up to say bye, I saw who the third guy was… Monty, it was Ryan," he said. "Look, he knows I saw him, and he looked spooked as fuck. Being at the mall early on a Monday maybe he thought was safe, but when he saw me, he flipped. He just shy of ran out of the store and Sunny and Jason followed," Hunter said.

"I don't get it. Monty, why would Jason be with your cousins? And I thought Ryan was in Europe, is he back now? Also, Hunter what are 'party favors,' like balloons and stuff?" Mandy asked.

"Party favors are drugs Mandy, just a clever way to put it when talking in public," Hunter said snidely.

I told them both that I didn't know if he ever went to Europe, or if he had been lying to everyone this entire time. I decided to fill them in on what had happened last Thursday and just be open about it. But I also decided to let them know that I knew who some of the men were now… "When the men were leaving, I saw there was another man driving a truck, and when I was at the picnic yesterday, I realized it was Jack's farmhand, Greg. But when the guys were getting in the back of the truck Thursday, I saw them too. I know who they are…"

I paused for a moment when Hunter looked up and said, "It was Sunny and Jason, wasn't it?"

181

"Yeah, it was them. How did you know? I don't know what they are involved in, but I think it is dangerous. But guys, there is more. Once they left the field, I walked over to where they were. There was blood on the ground and clippings of what looked like polaroid pictures. I also found a braided leather necklace that was broken and looks like its missing a charm. See, I kept it," I said while showing them the necklace.

"Monty, you know what this is, don't you?" Hunter asked. "I don't really know; it sort of looks familiar, but it's just a braided leather necklace, could be anything," I responded.

As I looked up at Hunter, he was holding the same necklace out from his shirt, as it was on his neck and with the charm still intact. The charm being an ichthys.

"You guys, these were the necklaces we got at church camp last summer. So, the one you found could be anybody's who went to that camp," Hunter said.

"Okay, so that is like everyone in our town. Doesn't really narrow it down that much and it's not like I can just see who is not wearing it any more, as I am sure hardly anyone still is," I said.

"Yes and no. Honestly, Monty, I feel like everyone still wears theirs. I mean your brothers always have theirs on, so do your cousins," Mandy said.

"Yeah, I guess they do, but still not sure it will lead to anything. One more thing I should mention. The reason I had us meet at the cemetery yesterday was not because Jack was working in the field, it was because when I went to the cow barn, Greg was in there talking to someone. I couldn't see them, but I know who's voice it was. It was Ryan's. I know he wasn't the man with the shotgun, that man was taller and older, I could tell. Plus, he and Greg were talking about that night and Greg was sort of filling him in, so Ryan wasn't there. I don't know if Ryan went to Europe when he said he went, or if he came back early or what, but I know he is back now, and I think he is trying to hide out. I just can't figure out how Jason plays into any of this. Sunny is a dirtball and lives at Ryan's house, so whatever Ryan got into, I get Sunny got mixed up in. But the Jason and farmhand Greg element just don't make any sense; this is where I am hoping Aunt Janet's news is good and can help me fill in the missing pieces," I said.

Mandy was feverishly making notes and sort of creating a diagram of information to follow. I love how her brain works, and her thoroughness is awesome.

"Okay, first we need to find out how long Greg has been working for Jack. We also need to find out where he lives and honestly how did Jack find him for the job. Monty, you must handle that, bring them something to have a reason to stop by and find out all you can. I think that might be a key to a lot of this. We need to find out, if we can, why Jason has been with Ryan and Sunny, so Hunter you have to go to that party. Jason likes you and I think he wants to show you something – that is what he means by 'entertainment,' so find out what that is. But don't drink at that party, you need to be totally with it. I am going to go over to the church and look at the camp records from last year. I will find out who on that list might fit the description, so Monty, do you have anything I can work with?" Mandy asked.

"Okay, maybe between sixteen and twenty-two or so, hair was longer, sort of shaggy, and he was tan like he works outside or has just been out a lot this summer. I couldn't get his hair color because it looked wet and the way the sun was hitting it, but I would say not blonde and not black, somewhere in the middle. But that is all I got. The men were blocking most of him. When they were berating him, they were saying he was sick, and they needed to either kill him and bury him, turn him into the cops or he had to run and get out of town. Once I realized it was Sunny and Jason, I am just trying to figure out who this dark and twisted soul is that has them willing to shoot someone or threaten to kill them. Like who the hell lives in this town, attends church camp, knows Sunny and Jason and is that fucked up? It just doesn't make sense," I said.

"That is why we need to go with Mandy's plan. It's a good start and once we piece some of this together, maybe it will all make sense. One last thing. Monty, your house backs up to the farmhouse and it only makes sense that you and Mandy sit back there during the party. I just don't have a good feeling about this, and it is better if you are there. We should even think about bringing a camera or camcorder. I don't know what Jason is planning, but if he is mixed up in potentially shooting someone, I don't want to be there alone," Hunter said.

"Actually, I was already planning to go there with my sister. Jason asked her to go, alone, with him, as sort of his date. She is very nervous too and I don't even think she knows what drugs look like. So, I will be there. I think I am going to put up a tent off to the corner of the cornstalks and just completely set up there. My brothers have binoculars so I can see all the way to the farmhouse, and I can just stay out of sight. You have to keep an eye on my sister, though; Eve is very smart, but very naive and I just don't know why Jason would ask her to go. I know she is super-hot, but she is not into that whole scene, so I am just super confused," I said.

"Ten-four. Okay, let's finish these letters, I need to get home and chill with my dad for a bit. If I want to get out of the house to go to a party, I need to be home a lot this week, so my parents don't freak out," Hunter said.

"Okay, folks, next letter," Mandy whispered.

Rebecca,

Amazing news, I am so glad to hear that you and Trent were able to meet up last week. He said that the last year has been so tough, but you and Mike have been a huge help. I know it's not official yet, but if your minister is planning on going to the new location when they build it, that could be a huge opportunity! I mean, he could be right there, you can watch over him and with the foster plan, this could all work out. I am not trying to get ahead of myself, but I really feel optimistic. And don't worry, I don't talk to anyone, so who would I tell? You know I support you in all of this.

Good news, I talked with Gary again, and he is doing so much better. Now that time has passed, he is willing to help us handle the farmhouse. He agreed to keep up with the property taxes and will work with the attorneys on assuring that Sebastian is able to get the home when old enough, or if all parties agree to sell, he will assure all proceeds go into a trust for him. He says he wants to sell it, as it makes the most sense, and I know you and Mike are interested in maybe buying it but can't afford it yet. So, I asked him to just work with us and when the time is right, I will make sure it is all taken care of.

Oh, Bec, Gary loves you and I know he would love to reach out if he could, but he says talking to you would just be too painful. You and Helen were in school together and grew up together and he knows you miss her so much and would love to just be able to talk about her. But he says he is not ready. When he sees a picture of you two together, his heart breaks all over again. He appreciates what you are doing to help with the farmhouse, and he loves that you and Mike live right there, but he is not ready yet. So, trust me, I tried, but it's just not time. I didn't know her like you did, but I am so glad you introduced us so many years ago. Not being married with kids myself, I have been so fortunate to have people like you, Helen, Angie (at one point in time) and others in my life.

I think he will be ready in time, just be patient.

Everything else is going smoothly and I have a meeting next week about becoming partner at my firm! Not to toot my own horn, but I think it is actually going to happen. So, stay tuned as a little Chicago visit might be in your future!

Tracey

One more insane similarity and family secret uncovered. *So, Grace's mom went to school with my mom. I need to find my mom's school yearbook and find her because I wonder how close they were? I mean, my dad tells us my mom had to buy this land, and it seemed like she pushed just to be close to the farmhouse, so, I wonder if Helen and my mom spent a lot of time there? Also, this letter is from over three and half years ago, and my parents never bought the farmhouse, so I wonder what happened with that plan. It's still abandoned, obviously.*

We all sat there and felt like we ran a marathon. It had been an intense few days, and it was like an endless menagerie of secrets. It all made sense to why my parents keep us so in the dark, because they were tied to some really messed up stuff.

"I can't even make this up, Monty, Mandy, you have got to look at this last letter. Holy fuck," Hunter said louder than he should in a library, as a mother and her two sons gave us the dirtiest looks.

Rebecca,

The months have passed, and I feel like we have not written much at all, but I realize I have at least gotten to see you and talk on the phone a few times, which decreases my friend guilt. Who knew getting a boyfriend would keep me this busy? I now know why people do it, though; dating can be super fun and it's not horrible when they are hot and have good grammar! I am falling so in love, and I cannot tell you how lucky I am. I am hoping he is the one, as I have never been this happy!

Okay, enough about my great sex life and utter happiness... I digress...

Trent is doing great in school and is keeping up with his visits to Sebastian, and the foster family have been so helpful and positive. They invite Trent to family dinners and send him photos and have been such a pleasure to work with. I had some contact recently about a plan to place him later, and they said no rush, whenever it works and whatever is best for him. We could not have gotten luckier with where he was placed!

Too bad I don't have all good news. Look, I know he is your brother-in-law, but Ted is a dipshit. Helen and Lisa were very different, and I get that Lisa is more submissive and drabber, but she sure knows how to pick them. I am glad Mike works well with Ted because I don't know who else would hire him other than his own brother. I think he is slimy.

As we all know, Helen was left the farmhouse. Lisa was left some bonds, money, a car and even a piece of land, not worth very much, down in southern Indiana. Lisa never had one issue with the farmhouse being left to Helen, and I'll be dammed if her or Ted have helped navigate any of this mess with Sebastian. They have had absolutely no contact with him and honestly do not know that sweet baby at all. They act like he never existed. But now that I have everything drafted where you and Mike can buy the house, and it would offer a large chunk of cash for Sebastian, Ted raises issue. He has no real play here, but he is saying it should just go to Lisa and that Gary has no right to handle it any other way. He is arguing that it is Lisa's more than Gary's and if it sells, all the money should go to them.

Look, Gary won't fight them. He is barely involved in any of it. Legally, we are fine, but I don't know if Ted keeps pushing, Gary will give up much of a fight. Like I told you last chat, I think we stop the sell, and leave it as is. Ted doesn't want the house, he just wants easy money and if there is no money, he will back down. I say, let the dust settle and we will go from there.

The good news is, Ted and Lisa don't know anything about Trent and have not seen a picture of Sebastian since he was a newborn. I don't think they will hinder our plan to move them there if everything works out with foster care and the church. I will not ruffle any feathers with Ted and just see how it all settles. He is just such a prick and somehow you put up with him.

Now that I am partner, I have a much easier schedule. I get to pick my own cases and I can do loads of pro bono work, which means I can finish all this up with Trent, Sebastian, and the farmhouse and all those hours can be covered by the firm. It's good to be a lady boss!

I will be out there soon, let's talk next steps with Trent and Sebastian.

Tracey

The three of us just looked up and if it all couldn't get any more intertwined, here we are. We looked at each other in disbelief and started to pack up our things. I was silent because I was out of emotion to feel at this point. I just wanted to go back to a week ago when all of this was still a twisted family secret. The term *ignorance is bliss* really made sense to me now.

"Hey, Monty, I know this is a lot to take in, but I think we made some progress and maybe this will help us find the man in the chair and maybe we can save him if they are still after him," Mandy said.

"Look, this might sound crazy, but this is all sort of cool, hear me out… This sleepy town you always say is boring and nothing exciting ever happens, now you just found out that your mom was best friends with a woman whose daughter was raped, had a child with the rapist and potentially murdered by him as well. Your parents illegally are fostering the dead woman's child, as they don't actually have him and helped move minister Bailey's stepson to our town after changing his name and are sort of hiding him out. Your Aunt Janet was the sister-in-law to minister Bailey, one of the biggest scandals during our lifetime. Your Aunt Lisa is Helen's sister and so in fact Grace's aunt and Sebastian's great aunt. Your Uncle Ted is slimy, but I think that is old news. And not to mention your cousins are caught up in some crazy scandal that might involve murder and let's not forget, you are friends with two of the coolest people in town. Boring my ass, this town is immersed in your family's shit…shit you only see on T.V.," Hunter said.

I shrugged my shoulders and didn't disagree this was like an entirely new world to me. But it also made my life so unrecognizable. I wanted answers, but I also missed the not-knowing, too. The issue was, I didn't even think this was all of it. There was no way this was the last letter either; my mom had to have others hidden. This ended on a cliffhanger, and we knew he finished school, changed his name, has custody, illegal or not, of Sebastian and moved to our town. So where were the letters talking about that? Why would my mom keep those separate? I was hurt and pissed and so incredibly frustrated.

"Look, you guys head out, we can catch up tomorrow. I need

189

to get my books from Cliff and head home. I need to be alone for a little bit. But I will talk to Edna and Jack tomorrow and let's all talk after, love you guys," I said.

We walked toward the door, and I just felt sad all over. I don't know why sadness was the emotion I had, but I couldn't shake it. When I got up to the checkout desk, my books were in a cloth bag with a note from Cliff.

Hey Monty

You and your friends seemed super engrossed over there, so I didn't want to bother you. Here are the books I think you would like and a little something extra. They are all checked out and ready to go. Thanks for always being a good listener when I need to vent. I love our friendship and I am grateful for you.

I hope you figure out what you were looking into... sounded very intense! I am here if you ever have any questions.

Cliff

I grabbed the bag and left. I hopped onto my bike, looked at my watch and realized I needed to be home in about thirty minutes, which was plenty of time. But the sky looked like the storm was passing back through, so I needed to hurry to avoid getting caught in it. I started to peddle and just began to cry.

Even though we found out so much today, I felt defeated. I felt like I didn't even know my life right now. I could not wrap my head around all of this; I felt like the more I learned, the more I didn't understand.

I am going to try to talk with Aunt Janet tonight and see if I can figure out what happened after that last letter from Tracey.

Chapter Nine

Secrets

I didn't remember much of my ride home, but at one point I was so glad I stopped at the store before the library. I had the steak sauce, I was on time, and I had books to prove I was at the library. I was not in any mood to deal with my parents if I messed up in some way, so my goal was to get home, eat and talk to Aunt Janet. Maybe her big news would offer me some solace.

When I pulled up to the house, there was an extra car in our driveway. I didn't recognize it at first, but as I got further up the driveway, I saw them exiting the car, Tate, and Sam. I started laughing, out loud, because I felt like I was being pranked in some way. I was not mentally equipped for any of this, so add surprise dinner guests and I felt like I was starting to actually lose my mind.

My laughing must have startled Tate, because he turned and sort of jumped as I rode past him and laid my bike against the side of the house. "Hey, Monty, what is so funny?" he asked.

"Oh, nothing, just thinking of something weird that happened to me today," I responded. But then I thought, *Great, now I am lying to a minister on top of everything else.* If there was a hell, I was losing any chance of avoiding it at that point in time.

"What brings you over tonight, did Mom invite you for dinner? It is supposed to be extra delicious," I shouted whil' walking over to the front door.

"Actually, no, this is sort of an unplanned stop in. Your mom dropped off some items at church today and in one of the jackets was this little pouch with earrings and a ring in it, and I wanted to drop it off to her. I don't think she intended on donating it, so I just wanted to make sure she got it back before it got lost with all the rest of the donations," Tate said.

"That is really nice of you, well, come on in and I will grab her for you," I said.

As I walked them into the front of the house, it hit me. What if Mom didn't tell Aunt Janet where Trent was? Well, if she didn't know yet, she was about to find out. To hell with it. I couldn't handle any more secrets at this point.

I walked in and saw my mom and dad in the kitchen and Aunt Janet on the back porch. I didn't see Adam, Eve, or the twins, but I heard the T.V. on downstairs and assumed the twins were there.

"Hey, I brought surprises," I smiled and placed the steak sauce on the table.

"Hey Monty, thank you for picking that up," Dad said. "Oh, yes, how was the library? And did you say surprises, what else do you have?" Mom questioned.

Before I could answer, Tate and Sam walked around the corner into the kitchen. They both said hello and as I looked at my mom, she turned sheet white and dropped her spatula onto the ground. That two seconds told me; Aunt Janet did not know where Trent was. I wanted to feel bad, but I didn't. My entire life felt like a totally twisted lie, so this one was on them. I would have no way of knowing since they had shielded us from everything, so how this played out was on them.

"Oh, hey, Rebecca and Mike, we didn't mean to frighten

you. I just found this pouch with jewelry in one of the donated jacket pockets and wanted to get it back to you before it got lost at the church. Don't worry, you don't need to add extra plates, we aren't staying," Tate said with a smile. As my mom stood there startled and unresponsive, Aunt Janet walked in from the porch.

"Trent!" she exclaimed.

"Everybody, umm, there is a lot to unpack right now. Monty, why don't you take Sam down to play with the twins, we are going to push dinner until a little later," Dad requested.

I grabbed Sam's hand and led him downstairs. The twins were ecstatic to see him, and he jumped right onto the couch and started watching shows with them.

I ran back upstairs and walked back into the kitchen.

"Oh, no, Monty, this is adult stuff, you need to go to your room," Mom demanded.

"No, I am not going to my room, I am not being treated like a little kid. I know everything anyway, so you don't need to lie to me any more! I know who Trent and Sebastian are and I know everything you have done… all of you! You don't need to hide this all from me, I deserve to be a part of this," I said, but no sooner did I say the words, did I regret them.

Fuck. What have I done? How will I explain how I know all of this? My head was spinning and as I waited for my dad to shout at me or shove me out of the room, he said, "Okay, but please listen and be respectful until you hear everything."

I looked over to Aunt Janet and she was sobbing while hugging Tate. He kept repeating that he was all right and that everything would be okay.

My mom, on the other hand, looked terrified. I couldn't tell if it was because Aunt Janet would know she had been lying to her, because Tate might find out some of the deception, or because I was there, and they would have to explain it all to me. But these types of situations were where my dad shone the most. He was poised. He got everyone's attention and told us to go sit in the living room. He even walked over to the stove, made sure the burners were off and made sure to grab a beer from the refrigerator before joining us. Calm. Cool. Collected... I love that about him.

"It looks like we have a lot of explaining to do and I just want to start out by saying that everything done, was done with love and good intention," Dad said.

He went on to say to Tate that they never told anyone where he was, other than Tracey. She helped get him through school, she worked with the social worker, and she was an integral part of all of this. He then told Janet that they never meant to hide it from her, but Angie being a liability and with her harassing her constantly, the less she knew, the better. My parents explained that they promised to help keep them both, Tate, and Sam, safe and that is what they had done. Moving them here had its risks because of Lisa and Ted, but they had not been the wiser, at all. Dad explained that Tate does not look anything like he did in the old news photos that were splashed all over. He was just a boy back then. Plus, before they even contemplated this idea, they made sure to understand if Lisa or Ted knew what Sebastian, now Sam, looked like, and they didn't have a clue. They had his newborn photo and one more from his first Christmas. But Helen and Lisa were estranged, and Lisa wanted nothing to do with Helen, Grace, or Sebastian.

Mom jumped into explain that it was very divided for her because she was so close to Helen but not Lisa, even now that Helen was gone. Lisa held onto grudges and wouldn't let the past go, so Lisa and Ted didn't play a big part when planning all of this.

Dad cut Mom off and said, "I love my brother, but I have kept him working for me through the years to keep him close. He has a history that I am not proud of, but with him close, I can be sure everyone remains safe. But I am not blinded by him being family either. So, I want everyone to know that."

The whole time my parents were talking, Janet was just staring at Tate. She didn't look mad, she looked happy, a little confused, but really happy. Her response lit the room up and made it easier for my parents to explain everything, honestly. Mom looked at Janet and told her that Tate had been here for over three years, and he had a life here now. He was running our church, although small and modest, he was raising Sam and he was a great father-figure for him. She said they shouldn't have kept all of this from her, but there was no way to explain it without explaining where Tate was, and they didn't want to put him at risk.

"Mike, Rebecca... I am not upset. I am not angry. I don't feel betrayed or even lied to. I trust your intentions and seeing you right now, Tate, it makes me feel so lucky to have friends who would go to this extent to protect you. My only concern is, well, I think your safety might be at risk. I don't know everything yet, and I am still peeling back layers here, but I think Ryan is looking for you. I don't know if he already knows you are who you really are, but I think somehow, in some way, he is trying to find you and his goal might be to hurt you. Maybe for Angie, but I am not sure. I thought at first, he was looking for me, but knowing you are living here, that makes more sense," Janet said. "Okay, we need to stop there, Monty, this is not appropriate talk for you to be here, you should not be listening to all of this," Mom said.

"Rebecca, Monty knows. We have been talking and she knows more than any of you think she does," Janet responded.

"I am confused, where does Ryan play into all of this? He is not even in the country, and he doesn't know Angie, does he?" Mom asked.

"Okay, Mom, Dad, that is where you are wrong. Ryan is here, in town. I saw him yesterday and so did Aunt Janet. He was in the field, in the cow barn, talking to Jack's farmhand, Greg. They were talking about harming someone, and Ryan said he didn't want to kill him, but he would try to talk to him first and if that didn't work, he would take necessary action," I said.

"What? Oh my God! Monty, what are you talking about?" my mom yelled out.

"Okay, everyone calm down. I have not seen Ryan at all. He has not been by the church, or my house, if he is up to something, I don't think it's about me. Honestly. But maybe I know what it is about. Ryan and I were close when I first moved here, he volunteered at the church, and we spent a lot of time together. I am a few years older than him, but he was probably my first real friend here. I know I am a minister now, and I believe in God, and I follow a path of honesty and goodness, but I am also human and not every answer to a person's struggle can be answered by God's word. Ryan was struggling and he didn't need me as a minister, he needed me as a friend.

"Ryan was getting deep into drugs, and he was drinking more and more. He would confide in me and tell me things about Ted and many things he brought up I didn't even want to believe. Ryan and I had a falling out about six months ago, when he showed up at my house. I was home alone with Sam, he had various drugs on him, and he was obviously drunk when he drove over. I told him he needed help, and his response was the only

196

help he needed was someone to kill his dad. I didn't know what to do. I know there is a history of issues between the two of them, but this was a big statement, and I was worried he was going to either harm himself or his dad. I didn't want to call Ted, of course, to come get him, so I called Daniel. He was on campus with Zach, so he couldn't help, so he sent Sunny to come get him. Jim and Loni were in town around then, so Sunny took Ryan home with him and he even called me the next day to say that Ryan was better. Ryan realized he was super messed up the night before and he really needed help.

"As far as I know, he didn't seek any help and he sort of kept spiraling. But he stopped talking to me. He wouldn't return my calls and he sort of ghosted. I know everyone in town sort of mentioned him not being around very much any more. But something I don't think anyone knew was at one point, Ted called me and demanded I told him what sort of 'shit' I was feeding into Ryan's head.

"Look, I didn't know what that meant. I never really gave any advice to Ryan other than he needed to step away from that lifestyle, because it was a dark path and there was no way it was going to end well. But Ted was heated and thinks I did something to Ryan or told him something, and I tell you all here and now, that is simply not true.

"Monty, I know you said you can handle this, but can you really? Because this next part is big and I don't want to alarm you," Tate asked.

"I am okay, this is not as bad as half the other things I need to fill you all in on when you are done, so go ahead," I responded. "I think the truth of why Ted was attacking me was that Ryan told Ted that he confided in me about what Ted had been up to and he thought I was going to rat him out," Tate said.

197

"I don't understand, what stuff had Ted been up to?" Mom questioned?

"Mike, I know you are his brother, and you are the epitome of a good guy, so it breaks my heart to say this, but he has been stealing from you, for a long time. I heard you talking at the picnic with a few others about there being a lot of theft at your jobsites lately, and that is no coincidence that now you are all seeing Ryan around town. Ted had Ryan taking things from jobsites for years, but it was definitely lower key. It looks like either Ryan has gone rogue on his own, or Ted just doesn't care any more. But Ryan told me that each time you do a job, Ted makes inventory sheets that have quantities of items on them. He said you never go over them in full detail, as that is his job, so if he adds some extra to piping, lumber, fixtures or whatever, you don't notice. So, either you eat the cost, or the home builder eats it on the total construction cost. He has been taking those items and doing work on the side. He had Ryan doing work for a while, Sunny and even some high schoolers in town I believe. He pays them under the table, and lots of times, he had Ryan exchanging drugs and alcohol for work. It kept the guys working quietly and there was no money trail. I could be wrong, but I don't think Ryan ever left for Europe, I think that was all a cover for maybe him taking bigger items, and to keep the heat off of him and Ted. I know he wanted to stop all of it with Ted, he never wanted to start, but Ted made him," Tate said.

"Sadly, I already know all this. I have been personally looking into all these missing items and I started cross-referencing order sheets, and nothing was adding up. I have a friend that works in security, and I asked about adding cameras to jobsites, but it was exceedingly expensive, and I wasn't sure it was going to prove anything. But my buddy offered to set cameras up for me for two nights for free, just to see if there was anything to my hunch. We set it up at the doctor's house I am building right now, the day the appliances, HVAC and plumbing faucets were being delivered. I personally locked up that entire house after delivery. I never do that any more, but I wanted to be sure, if something was missing, it was calculated and someone on my team was doing it. The next day, my buddy called me to his office early and said, they didn't even wait until it was dark before they broke in. A man walked over to the garage door, unlocked it with a key and loaded up everything into a box truck. He then left the side door unlocked, to make it look like whoever closed up for the day left it unlocked, so it wouldn't look so obvious.

"When I watched the video, it was grainy, but I knew it was Ted and someone else I didn't recognize. Before I saw this, I knew Ted had to be involved, because that shipment was not supposed to arrive for a few more days. I was there for delivery, no one else, and I called Ted when it arrived early and asked him to call the doctor and his wife let them know we could do another walk through in a few days to see the progress.

"Before the GM for that house called me to tell me it was all stolen, I called the doctor. Ted never called him. I didn't mention the items, I just was checking in and wanted to see if anyone from my office had reached out to offer an update on his home, and no one had. Once I talked to the GM, I called Ted and his response was, 'Thank God I got tied up yesterday and never called them to let them know it all came early. I'll go ahead and get the items re-ordered and pay for rush.' I knew then, Ted was behind all of it, and someone was helping him," Dad said.

"Oh, Mike, that is appalling. Why would he do that to you, why in the world does he need the money? You pay him well and they live in this shit town, no offense, I don't understand why anyone would steal from anyone, let alone their own family," Janet exclaimed.

"Monty, this might be something you don't already know, but I think you are old enough. We told Zach and Adam a little while back, we have not told Eve yet, but there are more family secrets to put out on the table. Ted has another child that he had with someone while married to Lisa. He was born just before Ryan, so he is grown now, maybe twenty-two or so. The reason Helen and Lisa stopped talking was really because of him. Helen had been pushing a relationship with the child on Lisa and Ted for years, but they wanted him to be completely forgotten about. From my understanding, Ted paid the mother to go away, and he used to send money a few times a year to keep them away. He has never met the boy and refused to have any association. Helen thought that was so incredibly heartbreaking and she tried to reason with Lisa, but Lisa stood by Ted, and it really pushed the two of them further apart. Your mom was very close with Helen, and sided with her, which caused friction with my brother and Lisa. She never believed the boy was Ted's, but Ted knew he was. Lisa would call the mother a liar and would say just about anything to discredit her... but she never held any of it against Ted. It didn't make a lot of sense. The mother had a drinking problem, but she came from a very hard life. Lisa and Ted used this as an excuse to explain why they couldn't know the boy at all. Saying there was no way to have her close to them in any way and still keep their family safe.

"The boy's mother really struggled to stay in one place and couldn't keep a steady job. She was not stable and after a while, Helen lost touch too. She helped move them closer to her and Gary many years ago, but one day Helen went by their place, and they were gone. She didn't know what ever happened to them, but they both sort of vanished. Maybe his son found Ted and wants money? Or maybe the mother did? Or maybe Ted got into something else like this again and needed money that he couldn't discuss with Lisa. I don't know, but I know Ted makes poor decisions and will never take accountability. I need to talk to him, but I don't know if he will ever be honest," Dad said.

"Mom, what was the boy's name?" I asked.

"Oh, wow, it's been a while. I cannot remember his last name, how horrible of me, but his name was... umm, oh, Peter something. His mom called him P.G., and the name was after her father," she replied.

"Does Ryan know about P.G.? Like does he know he exists, has anyone ever talked about it with him?" I asked.

"We told your brothers because I felt like I owed it to them to be truthful. Adam seemed to have an idea already, but Zach was very surprised. With Zach and Ryan being so close, it is hard to believe if Ryan knew that he wouldn't have talked about it with Zach. Ryan could know, but Lisa shields him so much, I just can't imagine she would tell him. It was something very scandalous for our family and once Ryan was born, everyone was very tight-lipped about it. Lisa pushed Helen away even more as Ryan got older, I truly believe to make sure she never slipped up in front of him and said anything. If I was to bet, I would bet he doesn't know, but everything is up in the air at this point," Dad responded.

The room was somber for a moment, while everyone was just taking it all in. I looked over at Tate's demeanor, which shifted, and was now sad.

"Hey, Tate, are you okay? You look upset," I asked.

"I'm fine, I'm fine... I have an idea. We need to talk to Jack and Edna and find out how they came to find Greg to work for them. I haven't met him yet, but the timing of his arrival and all if this happening seems very suspicious," Tate said.

"I actually was going to ask the same question to them, because I want to find out the connection with Greg and Ryan… why they were together yesterday in the barn talking about killing someone?" I asked.

"Monty, you are not to do that at all. Let us handle this, this man might be very dangerous, and you cannot get hurt!" Dad yelled.

"I am only saying, Jack and Edna love me, we have a good relationship. No one would suspect anything from me stopping by to bring over say some German chocolate cake and to just chat. Jack has told me so much about the fields and how he grew up and his kids, it is very normal for me to talk with them," I responded.

"Oh, honey, I didn't know that. That is so incredibly sweet. They are the kindest people, so I love that you have a relationship with them," Mom replied.

"Rebecca don't encourage her! Monty, it is too dangerous!" Dad yelled.

"Tate you could do some digging by way of trying to get him to join the congregation, that wouldn't seem out of the normal. You could go to their house, have lunch, and just talk about the help around the farm and if he might be interested in coming to Sunday service," Janet said.

"Mike, you are not going to agree, but I think Monty has a better chance. I don't do that to anyone, so it would seem abnormal, for sure. Also, what if Greg is there and thinks it is strange; I didn't contact him directly. Monty is a kid, and if she is just going to chat, she could at least get his full name and we could work from that. There would be nothing alarming to them or him if he is around, and it would seem very natural," Tate responded.

"Also, small thing I should mention, I ran out of gas in the field last week and Jack drove me back to get my four-wheeler and put some gas in for me. I could easily bring something by as a 'thank you' for that and then transition the conversation," I said. "Monty, are you fucking kidding me? Sorry, but seriously, how many times have you done that?" Dad screamed.

"I know, I know… I didn't want to tell you, but I think that this could work. When he was driving me back there, we noticed the new chain and padlock on the cow barn, so I could just start by talking about how things have changed through the years in the field and transition into how he found help and if he is ever going to retire. Something like that," I said.

"What chain and padlock on the cow barn?" Dad asked. "Oh, I thought you put it on. It was chained up last week, so when I ran into Thomas at the store today, I told him to page you to find the key. He said he was going to go work on the truck. But, Dad, the truck is running, I saw Greg driving it the other day in the field," I said.

I could not talk about the men in the field yet. They were starting to trust me, and if I brought that up, I would be locked in this house forever. I would work with Aunt Janet and try to figure out the rest of this, but until we figured out who Greg was, I didn't want to bring it up.

"Why would Greg be driving my truck? That barn has never been locked up and that truck hasn't driven in at least a year. If it is working, he must have worked on it. But I don't even know how he knew about it or why the hell he is nosing around our barn. That really pisses me off. That truck is not registered any more, and I sent Thomas down to work on it today and if he could get it up and running, I was going to plate it and give it to two of my guys. Do you think Greg has been driving it around? Thomas paged me hours ago and I never called him back. Shit, I am going to do that now. I want to find out if he was able to get into the barn at all," Dad said, and left the room to call him back.

"Well, one morsel of a clue is to start and find out who knew the truck was back there. If Ted and Ryan knew, they could have told Greg. Or, well, if he is working in the field, he could have just stopped by the barn and seen it. But how would he know it's not used and who it belongs to? Greg had to get information from somebody, I just feel it," Aunt Janet said.

"Well, if your dad didn't put the lock and chain on it, it only makes sense that Greg did. He must have thought it was abandoned, and if he got it working, no one would miss it. Or he knew it was there, whose it was, and once he got it working, he didn't want anyone to move it. But if Ryan was in the barn with him, Ryan knows it's our truck, so didn't he warn him to not use it?" Mom asked.

Tate was still sulking while sitting on the couch. Something was bothering him, but he was not speaking up. I was not going to ask him again, because it was obviously something that he didn't want to say in front of everyone. *Maybe I will go by the church this week and just see if he is willing to say more when there is not such an audience.*

We all waited in silence while Dad called Thomas. I was trying to organize my thoughts and everything that had transpired so far, while Mom looked confused and worried. But Aunt Janet was just smiling while staring at Tate.

"I know this is all unnerving, and I am honestly worried and not sure what to imagine any more. But seeing you... Trent... I mean Tate, is making my heart burst. I have missed you so much and I am just so glad you are here. You look healthy. You seem happy. Sam is with you, where he belongs, and I just cannot express how good this feels," Janet said while her voice trembled. "I feel good, and I love it here. I have never felt real family before, and I feel like I have that here. I feel so good that I want to pinch myself each day. Life has just never been like this for me, and it feels surreal every day," Tate said.

Everyone sort of smiled. Hearing that was the pick-me-up the room needed. But it didn't last long, as my dad turned the corner and slammed down his pager on the side table.

"Welp, Thomas was not able to get into the barn. He was going to cut the chain with his bolt cutters while there, but the gap in the door was big enough that he could see in and there was no truck inside! That fucker, sorry for my language, Monty, stole my truck! We don't need to talk to Jack, we need to call the police," Dad yelled.

"Let's all stay calm. Mike, you drive out to the field tomorrow before work and see for yourself and we can go from there. And maybe it wasn't Greg, maybe Ryan has it. We just don't know. Monty, tomorrow, you take Aunt Janet's cake over to Jack and Edna and find out what you can. Tate, stay safe. I know you are not worried about Ryan, but I am. If you and Sam want to stay here you are welcome to, just say the word. Let's all go sit down and have dinner and deal with the rest of this tomorrow," Mom said.

"Mom, I still have questions I want to ask…" I was saying as my mom cut me off.

"Monty, that is enough for tonight. We will talk more this week. I cannot take any more right now, and I just want to drink that good wine with Aunt Janet and appreciate everyone who is here right now," Mom said.

"Oh, I get you as a drinking buddy tonight, mark the date, it must be special!" Janet exclaimed.

"If you don't mind, I wouldn't hate a glass of that too, if there is enough," Tate said.

"Wine all around, break out all the good stuff, we deserve it," Dad replied, while walking over to the fancy wine rack.

I ran into the basement to get the kids to tell them to come up for dinner, but before I walked back up, I stopped at the hide-a-bed where Aunt Janet slept each night.

I never snooped in Aunt Janet's stuff, because there was really no need. She is an open book and will tell you anything you want to know. But there was a piece of paper next to her bag and it was the same paper we kept by our phone upstairs to take messages on. Something urged me to look at it; maybe it was the big news she was going to tell me. I could just ask her, but my adrenaline was intense, and I just had to look. I walked over and picked it up, as I unfolded it, it just read,

David R. Bailey did not report to his parole officer during the scheduled visit. Getting more details, call you later this week. Stay safe.

I wonder if Aunt Janet called her answering machine and was writing down her messages and someone left this for her? If minister Bailey did not check in, where was he? This was disturbing because he was not mentally well and was a perverted man who was willing to do who knows what to get what he wanted. I wondered if he was having Aunt Janet followed and if he knew she was here. Shit. My mind was now running wild, and I needed to calm down. I needed to talk to Aunt Janet as soon as we finished dinner.

Once we sat down, my mind cleared for a minute and all I

could think about was how good the food smelled and how hungry I was. Investigating criminals and really fucked up family drama gets an appetite going! The dinner was going well, and we all seemed to be calmed from the conversation when Sam became startled and screamed for Tate. He spilled the milk he was drinking onto the table and got it all over his long-sleeved blue shirt. Tate handled it well, and told him it was no big deal, and they could just take that under shirt off and easily wipe up the mess. He walked him back to the bathroom and came back a few minutes later, and Sam seemed fine. But he kept holding part of his arm and tried to hide it under the table. Simon screamed out, "Hey, is something wrong with your arm, did you hurt it or something?"

Oh, shit. The cut from the broken glass when his mom died. I forgot all about that detail from Cliff. That is why he always wears that long-sleeved shirt, to cover up the scar. Poor kid, this broke my heart. I looked at Sam and he didn't seem bothered by the question, but Sam was always very quiet, so I didn't expect him to even respond. Then, all of a sudden, he looked up at Simon and said, "I don't remember how I got it, but I hurt my arm when I was little, and I have this big scar, see." Sam lifted his arm above the table to show the scar that was about six inches long on his forearm and still very thick with a purple hue to it. He continued and said, "Tate told me I was super brave when I got it and it makes me strong like a superhero. I normally just cover it up so I don't have to talk to everyone about it, because people can be so annoying. Like give a kid a break, and don't ask silly questions about how they look!"

We all burst out laughing. Where had this kid been this whole time? We had hardly ever heard him form a sentence and here he was, being so clever.

"That's right, buddy. You are so brave, and people just don't have manners sometimes and bother us about the way we look. But you don't need to be ashamed of that scar or explain it to anyone; it is part of you, and you should wear it like a badge of honor," Tate lovingly said.

"Yeah, Tate got me this blue Superman shirt that I wear all the time to keep it covered up. It's my superhero shirt and it just reminds me about how brave I am," Sam responded.

I knew Sam had been through so much, but it is truly remarkable how far he had come with Tate. He seemed to be so adjusted and happy; to finally hear him speak up and interact with others was incredible. Tate was really doing something so wonderful, and I felt bad for ever questioning him and his role at the church. To overcome what he went through, and to raise a child that was not his after trauma and complete betrayal was beyond comprehension.

We all smiled at Sam and Tate and went back to shoveling in dinner as it was all so delicious. But soon after we cleared our plates, everyone just stared at the cake Aunt Janet made sitting so perfectly atop the cake pan on the counter. The adults all knew we were now saving it for Edna and Jack, but the kids were practically drooling over it. Delilah got everyone's attention and screamed out, "How much longer do we have to stare at the cake before you let us eat it? The chocolate is calling my name and I can't wait any longer!"

"Well, I was going to give it to the neighbors, but I think we can eat this one and I will just bake something else to be neighborly. How does that sound to everyone?" Aunt Janet asked. The entire table cheered, while Simon ran to get more milk from the refrigerator, Dad grabbed the pot of coffee and Mom set out plates to pass around.

"Adam and Eve are really missing out on something delicious," Delilah stated.

"Yeah, where are they anyway?" I asked.

We all sort of looked around and it appeared no one knew. Then Delilah popped her head up, with a mouth full of chocolate cake and said, "Eve is still with Olivia, she said she is staying there tonight. Adam was here earlier and then left with someone in an old truck. But he didn't even say bye to me, so whatever!"

"Umm, Delilah, sweetie, what old truck?" Dad asked.

"I dunno, it was super yucky. It didn't match and was all dirty and rusty," Delilah responded.

"Sweetie, what color was it?" Dad asked.

"Dad, I don't know, it was like a rainbow of colors. It was like white, blue, some green and orangy-red rust all over. He couldn't even shut the door when he got in, he just kept slamming it."

Dad looked at Mom and sort of froze. I placed my fork down on my plate and scooted my chair away. I felt sick to my stomach and didn't want to think of the possibilities. Janet covered her face with her hands and tried to hide her tears that were welling up. Tate didn't move, he sat still, and you could tell he was running through every scenario in his head. The shock of this revelation halted the rest of dessert and now it appeared we had more to figure out.

"Hey, kids, you want to finish your cake downstairs and watch a movie?" Mom asked.

They all screamed 'yes!' and ran with their plates in hand.

I didn't know what to say, and I just hoped he got in by choice and was not forced in.

"Okay, Monty, does Adam know anything about Ryan being back?" Aunt Janet asked.

"Yeah, he has known the whole time. He said he never left at all and has been up to something extremely shady. He was going to look into a few other weird things that have been going on and just some drama with school kids, but he doesn't know Greg. Maybe Ryan had the truck and Adam got in willingly," I questioned. "Does Adam know it's your truck, Dad?"

"Yeah, he does. He has ridden in it many times when he used to come to work with me. I have had it since your mom and I started dating," Dad responded.

"Okay, yeah, maybe he got in on his own and everything is fine. But maybe not. I am going to reach out to Ryan. We haven't spoken in a long time, but maybe he will talk to me. I need to see where he is mentally and see if he is being manic, if he is on drugs, or what. It's a long shot, but I have to try," Tate said.

"I know this might sound like a silly mom question, but where the hell is he staying? Even if Ted and Lisa know he is here and they are lying, they can't just have him at home and in plain sight. They have to have him stay somewhere, it's the only way this makes sense," Mom said.

"That's a good point. I am over at Ted's all the time, and I have never seen a trace of Ryan, and they never act strange when I pop over unannounced. I really don't think he is staying there. I see Sunny and Daniel all the time over there and they act totally fine," Dad said.

"Maybe this is a long shot, but what about Sunny and Daniel?" I asked.

"I don't understand… what about them?" Dad responded, looking puzzled.

"Well, Uncle Jim and Aunt Loni are gone, and if I remember from last year, Ryan will go over and get their mail and check on the house because they didn't trust the boys to go there alone. So, if he still has a key, couldn't he be staying there?" I asked. "Brilliant! That would be a very easy place to hide out, and they are not due back for at least another month. My sister said since the boys were doing fine, she was just going to stay with Jim until he finishes this tour. I have a key too; my sister doesn't trust her kids or Ryan even, so she gave me one a while ago to pop in every once in a while, to check on what Ryan was supposed to check on. Also, make sure the boys don't break in and throw any parties. For this tour, she said she gave her plants to her neighbors to care for and did a hold on their mail at the post office, so there was not a lot to do with the house. Jim even set up photocells on their exterior lights to come on each night. So, they didn't really ask me to do anything but drive by and make sure there were no issues or newspapers or anything outside. But to be honest, I have not been there in a few weeks. I just have not had the time," Mom said.

"I think everyone has something to do tomorrow. I just hope Adam comes home tonight safe and sound. Tate, if you will still try to page Ryan and see if he will call you. Janet and Rebecca, go to Loni and Jim's tomorrow, keep your mase with you. I am not taking any chances. See if it looks like anyone has been there. I am going to check out the barn and see if the truck is back tomorrow. I will use my spare key and I am going to move it and hide it if it is. Monty, you go and talk to Edna and Jack tomorrow. I can't worry about Adam right now. He is smart and if he knows Ryan was here the entire time, I am hoping he chose to meet up with Ryan and he doesn't feel threatened at all. I have faith he is not in any trouble. Sound good everyone?" Dad asked.

"Hey Mike, move the truck to my garage if it's there. I have two spaces and there is plenty of room. If you get it tomorrow, just page me and I will come and give you a ride back. Garage code is eight, nineteen, fourteen, enter," Tate said.

"Okay, everyone knows the plan. Let's have full transparency here. Is there anything else we need to cover right now?" Dad asked.

Oh, I don't know... The men in the field, the guy that might be dead, Sunny and Jason being there, the party Friday at the farmhouse, the farmhouse actually belonging to Sam, minister Bailey missing... you know, just normal family stuff. But now was not the time to add any more to what is going on. We had a plan; a good plan, and I would talk with Aunt Janet about some of the other things I had questions about. I was not about to add more right now and freak my parents out even more. This was the first time they had ever treated me like an adult, and I didn't want to lose that the minute after I got it.

We all sort of mumbled that there was nothing else. But when you looked around the room, *everyone* was holding secrets. It would just come down to who will share their secret first.

Chapter Ten

Keys

A few minutes after we finished discussing the plan for the next day, Tate and Sam left, and Mom and Dad went off to bed while Aunt Janet went to go take a long bath. Mom even left the kitchen messy, which was not like her, but I think she was very worried about Adam and just needed to go to bed and not think about it.

I helped get the twins to bed and changed into my pajamas before I went back into the kitchen to start to clean up. I didn't want my mom waking up to it being a disaster; she was dealing with enough right now. I loaded the dishes, cleaned off the table and counters and while I dragged out the trash, I saw headlights pulling up the driveway. The house was dark, as I didn't believe anyone else was still awake. You couldn't see me on the side of the garage next to the trash cans, but I still ducked down to be safe. Everything has me spooked these days.

I tried to see who it was, but the headlights were too bright. I heard a door slam, and then it slams again, I knew… the truck! I snuck back through the garage and tried not to let whoever was driving see me. I went back into the kitchen and waited for the front door to open, hoping to see an unscathed Adam come in. I waited and waited, but no one came. I walked through the house and didn't see anyone; I looked outside, and no one was in the yard, but the truck was gone. I went into the garage and there was Adam, thank God!

"Adam, are you okay, where have you been?" I asked in a quiet tone to not wake anyone else up.

"Monty, what are you doing up? I am fine and I will fill you in tomorrow, but I need your help finding something right now," he said.

"Okay, I won't ask any more questions, other than were you with Ryan?" I asked.

"Yeah. Look, he is mixed into something very serious, and I just need to find out how deep it goes. He wouldn't tell me much, he just told him he didn't go to Europe, that was a ruse his mom came up with. He was supposed to stay back and do some work for his dad, but he is not talking to Uncle Ted really at all. But Monty, I thought when I saw him, and he would be all fucked up, but I don't think he is on anything. He was the most clear-headed he has ever been. He looks like he is taking care of himself, I didn't see him smoke one cigarette, his pupils weren't dilated, and I didn't smell any liquor on him. So, something doesn't add up," Adam said.

"Sober Ryan, it's been a while since any of us have seen that... But the truck, why is he driving the truck? I saw someone in town driving it today and it wasn't Ryan or Greg, there is someone else using it, and I don't get why they would use Dad's old truck," I said.

"That's the thing. Tonight, I paged him, and I was shocked he called me back. I said I knew he was in town, and I had seen him around several places, so he doesn't need to hide from me. I said I don't give a fuck why his parents are lying about where he is, but I just wanted to hang and catch up to see what's going on. He literally jumped at coming to get me to hang and talk. He asked who was at home, and I told him the twins and Aunt Janet. Mom was actually here too, but she was taking a shower and

214

cleaning up and wouldn't be paying any attention. He didn't pull up the driveway all the way, but he pulled up a little, honked and I came out. The twins were both in the front yard when I left, they were swinging on the tire swing... I hope they didn't see him. When I saw the truck, I freaked out. I don't know what he was thinking driving Dad's truck to Dad's house! When I got in, I asked him and you will not believe what he told me," Adam said. "What?" I screamed. "Oh, and Delilah didn't see him but saw the truck. She described it to Mom and Dad, and Dad immediately knew it was his truck. But no one was sure Ryan was driving or not and if you were forced in or got in by choice." "Fuck. Look I will tell Dad I was with him and fill him in a little, but we cannot tell him or Mom everything. I need to know why Sunny and Jason are involved, what went down last week in the field and details about the party this Friday," Adam said. "Totally agree. We all talked tonight, and they filled me on a lot of the family secrets, so I feel like I can help figure this out, but no way I am telling them everything right now," I responded. "Okay, we both agree. So back to Ryan... He said he knew the church gave the truck back to Dad because it was falling apart, so he was working on getting it up and running all year. He said he was going to fix it up and then ask Dad to buy it from him. When I asked why, since he has a really nice car his parents bought him, he said he was working on completely separating from them. He said he found out some shit and he said they are not good people, and he wanted a clean start, without them. So, if Dad saw him driving it, he didn't care, because he would just show him he was serious about fixing it up and buying it off of him, and maybe even getting his old job back," Adam said.

"But that doesn't make any sense. Dad told me tonight; he knows Ryan has been stealing from him. He has Ted on camera

215

taking lots of stuff from a job site and Tate said that Ryan was helping him at one point," I said.

"Monty, maybe before, but that is not going on now, with Ryan at least. Look, I don't know exactly what he has going on, but he said he was handling something that should have been taken care of a long time ago. But he is trying to right a wrong, so I don't get why he would steal from Dad… I am going to meet up with him later this week, I will ask him about it. But I will bring it up in a way, so he doesn't suspect anything," Adam said. "Okay, just be careful. Dad was fuming tonight about it. He knows Greg has been driving the truck too and he plans on going to get it out of the barn and hide it from them," I said.

"Yeah, that's another thing that is weird. He never mentioned Greg, at all. I didn't want to bring him up like I knew anything, I had to make it natural and let him tell me what he wanted so he would trust me. But I did ask what sort of shit he was working on and if he was working alone. He said that there is a side project he is working on with some people, but it's something different, not for money, but a long project," Adam said.

"Do you think he means Sunny and Jason? He wasn't in the field that night, so maybe that is what he means; maybe they got something wrong that night," I said.

"That is what I am thinking. Like maybe something he is doing with Greg because Greg has to know more, since the talk in the barn you overheard. Maybe he got the other guys involved in some way and Ryan says it's not what it seems. Maybe Greg was trying to create a diversion or something. I don't know. But Ryan is opening up and I am going to figure this out. But I still don't trust that Greg guy, stay away from him. I am not going to mention the truck to Ryan if Dad takes it tomorrow. I am going to play dumb and see how it plays out," Adam said.

"Well, Dad was going to have Thomas work on it and get it running, so you could always repeat that if he asks about it if it goes away. Say you heard Dad talking to Thomas to go pick it up and fix it and that must be where it is. It shows you are sharing what you know, so he will maybe share more. I just want to know who Greg is to him or how they got mixed up with each other," I said.

"Good plan," Adam said.

"Okay, I am off to bed, today was exhausting," I said. "Wait, before you go, I need your help finding something," Adam said.

"Oh yeah, I already forgot... what do you need?" I asked. "Keys. I know you know now who the farmhouse belongs to now, but that is a whole other night to review. Mom and Dad have a set of keys to it. I stopped by there earlier today before Ryan picked me up and every door was locked. It doesn't look like anyone has broken in, so I don't know how much truth is in this whole notion that someone fixed it up before this party. I bet they are planning on just breaking in. The windows are covered, but honestly, they might have always been like that, I can't remember. But Mom and Dad used to have keys, and I thought I could go in and check it out and see what is really going on.

"Tracey sent keys with a letter a long time ago, but there are a lot of missing letters in the cooler now, so for some reason mom moved some of them but not all of them. She had to have moved the one with the keys and I want to find them," Adam said.

"See, I thought something was off. The letters just stopped and nothing for years, even with everything that happened after the last one. I knew there had to be more. I don't have a clue where Mom would move those to, but I will start looking," I said. "Thanks, Monty. I haven't looked too much in the garage yet, but I just don't think she would leave them here so close to the other

217

ones. I read a lot of the ones that are missing, she is hiding them from Dad, so I don't think she would keep them where he might come across them," Adam said.

"Why would she hide them from Dad?" I asked.

"Honestly, it's just some more stuff with Tate and Sam and Mom authorized some things that Dad would not be okay with, and she also made a few visits that were dangerous. It's nothing too crazy, but stuff a husband wouldn't want his wife doing," Adam said.

"Okay, I will do some digging, but promise to be safe around Ryan. I know he seems good, but we still don't know what he is into, and who is involved. And you and I know that him, and Greg talked about killing someone to shut them up, so that is majorly big! I think you are right though, whatever happened in the field might have been a mistake and Ryan didn't know it was going to happen. We need to figure out who the tall, other man is and maybe we can figure this all out... Okay, I need sleep, talk tomorrow," I said.

"Night, Monty," Adam said.

As I crawled into bed, I felt better than the night before. Yes, there was even more out there now, but it felt like we were getting somewhere. I was also not holding all the weight on just my shoulders any more. There were secrets that no one had the answers to, and that made me feel like I was in this with my family and not some outsider trying to peer in. To always feel like an outsider but then to finally feel trusted and needed was really nice. The next day would hold answers, but for that night, soft pillows and blankets were all I was focused on.

The next morning, I woke up to silence. The entire house was still, and I was worried I overslept and missed out on everything. But as I turned my head to see the alarm clock, it was just past seven, so I thought everyone else was sleeping in. I got out of bed and decided to shower and get dressed first. I never get any hot water in this house, and it is the one perk to being up early. When I walked out to the kitchen, the pot of coffee was already half gone and so was the paper. Looked like Dad got an early start on looking for the truck. I started to make some oatmeal when the twins walked in asking if I would make them some too. As I started the stovetop, the front door opened and shut.

I turned my head to find Mom peeling off her sunglasses and saying the day is already a scorcher.

"Mom, where have you been so early?" I asked.

"Well, I went to help Dad find what he was looking for, and he did. I just gave him a ride and came back," she responded with a mysterious tone to not say anything in front of the twins.

I sort of nodded and went back to finish making breakfast. As per usual, I ate in a hurry and wanted to get to Edna and Jack's as soon as possible, but we ate over half the cake last night, so I had to wait until Aunt Janet made something else. I sat at the table staring off for a minute, when Adam walked in, shocking Mom into tears.

"Ugh, Mom, why are you crying? It's just Adam. You are super weird," Simon declared.

"Oh, I am not crying, I was just thinking of something really funny, and it brought tears to my eyes, so you just be quiet and eat your breakfast. Adam, sweetie, do you want anything to eat?" Mom asked.

"No, I am okay. I am very okay. Just got in late from hanging with my friend, safely, and just need to grab some coffee and fruit then head over to the school for practice. But, Mom, I am fine, very, very fine," Adam responded while smiling at Mom.

Mom turned her body to wipe her eyes and she just stood with her hand over her heart. She was worried and I knew she still was, but seeing Adam offered a lot of relief. Within a few minutes, Adam was off to school and the twins were asking to go swim at their friends again. As Mom went to call their friend's parents to see if it was okay, she stopped in her tracks.

"Who cleaned up the kitchen? I just realized it is spotless and I left it a complete mess last night," she asked.

"I did. I didn't want you to have to deal with it today. So, I stayed up and made sure it was all cleaned up," I responded.

Simon started making kissing noises with his lips, insinuating I was being a kiss-ass, when Mom shut it down very fast.

"Simon, if you don't stop that right now, you can sit your ass in this house all day alone and Delilah can go swim without you. Leave your sister alone, what she did was selfless and not something to mock," she screamed at him.

My mom never really sided with me, and I never saw her snap at the twins like that either, but maybe this was a totally new Mom. Everything seemed to be turned upside down right then, so maybe it could be a fresh start for a lot of changes in the house. Simon immediately stopped as the risk of not swimming was too great to make a silly joke that might ruin it. Mom confirmed the twins could swim and was set to drop them off a little later that morning. Aunt Janet walked up just as Mom hung up the phone and started sifting through the pantry.

"Rebecca, I think I can make another cake with what you have here, just has to be a white cake, so I will do a nice fruit topping on it. Do you have any berries I can use?" Janet asked.

"I don't, I can run to the store and get some. But there is also a great produce stand by the high school that has the absolute best selections. I never know when they are going to be there, their hours are not dependable," Mom responded.

"How about this, I will make the cake now, and when I am all done, Monty you ride with me and we can drop the twins off for their swim date and you can show me where the produce stand is, does that work?" she asked.

"Works for me," I responded.

It gave me time to look for those keys and chat up Aunt Janet about what her big news was.

"Oh, that would be great! I would like to drive to the city and get Adam a pager. He has been asking for one for so long and honestly, I would feel better if we could find him more easily. So, if you can drop the twins off, I could head up that way now," Mom responded.

Mom wrote the address down to where the twins were going, even though I had known these kids their entire life and been to their house hundreds of times. But that is just how Mom is. I knew she wanted to get going, I could see it on her face. After last night, she needed to know if she could find Adam if she needed to. I was tempted to ask for one too but wasn't going to push my luck. Eve already had one; Oliva's parents gave her an extra one they had. It was ugly and sort of beat up looking, but it was free, and Mom paged her on it all of the time.

Mom just short of ran to the door and was gone within minutes. The twins went to put their swim clothes on and said they were going to watch a show downstairs until it was time to go. I offered to help make the cake and was ready for Aunt Janet to fill me in on her big news.

"So, how can I help?" I asked.

"Monty, I still want to talk to you about what I found out, but how about we do it after we drop off the twins. I want to work

221

on the cake and not to sound rude, but I bake alone. I also need to make a few calls, so let me work on all of that and we can catch up in the car," Aunt Janet said.

I smiled and nodded and went to my room.

I was not surprised she wouldn't let me help bake; I don't think she ever let anyone help her. She has a method and is very meticulous with her measurements, which are all in her head, and she has to keep the workspace very clean and anyone trying to help is just in her way. Plus, the sooner she is finished, the sooner I could go talk to Jack and Edna, so I didn't mind.

While sitting in my room, I started thinking about hiding places Mom might have in the house from Dad. She was not a good hider of anything, as we always find our birthday and Christmas presents even though our house is a good size, but there are not a lot of drawers or cabinets or just things you can hide stuff in. I knew Adam said probably not the garage, but I had to start there first. It had the most opportunity for hiding spots and I really couldn't think of anything better just yet.

I scoured the entire garage, top to bottom. Opening every container, drawer, and cabinet, and even checking in old gas cans, but nothing but dead bugs and lots of cobwebs. I was covered in sweat from rummaging around in there; Mom was right, today was unbelievably hot. I decided to take a break and get a snack and a drink from the kitchen. As soon as I walked in, I saw Aunt Janet cleaning everything off of the counter and setting the egg timer for the cake. It already smelled delicious throughout the house and the smell heighted my appetite.

I decided that leftover chocolate cake and milk was the perfect snack, and as I reached for a plate in the cabinet, Aunt Janet hollered at me to use a disposable plate instead. She just started the dishwasher, and she didn't want a rogue dirty plate in the sink. I thought she was joking, but she is obsessive about keeping cars, houses and just about anything clean and organized, so I didn't give any pushback.

I went into the pantry looking for any sort of disposable plates but to no avail. We had mini milk containers in the refrigerator that we pack in lunches for the twins, so I just grabbed that and stared at the cake, longing to eat it.

"Oh, for heaven's sake, Monty. Did you even try to look for a disposable plate? I know your mom has some, the twins were eating bananas and peanut butter on them just the other day," she said.

She opened the pantry, looking all over and she too couldn't find the plates. She just stood looking at me with her hands on her hips, laughing.

"I told you... who knows where Mom put them. She is a horrible hider of things unless they are things of usefulness, then she is a wiz," I said with a laugh.

All of a sudden, I remembered the picnic basket at the top of the pantry that we hardly ever used. We took it out to the lake a few weeks ago and it was filled with disposable cups, plates, forks, and napkins. I walked back over to the pantry and climbed up the shelves like a monkey until I could grab the handle. I grabbed it and jumped down, making a very loud thud sound when I hit the ground.

"Monty, be careful!" Aunt Janet exclaimed.

I opened the top of the picnic basket and there they were, a stack of disposable plates... *Cake, here I come!*

I grabbed a plate and a plastic fork before cutting the biggest piece of cake that would fit on the plate. I was barely breathing between bites; I think it was even better today than yesterday! The entire time, Aunt Janet just gave me this curious look, like

223

someone had been starving me up until this point.

"Sorry, I just really love your cake," I said, smiling with a mouth filled with chocolate cake and icing.

"Well, while you stuff yourself like a pig, we have just a few minutes left on the cake for your neighbors. Once I get it out to cool, we can take the twins and head into town for some fruit. I will whip up a fruit compote to put on top in two shakes when we get back, then you can go talk to them. I need to make one more quick call, so why don't you tell the twins to get their stuff together and that we are leaving in ten minutes," Aunt Janet said. I finished my last bite and then took my finger to wipe any leftover icing off the plate and into my mouth. *God, this cake is incredible.* I threw the plate and fork away and walked back over to the pantry to put the picnic basket away, so I didn't hear any grief from Mom for leaving it out. I climbed back up the shelves but lost my grip and dropped the basket. Nothing broke, thankfully, but it landed upside down, so the floor was covered in disposable plates and utensils. I started to clean them up while sitting on the ground when I glanced into the corner of the pantry. There was this weird wok with a lid; I had never noticed before. I didn't remember my mom ever making Asian food in it, it even had dust all over the top. All I could think was that it was a perfect hiding place.

I finished picking up the picnic basket and successfully placed it back on the top shelf. I crawled into the corner of the pantry and scooted out the wok. I opened the lid expecting a pile of letters and keys, but it was nothing more than the original instructions for its use and nothing else. I was right to think we had never used it, but I was still no closer to finding those remaining letters.

I put everything away and went to the basement to alert the

twins that we were about to leave. I walked around, looking at the walls, lifting up couch cushions and even opened the deep freezer that was down there, but nothing. I walked back up the stairs, feeling defeated. I was out of ideas. I checked my parents' room the other day, checked the garage, the pantry, the basement, and I really could not think of any place else – and then it hit me. When I saw the foster care paperwork, it was in my parents' bedroom and even though I looked there for the letters, there had to be something in that room where she kept all those papers. I ran into their room and just stared at the walls for a minute. I walked into the closet, and I noticed that the hangers were separated on the far right of the rack on Mom's side, but there were no boxes or shelves or anything below the opening. I just stood there, looking at the space, and I noticed above the rod for the hangers there was one shelf around the entire closet.

On Dad's side it housed loose ties, handkerchiefs, hats, random winter gear and just was overall messy but not overly full. On Mom's side everything was color-coded and organized. She had these clear containers without lids that each held a few items like scarves, gloves, large necklaces and old wallets and small purses. The containers were small, and you could see inside of them, so there were no letters to hide there. But at the far end of the shelf, she had her purses. My parents did not live lavishly, but Mom had several designer purses she collected over the years, picking them up on her Chicago trips. Eve always tried to steal them, but Mom kept them perfect. She covered them in cloth bags and only used them on special occasions.

Most of the purses were small, and could house a few letters, but that wouldn't make much sense. She had one larger bag, which was more like a tote that she used to pack her miscellaneous items in, then she would go to Chicago. It was

225

bigger than a purse but smaller than a suitcase. She kept it also in a cloth bag, and it sat against the wall since it was too large to stand up on its own.

I opened the cloth bag to see the tote inside and it was still in pristine condition. I think my mom bought it when she first had Zach, so it was impressive how well she had kept it over the years. As I pulled it out, I immediately could feel there were items inside.

I started to pull out the contents to where I found more letters, documents about Sam, an old license with Trent's name on it, some tickets, a random piece of torn cloth and just a plethora of items. It looked like a mix of items pertaining to Tate and Sam, some memory lane items from when her and dad were dating, some items from when she lived in Chicago, plane tickets from years ago and the cloth I couldn't make sense of. But within all the contents, no keys. I needed to get ready to leave with Aunt Janet but took a quick peak at the letters first. They were almost all Aunt Janet, Tracey and a few that were loose and not in envelopes. I didn't have time to keep snooping, but at least I knew where I could go back to for answers if needed.

I put everything back into the bag and perfectly placed it onto the shelf. I was disappointed I didn't find the keys, but at least I could find out whatever happened to Tracey after the last letter left off.

I ran into the living room where the twins were waiting by the door and Aunt Janet was fumbling for her keys and purse before we could head out.

"Okay, troops, it's time to get on out of here. Make sure you have everything you need, because I don't have a Mom bag filled with goodies to save the day," Aunt Janet said with a smile.

We all piled into the Bronco and within minutes the twins

226

were dropped off and we were heading into town. I looked over at Aunt Janet and didn't want to blatantly ask her again about her big news, but I was on the edge of my seat. My interest must have been obvious because she looked over at me and said, "Okay, are you ready for a doozy?"

"Yes! I am dying to know what you found out," I said. "Monty, all of this just has so many layers and every time I think we are closer to understanding, more piles on and makes it all make no sense again. I called my answering machine to collect my messages, and the older ones from last week were from Angie, asking for me to talk to her and help her find Trent. So good news is, she doesn't know where he is as of Friday last week. The bad news is, she is still driving me nuts. But then I had a message from one of you mom's old friends, Tracey. We knew each other, sort of, back in the day, but we weren't close. Tracey was friends with Angie the summer your mom lived in Chicago because her cousin was dating her. Once Trent, well Tate, was placed here I guess, she felt it was time for us to reconnect. She reached out one day to have lunch and we have been friends since.

"I am sort of bummed to know she helped so much with Trent and left me out of knowing a lot, I mean he is my nephew, but I guess he is family to her too, so I moved passed it. Anyway, she left a message out of the blue to say that minister Bailey didn't report to his parole officer. She said that he called and said he was interviewing for a job, and he forgot all about the check in and would reach back out in a few weeks. Well, he is not really able to do that, but of course no one has done anything about him missing it. Fucker gets away with everything... I digress... the weirder part is this: I called Tracey back and she said that she sent one of her law firm's Private Investigators over to his and Angie's house and it doesn't look like Angie is there either. I know she has been stalking me, but she is always home at night, and she doesn't do much at all. The PI said it looked like no one had been home for several days, because there were newspapers out front and the grass was overgrown and the house looked sort of abandoned," Aunt Janet said.

"Okay, if you don't think Angie knows where Trent is, that's good. But where do you think she is? Do you think he is really interviewing for a job somewhere?" I asked.

"Maybe, not a completely crazy notion, but where is Angie? He would *never* take her with him to a job interview. You don't know their past, but he treats her horribly. When all of this came forward, she never talked, she never told her story, but she did support him. However, he blamed her for all of it and said she set him up. The only reason he went back to their house, is he had nowhere else to go when he got out, at least for now, and he had to show residency with his parole officer," Aunt Janet said.

"Do you think she is okay?" I asked.

"I don't. I know I shouldn't care, but him missing, weird, but her too, well, it just doesn't make sense. If he did go interview for a job, I want to know where. If the church is going to allow him to work again, I might actually lose my mind. But whatever he is doing, I feel like Angie is not safe. So, I talked with Tracey, and she is doing some digging. She is trying to find her car and see if there are any leads. I am going to remain patient and although I think she is not a good person, Angie is still my sister and I don't want her getting hurt or killed because of this monster," Aunt Janet said.

"Okay, did you tell Mom?" I asked.

"Not yet. I was going to last night and then I saw Trent... I mean Tate, and it threw me. I didn't want to worry him, and it

228

just wasn't the right time. I will, for sure, just want to hear back from Tracey first," Aunt Janet said.

Right as she finished, I pointed for her to turn to where the produce stand is, but unfortunately, no one was there today.

"Well, shoot. Want to go over to the minimart?" I asked. "Not a lot of other options, so let's go to your shitty minimart. I might have to just get some store made icing, I doubt there will be any fruit worth buying," Aunt Janet said with a snarky tone.

We pulled into the parking lot and got out of the car. As we walked inside, she fumbled putting her keys in her purse and they fell onto the ground. I ran to scoop them up to hand them to her and noticed this very interesting keychain I didn't remember.

"Hey, this is very cool, any significance behind this keychain?" I asked.

It was a silver circle with three rhinestones placed on it, in a sort of triangle pattern. It had some worn off engraving on the back of it and was just very beautiful and unique.

"Oh, sadly, no. Your mom gave me spare house keys years ago, and this was the keychain they were on. A key to your house, a key to your dad's office and the third key I am not even sure what it is to. Maybe the backdoor or something. I don't know. In the years I have had the keys, I have never used any of them. You all just welcome me in, so I never have to break in," she said and laughed.

Of course. Aunt Janet had the keys. This had to be them, I didn't recognize the keychain at all, so if it was Helen's, that made a lot of sense.

I just laughed to myself. I had turned the house upside down looking for these keys, and I was sure that the third key was to the farmhouse. What better way to hide it and know it's safe than with Aunt Janet? Now I just needed to get the right key off of the ring later today and give it to Adam. He was not going to even believe I found it.

"Well, I love the keychain, I will have to ask Mom where she found it," I said as we walked into the store.

Just like Aunt Janet predicted, the fruit was all shitty and nothing was good enough to use. So, she got some maraschino cherries, vanilla frosting and some tiny chocolate chips and said she was going to decorate the top of the cake and call it a day.

We checked out of the store and got back into the Bronco when Aunt Janet grabbed my knee and squeezed it hard.

"Oh my God, what is it, what?" I yelled in pain.

She pointed her finger over to the right of the car, where I saw Sunny, Jason and a tall, older man getting into a box truck at the corner of the parking lot.

"Sorry, Monty, I didn't mean to scare you, just getting your attention, that's your cousin Sunny right there, isn't it?" Aunt Janet asked.

"Yes, and the other boy is Jason – he goes to my school," I said.

"But the tall man, I know him too. I know his body; he is just dressed differently than he normally is. You know who that is, don't you?" she asked.

"Aunt Janet, it looks like just like the man in the field, and I think I saw him again yesterday by the library, but I can never get a good look at his face, so no, I don't know who that is," I said in a huff.

"Sweetie, it's your Uncle Ted. I always see him in dress shirts, dress pants and even ties, never in casual work clothes. In jeans, a torn shirt and hat, he looks very different, but that is definitely him... But wait, what do you mean he looks like the man in the field? That's your uncle, you said the tall man had a shot gun and was threatening to kill someone. Ted wouldn't do that," she said while her voice trembled.

"Aunt Janet… it's him. I know it's him. That is the same man. And I didn't tell you, because I was figuring things out, and really scared, not knowing who to trust, but Sunny and Jason were the men standing on each side of him. I saw their faces when they got into the truck. Jason was covered in blood and Sunny was holding a handgun. When I was riding to the library yesterday, he was driving the truck in town, and I saw him. He saw me and pulled his hat down and shielded his face with his hand, so I couldn't get a good look again, but it was the same man in the field. But that makes sense if it is him because he didn't want me to know who he was… I think I am going to be sick," I said while opening the car door and continuing to vomit onto the ground.

"Honey, are you okay? Fuck… what do we do? Should we follow them," she asked in a panic.

I pulled myself up and shut the car door. I rummaged through her purse to pull out TicTacs to get rid of the puke taste while just staring at the box truck. My head was spinning; I didn't know what to do.

"Okay, your car is too noticeable; we can't follow them, he will know. Let's pull out behind him and see where he goes, but after a few minutes, we have to turn opposite of them, so it is not obvious. I am going to get into the back, so Uncle Ted can't see me. He might already think I saw him yesterday in the truck and I can't risk it. Follow him for a little and see which way he is going," I said.

As I finished trying to devise a shitty plan, the truck started moving. So, I climbed over my seat to get into the back and stayed down low. Aunt Janet followed but stayed a few cars behind them. We made the first two turns with them, but when we were going to turn opposite, they got onto FM250, like they were going to our house. We had to turn with them to get home, but it didn't make sense where they were going. They passed our house and kept going. Ted and Lisa's house was on the opposite side of town and there was really nothing back this way other than the old farmhouse, Jack's house, and the church. Maybe they were looking for Greg, which made the most sense.

No matter where they were going, I really didn't want to find out. They were up to something that could not be good, and we needed to steer clear of them at all costs.

I looked at Aunt Janet as we parked the Bronco. My heart was pounding, and I felt sick. Everything this past week had been life-changing, but if Uncle Ted is the man in the field, I felt completely gutted. He was like a second dad to me, and the actions in the field were that of a sociopath, not my endearing Uncle. To involve Sunny too, just showed he was not at all who I thought he was. I could feel my whole life sort of crumbling down.

"Aunt Janet, I am not totally sure where they are going, but I think we both know, we need to get into that farmhouse. I think we will find answers there," I said.

"We need to talk to your parents first. Should we page your dad?" she asked.

"No, don't call him yet. Adam has been working on this already and was looking for keys to the house, that Tracey sent to mom a long time ago," I said.

"Monty, how in the world would you and Adam know that Tracey sent keys to Rebecca?" she asked.

"We know a lot of shit we shouldn't know, but trust me, Adam knows what he is doing. I trust his plan, I really do. And the craziest part, I think you have the key to the farmhouse," I

232

said.

"What? No, I have house keys to your house and your dad's office, that's it," she said.

"That third key, I think it's to the farmhouse. Our back door is set to the same key as the front door and look at this key, it is completely different and much older than the others. Then I was staring at the keychain, look at it, it looks like three birthstones… Gary, Helen, and Grace. The back is worn off, but if you hold it up and tilt it, it reads, 'the farm is our forever home.' I bet these were Helen's actual keys, and Tracey made sure mom got them. They were so close, it makes sense. Let me send Adam back there when he gets home. He knows what to look for, he will be safe and let's not tell dad all of this in case we are wrong. He is already pissed, and I don't want to add drama if we are not on the right trail," I said.

"Okay, but Adam can't go back there alone. He has to take someone with him. But if I have Helen's key, do you think Ted is using Lisa's?" she asked.

"That makes sense I guess," I said.

"Okay, I am going to trust you and Adam, but if anything seems funny, I am calling your dad. For now, let's go finish this cake and get it over to the neighbors. We still don't understand the entire Greg part of all of this and why he would be with those guys in the field without Ryan, so we need to figure that out. Not a word to Adam until I am with you. I will give him my keys after we all talk, together, and have a safe and solid plan," she said.

I nodded and carried her purse and the grocery bag into the house. I set them both down on the counter and went back to my room. Some of this was finally making sense and it felt surreal. But I was also not feeling so good all of the sudden. Might have been nerves, or too much cake, but it felt much worse than that.

233

Chapter Eleven

Lost

I sat on my bed, holding my pillow, and rocking back and forth. I could hear my heart beating while every noise in the room sounded like a siren. Each tick on my alarm clock felt like a year, as time was slowing to a snail's pace. The drama, the scandal, the lies, and deception were all amenable. I could handle Ryan or Sunny getting involved in something stupid and illegal; they always walked that line and eventually it caught up to them. I could even understand what my parents did for Tate and Sam because yes, it bent the law, but it was the humane thing to do. Fuck, I didn't even feel shocked by the fact minister Bailey was Aunt Janet's brother-in-law. I could compartmentalize everything. I could rationalize all of it. But I could not accept that Uncle Ted probably shot that man in the field. I could not move on knowing that he was involved in something that hurt my family and hurt others. I wanted to wake up from this bad dream, except it was my real life. I was never going to be the same again. My entire family was never going to be the same again. My entire life was changing in this moment, and it was too much to endure. Tears streamed down my face. I was not an emotional person, but this had broken me. I didn't want to open my eyes. I didn't want to learn any more shit about my family. I wished I could just forget it all, but I knew that there was no chance of that. This was my new normal and I was freaking out.

I must have dozed off during my mental breakdown because I was startled by Aunt Janet caressing my arm nearly two hours later. I shot up out of bed, startled, and asked why she let me sleep for so long.

"Monty, your body needed to rest. Nothing going on that couldn't wait a little longer while you slept. Your mom is home now and getting things ready for dinner. She asked if I could go pick up the twins, so I thought I could drop you and the cake off at Jack and Edna's, get the twins and then come pick you back up. Does that sound okay?" she asked.

"Of course. Thanks for letting me sleep. I do feel better. I will be ready in just a few minutes," I answered.

I packed up my backpack and ran some cold water over my face. I couldn't tell if it was all of the stress or if I was actually getting sick, but my head was pounding, and my stomach was twisted and nauseated. I wanted to keep pushing through to figure this all out, but I felt really worn down and even though I had just woken up, I felt like I could go back to bed again. I walked into the living room to see Mom sitting on the couch reading a letter. I was not sure if it was something new, or if she was reading something from the past. I was curious, but barely felt well enough to ask.

"Hey, Mom, I am not feeling great, is it okay if I go take some aspirin from your medicine cabinet?" I asked.

"Oh Monty, of course, let me get it for you. Hold on just a moment," she responded.

Mom placed the letter face-down on the arm of the sofa and leapt off to go get me some medicine. Aunt Janet walked back into the room with the cake placed in this very nice plastic container you carry from the top. She had her shoes on and purse in hand, ready to go.

"Monty, honey, here you go. Here is some Pepto as well, you look a little green. Are you sure you are well enough to go to Jack and Edna's? Because you don't have to, maybe this is a sign for you to stay in and we will think of something else," Mom said.

"I don't feel great but let me take that and drink some water and I am sure I will be fine. I haven't eaten much today and hardly drank enough water, I am probably just dehydrated," I answered.

Before I could turn toward the kitchen, Mom was running back into the living room with a full glass of water. She is such a good mom when we don't feel well. She caters to us endlessly and thinks of everything.

I really am very lucky to have her.

"Okay, take the capful, the two aspirin and drink this entire glass before you go. If you feel ill at all, call me and I will be right over to get you. Do you promise?" she asked.

"Of course, I promise," I answered.

I took everything she handed me and shrilled a little after the Pepto… it was such a gross texture. I still felt pretty bad, but I really wanted to try to get answers. My motivation outweighed the sickness, and I knew this conversation would be worth it.

Aunt Janet pulled into their driveway and both Edna and Jack were on the porch. I got out of the car, thinking I was going to do this alone, but then Aunt Janet followed me. I didn't know her intentions, but maybe she had an idea.

"Monty, what a pleasure seeing you! What brings you by today and who is your lovely friend?" Edna asked.

"Hi there, I am Janet, I am an old friend of Rebecca and Mike's. I am staying with them for a few weeks to enjoy some time in the quiet countryside. But I realized, in all my years visiting, I have never met the people who care for the land behind their house. It honestly gives me so much joy; being here is such a great break from the big city. So, Monty said she wanted to say thank you for helping her out the other day in the field, so we made you a cake and I wanted to drop it by with her and say hello, if that is okay?" Aunt Janet said.

It was so smooth and natural and gave me an easy introduction to talking about what they do here, for how long and who helps them maintain it so well… *She is brilliant!*

"Well, that is so lovely. I guess Monty told you that Jack here has quite the sweet tooth and by the looks of it, he is ready to dig into that beautiful cake," Edna said.

They led us both inside and sat us down in their dining room. I had maybe seen this room once before, but never got to sit in it. It was very clean and quaint with beautiful details everywhere. The walls had this olive-green wallpaper with tiny pink and yellow flowers that were patterned in vertical vines. There was a large China cabinet with stunning white plates and bowls with blue and gold details on the edges. There was a large window with black and white framed photos hanging on either side, all being generations of pictures of their family. In the center, there was a large, maple table with ornate chairs surrounding it. Each had details on the back and arms and a light pink cushion to sit on.

As soon as I scooted my chair out to sit, the man sitting in the chair, in the field, flashed before my eyes. These were the same chairs. I counted around the table to find seven – it appeared one was missing. As Edna and Jack sat down with us, holding plates and a beautiful silver tea kettle, I had to ask.

"Oh, I love this table so much. It reminds me of something I have seen before, maybe at one of my grandparent's houses. Any fun stories about it?" I asked.

"Hmm, well, we have had this table in here since I was a boy. I am not sure how old it is, but as old as me and that is saying a lot. The chairs are starting to wear more now, and Edna has covered these cushions maybe a dozen times. We will probably have to upgrade them soon, as we already lost a chair and I foresee more going soon," Jack said.

"Oh, how did you lose a chair... did it walk on out?" I asked with a chuckle.

"You are too funny. No, it was very wobbly, and I tried to tighten it and adjust the legs but couldn't fix it. I tossed it out next to the barn months ago, and plan on using it for firewood this winter," Jack said.

Okay, that's it, Greg found it out there and used it on the man in the field. That was it, it was discolored and damaged.

"I sure hope you get more time out of them though; they sure are stunning. Your entire home is beautiful, I love how well-maintained everything is. So many original pieces in pristine condition. I might one day have it in me to leave the city for good and settle down out here. Just have to find a place as nice as this," Aunt Janet said.

"Well, you should talk to whoever is fixing up the old Neddles' farmhouse in the back of the field. I have seen a few guys going in and out of there with tools and appliances, and it looks like they are fixing it up to move into, or maybe sell. I thought when the owner's died and then one of their daughters passed away, it was going to be forgotten, but I am so glad someone is fixing it up again. It was a beautiful home with amazing wood features, gorgeous floors and they even had a full concrete storm cellar in the house. So, if a storm came through you didn't have to go outside to climb in, they had stairs right inside the house. I always thought that was such a neat feature. It was so sad to see it deteriorate like it did, but glad someone is taking pride in it again," Jack said.

"Oh, you don't say. I will have to find out who is working on it and see if maybe I can snag a deal on it," Aunt Janet said.

Edna cut the cake and was passing out slices, but I felt awful and couldn't eat any. I waved it away, which says a lot, because I never turn down cake. I poured some of the tea and put some lemon and honey in it which was soothing to my sour stomach. But against what I hoped, I was definitely getting sick, at the worst possible time.

"Sorry, please don't find this to be rude, but how do just the two of you take care of all of this? I am sure you have seasonal help because it is just so much for two people," Janet inquired.

"It is far from just the two of us so, so you are not rude at all. We have crews who help, depending on the season. We work with some other local farmers and sort of share the teams in rotation, which works out great. We like to always keep one full time farmhand for the everyday, because it really has become too much for just us. We hope to retire in a few years, we just have to figure out what that really looks like for farmers. Because we do not want to ever say goodbye to our land, but we are nearing the day when we won't be able to handle much of it on our own. So, for today, we rely on Greg to get us through, and we will just handle it all, day by day," Jack said.

"Yeah, I met Greg the other day at the picnic; he seems really nice. But in this small town, how in the world did you find someone new to Blakesville who is capable of doing so much?" I asked, while trying not to appear too insistent.

"You know, it was so fortuitous. I was in town a few weeks ago at the tractor and seed store talking to an old friend that works there. I was asking if he knew of anyone looking for more full-time work as a farmhand. He told me to post on the bulletin board there and said all the farmers have good luck doing it that way. But as I was checking out, a young man approached me and said he was looking for just that sort of job. He had stopped in to pick up a few things and was also asking around for work in the area. We talked and I offered him a job on the spot. Greg started the next day, and he has been so helpful. It's like he already knew the fields and familiarized himself to the area very quickly. We have been so blessed to have him," Jack said.

"That is great. See, this is why I love small towns, that sort of stuff would never happen in Chicago," Aunt Janet exclaimed. "You are from Chicago? What a great city. Jack used to take me to see shows up there many years ago, it is so beautiful," Edna said.

"Well, a small suburb outside of Chicago, but yep, I am a city gal. However, the country is looking pretty good these days," Aunt Janet said.

Aunt Janet was making the entire conversation very easy and smooth, but we still needed to get what we came for, so I had to be a bit pushier.

"That is great you found Greg, is he from near here or does he have family here?" I asked.

"You know, he never said where he was from, just that he was new to the area. He is staying in a rental a few miles away. But I really don't know what brought him down this way in general. I am just glad to have him. His last name is very distinctive, and I don't know anyone else in this area with it. It's Swanker, which makes me sort of giggle when I say it," Edna said.

"That is a funny name, very unique. I am so glad you have him here, you two deserve someone to help you with all of this.

But always know if you need anything, me and my family are always here. We are happy to help in any way," I said.

"Thank you, Monty, we are very grateful for you and your family. Also, thank you Janet, this cake, it is wonderful! I plan to pack some in my lunches the rest of the week," Jack exclaimed.

"Well, we should let you both get back to it, but it was so lovely to finally meet you. Monty talks about you both often, and when she wanted to send thanks to you, I just had to meet the amazing people she speaks so highly of. I might do some more baking while I am here, but Monty said that your apple pie Edna is perfection. So maybe we can have a trade in the coming weeks. Your apple pie for whatever my specialty is... have to ask Monty what that is," Aunt Janet giggled.

"Deal," Edna said with a smile.

We both stood up and I gave Edna and Jack a small hug and walked out of the house. When we were getting into the Bronco, we saw Greg in the distance by the barn. He was moving bales of hay and was wearing overalls with no shirt. I didn't mean to stare, but I couldn't take my eyes off of him. He was such a mystery and I just wanted to know why he was here. As I looked, I noticed he had a tattoo on his right shoulder that did look familiar. The Chicago Cubs logo.

"Aunt Janet is that the symbol for the Chicago Cubs?" I asked.

"I am not sure, as my eyes are not what they used to be, but it sure looks like it," she responded.

Gave maybe a hint that he was from Chicago or Chicago area... or he was just a fan. My entire family are fans, so I was not sure it offered any leads at all. But I was doing what Mandy would do and added it to my list of information to keep it all straight.

"Hey, I am really glad you came in there with me, you were so good. I have something to tell you that I realized while there. We might not know where Greg came from or what he is doing, but the chair that the guy was sitting in last week was their missing dining room chair. I remember the details perfectly. So, whatever happened in the field, for whatever reason, Greg knew he was going to need a chair, because he planned on doing who knows what to that poor guy. I hope Jack and Edna are safe, I just hope he doesn't harm them in any way," I said.

"Whatever he is after, I don't think it has anything to do with them. I think he took the job because its cash and gives him a reason to be seen. But why he is here has nothing to do with them. I don't know for sure, but he came here to this town for a reason, I just don't know what that is. I am hopeful that they are just a cover for whatever he is doing, but we should keep an eye on them for now, to be safe. Now we really need to get into that farmhouse. Jack saw people working in there, but it obviously wasn't Greg, or he would have recognized him. I just can't figure out how this is all connected," Aunt Janet said.

The drive to pick up the twins was completely silent. We both had scenarios going in our heads and we just kept trying to piece it all together. As soon as the twins climbed into the car, the silence was broken. They were screaming and giggling and telling us all about the great day they had. They looked exhausted but I was jealous of their innocent day. I wished I could go back in time and just be ignorant of all of this and have my only concern be a sunburn and pickle skin.

As soon as we walked into the house, Adam greeted me with a concerned look. I wanted to talk to him, but I felt like I was going to be sick again. I held up one finger and then ran to the bathroom – yep, sick. Whatever I was coming down with, it did not care that I did not have time to be sick. I sat in the bathroom for a few minutes and then ran cold water over my face, hands, and forearms trying to cool down. I was starting to feel feverish, and my eyes were bloodshot and burning.

I walked out of the bathroom and into my room, where I plopped down, lifeless onto my bed. I had about thirty seconds of silence before Adam knocked lightly on the door and walked in.

"Hey Monty, are you okay? You look really bad. I hate to even bother you, I do, but any luck with those keys?" Adam asked.

Before I could turn my body to answer, I heard my bedroom door slam shut. I shot up and looked over and Aunt Janet was standing there, blocking the door, while standing next to Adam.

"Adam, Monty told me about the keys and after she looked all over the house, she thinks I had them this entire time. Here, on my keychain your mom sent me this set of keys for your house and your dad's office, but there is an extra key, and it doesn't look like the rest. Monty thinks it's to the farmhouse and maybe these were Helen's keys and that Tracey sent to her. It seems nuts, but everything right now does, so I don't even know what to think," Aunt Janet said.

Adam grabbed the keychain and looked at the keys in detail. He looked over at me, I think puzzled that I involved Aunt Janet like I did, but he had to know it was the best decision. Before he could respond, I began to feel sick again. I grabbed my desk trash can and puked, again. I felt horrible and was getting worse by the minute.

"Monty, you are really sick. I am going to go get your mother. Adam, don't you leave this house before we talk," Aunt Janet said while walking out of the room.

"Monty, this could be the key, it makes the most sense... I did some digging today, and I think Ryan brought Greg into town. They know each other somehow, and he got him to move here. So, I am not sure he is anyone more than one of Ryan's goons, getting involved in whatever shit Ryan gets into. I know he said he is working on getting better and wants to prove to dad he is not a fuck up, and I want to believe it, but not sure I do. Greg is not from here and just showed up one day when Ryan 'so-called' disappeared... but why?" Adam asked in a whisper.

"Talk to Aunt Janet, she can fill you in on today, a lot went down. We found out his name is Greg Swanker, or at least that is the name he gave Jack and Edna. They said he has been wonderful, which is opposite to what I have seen and heard so far. Oh, and Jack did mention that he has seen people working on the old farmhouse, and it obviously isn't Greg, or they would recognize him. But someone has something going on there, and if you go over there, you can't go alone, someone might be in there working," I said.

"I won't, something really strange is going on and I don't want to risk it. I think Zach is coming down on Thursday, so I was going to just leave it alone tomorrow and do some more asking around and see if he will go with me then. He is so anti-drama, it is going to take an army to convince him, but it's worth a shot," Adam replied.

I was sort of dozing off when Mom came in. She shoved a thermometer into my mouth and gasped while saying, "One hundred and three point two... Monty, you are really sick!" I didn't remember Adam leaving the room, and I was not totally sure, but I think I took medicine my mom gave me, and the rest was a blur.

The next morning is murky, with little I can remember. I was in and out of sleep and I had not broken my fever yet. I heard shouting throughout the house and the phone rang over and over again. I wanted to get up and see what everyone was doing and check on Aunt Janet and Adam, but I couldn't move. I wasn't puking any more, because there was nothing left in my stomach, but my body was achy, I was switching between chills and sweating uncontrollably and when I tried to open my eyes, they burned like someone was pouring chemicals into them. I was the person who goes to school sick and had perfect attendance, so to be motionless in bed was new to me. I was sound asleep when I was startled awake by Mom shaking me and saying my name.

"Monty, I need you to wake up and drink this. You are going to get dehydrated and that will make you even sicker," she said.

She handed me purple Pedialyte, which doesn't taste great, but mom always gives it to us when we are sick… no matter what age. I held my breath and drank it down, while she handed be some cold and flu medication and two graham crackers. As I chewed while my eyes remained closed, I heard my mom crying. I opened my eyes slightly, to see her wiping her eyes and clinching her fists.

"Mom, are you okay?" I asked.

"I am struggling with all of this right now. I am really worried about Tate and Sam, and I think they could be in harm's way. I also don't get who this Greg guy is, and it is really bothering me. To top it off, when Dad found the truck yesterday, inside of it was a loaded shotgun, a handgun and tons of weird items that just don't make any sense. I don't believe all this is happening in our backyard. I want everyone to be safe, and I don't even know what that means at this point," Mom said while tears streamed down her face.

I didn't have much to say as Aunt Janet could fill her in, and

I had hardly enough energy to drink fluids and chew on crackers. I just grabbed her hand and squeezed it, then laid back down. I had no idea of the time, but I just needed more sleep. As I started to doze off again, Mom said, "Mandy called a few minutes ago and I told her you were under the weather. She just said if you feel up to it later, give her a call back. She wanted to talk to you about summer camp... whatever that means."

She got the list of male campers from last year, which was great news. I wanted to call her, but I literally didn't have the energy yet. Maybe after some more sleep and if the medicine kicked in, I would be up for it. But right then, I just needed to focus on feeling better.

I slept the entire day away. When I woke up, it was just past five-thirty, and the house was in a frenzy as everyone was getting ready for dinner. When I got out of bed, I took my temperature and it was finally back to normal, but I was weak and still felt shitty all over. I walked into the kitchen to be greeted by my mom asking me what she could make me or get for me, while Simon chimed in and said, "I am glad you are feeling better. I did your chores today, so you could rest." I must have given everyone a scare because no one in this house likes to do their own chores, let alone someone else's. I poured some orange juice into a tall glass and sat at the table next to Simon. I smiled at him and mumbled a 'thank you' under my breath. The house smelled amazing, my mom made homemade chicken noodle soup with fresh bread and a large fruit salad with whipped cream on the side. I didn't have much of an appetite, but soup and fruit were exactly what I needed. Mom knew best, again.

"Hey, Monty, Hunter called for you and Mandy called again, I left the messages by the phone" Eve said. "Also, Mom, Adam said he was not going to be back for dinner but would be home by around seven. He was meeting up with some guys from school and then he said he needed to return some videos he rented. But he said to thank you again for the pager and the roll of quarters and not to worry, he will be back on time, if not, page him."

My dad was very quiet at the table but kept looking at me once the twins and Eve left the table. Aunt Janet and Mom were acting as if nothing was wrong, chatting the entire time. As soon as everyone finished, Eve went off to her room to work on posters for the church fundraiser for next week and the twins ran outside to play. I could feel Dad looking at me, wanting me to ask him what he found out.

"Hey, Dad, so, anything new today?" I asked before laying my head onto my hands, placed on the table, because whatever I had, it was still kicking my ass.

"I want you to rest, so I was just going to fill you in tomorrow. But if you are okay, let me give you a little update from today… I got into the truck, and you were right, it's definitely running. I drove it straight over to Tate's where we parked it in the garage and started inspecting it. There was blood in the truck bed, rope, trash, and a lot of other very strange stuff, but one item I thought was very bizarre," Dad said.

I sort of popped my head back up to pay attention, and as I looked at Dad, he looked over at Mom and Aunt Janet, so he had obviously already told them, and it seemed big.

"What, Dad, what was so weird?" I asked.

"There was a bag shoved under the driver's seat, like an old messenger bag, with letters, papers, receipts and what I thought was just garbage. But Tate told me to dump it all out before I trashed it, and at the bottom there were several polaroid pictures. I left them with Tate to keep stored safely because they are not something you or anyone should be seeing. Without getting too graphic, the pictures were of young girls asleep, or rather passed out, half dressed in very compromising positions. In some there were pictures where you could see a man in them, but no face. Monty, these women look like they had been drugged and taken advantage of. It shook me to my core and Tate had to help me off the floor," Dad said.

Mom looked horrified and was squeezing Dad's hand. Aunt Janet had already gotten up from the table and was standing by the sink pouring herself coffee, but her hands were trembling, and she was visibly upset.

"Dad, do you think Greg and Ryan are doing this to girls?" I asked.

"I would never accuse anyone of such a crime, but the photos were in my truck that they fixed up and have been driving. They are involved somehow, and I now think we need to involve the police. I am worried this is currently going on and we cannot let anyone else get hurt," he said, his voice cracking, as he was trying not to cry.

"Look, I know you don't want to show me the pictures, but if I saw them, I could tell you maybe who the girls are. Like, if they go to my school or not," I said.

"Oh, Monty, no, we can't do that. We need to go to the police; they can look into this properly. But before that, we need to make sure your father is not connected to anything done in that truck that was illegal. So, let's keep all this here, at the table for now and let's think of what to do next," Mom said.

"Monty, we know Greg was in the field and if these pictures have anything to do with why they were threatening someone, Greg is tied to that. He took the chair from Jack's, he has been driving the truck, he knows Ryan and now we need to figure out who he is. I left a message with Tracey, and I am just waiting to hear back. I want to know if she can dig anything up on him," Aunt Janet said.

"Adam thinks Ryan brought Greg here, like he knew him somehow and he got him to move here. So, we need to focus on getting Adam to talk to Ryan and see what more he can find out," I said.

We all sat around the table looking at each other, and it felt like everyone was still holding back something. Maybe we all needed to tie up our own loose ends and then come back together to share what we know, but only after we made sure it would help solve what the hell was going on.

I slapped my hands on the table and stood up, physically having to push myself out of the chair. The soup helped, but I was still weak and needed to go back to bed. I told everyone I was going back to my room and was going to call Mandy and Hunter before going back to sleep. I walked past the phone, picked up my messages from Eve, and went back to my room, where I crawled back under the covers and barely had the energy to pick up the phone to dial.

I grabbed my phone and went to call Mandy, but as I looked at Eve's note, I stopped and sat up. The top of the sheet simply said to call Mandy back. The next line down said to call Hunter back, but not until after seven at night. But there was a third message Eve didn't mention at the table, and it read,

Page Adam, he said it is urgent and he needs to talk to you as soon as you get this.

Strange that Eve wouldn't mention it in front of our parents. Instead of dwelling on the details, I just paged Adam right away and sat by the phone waiting for him to call back. He didn't take long at all, and I answered, and Mom did at the same time.

"Mom, I got it, it's for me, please hang up," I said in a stern voice.

"Okay, sweetie. Feel better," she said before hanging up.
"Monty, are you feeling any better?" Adam asked.

"A little, but I have absolutely no energy. I ate some soup but now I am back in bed. So, what is so urgent you needed me to page you?" I asked.

"So, I went to practice and saw Jason there. I sort of made small talk with him after and he asked me about this girl I dated a while back, then if he could get her number. I said it wasn't my place to hand out her number and sort of mentioned that he just asked Eve out and that I wanted to know his plan. I told him he is not to fuck around on my sister, and if she wants to date him, that is on her, but I am not going to help him hook up with other girls at the same time… but he sort of cut me off and said he was into Eve, and this other girl is for his buddy. I didn't want to seem too interested, but asked, like who else would he know that wants her number who couldn't get it themselves. He wouldn't say, but said he was cool and it's no big deal if I don't give it to him, they will get it," Adam said.

"I don't get it, so he wants a girl's number, what does that have to do with all of this?" I asked, completely puzzled by all of it.

"That's the thing, this girl is a nice girl Monty, but she really likes to party. She drinks a lot, can get sloppy and she sort of puts herself in compromising situations. When she is drunk, there is no reasoning with her. I tried to get her to leave a party when we were dating, because she was too drunk to be around anyone, and she got pissed at me, and told me to leave without her. I stayed just to keep an eye on her and creepy assholes from school were all over her. I got into a fight with a guy who was trying to get her to go back into a room with him when she could barely keep

250

her eyes open," Adam replied.

"Okay, maybe this is something. Have you talked to Dad at all today?" I asked.

"No, I have been out almost all day. What happened with Dad?" Adam asked.

"Well, he found the truck and he moved it over to Tate's. While there, him and Tate went through everything and found really weird stuff like blood in the bed, rope, trash, and a bag with letters, receipts, and other garbage, but at the bottom of the bag were polaroid pictures of girls... in umm, well, compromising situations..." I said.

"Okay, that might be something. But they were yelling at some guy and threatening him in the field. If they are the ones doing that, like, how bad is the stuff that guy was doing? I mean they shot at him and if they are potentially raping girls, I don't get it," Adam said.

"True. I don't know, but that has something to do with all of it. We need to figure out who the guy was in the chair. Mandy has the list of everyone who attended camp last summer, and unless that necklace fell off of Sunny or Jason, it belongs to the guy in the chair. Maybe if we figure that out, we can make sense of all of this," I said.

"It's not Jason's necklace, he had it on at practice today. But you are right, that is a big piece to all of this. Also, Ryan wants to meet up tonight, but I need to get home and have tons of shit to do. I know I can get more out of him, so I am going to meet him tomorrow. I don't know if he knows about the truck yet, so I am going to play completely dumb. I'll offer to pick him up, so maybe I can figure out where he is staying. Also, Zach is coming over tomorrow, and said he would help me with some stuff... but I didn't tell him what the stuff was. So, we will see. Okay, I am leaving my buddy's house now, stopping by the video store and then home. Get some sleep and let's talk in the morning. It's supposed to rain, so practice is cancelled if it is, so maybe I can get with Ryan early before Zach gets in town," Adam said.

"Sounds good, night," I said and hung up.

I picked the phone back up and dialed Mandy. She must have been waiting by the phone, as she picked up after one ring.

"Hey, Mandy, sorry, I have been asleep all day. Did you find anything out?" I asked.

"Monty, I didn't mean to stalk you, I think I called you like five times, but this is huge, and I just didn't know what to do," Mandy said frantically.

"Okay, I am here, what's going on?" I asked while worried from the sheer concern in her voice.

As I listened to Mandy, she obviously was taking all of this very seriously. She of course took tons of notes and read them back to me. It took me a minute to realize I needed to sit up and focus on what she was saying, as I didn't realize it was a novel of information, but all worth knowing. I leaned into her words, and she was right, it was a lot to take.

She began with how she was able to get the information and that alone showed Mandy's true dedication to finding answers. Mandy went into detail, explaining every minute of her day. It started as she went to the church to start digging and Tate was there with the secretary, Diane. She just told them she wanted to look over the summer camps from this year and going back a few years, to go over attendance, activities, fees, and overall feedback to see if she could find a way to get attendance up, and in turn, make a little more money for the church. Diane said it wasn't a problem and gave her a stack of folders. Diane sort of gave Mandy the go ahead to go through whatever she needed, which was exactly what we needed.

Diane sat Mandy at a desk behind hers, in front of Tate's office and apologized profusely about the filing lacking organization. The files were all loose and just filled with the enrollment sheets but no master copy. Mandy, of course, offered to type them up as she sorted them and would place a summer roster sheet in each fold when she was done. Only Mandy would be so obsessive of the lack of structure in the files that instead of just looking for what she needed, she also organizing the entire system for the church so she could leave for the day and not stress about the messy files for weeks on end.

Diane was super grateful and said lunch was on her for all Mandy's help. Tate also offered to help if Mandy needed it, since he ran the past three years. The plan was going smoothly from the start so as I listened to Mandy, I knew there was a twist coming.

"Monty, here is where it got weird as soon as I started digging. I pulled 1995 first, because we know that is the year of those necklaces. This year it was the trucker hats, so I wasn't as concerned about 1996. As soon as I got started, Diane left to grab us lunch from the deli in town, so it was just me and Tate in the office. The phone kept ringing, and Tate was already on the phone, so I motioned into his office to see if he wanted me to answer it and he nodded yes, and smiled, so I did. I picked up the phone and it was a man, very angry, calling me Diane, and he was demanding to talk to Tate. He was frantic, rude, and practically yelling into the phone. I tried getting his attention and told him this was not Diane; I was just helping out in the office while she ran out to lunch and told the man Tate was already on another call. He kept screaming, saying he would wait and if he didn't get on the phone, he would drive over here right now and make Tate talk to him.

"I thought this was strange, so I asked who I was speaking with, and he said it was none of my business and just to tell Tate to pick up. I asked again and said I was not going to bother him on his call without knowing who was demanding to speak with him, and he again refused. So, I got very stern and said that I was going to hang up on him if he didn't calm down and give me his name immediately... it was completely out of my character, but he had my blood boiling with how incredibly rude he was being. He finally said to just tell Tate it's an old roommate, and if he didn't stop avoiding his calls, he would be outside the church waiting for him. So, I told him that Tate was finishing his call and leaving, so coming by here would be pointless. This wasn't true Monty, but this guy sounded crazy, and I didn't want him showing up when I was there. He told me to tell Tate he was out of patience, and he would tell everyone what he knows, if he didn't call him back. He left me his number, and hung up," Mandy said.

"No name?" I asked.

"Monty, listen, I am not done. It gets crazier. Just a few minutes after the man hung up on me, Tate was off the phone, so I walked into his office and told him about the call. Before I could say it was his old roommate, he told me that some crazy man keeps calling here to talk to him and Diane will not patch him through until he calms down. He refuses and always hangs up. It's been happening for a few weeks, but he has never shown up, so he thinks it's either someone pranking him or something like that. I then said, well, he didn't give me a name, but I demanded he told me who he was, and he said it was his old roommate.

"Monty, Tate paused for a long minute and looked at me and asked if he gave any more details about who he was, but the man didn't. Tate said he lived with a few guys over the years before moving here, but none of them would ever act like that, so he looked very confused. Then he sort of stopped in his tracks and looked at me and said he thought he might know who it was. He looked concerned and before he said anything else, I handed him the phone number. He was in total disbelief, he said he had never left a number with Diane before. I asked if he was going to call him back and he said not right now, he had to think about it. He then shut his door and didn't come out for another few hours… it was super bizarre," Mandy said.

"That is so weird… you and I know he is minster Bailey's stepson and he moved here in hiding, so this means that someone found him. This is really bad, Mandy," I said.

"I know, that is why I had to tell you, but there is even more… it was a day, I am telling you. I started going through the 1995 enrollment forms and it is everyone we know. The camps are always divided between girls and boys and then we have those shared activities, but not everyone attends, so I was hoping maybe there was someone we never saw who attended, but nothing. I was going through the names, and it was almost all kids we know, and your family were like all the male counselors. A few names sound familiar, but I can't picture a face so maybe one of them, but they were young, so not sure it makes any sense. No one from memory that would fit that description you have, I don't think. If it was someone from that camp, we had to know them…which freaks me out even more. I made a roster sheet and made a copy for us, so I have it if you want to go over it tomorrow," Mandy said.

"Adam made a good point earlier; it could be Sunny's necklace as well. He was in the field, so his could have fallen off and maybe that is why he was looking all over the ground before they left. I don't know. Jason had his on today, Adam said, so it's not his. The call for Tate adds a new twist, but the roster might be a dead-end unfortunately," I said.

"Yeah, sucks because I feel like we are just going in circles on this. One more thing you need to know... When I was leaving the church, Diane thanked me profusely and gave me this little change purse as a present for my help. I guess it's a sample for next summer's goodie bags; it was very sweet and thoughtful. I was walking around the back of the church where I left my bike looking at it, not paying attention and walked right into Ryan. I know you know he is back, but no one else does, I didn't think. He was definitely trying to be in disguise as it was about ninety out and he had a hooded sweatshirt on, baggy jeans, a backpack, and sunglasses, I barely recognized him. I was startled and said excuse me, and he looked right at me, as I went to say his name, he just ran off... Monty, it was very strange," Mandy said.

"Ryan was at the church... what the hell was he doing there in the middle of the day?" I asked.

"He was behind it, and he never came inside while I was there. When he ran off, he headed down the hill toward the cemetery. He looked like he was either looking for something or waiting for someone, but that person was not me and he was spooked. Whatever he has going on is super dubious. I peddled home as fast as I could. I would have just gone to your house, but you were sick," Mandy said.

We finished up the call and decided to meet up tomorrow around lunch time. I needed to call Hunter, but I could barely keep my eyes open. I looked over at my clock and it was seven o three and he said not to call until after seven. I thought maybe I could take a quick nap before calling him back because I was fading fast, then the phone rang.

Dad knocked on my door and opened it slightly to say Hunter was on the phone for me. *There goes my power nap.* But maybe he had some news that might be more useful than the dead-end roster. I smiled at Dad and said thank you, then picked up.

As I waited for Dad to hang up from the living room, I could hear Hunter breathing heavily, like he just got done running. I heard the click from him hanging up and just started with 'hello.' "Mandy! Where have you been all day?" Hunter demanded with a very coarse tone.

"Hunter, I have been so sick since last night, I have just been in bed. I am just now trying to get all caught up, but I still feel like garbage," I said.

"Listen, I couldn't even get Jason to mention a party, let alone invite me to it. Which is weird. That guy is not great at keeping secrets and if it was just a party, he would say so and just not invite people he didn't want to come. I saw him talking to your brother today at practice then Adam left and didn't shower with everyone after. I went into the locker room and just tried to listen to anything Jason was talking about, but he wasn't saying anything at all. The only thing I heard is that he has a date with Eve, but he didn't say when or offer any details... again, weird. You know Jason, he is slimy and if he is taking a hot girl out, he is going to talk about it," Hunter said.

"Oh, so you think my sister is hot?" I asked with a chuckle. "Oh Monty, come on, you know what I mean. Focus. So, after I couldn't get anything from him today about a party or anything at the farmhouse, I decided to follow him... by the way, my mom is pissed at me, because I was gone all day and I never told her where I was, so I might be grounded now, waiting to hear my punishment... but I think it was worth it. I knew Jason and some

257

guys were going out to the public pool up north and some said they were heading to the mall after. So, I convinced one of my buddies with a car to do the same. We went to the pool and there were tons of kids from school there, and the entire place was packed. My buddy saw some people he knew, so he went off with them for a bit and I sat by the snack stand at a table with an umbrella just trying to see Jason when he got there. As soon as Jason showed up, your cousins soon followed," Hunter said.

"Who, Sunny and Daniel?" I asked.

"No, Sunny and Ryan. They were just past the entrance around the corner by the showers. I was close by them and could see what was going on, but it was really hard to hear. I watched Ryan hand Jason a small cloth bag and Sunny then handed him some cash, rolled up. Jason immediately shoved it all into his backpack and then something went down between him and Ryan. Ryan was visibly upset, and Sunny had to separate the two of them. I tried to listen to what they were saying and all I could hear was Ryan telling Jason to stick to the plan and go to where they all decided on Friday. Then Sunny said something about a gun and that it was where he left it for him. Jason was nodding and seemed to agree, and I couldn't hear what he said, but it was something about time, or what time or where this time… Monty, I tried but there were just tons of kids splashing and laughing, I just couldn't understand," Hunter said.

"What do you think was in the cloth bag, was it small like to hold drugs, or like small to hold weapons, or what?" I asked.

"I didn't think it was drugs, it was bigger than that. It looked heavy like it held equipment or something. It was a little smaller than a plastic grocery bag. But when they handed it to him, he freaked a little. But Monty, you won't believe what I did," Hunter said.

"Oh, Hunter, what in the world did you do? You have me freaking out over here," I said.

"Well, Jason put his backpack under a lounge chair and threw a towel on top of the chair, so you couldn't really see the bag. He then went down to the area where all the girls were and was being his sleezy self, so I grabbed his bag," Hunter said.

"What in the world! Did he catch you?" I screamed.

"No, but I ran into the bathrooms and locked myself in a stall to go through it all. It was five hundred dollars in cash and in the bag, well, it was really bad Monty. It was a polaroid camera, some pictures, and a bullet shell. The pictures were of Jason standing next to girls, passed out and some of them, well, what he was doing was illegal. That's all I am going to say. I know Jason is a bad guy, but he is worse than I thought. This bag, I think, was blackmail on him. There were also pictures of some other guy, but no face doing some of the same things. I was able to sneak his bag back under the chair before he noticed it was gone. My buddy wanted to stay longer, and I actually hitched a ride to the mall with your cousin Sunny. Ryan wasn't with him any more, but Sunny saw me and said 'hi' and asked what I was up to. I said I was going to head over to the mall, and he said he was too and offered me a ride," Hunter said.

"Hunter, are you completely mad? After seeing what was in the bag, you know they are up to illegal shit, and you ride with them? I don't believe you; you could get yourself killed for all you know," I screamed.

"Well, the risk was worth it. Guess what Sunny asked me to on Friday… a small, little party at the old farmhouse. He said it's super hush, and no one knows about it, and I can't bring anyone. It is going to start a little later than Jason had planned, because they have some stuff to do before, but I can swing over at ten-

259

thirty, alone. I said I would try, and he sort of fist-bumped me and dropped me off. He was heading over to the food court to meet up with some more people, and I didn't see him again," Hunter said.

"I am still pissed at you, but holy shit, my idiot cousin invited you. But what the hell are they all doing before the party that it is all pushed until later, I wonder," I asked.

"I am not sure, but I am not sneaking around to find out. I will go to the party, but you have to wait in the field. I think whatever they have planned is bad and I need to be ready to get the hell out of there and may even need an alibi," Hunter said.

"Are we insane? Should we just go to the cops and call them out on the party?" I asked.

"I thought about that too, but only a handful of people are invited and if cops show up, they will know someone snitched and with how fucked up all of this is, I don't want them coming after me. I wish I could bring my camera, but Sunny said it was super exclusive and they are carefully watching everyone and everything coming in, so I can't risk it," Hunter said.

"Today just feels overwhelming, and I still feel awful, so I am going to try to get some more sleep. If I am feeling up to it, I am going to meet Mandy around lunchtime. We haven't decided where yet, but if you are not grounded for life, maybe you can join," I said.

"Sounds good, feel better Monty," Hunter said.

We both hung up and I closed my eyes while dragging my arm back under my pillow. I was done and just needed to rest some more. My body was still achy and all I could think about was sleeping. There was so much that happened today, but I couldn't even process it all, I just needed sleep and then could have a fresh start tomorrow. Before I dozed off, I kept thinking about one part of what Hunter said over and over again, that Ryan got into an argument with Jason. It was a small detail, but it stood out. It seemed like whatever was going on, Ryan had the upper hand, so why pick a fight? I wrote that down in my notepad just in case my deliriously sick brain forgot. It might not mean anything, but I guess I'll find out.

I glanced at the clock one last time and it said seven-forty-seven... and that was the last thing I remembered until I woke the next day.

Chapter Twelve

Blackmail

The next morning, my head was still aching, but I felt surprisingly better. Before I did anything, I had to brush my teeth and take a long hot shower because I felt gross all over. I was still not one hundred percent back to normal, but I was getting there. I got dressed and went out to the kitchen to find the entire family; and it was complete madness. Dad was still there, and Adam and Eve were even sitting at the table. The twins were fighting over the last of the orange juice, while Aunt Janet was drinking her coffee and laughing at the chaos. As soon as Mom saw me, she ran over to feel my forehead and was relieved that my fever was gone. She then snatched the cup of orange juice that Delilah argued away from Simon and gave it to me. She rushed me to a seat and told me to take it easy while she made me some toast and berries. I didn't mind being catered to like this, it was really nice, and when I am sick, my mom can still make everything so much better.

While I sat at the table, I noticed it was another rainy day, with dark skies and the wind was really picking up out there. You could see the branches of the trees swaying while rain hit hard against the windows. I was in a trance staring out the window when my mom placed my breakfast in front of me and two pills.

"Mom, what are these?" I asked.

"You look a lot better, but I want you to feel better too. They are cold and flu pills, should help you continue to feel on the up and up today. But eat some breakfast before taking them, so they don't upset your stomach," she said.

I did as she asked and was willing to do anything to feel better than yesterday. Once I finished eating, I sort of looked around and everyone was acting a bit strange, well, other than the twins. They were arguing as usual and deciding which puzzle to work on today. I didn't know what I missed while being near death the past thirty-six hours, but something was up.

"Hey, so what has everyone been up to since my sudden, sick departure the other night? I feel like I need to be updated on the Patterson household drama," I said with a giggle.

"Well, Zach is coming over today, which is very exciting, and I am making lasagna, if that is newsworthy enough for you," Mom said.

"I am going to watch your mom make lasagna while critiquing her sauce, because you all know that I am part Italian and she should listen to me," Aunt Janet said while making herself laugh out loud.

Adam seemed distracted and Eve just acted annoyed when anyone spoke.

"Rebecca, I need to head out to two job sites this morning but should be an easy day with the rain. The forecast says it's going to be like this all day, so only my interior guys are working, which is a small crew. So, I am going to just grab some stuff from the office and work on it here this afternoon; so maybe we could go grab lunch together?" Dad asked.

"Umm, yeah, Mike, that sounds good. Let's meet at the diner at one. I have a lunch coupon for there and today they have meatloaf which is always good," Mom said.

Okay, I didn't know what was going on, but my parents

never got lunch together, and this felt so scripted. Also, why would my mom know it was meatloaf day; we had not been there for lunch on a Thursday, maybe ever, so something smelled fishy. Before I said anything, Adam looked at me and I knew he felt the same way. My parents were hiding something, and I thought they were hiding it from Aunt Janet too. She didn't seem phased by their little awkward skit and just volunteered to watch the twins while they met for lunch.

"I can stay with the twins today. I brought a few books to read while here and haven't done much reading, but with you guys gone, me and the twins can do puzzles, read, and snack on candy and soda," Aunt Janet said while winking at the twins.

"Janet, please don't fill them with sugar all day! We have lots of great fruit and healthy snacks for them to choose from," Mom said.

No one answered Mom; everyone just sort of laughed and nodded, knowing that Aunt Janet was going to play by her own rules if left in charge.

"Monty, I want you to take it easy today. Maybe lay down some more this morning and just drink lots of liquids. Don't overdo it, promise me," Mom said while looking at me like I was still her baby.

"Of course, Mom. I am much better, but still not back to normal. I am going to go lay down and maybe watch some T.V.," I said.

Everyone got up from breakfast and scattered all over the house. Eve was acting strange, and I knew something was wrong. I stopped by my room to grab a sweatshirt and headed down to her room to see if she was okay. As I knocked on the door, I saw Adam was already in there.

"Oh my God, you guys I am fine. Look, I was going to go

out with Jason tomorrow and he just totally cancelled on me. There was some secret party and he asked me to come, and he said it's cancelled now or whatever, so we are not going to hang out," Eve said.

"Oh, the party is cancelled? Huh. Umm, why don't you guys go do something else instead?" Adam asked while sounding very interested.

"He said he has something he needs to do now and maybe we can catch a movie or something on Saturday. He was acting super weird, so I don't even care. Just annoyed because all my friends have plans tomorrow, and now I am just a loser with nothing to do," Eve said.

"Eve, you are not a loser, he is. He is so sketchy; be glad he is busy. Every guy in school is obsessed with you, pick anyone else and they will jump to hang out with you," I said.

"Thanks Monty... hey, Adam, do you think that guy Paul you play with is seeing anyone?" Eve asked.

That was super-fast. I didn't think she even liked Jason, he is just ogled by all other girls, so he seemed appealing, but the reality was that he was awful.

"Eve, yeah, Paul is single and has asked me about you before. Look, you are my sister, and it grosses me out setting you up, so keep me out of it. But here is his pager number. Page him and I am sure he would love to take you out. Just don't tell me about it, I do not want to hear anything about him and you," Adam said while writing down his number.

Eve's entire mood changed. She seemed fine that the party was cancelled and already seemed over Jason. So that was one less thing to worry about. I walked into the hall to head back to my room when Adam grabbed my arm and yanked me into his.

"What the hell, Adam, you nearly broke my arm!" I

screamed at him.

"Sorry, I didn't mean to pull so hard, but that party is *not* cancelled. I got home last night just after seven and was talking to Aunt Janet downstairs. She filled me in on everything, and what the hell, Monty, you didn't tell me you discovered the other man was Uncle Ted," Adam said.

"Oh, shit, sorry. Adam, I have been deliriously sick. I would have told you today, I talked to Hunter and Mandy last night and found some more stuff out, I can fill you in now," I said.

"Well, first, while talking to Aunt Janet, she said she talked to Tracey, but it was a bad connection on her car phone, I guess. So, she is going to call her back today to look into Greg. She also told me about the shit in the truck, which is completely fucked up. But then she said Tate called her last night and said someone has found him and he is super worried. He wouldn't tell her who it was, but he and Sam might come over here and stay for a few nights," Adam said.

"It's his old roommate, whoever that is. He called the church when Mandy was working yesterday, and she spoke to him. She said he was aggressive, belligerent, and demanded to talk to Tate. She said he thinks he knows who it is, and he has his number to call him back, but she said he looked uneasy," I said.

"Do you think it's minister Bailey? I know 'roommate' would be a weird term to use, but Tate lived with him, maybe it's code and he said it to make sure Tate knows he found him. That's what me and Aunt Janet think, she said he has not checked in with his parole officer, so he could be here in town. If he knows where he works, he can easily find where he lives," Adam said.

"I didn't even think of that, but shit, it could be him. Do you think that is why Mom and Dad were being so weird today? They never go to lunch, and I saw you when they were talking, they

266

we're acting so strange and you noticed it too," I said.

"No, they are meeting with the social worker. I think someone at school said something was weird on Sam's re-enrollment form and they have a meeting with them and Sam today at the school. I heard Mom and Dad talking about it last night. It shouldn't be a big deal, just have to make sure Sam is versed on what to say," Adam said.

"Well, hopefully there are no issues. I swear, everything seems to be hitting all at once. It's nuts," I said.

"Well, you ready for one more surprise?" Adam said.

I looked at Adam, not ready for one more surprise, but I nodded yes and braced for impact.

"Ryan called the house last night. He disguised his voice and told Mom when she answered it was Phil from football... by the way, there is no Phil on my team, but Mom wasn't the wiser. When I got on, I gave him my pager number and told him to just page me first and I would call him. He said okay, but he has been staying at different places to make sure to call back any number he leaves, to which I agreed. He called to tell me the truck in the field was gone and he is freaking out because there was some stuff left in there that he needs back. He asked me if I knew where Dad took it. I totally played dumb and said I have no idea and I didn't even know that truck was on Dad's radar at all. But here is the weird part... when I asked him what sort of stuff was in there that he needed, he said some papers. He didn't mention the pictures or the part where there was actual fucking blood in the truck bed," Adam said.

"Papers, I mean Dad said in the bag there were letters, papers and trash, do you think he really means the papers, like something in there he needs back?" I asked.

"Maybe. We need to go to Tate's house and look at that bag,"

267

Adam said.

"Something you need to know – Hunter followed Jason yesterday and he met up with Ryan and Sunny and they exchanged money, a camera, and some illicit pictures, just like those in the truck. But these pictures had Jason in them, where maybe they were blackmailing him to do something for them," I said.

"What the fuck? See, I knew there had to be some crazy reason Jason is involved. I am sure Sunny caught him doing some crazy shit and wrangled him into all this that way. What a sicko… Okay, good news is that Zach is going to be here later this afternoon, so we have most of the day to dig into this. Plus, I have no practice and nowhere to be. We know Tate is not home around lunch, because he will be meeting Mom and Dad with Sam for that meeting. I say we go into his garage and look in the truck," Adam said.

"I have his garage code, so we can easily get in. But Dad said the important stuff was put away, so no one would get to it," I said.

"Yeah, but from what you and Aunt Janet said, the papers were not mentioned as important. Maybe Ryan is not lying, and the papers are really what he needs. Aunt Janet said there were no men's faces in those pictures, so maybe Ryan doesn't really care about those. But we need to see what else is in that bag to see if maybe that is what will make all this make sense," Adam said.

"Okay, let's do it. Let's swing by the church and see if Tate's car is there. If it is, we head over to the house. I am supposed to meet up with Mandy and Hunter later today and look at the roster from summer camp last year. I think the broken necklace might be Sunny's, because Mandy said there was no one we didn't know on that list and no one who met my half-ass description, so it's probably a lost cause. But I want to put my eyes on it just in case. But how do I get out of the house with you? Mom will be super suspicious," I said.

"Don't worry, I have an idea. Just be ready at ten," Adam said.

I had a little over an hour before we left, so resting for a bit longer sounded perfect. I crawl back into my bed while listening to the rain against the window, just thinking about the past week. Life would never be the same. Everything that transpired through the weeks, months, and years had altered the life I know. In the end of all of this, no matter what we found out, members of my family could end up in jail, Tate and Sam could be in imminent danger, and the dynamic of my family would be different. Just a week prior, I stressed over too many chores and not enough time with my friends and now I was trying to solve potential crimes while uncovering some completely fucked-up family reality. Nothing about sitting there waiting to go break into Tate's house was normal, yet, after this week, it didn't even phase me. I'd always wanted my family to be more interesting, but I thought maybe a hidden tattoo on Mom, or a splurge expense by Dad, not all of this. So much had been uncovered, but I worried that the most horrible parts were still out there waiting. Then, in moments of distraction or false optimism, I felt like maybe the hardest was behind me. When we filled in the missing pieces, everything would make more sense and not be as bad as it seemed right now...

I remained hopeful that in the end something good would be found. This couldn't all be for nothing; I had to believe there was a reason this was all being unveiled.

I couldn't sleep. My mind was spinning, and the medication

Mom gave me felt like a shot of adrenaline. So, I crawled off my bed and started looking at old photo albums I had of me and my friends. I just needed a distraction for a minute.

When I looked at them, everything felt lighter. I just wanted to be in this moment right then, not thinking about anything sinister that might be waiting to be uncovered. Fun pictures with friends felt normal... I missed normal. In lots of pictures, I am hiding from the camera, so if I am in a picture, I can barely be seen. I am hiding under a sweatshirt, behind someone or I have my hand blocking the camera. *I know I do this because I have zero self confidence in my looks, but I need to stop. I want these memories to last and if I am missing from all the pictures and I fade into the background, I worry my memories of those good times might fade too. I need to not be so hard on myself.*

I looked at the clock to see I had a few more minutes before it was time to go, so I opened the most recent album Mandy made me from church camp last summer. Hoping maybe there were a few good ones where I was not hiding.

Cautiously, I opened the album, hoping to see a few pictures where I looked happy to be in the picture. I am lucky because Mandy is really good at memorializing everything we do. All of our pictures are just the three of us, because we constantly snuck away from group activities to go hiking, swimming in the pond or to break into the food hall to get the best snacks to hoard in our cabins. Since Mandy insisted on documenting everything, there were a million photos she didn't even put in the albums. She likes to take artistic ones and scenic ones and hates if we try to pose. She likes to get very candid photos of us. There are always a few posed ones with the timer, so she can be in them, but only a handful on any roll of film.

I quickly scanned all of the scenic ones, looking for

270

anywhere I might actually be looking and smiling at the camera when I noticed something unexpected. I'd looked at this album a dozen times since she gave it to me and never noticed anything abnormal. The first few are of Hunter acting crazy and one of all three of us posed next to the camp check in, then a lot of scenic ones. I generally scan over these quickly until I get to ones with people in them again, not really paying attention. As I slowly flipped each page in the album, I noticed that in three separate shots, there was a large tent and makeshift campsite setup deep in the woods I had never noticed before. We hike on the north side of the creek and never cross it, and the tent was just on the other side. Where we were in the pictures is quite a distance away from the church campsite, and we were not technically allowed to explore this far away. They gave us each a map when we checked in showing where we are permitted to be and during what hours and where is restricted, to assure no one gets lost or hurt. But of course, we never listened.

As I looked at the pictures closely, you could see two people sitting inside the tent in one shot, but it was hard to make them out. The tent was far in the background from where we were standing, but there were definitely at least two bodies. In another picture, one of the people is getting out of the tent, but you can only see the backside of them. Then in another shot, Hunter is stretching his arms out to pose in front of me and it was blocking the tent, but you could see the person's entire profile.

Fuck.

I pulled the pictures from the album and slid them into my backpack. I ran into the living room to see what sort of scheme Adam had concocted so I could leave the house. My heart was racing. I needed to call Mandy and see if she still had the negatives from this roll of film or if there were other pictures she didn't share in the album she made. I didn't know who the other person was in the tent, or why it was there, but I knew the person who was getting out of it, and I needed to figure out what the hell they were doing out there.

I went into the living room where Aunt Janet and Adam were talking. Adam sort of looked at me and nodded his head toward the door, motioning me to leave. Aunt Janet smiled and gave me a shooing motion with her hand, so I didn't wait for any more explanation, I just left. I got into Adam's car, which was filthy and smelled like sweat and icy hot, then just waited for him to get in. As I sat there, I started placing trash from the floor into an old fast-food bag and throwing dirty socks and random shoes into the backseat. It looked like he lived in this car and had never cleaned it in his life. As soon as I got everything in the passenger area clean, Adam got into the car.

I couldn't feign my disgust for this car, and without saying a word, he just rolled his eyes at me. I think my face was clear and I was completely disgusted.

"Monty, Aunt Janet is telling Mom, if she asks, that I am running out with you to rent some movies, drop some books from the library and buy some Gatorade. By the time we are back from doing all of that, Mom will be gone, so we are fine. She might not even ask about you; she seems pretty frantic about this meeting, so don't worry. Also, Aunt Janet said that the bag, rope and all the stuff other than the trash that was in the truck is still in Tate's garage. The pictures aren't and dad didn't say where Tate put them, but they are locked up somewhere. Dad doesn't want anything left in the truck. He wants to stay far away from whatever has been going on with it, so she said Tate already cleaned the entire thing, inside and out," Adam said.

"Okay, thank you. I have the code, Tate gave it to Dad right in front of me, and I don't know why at the time I thought it was important to remember it, but I did. Don't forget to drive by the church first to make sure Tate's car is there. I don't want to get caught in his house," I requested.

Adam nodded and took off down the driveway. The rain had not let up at all, and the skies were so dark it looked like it was nighttime. As we pulled into the church parking lot, Tate was standing out front under the awning talking to someone. I didn't recognize them, but it was raining hard and could have been anyone.

"Shit, he looked up, we need a reason to be here," Adam said.

"Umm, okay, I got this, drop me close to the door," I said.

I jumped out of the car and saw that Tate was talking to our previous minister. I smiled at both of them and screamed hello, so they could hear me through the storm.

"Monty, what are you out doing today?" Tate asked.

"I was just heading into town to get a few things and wanted to stop and see if there was anything I could help with for the fundraiser coming up. Was just going to check out the signup sheet with Diane if that is okay?" I said timidly.

"Oh, that is wonderful, but she is not here this morning, not feeling well. But if you trust me, I can look at the sheet and find something on there that you can do, alone and not be bothered," Tate said with a smirk on his face.

Shit. Well, I guess I have never hidden my dislike of people and being social, but that was pretty on the nose and embarrassing...

"Yeah, you got me... and yeah, I totally trust you. Pick anything, I can hide in the basement and do alone, if possible," I said and smiled back at him.

273

I ran back over to the car and was already soaked. Probably not the best after being sick, but we had to cover our bases here.

"We good?" Adam asked.

"Yep, but let's not waste any time. We can't get caught," I said.

Tate's house was not far, but that ten minutes felt like an eternity. I started to feel more nervous with every passing second and out of everything that has transpired the most recent few days, something about this had my stomach in complete knots. Adam, on the other hand, appeared completely calm and unaffected. He started jamming out to Nirvana as loud as his speakers would go, while my ears began to ring. It was pretty unbearable, but I wasn't about to complain. Adam had been so helpful with all of this, so if he wanted my ears to bleed, so be it.

As we pulled up to the house, Adam went past it and parked on the opposite side of the street to be safe. We walked over to the house and looked in the windows, just to be sure no one was there. Sam attended a summer camp through a daycare in town on the days when Tate worked, and it looked like he was there for the moment. The coast was clear. My heart was beating out of my chest. The rain slowed to a light mist and the entire street was overtly quiet… which eerily made breaking into the garage seem even worse.

We walked over to the garage and through the top window, we could see that the truck was just inside. Adam and I looked at each other nervously before I punched in the garage code. The door opened and it seemed like it was the loudest noise on the street. We ran under the door before it opened fully, and immediately Adam hit the button on the wall for the door to come back down. We were in the garage, and we were both panting. We hadn't even run, but I think it was finally hitting Adam that

274

we just broke into a house and were looking for something potentially holding all the answers we were looking for... we just didn't know what that was.

We each took to a side of the garage looking for the messenger bag from under the seat. But before I could say my side had nothing, Adam alerted me that he had it. He held up the bag and I walked over to him. The extreme nervousness made it almost impossible to open the clasp, but after a few failed attempts, we got it.

I reached in and started to pull out piles of what seemed to be garbage, immediately thinking Ryan was lying. Sorting through each handful, we found scribbled notes with nothing really on them; old receipts, which I separated and set aside, some old mail, which I also set aside in case the addresses meant something and crumpled up photocopied documents. There were small confetti pieces at the bottom, stuck to the walls of the bag which looked like photo clippings. There were also two pens that came out when I shook the bag upside down. We emptied all of the loose paper and then I unzipped every pouch and pocket inside of it. At the bottom of the front pocket, I reached in my hand and the first thing I pulled out was an Ichthys charm. It was broken at the top and looked like it was the missing one from the necklace I found on the ground. I couldn't even believe it. I just squeezed it in my hand for a minute and tried to take this all in.

In another pocket there was a keychain with a small key, something that would go to a padlock or locker and next to it, a large key... just like the one Aunt Janet had on her keyring. Adam pulled Aunt Janet's keys out of his pocket, and we compared the two to find they were a perfect match.

"I think it's safe to say that the key we have is going to open the farmhouse," Adam said.

I just looked at him and shook my head. This was just all unreal to me. I finished going through the bag and didn't find anything else. I placed everything we found into neat piles and stacked them up. We agreed to take them with us and go through it all, just in case what we were looking for was super small and rushing right now we might miss it. Adam walked over to the truck and opened the doors and looked all over. Aunt Janet said that Tate cleaned it all out, but he wanted to be sure. He moved the seats around, checked in the glovebox and even opened the dashboard up to make sure nothing was hidden inside. He walked around the entire truck and then just stopped at the back of it. I didn't know what he was looking at, so I walked over to where he was.

"Adam, what is it?" I asked.

"I didn't notice this when I rode in here with Ryan, but do you see the trailer hitch? Was that there when you saw it in the field?" he asked.

I looked down at the trailer hitch and saw the Ichthys still hanging from it.

"Actually, yeah, it was there. I noticed it when Greg was driving away last week. Why?" I asked while looking puzzled.

Adam didn't answer me. He just got down on the ground and started manually twisting off the bolts holding it there to remove it. Once he got it off, he shoved it in his back pocket and didn't say a word. He walked over to the bag and put it back where he found it and told us we needed to go. I followed him through the side door, we manually locked the handle before we closed it behind us, and we ran back to his car. The rain was starting to really come down again so once we got back to the car, we were drenched.

"Monty, I have some clothes in the back if you want to grab

a dry sweatshirt. Can you hand me that gray t-shirt on the floor behind me?" he requested.

I grabbed both and took off my wet sweatshirt and put on his nice dry one. He swapped his shirt and started the car. He still wasn't talking about the Ichthys trailer hitch, and I wanted to ask, but if he really wanted to talk about it, he would, so I let it go for now.

As we started our drive back, I sorted through the receipts first. There were several with Illinois addresses on them, which I found peculiar. Mostly snacks from gas stations and minimarts; the items weren't helpful, but the location might have been. There were some from the tractor and seed store in town that were recent, and the items were extremely odd. Twenty-five feet of rope, nine-inch gauge chain, two keyed padlocks, one combination padlock, deadbolt, different hand tools and some various other items I couldn't recognize from the description. Then there was one receipt that I kept looking at and something about it seemed familiar. It was for pizza, nothing about the name and location meant anything to me, just the order. The pizza toppings were very strange and even though they didn't spark any specific memory, I couldn't help but think it meant something. I took a hair tie from my backpack and wrapped it around the receipts, with the ones I felt were most important on top. Then put them back into my bag.

Next, I looked at the envelopes. I looked into each one of them, but there was nothing inside, so I focused on anything on the outside of them. Some were blank, some just had Ryan's name on the front, and a few had scribbled addresses and phone numbers on them. Only one had an actual address and postage, like it went through the mail. There was no return address, but it was made out to Ryan, postage was dated for May 1996, the

277

address was a PO box in town. It didn't make sense why Ryan would have a PO box, when in May he still lived with his parents and could have had stuff mailed there.

The last bit was probably over fifty loose pieces of paper that were too hard to go through in the car. Looking into the bag was making me carsick and I need to look straight forward for a minute. I was still holding the single envelope in my hand when Adam looked over at me.

"Monty, did you find anything?" Adam asked.

"A few odd receipts I will dig more into, and this envelope made out to Ryan, but addressed to a PO box in town. I just can't figure out why he wouldn't have his mail go to his house, unless he was worried Ted or Lisa would find it," I responded while holding it up.

"I have an idea, let's take a little detour to the post office," Adam said.

Adam completed a full U-turn in the middle of the road and was driving like a maniac. I am not sure if I was feeling carsick from his driving, from reading papers or from being actually sick, but even with the rain, I had to roll the window down a little to get some air. Adam must have noticed my green face and slowed down and began to sort of follow the traffic laws.

Within a few moments we pulled into the post office and parked.

"Adam how are we going to get anything from here? We are not Ryan," I asked.

"No, we are not, but we have the same last name and let me just see what I can do," Adam said.

We walked inside and Adam looked at his options of people to talk to. A young male, an older male and a much older woman with gray hair, glasses, and shaky hands… that was his target. He got into her line and prepared to work his magic.

"Hi ma'am, so sorry to bother you, but I am Mr. Patterson and I have a PO box here with my brother and I am unable to find my key, is there any way you can open it for me?" he asked while giving puppy dog eyes and a corny smile.

"Oh, hunny, let me look that up... well, are you Ryan Patterson?" she asked.

"No, I am his brother, Adam Patterson. Here is my ID, I should be listed on there too," Adam said, while lying through his teeth,

"I am so sorry, but the account was only setup under Ryan Patterson and without him here, there is nothing I can do. Do you want to call him and have him meet you here?" she asked, while trying to be ever-so-helpful.

"I can't, he is out of the country, which is why we set this up, so I could pick up his mail. I don't know how it got missed putting my name on there. I came in here with him and set it up and signed my name... very peculiar," Adam said.

"I am so sorry, the person that opened the PO box is named Frank Tother. He is not in today, but will be tomorrow, if you want to meet with him, he might be able to help you out," she said.

Adam thanked her profusely and we went back to the car. It was a good effort and quite the acting skills from Adam. We climbed back into the car, and it felt like an actual lightbulb went off in my brain.

"Adam! The small key from the bag, could it be for the PO box?" I asked, while pulling it out my backpack.

"Shit, maybe. You stay here, let me go back inside and check," Adam said.

Within less than a minute, I saw Adam walking back to the

279

car with a handful of mail in his hand. Holy shit, it was the right key.

"Monty, you are a fucking genius. I just thought that key would be for the lock on the barn or some shit. The key opened it right up and it looks like he is getting all of his mail sent here. Maybe to keep up the ruse that he is in Europe, but I think it is something more. You take a look at everything, and I'll head back to the house so we can go through the rest," Adam said.

I sifted through the stack, it wasn't a lot, a few newsletters, a magazine, a bill for the actual PO box and one handwritten envelope. The handwriting was the exact same as the one from the messenger bag, as the way the R was in Ryan was very large and unique. The difference on this letter was that it had a return name and address: Brenda Hobbs.

"Adam, this one is from the lady Ted had the kid with. Ryan must have gotten the PO box to communicate with her so Ted and Lisa wouldn't find out. I wonder if there are other letters in the bag from her," I said.

"We need to open it and see what it says and maybe find out how long they have been talking," Adam said.

"Okay, let's just get home and look at all of this at once. We are five minutes away and this is a lot to mentally unpack. I also want to call Mandy, I have something for her to look into for me from church camp," I said.

"Okay. What from church camp? You know I was there, so you can ask me," Adam said.

"Yeah, nothing about the actual camp. She took some pictures that week and I want to know if she has any more, she didn't show me. I saw something funky in one she put in my album and just wanted to see if she had a different angle or something. It might be nothing, but at this point, I am looking at everything I can," I said.

"Okay, let's get home, grab something to eat and let's empty all this out in my room. I have a couple of pages I need to call back first. One is Zach and the other is a weird number I don't know, so it might be Ryan. I want to keep him talking too, I think he is the answer to all of this weird shit," Adam said.

We pulled back into the house at just after twelve and Aunt Janet was just preparing lunch for the twins. On the stove was a saucepan, where it looked like she was also making her own sauce for the lasagna tonight, proving once again that she didn't trust Mom's non-Italian cooking skills.

"Hey, you two, did you get everything you need? Monty, are you feeling any better? Your mom just left a little bit ago; she said she had to make a stop before heading to lunch, but she plans to be back before three. I am re-heating soup from last night and making turkey sandwiches on the side, either of you want any?" she asked.

Adam and I unanimously said 'yes' and sat at the table. "So, Aunt Janet, you don't trust Mom's skills enough to let her make the sauce?" I asked while laughing.

"Well, to be perfectly honest, no. It is always bitter, she never cooks it long enough or adds enough sugar and well, I love lasagna and want it to taste good! So, sue me," she responded.

Everyone laughed. She was right. My mom is a great cook, but her tomato sauce always tastes funny, so seeing Aunt Janet step in was actually a relief.

"I am feeling a lot better, thanks for asking. I am still a bit off, but the medication helped and some more of that soup sounds perfect," I responded.

She served all of us a large warm bowl of chicken, noodle soup, half a turkey and Swiss sandwich she pressed so it was hot, slices of pear and fresh squeezed lemonade. Even her presentation was fancy; I love when Aunt Janet makes our food, she is incredible at making leftovers look good!

We all started eating with very little talking at all. Adam was the first to finish and excused himself to make a few calls. I was eating very slowly; I felt like my stomach had shrunk while being sick and I was full after a few bites. The twins were chastised for throwing food at each other and arguing until eventually Aunt Janet told them they were done and to each go do something alone for thirty minutes. They agreed and Delilah ran to their room, while Simon went downstairs.

"Lord help me. I love those kids so much, but when they are confined to the house and can't go outside, they are lunatics I tell you. I need just a minute of sanity," Aunt Janet said.

"I completely know what you mean. The rain is not letting up, so as crazy as they are now, it will only get worse by this evening. Just wait. You might choose to sleep outside just to avoid their craziness tonight once they have been in the house all day," I said while clearing the plates and letting Aunt Janet take a minute to breathe.

"Thanks for your help, Monty. Wanted to let you know, Tracey is supposed to call me around three today. We tried to talk before, but she was on her car phone and couldn't understand anything I said. This new technology is so ridiculous. If it's not going to work, then why are they even selling it? When she picked up, it sounded like she was inside the dryer. Anyway, I will talk to her about Greg and see if there is anything we can find out about this guy that might be useful," Aunt Janet said.

I nodded and finished clearing the dishes and putting everything away. I went back into my room to call Mandy before digging into the letters with Adam. I picked up the phone to dial, but Adam was still on the phone, so I hung up quickly. Instead, I grabbed my backpack and went to his room. If I waited there, it might hurry things along, I was anxious holding potentially something in my backpack and I still want to call Mandy to have her check her film.

I walked into Adam's room, just as he was hanging up the phone.

"Monty, hey…" Adam said.

"Umm, okay, is everything all right? Why are you all of the sudden solemn and acting strange?" I asked.

"Zach said he just might not be able to make it tonight, he has to handle something first and doesn't know if he wants to make the drive after. I told him it was important, but he is still not sure. But it won't be this afternoon if he does come, it will be later tonight. Which means, I need to go into the farmhouse alone, or take you or Aunt Janet or something," Adam said.

"Okay, I can do that. I feel super freaked out, but I want to know what the hell they have been doing in there too. Let's go through the rest of this stuff and just do it. The longer we wait, the less nerve I will have," I said.

"One more thing… that other number was Ryan, and when I talked to him, something was very odd. I asked him what was up, and he just kept asking if Zach has been around at all. I told him that he usually comes every weekend, and he was supposed to come today. I talked to him before I talked to Zach, so I assumed Zach was still coming. Ryan said he had been trying to get a hold of him but no luck. He said he even went to campus to look for him and couldn't find him. I then asked him if Zach knew he didn't go to Europe and he sort of mumbled yes… So why wouldn't Zach tell us is all I am thinking… But the part I thought stranger is, why wouldn't Zach call him back? They are best friends and that is just not like him at all. Ryan said he was borrowing someone else's car today and would page me later to meet up. He wanted to tell me something but didn't have time just now," Adam said.

"Are you sure he is not on drugs right now? He is acting manic, and what also doesn't make sense is the other day Zach called here and asked when Ted and Lisa were here, if they mentioned when Ryan would be back from Europe. Why would Zach even ask that if he knew he never left. Zach never lies and that whole call seems so weird now. I wonder what Ryan wants to tell you and why there is some sort of disconnect between the two of them. Also, no offense, but why is Ryan confiding in you? You two have never been close and something just doesn't add up," I said.

"I think he is just defaulting to me because Zach is dodging him. He might be on drugs, he seemed clean the other night, but that was a very strange phone call, and you're right, something just doesn't add up. Zach also might be just getting his own life at college and done with Ryan's bullshit. It's like a fucking roller-coaster with him, so maybe enough is finally enough for Zach. I am going to try to meet with him later, I'll take a few of dad's beers and meet him at the park. Maybe that will loosen him up and he will tell me what the actual fuck is going on," Adam said.

"Our family is so fucked up…" I said.

"And on that note, let's dig into whatever shit all of this is," Adam said.

I held up the envelope from the PO box first. I opened it slowly and held my breath as to what it might actually have inside. The return address was White Plains, IL, so she was still in the state, but I wasn't completely sure where that was in comparison to Oak City, IL. I thought for a moment on how Ryan found her, but maybe she found him, or maybe they have been in contact for years. I opened the envelope, and it held a single letter inside. The letter was handwritten in beautiful cursive on nice stationary paper.

Ryan,

It's hard to believe that you and P.G. are all grown up now, I wish I would have been able to know you more through the years. Like I told you before, I never knew about your mother when I met Ted and if I would have, I would have never been with him. I promise you I am not a homewrecker. The stories he fed me were all lies but it's too late now to do anything about it. I don't know what he told you over the years about me, but please know that I was not all these bad things. I was gainfully employed when we met, with a very good job, and yes, I have had some issues with drinking, but I always took care of myself. I was recently divorced but I had my life together when we met.

My pregnancy with P.G. was dreadful and I was placed on bed rest the last few months before he was born, where I eventually lost my job, and everything began to spiral. I never wanted money from Ted, I just wanted a father for P.G., but your mother made it clear that was not an option. They paid me off and threatened me if I made any contact, so I backed away. I never touched that money, I set aside every penny of it for him. It is still in an account to this day.

Your Aunt Helen was truly a Godsend. She helped us, supported us, and made sure P.G. was afforded the life he deserved, not the one Ted cast down upon him. When I was at my lowest, P.G. was barely a teenager and I had no resources left. I was sick and the medical bills never stopped coming. I worked various odd jobs to try to make ends meet, but I was in and out of the hospital battling for my life. I couldn't be a mother. I tried talking to Ted, but he showed up at my door threatening that if I ever contacted him again, he would make sure no one heard from me or P.G. ever again. I don't mean to cast this image of your father, but that is the only image I know. He was frightening and I had to find some other way to make sure P.G. was taken care of, especially if I didn't make it.

My heart breaks that P.G. has still not reached out to me, I did what I thought was best, I had no idea what was actually happening. When everything came to light, I went to Angie immediately to get P.G., and she said he was already gone, and she had no idea where he went. She assured me that none of it was true, and that David was wrongfully accused. I wanted to believe her, but if that was true, why would P.G. run? And not come to me?

I only let P.G. stay there because I had no place to really call home back then. Helen went to that church; she knew them well, and they offered to let him stay there while I got better. I was a mother without options, and it all made sense at the time.

I am better now. My health is great, I have a wonderful career working for the phone company, I am married again, and I am the person I was meant to be. But part of me is missing, because I have looked everywhere for P.G., I really have, and I cannot find him. I miss him. I want to apologize for anything he went through in that house. I want to be there for him. I just need to find him.

I sent you everything I have so that maybe you can help. I am so glad you reached out when you did, knowing you are looking for him too means everything to me.

It's been over eight years since I have had any contact with him; I feel empty. I know in my heart he is alive, but I don't know where you can find him. I wish I did. You have my number and my address, please let me know how I can help.

Please know, I am here and want the same as you do; to find P.G.

Brenda

I finished reading the letter out loud, but Adam didn't react as I expected.

"So, Ryan has been looking for his half-brother and through that, it was uncovered that he was the boy who was living with Angie and David Bailey that Aunt Janet mentioned. He was also mentioned in the depositions from the victims that came forward. How fucked up," I said.

Total silence. Adam didn't move. He didn't respond. "Adam, did you hear me... P.G. is the boy that was living with minister Bailey, he has to be the boy that the victims talked about being in that basement room with them. Ryan is looking for him!" I exclaimed.

Adam just sat there staring at some paper. I couldn't shake him back into reality. He was in a trance. I started waving my hand in front of him and eventually just shoved his shoulder and screamed his name, "Adam!"

"Monty, Ryan is not looking for his half-brother..." Adam said and then trailed off.

"Yes, he is! Didn't you hear anything I said?" I said while giving Adam the most puzzling look.

"No, Monty, he is not looking for him. He found him," Adam said and held up a piece of paper that was crumpled up from inside my backpack. I reached for it and Adam was right, he wasn't looking for him, he found him. The paper was a photocopy of a birth certificate for *Peter Gregory Swanker, Mother Brenda Hobbs, Father Theodore Patterson.*

"Monty, she said in the letter she was recently divorced, so

287

maybe Hobbs was her married name and Swanker was her maiden name. Greg is P.G., Ryan's brother and Ted's son. Fuck… Greg is the boy who was living with Minister Bailey being abused alongside Tate. Ryan wasn't lying. He did find out something fucked up about his parents and maybe he was trying to fix all the shit they created. That's what all of this was. Everything led back to finding Greg and making Ted pay for being a complete deadbeat dad," Adam said.

"But in the field, Greg was with Ted in the truck. If Ryan was looking for Greg and trying to right some wrong, why would the two of them be together? Do you think they made amends or something?" I asked.

"Maybe, or maybe Ted doesn't even know it's his son. You even said they look nothing alike, and he had no contact with him and never saw pictures or anything. Helen even died before the whole scandal with minister Bailey, so Ted probably has no idea that his son was the boy from the stories or Jack's new farmhand. But I still can't figure out who the guy in the chair is and what he has to do with all of this. Ryan looking for Greg makes total sense. Sunny helping him even makes sense, they are like brothers. Doing some side work for Ted, which happens to fuck over dad, might be just a way for Ryan to be setting Ted up. Maybe Ryan just told Ted that Greg is a friend looking to make some extra money and that's how they all got connected. That would track… but who were they threatening and why?" Adam asked rhetorically.

We both sat there rummaging through the rest of the papers, but there really wasn't anything else that we could decipher. There were some addresses and lists of items, and we only assumed those were jobsites Ted gave to Ryan to steal stuff from, so we kept those separated. There were also some papers with phone numbers scribbled on them, but no name or anything with them. I saved those and thought about trying a payphone later to call them. Then Adam picked up a final piece of paper and it was a date and a name. The name I knew. I knew it really well – Bruce Janson. It was Cliff's roommate, and I saw Ted in their house, so he was connected somehow, I just didn't know how.

"Adam, I know who this is; he lives with my librarian friend Cliff. He is who Ted was talking to when I saw them the other day, I just didn't know it was Ted at the time. They know each other casually Cliff said and its more of a business friendship. I wonder why his name is here. The date is tomorrow... so maybe that is something we can look into," I said.

"Maybe. But let's get to the farmhouse now. If Ted has been having them fix it up with stolen stuff, then that might be the long game. Ryan could be getting Greg to help and then plan to go to dad and get Ted fired or arrested. Or maybe they are trying to blackmail Ted... the farmhouse has to be the answer. Let's go now, before Mom and Dad get home," Adam said.

Chapter Thirteen

Locks

It was still raining outside, so me and Adam drove around the farmhouse instead of taking our four-wheeler. Before we left, Adam went into our garage and pulled out a crowbar and large rubber mallet. I looked at him like he was crazy, but he assured me it was only to be completely safe. We parked just past the house, halfway onto the neighbor's driveway and stared at the farmhouse for a few minutes before we got out of the car. I grabbed the mallet, and he had the crowbar in hand. We walked around the exterior of the house, and it was obvious people had been there. There were footprints all over, the windows were completely blacked out, there was a new deadbolt on the back door. As we motioned toward the front deck to try our key on the door, we noticed a long extension cord running to the house. They were stealing power from the neighbors and had tried to cover most of the cord with leaves and tree branches, but the rain was washing away their attempted camouflage. Someone had definitely been here, but hopefully they were not there just then.

We stepped onto the porch and Adam looked at me with actual worry in his eyes. He always seemed so brave, so this was something I was not used to. He pulled out Aunt Janet's keychain and put the older key into the deadbolt... perfect fit. Adam opened the door and pushed his hand back for me to stay outside while he investigated into the entryway first. There was not a noise; the lights were all off, except one in the kitchen and it didn't appear anyone was there.

We walked into the first room, and it was still rundown, with wallpaper peeling from the walls, the floors were old and needed to be freshly sanded and stained. It was fully furnished like someone was living there, but everything looked to be over twenty years old and was in grave condition.

We walked into the kitchen, and it had a new stove, refrigerator, countertop microwave and a newer looking sink. The appliances didn't look to be hooked up yet, but they were in their place. What didn't make sense is that these were not high-end appliances like dad installs in his custom homes. They were very low-grade and basically something one would see in an apartment or starter home. The cabinets were freshly painted white, but the work was shotty with paint drips on the sides and front and the hinges were painted over completely. There was construction debris in the corner by the dining room table, appliance boxes, used painters' tape, hardened paint brushes and empty paint cans. The countertop was an original butcher block, but it had been freshly sanded and oiled. The space had been worked on, but it was not at all what we were expecting to find.

Around the backside of the kitchen there was the cellar door, just like Jack and Edna mentioned. Everyone around us had cellars for tornados, but most of them you have to go outside your house to get in, no one really ever had one inside like this. There was a new combination deadbolt on the door, with fresh drill marks with splintered wood. The receipt I found in the messenger bag listed one combination lock and it looks like here it was.

We looked at the half bathroom near the kitchen and it had a newer toilet and a new vanity that was installed, but the new faucet was not connected yet, with pipes projecting from the wall.

Just past the half bath was the main bedroom, where the floors were in the same worn condition as the living room. There was a mattress on the floor, blankets, pillows, and an alarm clock plugged into the wall, set, and obviously being used.

We walked up the stairs to find three bedrooms and one full bathroom. The bedrooms were cleared with a mattress in one of them that had no bedding on it and a futon-style sofa bed in the other. It was black and had visible stains on it but didn't look old. The rooms looked like the wallpaper was all stripped and was being prepared for painting. The floors were sanded but not yet stained; however, they were all in the process of being updated. When we walked into the bathroom, we were both startled.

The bathroom had not been touched, it looked to be completely original. Gold tiles and matching bathtub, a small window in the shower that had fifteen layers of paint on it. Broken floor tile and a toilet that had seen better days. But the style and condition of the bathroom is not what startled us, it was the blood splatters in the sink and on the faucet handles and some more on the mirror, which caught our attention. Maybe whoever was staying here simply cut themselves working on the house, but my stomach pitted out when I saw the blood because it felt like it was from something else. The shower looked to be freshly used, with water droplets at the base. There was a discolored towel hanging on the back of the door that also had light pink stains on it, which looked like blood residue and there was a single bottle of shampoo sitting in the bathtub.

It looked like Ryan was staying here and fixing it up. But nothing looked like stolen items from Dad's jobsites. The workmanship was a novice, and it didn't look like it was something Ted would be doing in order to sell the place. It didn't make sense.

"Monty, I was hoping this was going to be the answer, but I think it's just Ryan trying to fix it up for himself. I don't know how much he knows about Tate, Sam, or even the real story of Greg, but he actually might just be trying to get his shit together and this place is abandoned and has been for years. Maybe he is fixing it up and will try to buy it or rent it or something. Fuck… I was really hoping this would answer everything, but it just looks like he is crashing here. I am going to give him the copy of the birth certificate and the keys," Adam said.

"What, why? What about the blood? What about the new lock on the cellar, why would he put that on the door?" I asked.

"Monty, when you do construction, you cut yourself; that just happens. The blood was a lot, but I am sure that is what it is. The deadbolt, maybe that cellar is creepy as fuck and the door wouldn't stay shut, I don't know. But this doesn't look like anything is happening here other than he is working on it and maybe sleeping here. I will tell him I don't know where the truck is, but dad cleaned out the truck and put everything in the garage. I will just say I went through it and figured this is what he is looking for. I will tell him I know about the farmhouse and maybe he will tell me what the fuck is going on. I am completely out of ideas at this point. It's our only hope," Adam said.

"Adam, I trust you. I just want this all to be over, so you do what you think is best," I said.

We walked back to the car when the rain finally let up a little. It was still coming down but was much more manageable now. We got into the car and pulled back onto FM250 to head home. Adam looked defeated. I felt defeated. We had a few more answers, but they still didn't explain so much.

We pulled into the house and everyone's cars were there, including Zach's. I squealed, jumped out of the car, and ran into the house. Zach was sitting on the couch being attacked by the twins with questions, while Aunt Janet sat in the kitchen with Mom and Dad. As I walked over to say hello, I saw Sam sitting at the dining room table having a snack. Maybe Tate was coming to get him later, since they had that meeting today.

"Zach, what the actual fuck? You said you weren't coming this afternoon, what changed your mind?" Adam said quietly so Mom and Dad wouldn't hear him curse.

"Hey, man, I just decided to move my thing around and come help you out. Plus, a home-cooked meal sounded too good to pass up. I have lived off of ramen noodles and Kool-Aid for over a week. So, what is so urgent you need my help with?" Zach asked. "Actually, Monty helped me, and it turned out to be nothing.

No worries. I will let you get settled, let's catch up in a few. I need to call someone," Adam said while walking toward his room.

He must be trying to reach Ryan and plan a meetup. We couldn't figure anything out on our own, so complete honesty is the only route now.

"Zach, I am so happy to see you! It feels like it has been forever, and it has been quite the week! I have so much to catch you up on. How was your move? Do you like your roommates? How did you decorate your room? Ahh, I want to know everything," I screeched while leaning down and giving him a huge hug.

"Woah, watch out there, be careful of my leg," Zach said. "Oh, sorry, did something happen?" I asked while backing away.

"Oh, umm, just my dumb roommate dropped the couch onto my foot when we were moving, and I then fell forward and bruised my knee and shin pretty bad. It's getting better, but still really sore," Zach said.

"That sucks, so sorry. Let me know if you need anything. I am going to grab a snack, make a quick call, and then I want to hear everything," I asked.

"Let's catch up before dinner," Zach said.

The moment I walked into the kitchen, Mom, Dad, and Aunt Janet cornered me by the sink. I was completely caught off guard and was freaking out that they had something really bad to tell me.

Aunt Janet whispered low, under her breath, "Monty, Greg is Ted's son. Tracey called me back and said she didn't have to look up the name, she knew it was him. So, Ryan must have reached out and wanted to get to know his brother."

"Yeah, but there is much more to the story than that. Adam and I already found that out," I said while grabbing a yogurt from the refrigerator.

"What do you mean there is more to that, that is huge?" Dad said while trying to take his voice back down to a whisper.

"Yes, it's big news, but there is more to all of this… did you know that Greg is also the kid that was living with minister Bailey? He is the kid that you saw at the house Aunt Janet, years ago. His mom, Brenda, needed help because her health was really bad, and Helen said the minister from her church could help. Helen moved Brenda and Greg closer to her and he started staying with Angie and minister Bailey while she was in and out of the hospital. I don't know how long this was going on, but it is definitely him. When minister Bailey was arrested that day at the church, he took off and didn't tell anyone where he went. It was around the same time Tate left too. His mom couldn't find him, and Angie told Brenda she had no idea where he went. He had to be around sixteen or so by then. He is just so short, and I think they abused him really badly, so he was malnourished and looked frail, so everyone thought he was much younger," I said. "How in the world did you find all this out?" Mom demanded.

"I can't say, yet. But trust me, it's true. Ryan somehow got Greg to come here, but I don't know why yet. I still don't know how long they have been in contact or why Ryan is hiding from everyone, but things are slowly coming together. Where we are still stuck is trying to figure out who the guy in the field was or what is totally going on," I responded while taking a large bite of yogurt.

"Oh, Monty, I know Greg. I saw that child many times, but they always just said it was a friend of Tate's I had no idea. He had it worse than any of those kids, like truly horrific. It makes me sick to think about. Do you think he is here for Ryan, or do you think he is looking for Tate?" Aunt Janet asked.

"Aunt Janet, the 'roommate' caller for Tate, it has to be Greg. We were wrong; it's not minister Bailey, it's Greg. That is why when Mom said P.G. in front of Tate the other night, his mood changed. He had to know it was the same person and he was linking it all together," I exclaimed.

"Okay, Monty, I feel like you are too far into this. Greg had a troubling past, and we have no idea who he really is as a person. You need to stay out of this and let us handle it moving forward. We will see Tate later today when he picks up Sam and we will just talk to him and see what he wants to do," Dad said.

I shrugged my shoulders and walked into my room. I was not stopping now, but they could think they had this under control, I knew they didn't. I gave them enough information so that they would share it with me, but I knew I couldn't trust it all with them.

I plopped down on my bed, picked up the phone and called Mandy to finally ask about the roll of film. When she got on the phone, she laughed at me when I asked if she still had it.

"Monty, I keep all of the film rolls, so of course I still have it. I don't think there were a ton of pictures I didn't include in your album, but I know a few were blurry or just weren't great so I left them out. Is there anything particular you want me to look for?" Mandy asked.

"Yes. So, when we were hiking like on the second or third day, when we were by the creek, I can see a tent over the creek with people in it. I want to know if you have any other pictures from then, so maybe I can really see who it is. I just can't figure out why anyone was camping out that far and in one picture I think I can make them out, but I am just not sure," I said.

"Okay, let me run down to the school and work in the photo lab to look through them. I am free now; I will see if my mom can drop me off. Is it okay if I just come to you after?" Mandy asked.

"Yep, perfect. Thank you so much. See you in a little bit," I said and hung up.

I sat on my bed wondering what Mandy might be able to find when my door creaked open and Zach sort of hobbled in.

"Hey, your leg really looks bad, did you go to the doctor?" I asked.

"No, no, it's just sore. You know me, I am so clumsy, I am used to injuries like this," Zach said.

I laughed a little, but something about Zach was off. He didn't seem like himself. He could just be tired from moving all week, but he seemed distracted and bothered by something.

"So, Monty, what was all the whispering in the kitchen and what were you and Adam out doing? The house feels like it is filled with secrets, so someone needs to catch me up," Zach said. "It is so much; I don't even know where to start. But, in short,

297

Uncle Ted has another son, he wasn't in his life growing up and really treated the mother badly. But somehow Ryan found him and moved him here and now he is working for Jack and Edna, but under a slightly different name. They are up to something, but no one knows what, which is what Adam, and I were looking into. Oh, and Ryan is definitely not in Europe, probably why you two can't get a hold of each other, maybe he is hiding from you or something, unless you already know he is still here. Plus, dad caught Ryan stealing from a jobsite, but dad thinks Ryan might be forced to because he said Uncle Ted has been stealing stuff for a really long time; still trying to figure that out too.

"Also, Aunt Janet is related to some super twisted guy who horribly abused kids and was in jail, but now he is out and one of the kids was his stepson, Trent. Also, Ryan's half-brother Greg used to stay with Trent, and he was abused too, but everyone says he had it worse than anyone else. In a surprise turn of events, Trent is actually Tate, and mom and dad helped move him here. Then Sam is actually mom and dad's foster kid, but Tate raises him and they are all caught up with lies with the school and everyone in town, but they do it so Tate can be with Sam, because technically it is his half-brother I guess, because his step-dad, the bad guy, raped a young girl and got her pregnant, but she is dead now and some think she killed herself and some think the minister did it. The topper in all this, we can't figure out is Uncle Ted, Sunny, Greg and this guy from school, Jason, were all in our field last week threatening someone and no one knows why or who it was. We just can't figure out how they are all connected.

The part that Adam and I are most confused on is Greg is Ted's son, and they were together, so like, does Ted know it's his son, or is Greg just tied up in who knows what without Ted even knowing who he is? But like, who was the guy and why were they threatening him… it's super frustrating because we figured out so much, but that last part just doesn't add up," I said and then gasped for air. That was a lot in one sort of breath.

"Monty, how does anyone know about the guys being in the field, did they tell someone?" Zach asked while looking perplexed

"Oh, no, I actually ran out of gas, so I had to walk home. I stopped to look at that elm tree like I always do and saw all of it. I thought they heard me at one point, but then there were shots fired, but I fell over and couldn't see what happened. When they were driving off, I saw Sunny and Jason's faces in the back of the truck. Then I recognized Greg later when he was with Jack. I didn't know it was Uncle Ted until much later, Aunt Janet helped figure that out…" I was still talking when Zach cut me off.

"The guy you said they were threatening, you saw him too," he asked with tears in his eyes.

"No, I never got a look at him. Why are you upset, Zach?" I asked.

"Just, worried about you. I mean wow, something really bad could have happened to you and I would never be able to live if you were hurt," he said.

I walked over to hug him because he looked really upset. As I was hugging him, Adam walked into my room.

"Hey Zach, I think you lost this…" Adam said while tossing something into the air.

Zach reached his hands up and caught it. I couldn't see what it was, but it spooked Zach while Adam's face was furious.

"Guys, what is going on?" I asked.

"Why don't you ask our brother, Monty? Ask him why the Ichthys trailer hitch I got him two summers ago after his graduation was on Dad's work truck Ryan has been driving around. I know it's been on his car until I guess recently, because at church camp in June he had it on there, but magically it was on the fucking truck in the field this week. And I know it's the one I gave him, because I carved on the back of it… look at the back of it, the carving is still there! Fucking explain it, Zach. What the fuck is going on?" Adam yelled.

"Listen, it's nothing like that. It broke off my car while I was hanging with Ryan one night in June. Ryan said he could fix it, so I gave it to him; that's it. I really haven't seen him lately to get it back; he has been dodging me and acting really weird. The whole Europe story I knew was bullshit from the start. Uncle Ted signed him into a rehab clinic a few hours away and was paying for all of it, but only if Ryan did some shit for him, which must have been stealing from Dad. Ryan wanted to get clean, so he went, and the whole Europe story was to save face for Uncle Ted and Aunt Lisa, as they act like no one knows Ryan has addiction issues. But after a week or so, Ryan left and has been completely dodging me since he has been out. Uncle Ted said he paid for a month in the clinic, but Ryan was released after a week, for nonpayment. That is like the last we really spoke, but I knew he was around here. So, I started looking for him and following him around a few weeks ago because I knew something weird was going on. I don't know why he would put it on Dad's truck, but he is acting bizarre, and I swear I don't know why," Zach said.

There was a long pause while we all just looked at each other. I trust Adam and Zach but something about all of this doesn't add up. Someone is not sharing everything they know.

"Hold on, wait, Zach, you didn't say a word about anything I just told you, aren't you shocked by any of it? This is life altering stuff, I would think you would be more concerned," I

said.

"You guys, Tate and I were very close, I've known the truth for a long time about him and Sam. I also read all of Mom's letters forever ago, so none of this is new for me. I am actually the one who told Ryan about his brother when we were in high school, he had no idea about any of it. I helped him find Greg and they have been in contact for a while now. I think Ryan recently contacted Brenda to get some of Greg's personal documents so he could get his life together. That is actually about the time he started dodging me, when he started talking to Brenda," Zach said.

"Okay, let's say all of this checks out, why is Ryan dodging you and acting bizarre? What was going on in the field Zach, I know you know," Adam said.

"Look, let's put the Ryan shit aside. I don't want to talk about it here, plus I am still not totally sure I know what is going on. Let's just get with Ryan, together... it's the only way to make sense of all of this," Zach said.

"Where does Sunny fit into all this? Or the Jason guy? Why were they in the field?" Adam asked again.

"Look, in my opinion, Sunny is being misled by someone; nothing is really what is seems," Zach said.

"What the hell does that mean?" Adam demanded.

"Adam, just trust me right now. Let's not talk about it here. If Ryan is willing to meet with you, set that up. Try to get him to meet you at the farmhouse tonight when it's dark," Zach said.

"So, you know about the farmhouse? That Ryan has been staying there?" I asked.

"What are you talking about? Ryan has been staying at Sunny and Daniel's house. I followed him several nights and he has been sleeping in the basement there. I only said the

301

farmhouse because it's abandoned, and me and Ryan used to meet there a lot and hang out. After that party got busted last year, he told me he had his mom's key and so we would go and chill in the living room. Sunny and Daniel came sometimes, too," Zach said.

"Zach, someone is staying there, we were just there today. Do you think its Greg, then?" Adam asked.

"How do you know someone is staying there?" Zach asked. "There is a bed setup, with an alarm clock and the shower was freshly used and there was blood in the sink and on the mirror. Someone has been fixing up the place, it is noticeably repaired and that kid Jason from school is supposed to have a party there tomorrow and he also knows it's fixed up; he told Eve all about it. We just assumed since Ryan is hiding out, it is him," Adam said.

"You have been in the house, when?" Zach said. "Recently, Zach, recently," Adam replied.

I didn't know what was going on with these two, but there was thick tension, and I don't know who was trying to peacock more. It was uncomfortable and very strange for the two of them. "Fine, I will get a hold of Ryan, and see if he will meet us there tonight. Everyone keep your mouth shut about all of this, something smells funny about it, and I don't know who to trust, and Zach that means you too. You know something you are not telling us and its bullshit. I have no allegiances here, so if you are mixed up in whatever this all is, I am not covering for you," Adam said while storming out of the room.

Zach just looked over at me with a solemn face and walked out as well. I didn't know what to think, but I agreed with Adam; Zach knew a lot more than he was saying and I was not totally sure he was being honest with what he told us. Ryan wasn't in the field with the others, but knew about it, but why wasn't he there was my big question. Also, if he was trying to get away from his dad completely and was helping Greg out, why was Greg with Uncle Ted? Did Ted even know Greg was his son at this point? Every time we got close to figuring out what the hell was going on, someone threw some other information in that made it all unclear.

I couldn't sit here and dwell on all of this right then, I was still hungry, tired, sick, and just needed to focus on something else. I got up to go talk with Aunt Janet when Eve came barreling into my room. She looked frantic and had tears streaming down her face.

"Monty, why don't you like Jason? What do you know that makes you hate him so much? You have to tell me, right fucking now," she screamed.

"Eve, what are you talking about? You know why I don't like him. He is an asshole to every girl he dates; he lies, he is into really shady things, and I think he is overall a very, bad guy. Why are you so upset, did something happen?" I asked.

"Last night he was out with some people from school over in the park and I guess everyone was drinking and some were smoking weed. Somehow, he convinced some girls from your grade to go with him to an after party, but he didn't say where. I don't have all the details but one of the girls just woke up in the back of the school parking lot this morning, missing some of her clothes, with no shoes on and she had blood on her, but she wasn't bleeding anywhere. She called Olivia for a ride because she knows Olivia's little sister, and she didn't want her mom to see her in the state she is in. The other girl, they can't find," Eve said.

"Who are the girls?" I asked.

"Katie Tanner and Maggie Gray. Maggie is still missing, and

Katie said she thinks they were drugged because she hardly drank anything and blacked out most of the night. She has flashes of someone on top of her, taking her clothes off, but she was in and out of it, not remembering too much. She said Maggie was even worse than her, she was puking at one point, and she remembers there being other men there with Jason, but she doesn't remember their faces. Jason got them to wear a blindfold on the car ride. He said it was fun and the only way they would bring freshman to their hangout is if they kept the hangout a secret. Olivia took Katie to her house to take a shower and get dressed. But Monty, this is bad. We have to help them find Maggie. I tried calling Jason and Olivia drove past his house, but his car isn't there and he wasn't home," Eve said.

"Okay, we need to borrow Adam's car and go look wherever Katie thinks they might have gone. We need to talk to her and get her to remember anything she can. Any depictions, voices, visuals, anything at all," I responded while grabbing my backpack.

I walked down to Adam's room to ask to borrow his car. Once I filled him in on what was going on, he refused to stay back; he wanted to help. We all knew these girls and had for a really long time. I used to be friends with them when we were younger, but as the years have passed, we drifted apart. They are in the popular and attractive crowd, which is not my crowd at all, but they have always remained nice and cordial to me and never made me feel excluded. We just have different interests now.

Katie is tough, extremely athletic and I have never known her to party or to drink. Maggie, on the other hand, is a follower and always worried about fitting in. She is beautiful and sweet, but she lets people walk all over her if it will let her fit into a certain crowd. Out of the two of them, her missing worries me more because she never pushes back, even when she is uncomfortable. She is easily taken advantage of, which is probably why Jason was hanging around her.

I ran into the living room and told Mom and Dad we needed to go help a friend from school. Before Mom and Dad could ask any questions, the three of us ran out the door. We went to Olivia's first to get her take on what happened. She explained that Katie called her from the payphone near the gymnasium and when she got there, she said she had walked from the other side of the parking lot where she woke up. She was missing her bra, shoes and part of her shorts were torn and she was in the grassy area near that back road that the buses use to enter and exit.

She said she had maybe one and half beers all night, as she is not into drinking. Jason took a liking to the two of them right away and Maggie was following him around like a lost puppy. He asked them to go to the after party with him and some friends but was clear he had to blindfold them, because it was a super-secret location, and no one could know about it. Katie was not interested in going, but Maggie was begging to go, so she agreed. She immediately threw her beer away and grabbed a water bottle. She said the way Jason was acting was strange and made her uncomfortable, so she wanted to be fully alert in case she needed to get out of there.

They got into his car, and he tied a long tube sock around their eyes. He drove for only a few minutes and stopped, and two more people got into the car. She didn't recognize their voices and then they drove a little further and stopped. He turned off the car and escorted them out. Jason said they just needed to stop off and get some supplies and then were going to the party. They were led into a house, and she knew there was carpet, because she could feel it while walking. He sat them down on a couch and

305

then things started to get gray. She had the same water bottle the entire time, and had not been given anything else, but after being on the couch only a few minutes, she started to fade in and out. The next parts were all more difficult to remember and she said we needed to go talk to Katie.

We got back into Adam's car and drove to Katie's house and as we pulled up the sun was starting to go down and I realized it was already nearly seven o clock. Adam's pager was going off non-stop and he said mom was blowing him. When we got to Katie's, Adam asked to use her phone first to call Mom and explain we are fine and to eat without us as we would be there shortly.

Katie came outside and was noticeable shaken. Eve gave her a hug and explained that we were only there to help. We explained that she didn't have to go over all of it again, as Olivia filled in a lot, we were only trying to get through the parts once she was on the couch. As we looked at her, tears were streaming down her face. Her hands were trembling, and she was barely holding it together. At that moment, Adam walked out and nodded at me and Eve, so we knew Mom and Dad were taken care of and we were okay to finish talking to Katie. Eve squeezed her hand and asked her if there is anything she could tell us so we can help find Maggie.

"Maggie's mom keeps calling me and I don't know what to say. She called the police and they said since it has not been twenty-four hours, they cannot do anything yet. But I know she is hurt. I know wherever she is, she is not safe," Katie said and began to sob.

"Take your time, we understand this is horribly difficult. Have you talked to the police at all? Have you told them what you know?" Adam asked.

"I didn't say anything at first, because I didn't want to get into more trouble with my mom. But as the hours passed that we couldn't find her, I finally told my mom the truth and spoke to the police. They just think we are dumb high school kids who got drunk and blacked out. They really didn't take anything seriously at all. I was not drunk at all. I was drugged and I am sure of it. I got the water bottle from the cooler, and I opened it myself. But I dropped the cap somewhere in the grass, it was dark, so I didn't bother looking for it. I carried that water bottle into the car, and had it when we got to the first house, where we got out. I heard three distinctive voices, one was Jason's, but the other two I didn't recognize. One of them sounded older, like a dad's voice, but the sock was tied around my head, and over most of my ears, so I couldn't hear very well. We were at that house for only a few minutes. But while I was sitting on the couch, I started to feel dizzy, and I felt confused. I whispered to Maggie how she was feeling, and she said fine and giggled. She was drunk and I just needed to keep it together for her to be safe. The men were laughing and joking around and kept asking if we were ready to party. When they started the car back up, I said I didn't want to party, and I want to go home. Jason told me to relax and said we were almost there, and if I didn't like it, he would take me home. Maggie kept giggling and acting ridiculous in the car, wooing, and not acting like herself at all.

"We only drove maybe ten minutes if that, then we got out and they led us on foot for what seemed like forever. Maggie kept falling and that is where I lost one of my shoes. The sandal broke and I tried to say something, and they told me to be quiet, so I just kept walking. At this point, I knew we were in trouble. I knew they were going to do something really bad, and I felt sick and started to cry under the make-shift blindfold. We stepped up two steps onto a wooden deck that was splintered and had chipping paint. I could feel it under my one bare foot. He opened the door, and I heard them move stuff around and then a light came on.

"When they took off the blindfolds, my vision was completely blurry. I couldn't make out really anything. One of the men kept asking if I wanted anything else to drink, while I heard someone else in the background keep saying to leave me alone and just let me sit there. The third voice sounded worried and kept mumbling something about 'this was not what they had in mind,' and he wanted everyone to go. The guy talking to me was the one with the deeper voice, he sounded older. I couldn't see his face, I can remember his voice and that he was taller than the other two, but that's it. I could see a shadow walking up the stairs and I knew Maggie was with them. She wasn't sitting next to me any more and although I kept blinking, my eyes wouldn't clear. I think she was with Jason; I couldn't see. I leaned back on this gross couch. I remember rubbing my hands up and down it, thinking it felt dirty and was a gross material. I tried to keep my eyes open, but I couldn't. They were heavy and my body felt almost paralyzed. The taller man was on top of me at one point. I remember him taking my shirt off and whispering disgusting things in my ear. He carried me somewhere, I feel like a bed, but I am not sure. I kept saying no, but he kept shhing me. He said it was okay and this is what I wanted. I don't think he ever took my shorts off, but he tried and that's what ripped them. The other guy, I think pulled him off of me. I remember a flash of them arguing and fighting and I don't know what happened after that, I completely blacked out.

"The next thing I remember, I was in the parking lot. There was blood on me, but I wasn't bleeding anywhere, so it wasn't my blood. I wish I remembered more, but they had to have put something in that water bottle, it's the only way I would have felt like that," Katie said and began to cry again.

"Katie, you did great, this is really helpful. The place where you blacked out, did it have carpet too. Can you remember anything about the floors or walls or layout?" Adam asked.

"It wasn't carpet, it was wood, and it smelled like fresh paint inside. The couch is what I really remember. It was this corduroy material that felt like it had a layer of grime on it. I remember rubbing my hands up and down it and thinking my hands were almost sticky from just touching it. But I don't remember the layout or walls or really anything visual. I know there was a staircase to the right of where I was sitting on the couch, as I remember shadows walking up it. But that's it," Katie said.

Right then, her mom called for her to come back inside. Eve was crying, I had tears I was trying to hide, but Adam, he didn't look sad, he looked alarmed. He figured something out. He started walking to the car and yelled for us to come on. He started the car and peeled out of her driveway.

"Eve and Monty, I am going to drop you at home, I think I know where she is," Adam said.

"The hell you are! We are coming with you; you are not going alone!" I screamed.

"Then we need to get Zach, just in case what we walk into is what I think," Adam said and pulled into the house.

We all got out of the car and went inside to get Zach. He was just finishing dinner and he saw the look on Adam's face and knew something was wrong. Mom and Dad were yelling at us as soon as we walked in, demanding to know where we had been, but none of us said anything. We were just following Adam and what he was doing, which pissed them off even more. He ran back into his room saying he needed something, while me and

Eve took the brunt of the parental interrogation.

"Monty, I will stay here and fill Mom and Dad in. You three go and call me the minute you know anything," Eve said.

"I demand you tell me what the hell is going on," Dad screamed.

Mom and Aunt Janet looked worried while Dad was vehemently upset.

"Go, I'll explain," Eve said again as the three of us ran out of the house.

"Zach, you are coming with us, get what you need, we are leaving now," Adam yelled as he ran out of his room and out the front door.

Adam went into the garage first, while we got into his car. Zach sat in the front seat and slid his right leg into the car, slowly, while making pained noises. For a moving accident, he seemed to be in a lot of discomfort and his leg was very immobile; it didn't add up. I watched his face as he settled in, and he is either lying about how he got the injury or lying about what the injury is. I just have to figure out how to get him to tell us the truth. As I leaned back into my seat, there was a knock on the car window. I looked and saw Mandy standing there.

"Zach, roll the window down," I said.

"Hey, Monty, here is what I have. Take a look, I think it might be what you were looking for. Where are you going anyway?" she asked.

"Thank you so much!" I said as I reached for the envelope and looked at her face. She found something in the pictures and from the looks of it, it was not good. "It's a long story, I will call you later. Thank you again," I said while I saw Adam walking back to the car. Mandy backed away from the car, not breaking eye-contact with me. She was acting strange, so I knew whatever she found was a piece of the puzzle. I shoved the envelope into my back pocket and would look at everything when alone. Now was not the time.

Adam jumped into the car and handed back to me a giant pair of bolt cutters. He didn't ask what Mandy was doing there; he was preoccupied and totally focused on finding Maggie. When I looked at the bolt cutters and then looked at him in the eyes, I immediately figured out where we were going.

"Adam, you think she is in the cellar, don't you?" I asked as my voice trembled.

"Only one way to find out. But the way Katie described the couch, it has to be the farmhouse. I touched the couch as I walked by it earlier today and I would describe it the exact same way… also, I called Ryan at the last number he paged me from, and he picked up. I told him to get his ass to the farmhouse right now. He tried to ask me why, but I just hung up. We need to go now," Adam said.

"What the actual hell is going on?" Zach said.

No one answered him. I thought Adam and I were feeling the same way and the less we told him right then, the better. He was not being honest with us, so we just had to be cautious. Adam was bringing him for backup, not because he could trust him.

"Adam, should we call the police now?" I asked.

"No, let's just wait and see if we are right. If we are, we can use the phone at the neighbors. I just don't know what we are walking into, so let's just be prepared," Adam said.

We drove past the farmhouse thinking the small little bridge on the driveway was still broken, but Adam looked over and saw new boards holding it together that we didn't notice earlier when we were here. The rain had finally stopped, but the entire driveway was practically flooded from all the rain overflowing

311

the creek. Adam backed up slightly then turned down the driveway. My heart was racing, while Zach looked less confused and more nervous.

The three of us got out of the car, I carried the rubber mallet again as a precaution. Zach followed suit and grabbed the crowbar, while Adam took the bolt cutters. We walked to the front door, and I looked around us. The sun was practically gone but as I did a three hundred and sixty just to make sure no one was around, there it was. One shoe, covered in mud and lying in a puddle next to washed away foot imprints.

My stomach dropped. I didn't say a word; my mind was talking but my mouth wasn't working. So, I just followed Adam onto the porch to open the door. As we went to use the key again, we realized the door was unlocked. There were several lights on inside, and this time, we knew we were not alone. We walked into the house, and it was quiet, but you could feel the unnerving presence of someone else. I walked through the living room to go around to the cellar door. I wanted to touch the couch and solidify what Katie told us. To the touch it was sticky, grimy corduroy, just as she described. Adam and Zach walked through the kitchen, we met at the same time at the cellar door. Adam lifted his bolt cutters to remove the deadbolt from the door, but he didn't need to use them; the lock was off and on the floor. The door was free to open.

I was numb. I couldn't move. I kept trying to move my hand up to open the door, but I felt paralyzed. I had never felt fear like this before. I looked at Adam's face, and he was acting stoic, but his pupils were dilated, his eyes were opened wide, and his right hand was against the door, but he still had not moved it over the doorknob to open it. Zach looked like he had seen a ghost. He wasn't talking or asking questions any more, but something told me he knew what we were going to find down those stairs. We all sort of took a breath together, then Adam turned the doorknob. There was a small light on at the bottom of the stairs to the right. Adam went down first, then me, Zach last. Each step felt like a mile. Each creak sounded like an alarm. Each breath felt like a gasp. I was not prepared for this, and I felt as if I was going to pass out. When Adam reached the bottom of the stairs, he turned to the right and he screamed so loud that Zach missed a step and slid down the final few, catching himself on his bad leg, in a strange bend that looked uncomfortable.

I took my last step and looked where Adam was looking, and I was horrified. I didn't make a noise, I just leaned forward and puked onto the ground. I had chills all over my body and I couldn't catch my breath. I turned to Zach who was sitting on the last step holding his leg, he was looking at the ground, not even to what alarmed me and Adam. I looked at his hand and there was blood all over it from where he was holding his leg. He had not hit it on anything, so the blood was due to re-injuring a wound. And my heart sank.

He was the man in the chair. The wound was from a gunshot to the leg, not moving a couch. I looked at him in the eyes and he knew that I knew.

Chapter Fourteen

Justice

I collapsed to the ground and had to look away from Zach. I couldn't see anything. I felt like my world was closing in on me. I was blinking but could only see black with tiny speckles of light. My ears were ringing. I felt exactly how I did in the field, but this time I wasn't quiet. I finally screamed out lout as I began to sob. Zach placed his hand on my shoulder, but I pushed him away and pulled my body close to the wall. I wanted to be as far away from him as possible. I was sinking into despair as Adam screamed at both of us to help.

"What the fuck you two, get up and help me get him loose!" Adam screamed.

I looked up and saw Adam trying to find a way to unshackle the man. He was half naked, covered in blood. His eyes were black and blue, his lips swollen and chapped. He had lacerations on his arms, legs, and back. He was covered in soot and had a gag in his mouth and a blindfold over his eyes. There was a bucket next to him which looked to hold food that was not suitable for a pig. The area had some light, but it was dim, the floor was wet, and the conditions were completely deplorable.

I walked over to Adam to try to let the man loose, but everything was connected by chain and a keyed lock. Adam tried the bolt cutters on the chain and was struggling to get them to cut through. They were dull and the chain was thick. The man was mumbling something, so I took the gag out of his mouth and as I uncovered his eyes, I recognized his face.

Minister David R. Bailey.

I dropped the items and backed away, trembling in fear. Adam looked at me, then looked at him and stopped in his tracks. We turned to look at Zach and he was just staring at us, emotionless.

Adam looked at him and dropped the bolt cutters. He started to back away. "Bailey... what the fuck are you doing down here? How are you here at all?" Adam asked.

Before he could answer, we heard Ryan's voice.

"Adam and Monty, I need to you back the fuck up, right now," Ryan said.

We turned to see Zach, Ryan and Greg standing at the bottom of the stairs. Ryan was holding a gun, pointed at us. Zach stood with them. He didn't stop them or try to help us. He just stood there.

"What are you doing? What, are you going to fucking kill us? You are sick fucks," Adam screamed.

"Look, no one is going to get hurt, but I really wish you hadn't been digging at this. It is not what it seems, and things are just a little out of sorts. Let's go upstairs and work this all out," Ryan said.

"There is a half-naked man chained up here in the basement, and no matter what he has done, you don't have any right to leave him here. What is your plan? This cannot end well for anyone, and now you are threatening your family. Who are you, Zach? I don't even recognize you right now," I said while holding Adam's hand tightly.

"Up the stairs, now. I am not asking," Greg said while walking behind us and practically pushing us up the stairs.

When we reached the top of the stairs, they sat us on the corduroy couch while they moved over to the doorway. They were trying to whisper, but the house was small and underfurnished, so every word echoed and there was no way to hide that Greg and Ryan were not happy with Zach being there with us.

"Where is Maggie? Whatever the fuck you have going on here, we don't care about. It's your sick fucking project. We just want to find Maggie and get her home, so where is she?" Adam asked.

"Who the fuck is Maggie?" Ryan asked.

"One of the girls that was here last night. The one that was not dumped and practically left for dead in the parking lot. You drugged her and you did something with her," I screamed.

"Monty, there are no girls here. I don't know what you are talking about. Look, this looks bad, but it really isn't what you might think. Baily is a horrible guy who has gotten away with acts that he should have gotten the electric chair for. But he didn't. Instead, he is out, and out early to do it all over again. I don't know how much you know, but all we are doing is what he did to endless kids. He killed a girl, and he doesn't deserve to live. We would rather bring him to justice and rot in jail than let him go free to do this all over again. Because he will do it again. When we picked him up, in Illinois because he was interviewing for another job in the church that has an entire group for troubled teens. That is exactly what he wants so he can do this shit all over again," Ryan said.

"Monty, we really don't know about any girls being here."

Zach stopped mid-sentence and looked over at Ryan, it was like a lightbulb went off. "Oh, shit," Zach said while grabbing Ryan's arm and pulling him over to whisper in his ear.

"You do know, you are a fucking liar! You do know…" I said while I couldn't hold back the tears.

"Monty, please listen. We don't know and haven't done anything with any girls. But I think we might have an idea of who will know where they are. Ted is involved in some bad stuff, like really bad, trust me. We have been helping him on some side shit, just to get him to trust us, but we only did it to follow him and get blackmail on him. But he is getting sloppy and his whole world is about to come crumbling down. Ryan already told him he is out, which is why he has been avoiding him. I haven't done much more than fix up that damn truck to get him to tell me just about every shady thing he has done. He is arrogant about stealing from your family and he thinks he is invincible… but believe me, he isn't. Listen, last week, I saw you in the field. I was waiting in the truck while Ted was doing his holier than thou threat, and I was looking off in the distance and saw you. That is why I was so startled at the picnic. I didn't tell anyone else I saw you, but I told Ryan I didn't know if we should trust you. There is so much to all of this you don't know, and I am happy to fill you in, but I didn't know who you were talking to and what that would mean for us.

"You need to know, the field shit, was staged with Zach.

What Ted was talking about were photos he found in a bag left on the truck, but they were my photos, not Zach's. But we needed Ted to continue to trust me, so we said the bag was Zach's. They are all pictures I have of minister Bailey and the victims; they are just some of the photos that he kept as his trophies. But most are with young boys, and they are graphic and truly horrific. When I left after Bailey was arrested, I took them with me, and I also have probably a hundred more with his face in almost all of them. I also have videos too. Me leaving the bag was a huge fuck up and so, we panicked, and Zach agreed to help us. He knew our plan with Bailey, so he was the only person we could go to. Bailey was trying to kill me while I was there. I had no one to help me. I couldn't go to my mom at the time, she was so sick and on so many medications, she couldn't help me. So, one day, I called Ted because I was starved, beaten, raped, and practically left for dead. I tried to tell him who I was and what was going on, begging for help, but he hung up on me. He knew it was me and, in my heart, he knew it was all true and he did nothing.

"When Ryan convinced me to come here and deal with Ted, I kept replaying that moment and that is what pushed me. We didn't know that the same week I was set to come, Bailey would be released early from prison. So, our plans shifted, and Bailey is being delt with, but my focus remains on Ted. He doesn't even recognize I am his son for Christ's sake. He doesn't know me and is so fucked up, he trusted me within minutes of meeting him to do illegal side shit for him. He is an idiot, but Monty, he is who I think might know where Maggie is. He has been getting Rohypnol from Sunny and giving it to women he is sleeping with. He is no better than Bailey and I think he actually thinks he can get away with it, because Bailey wanted his victims to remember him, Ted drugs them so they don't know what happened. Sunny has been selling drugs for a long time, but easy shit. He started selling GHB and that's when shit really started to fall apart. Sunny started noticing his stash was low and realized Ted was taking it. So, one night he followed Ted and saw him with Jason and young high school girls. From that point, Sunny has been done with dealing and trying to figure out what to do. We have been trying to help, but Ted is out of control.

"Sunny took some pictures of Jason with drugged girls and

even gave him back money he had paid Sunny for the GHB and told him to stay the fuck away. I think he has pictures of Ted too, but Sunny is scared of Ted as he has been acting frantic the last few weeks. We have a few photos that Sunny gave us, but none have Ted's face in them, but Ryan knows they are him. All of this is fucked up, but if there is a girl missing, we need to find her, now," Greg said.

Adam held my hand tight, and we both knew Greg was telling the truth. But it didn't change that there was a half-naked man chained up downstairs. Zach helped them get him here and had been covering for them, and I just couldn't figure out what the plan was. I looked at Adam and the terror I was feeling was hard to hide. Adam squeezed my hand and then let go as he stood up off of the couch and walked over the three of them.

I was still in shock. My ears were ringing, my vision was blurred, and I felt my entire body shaking. There was a knot in my stomach, and it felt like I was floating outside my body. Nothing about this was real. I just sat and watched Adam calmly talking to them, like they didn't just kidnap a man, chain him up and perform who knows what type of torture on him. How the fuck was this my life right now? I kept looking at the door to see if I could make it if I ran, but I didn't think I could. Plus, where the hell would I go since half of these fuckers are my family who I can't just hide from. My fear turned to rage the longer I sat there, and I just wanted answers. But more than anything, I want to find Maggie; it was the only thing I could focus on.

"Where do we find Ted and where do you think Maggie is? Does he have a spot he goes or what? She was here, she and Katie were both here, Katie described it in detail. So why would he drop one of them and not the other? I can't fucking deal with the sick and twisted shit you have going on in the basement right

319

now, I just want to find Maggie before something even worse happens to her," I screamed.

Adam looked at me and sort of motioned for me to sit down and shut up. He was working on something, and apparently, I was messing that up. I sat back down and no longer felt sad, or scared, I was angry and wanted to get the fuck out of this place as soon as possible. Ryan walked over to me and motioned for me to stand up then walked me and Adam outside. We got back into Adam's car and Ryan got in with us. I didn't know the plan, but Adam seemed calm, so I was going to trust he knew what we were doing. We pulled out of the driveway, and I just stared back at the house. The windows being blacked out made it look like no one was there. But I knew. I knew in there my brother was breaking the law. There was a felon in the basement chained up and enduring torture. I knew that by the time we told anyone, he wouldn't be there any more. They were going to make him disappear. Greg had everything he needed to put him away for life, so what he was doing was personal. What he was doing was not about justice for all of the victims. It was justice for him. I sat there and stared until the house disappeared into the distance. I felt a sense of relief leaving the house. It felt heavy, dark, and sinister and I needed to get out. I need to focus on Maggie right then.

As I was sitting in the backseat, I felt the crumpling of papers in my pocket. I had completely forgotten about the pictures from Mandy. I pulled them out of my pocket while I watched Ryan navigate to Adam where to go. The car was dark, but the light coming in from other headlights and some streetlights were enough to see. As I pulled them out, the first few were the same I had in my album already. The one with the silhouette was there, but Mandy did have more. The next few were exactly what I wanted. You could clearly see a man's face in the tent and then out of the tent, then someone helping him carry a female body out of the tent. As I looked at the pictures, I held my breath. Fear took over my body again. Ted and Zach were in those pictures. They were carrying a lifeless body out of the tent.

A young female. Tattily clothed. She was maybe my age, and her body was lifeless. They didn't stage the incident in the field with Zach; Zach and Ted staged it against the others.

"Ryan… it's not Ted, Jason, and Sunny in all this. It's Zach and Ted. Let me guess, Jason gets the girls, Sunny supplied the drugs, and Zach and Ted are the ones raping them. The side work was a way to get them in to see who he can trust, but he strategically asked you to get guys who had sketchy backgrounds so he could get them to stay quiet. But it wasn't because he is stealing from Dad, they would have no way of knowing what items he paid for and what items were stolen. He wanted this motley crew of guys to help find and drug girls for him." I handed him one of the pictures showing the two of them carrying the girl out of the tent. It said everything.

Adam pulled over on the side of the road, looked at Ryan and then back at me. Tears welled up in his eyes. I think Adam was figuring this all out before me, and this picture solidified his biggest fears. Adam pounded his hands on the steering wheel and screamed at the top of his lungs. Ryan touched his shoulder and looked at him. Ryan knew all of it and was protecting us. Protecting Zach.

"Look, I helped Greg get minister Bailey here. I didn't know his full intention and I know it was kidnapping, but I did it for him. He is my brother, and I learned every fucked-up thing that man did to him, and I felt I owed Greg my help. I have been a fuck up for a long time, and I decided to get clean and offer some

321

value wherever I could. I don't care if it is illegal, that man deserves whatever Greg chooses to do to him. I only helped move him here, but everything else is on Greg. I had him in Sunny and Daniel's basement, and I realized Zach had been following me around and I worried he saw Bailey, so I moved him to the farmhouse last week. Monty, that is what I was doing when everything happened in the field. I put the new lock on the cellar door and gave a key to Greg and I kept one. When I went into the house, I noticed someone had been staying there and some things were fixed up, and I couldn't figure out who did the work or was staying there. Once I moved Bailey, I went looking for Zach. I knew Sunny shot him on accident in the field, so he was going to be in a lot of pain, resting up someplace. But he was nowhere on campus and really nowhere to be found. Then it hit me, this storage building dad has where he keeps all the shit he steals.

"He keeps his box truck there and he has an entire bathroom and sort of makeshift bed set up there. That's where I would guess that girl is. But if I was to speculate, Ted wasn't alone with them. Jason probably reeled them in, and Zach and Ted were the ones who dropped the one girl and might still have the other one. Greg knows all of this about Zach, and he will keep him busy at the farmhouse for a little while. You can trust Greg, but I can't say the same about your brother. There is no phone there so they can't call and warn Ted, so this is our chance," Ryan said.

Adam nodded at Ryan and wiped his eyes. Zach, our big brother, the good one, the one that supported us and never broke the rules was now the villain in this puzzle we had to seek the truth on. Ryan explained where the storage building was, which was just outside of town, maybe a mile or so from the town square. We drove down Main Street, passing Cliff and Bruce's house. As I looked, I yelled for Adam to stop. There in the window was Bruce, Ted, and Cliff in what appeared to be a heated argument. Just like the other day, but Cliff was acting as sort of a barricade between the two of them.

"There's Ted with Cliff and Bruce, what should we do?" I asked.

"How do you know Bruce, Monty?" Ryan asked while turning toward me.

I explained my friendship with Cliff and my basic knowledge of his roommate Bruce and where they lived on the square. I also explained how I saw Ted there the other day, fighting with Bruce and then taking off in the truck. The more I explained, the more Ryan looked surprised. I didn't get why he was looking at me the way he was, but he looked melancholy and before I was finished, he interrupted.

"Monty, Dad personally asked to work with Bruce at the bank. He has been sloppy on covering the deposits he is making each week on the side business and Bruce has gotten suspicious. The reason Ted wanted Bruce personally to handle his account, is so he could blackmail him if he ever raised any flags on the account," Ryan said.

"What, because he is gay? Everyone in town knows Cliff and Bruce are more than roommates, it's not really breaking news and a way to blackmail him," Adam said.

"No, the blackmail is that he is one of Bailey's victims. Bruce went to Bailey in high school because he was feeling different and thought he might be gay. Thought the church could fix him, but instead, Bailey abused him sexually just before his arrest. Bruce never filed charges because he thought it would damage the case because he was gay and worried it would somehow lighten the crime; like he wanted it to happen. Bruce knew Trent and they had some contact over the years. When

Trent moved here and became Tate, Bruce moved too. Dad followed that entire case, and he knows more than probably any of us.

"I don't know all of the details but do know that Bruce brought up the accounts several times over the last few months and each time he threatened to out him and his abuse to the town. Bruce was getting fed up and told him to do whatever he wanted to. That he had done nothing wrong, and he was still going to report him. I don't know what has been going on the last few weeks, but I am guessing they are arguing about that," Ryan said.

But of course, Bruce was involved too. Everything was coming full circle, and all those missing puzzle pieces were falling where they may. I heard Ryan and I believed him. He and Adam actually were the only people I felt like trusting just then. We decided to keep driving and just hope Ryan was right and we might have found Maggie at the storage building.

As we pulled up, there was no way of knowing if there were lights on inside, as there were no windows. There was a large garage door, sizable enough to fit a box truck into. The building is in good condition; newer looking steel building with a gravel driveway and parking lot, a large roll off dumpster off to the side and if I didn't know everything inside was obtained criminally, I would assume it was a legit business that was just missing a sign.

We walked up to the door, and we realized Ryan didn't have a key. He assured us not to worry, as he knew where Ted kept it. He walked around back and returned quickly, with a key in hand. Even though we knew Ted and Zach couldn't be inside, we were all nervous. We hoped to find Maggie inside, but part of us worried we wouldn't and that we would never find her.

Ryan opened the door and immediately we could hear a

clock radio on in the distance. There were no lights on in the main storage area, but you could see a sliver of light shining from under a door toward the middle of the large room. Ryan pointed and said that is where Ted had a makeshift bedroom and bathroom and where he kept his books and anything he didn't want the helpers going through. We tiptoed back to the door, not knowing what we were going to find.

Adam pressed the door open and there she was, lying on the floor, covered in blood. Jason sat next to her, trying to give her water and it appeared he had been trying to bandage the wounds she had. When he saw us, he didn't jump or worry; he waved us over and begged us to help save her. He said that Ted and Zach were out of control and left her for dead. They told him to drop her in the parking lot with Katie and just leave them, but he couldn't do it. He was begging them to stop the night before, but they were seditious and kept giving her more GHB and vodka and they took turns raping her. Ted was extremely violent, and Zach was no better.

They were taking Katie's clothes off and trying to do the same with her, but he lied and said he wanted her first and took her upstairs in the farmhouse. He laid her down and told them she was sick and puking and a total mess they didn't want to deal with. He tried to convince them to do the same with Maggie, but something happened in them last night and he said he was terrified to be there, but he couldn't leave the girls. With Zach's gunshot wound, he was standing a lot and pinned Maggie against the wall in the half bath and lost his grip and she fell and hit her head on the exposed pipes over the vanity. She has been bleeding from the head all day and she needed medical help, but Zach and Ted would kill him if he took her. He had been there trying to keep her awake and control the bleeding, but she was falling out of consciousness, and he was worried she was going to die.

We looked at each other and didn't ask any questions. We sat her up and Adam took off his sweatshirt and placed it over her nearly bare body. We all picked her up and carried her to the car. Jason looked relieved and not worried about what this meant for him; he just looked calmed we were there to help. He didn't care about himself; he just didn't want her to die.

Adam drove as fast as he could to the hospital, while I held a makeshift bandage over her head and Jason held her body up. I had never seen anything like it before. She didn't look like she should be alive; she was, but barely.

When we arrived at the hospital, we all carried her in. Adam explained that we had found her at the address of the storage building, and she appeared to have been raped and severely abused. He asked them to give her a rape kit and I then gave them her name and her mother's phone number.

The administrator asked if we knew who this did, as it didn't look great for any of us. She was wearing Adam's shirt; Jason was covered in her blood and Ryan was offering very specific information, like he was framing someone. I didn't know what to say, when Adam suddenly said, "Zach Patterson and Ted Patterson did this. She has been drugged, raped, beaten, and left for dead. Jason will stay here and give a statement to police when they arrive, but he needs to call his parents first and have them present with him… Jason, not a word until your parents are here with you."

That was it. We turned around and left. This girl's blood was all over us. The image of her lying on the floor covered in bruises, missing her clothes, and appearing lifeless will linger with me for the rest of my life. But we found her, and at least now she had a chance.

We walked out of the hospital, got back into the car, and sat there. What the actual fuck would we do now? I always played like I was all grown up and knew what to do, but all of this, every moment of this proved that I was a kid and needed to stay in my fucking lane. I felt dead inside, and after everything I had learned, I didn't think I would be able to go back and be my fifteen-year-old self. I was changed. I was damaged. I was broken. I wanted to start crying, but all of my tears were gone. I sat emotionless. This. All of this. It had broken me. I was gutted and not sure I could recover.

We sat in the car for ten minutes without speaking. We were motionless. We were mute. We just sat there deep in our own feelings just processing the last few hours.

"Adam, the cops are going to be all over the storage building any minute. I think we should go to your house and talk to your parents. The police are going to be looking for Zach and I think you know now that he is the one that has been staying at the farmhouse, fixing it up. He planned on making it a place for him and Ted to take girls and stay off the grid. The police are going to be there too, so let's talk to everyone before I am arrested. I want to make sure everyone knows the truth and I will own what I have done for my dad, for Greg and with Bailey. I can handle what is next for me. But I want everyone to know the truth first," Ryan said.

Adam turned the car on and drove slowly back to our house. He went out of his way to go down Main Street so we could look at Bruce and Cliff's house. There were no lights on, and it appeared Ted wasn't there any more; but where is he now was all I could think about. He kept driving until he got to our driveway. When he pulled up, Tate's car was there, Aunt Janet's car was there, and a car I didn't recognize was there. We all got out, and

I looked at Adam. He reached for my hand again. I grabbed it and squeezed it tight as we walked through the front door.

I was looking at the ground, waiting for my dad to start shouting at us as the door closed behind us, but the room was silent. My hand felt as if it was going to break, as Adam tightened his grip to an unbearable pressure. I looked up and saw Minister Bailey yielding a gun pointed at the room. My parents, Aunt Janet, Tate, Sam, Greg, Eve, and the twins were cowering together. Bailey was in filthy, soiled clothes, covered in lacerations, didn't have any shoes on and blood was seeping down onto his hands. His eyes were black, sweat was dripping down his forehead and he wasn't trembling at all. In fact, he stood as a statue with the gun pointed at everyone.

As Bailey saw us come in, he was startled and screamed for us to stand with everyone else, so we did. I stood between Greg and Tate, while Ryan and Adam went over next to the twins and Sam.

This man was just in chains a few hours ago; now he was in my home, ready to kill all of us. I looked at Greg, furious; this was all his fault. But his face told me it was something else. He took his finger and drew letters on my forearm – Z A C H

Zach let Bailey go.

Chapter Fifteen

Sixteen

Minister Bailey paced back and forth in front of us, waving the gun around carelessly. My mom was shaking and uncontrollably crying, while my dad simply tried to console her with very little movement not to alert Bailey. Aunt Janet's face was scathing. She had surpassed fear and worry and was filled with rage and resentment. The twins and Sam were scared, but I didn't think they were fully grasping the magnitude of what was going on. Eve kept looking at me, confused. I didn't think anyone ever filled her in on anything going on, so she didn't comprehend who this man even was, let alone why he was there. Tate and Greg were shells of who they were just the last time I saw them. Bailey had a power over them that was remarkable. They were timid. They were hunched over slightly and avoiding eye contact with everyone. They obviously had post-traumatic stress from their childhood and when we saw Bailey in the cellar at the farmhouse, Greg had control. He didn't fear Bailey because he controlled what he could do. But now, Bailey controlled all of us, and it felt like all of their trauma was flooding back to them.

Adam and Ryan were trying to appear heroic, but everyone was so powerless, the brave façade didn't go far. We all stood there, no one doing anything but fearing this man; then something inside of me snapped. I was tired of feeling numb, confused, and powerless, like I had all week. If he was going to shoot us, he only had six bullets, and there were eleven of us. So 'why the fuck not' kept repeating in my head…

"Baily… what do you want? You have us here, now what? You're angry at Greg. I am sure you are angry at Tate. Fuck, you are probably angry at your real son, Sam, for simply existing. But what's your plan? Try to shoot us all, you don't have enough bullets. Try to rape and beat us all, you are outnumbered. Try to purge us of our sins, sorry, but we have our own minister these days. So, what now… you hold us hostage indefinitely? Grace is already dead by your hands… do you want to shed more blood? Is that what does it for you these days? If you want to shoot someone, shoot me. After learning all about you and your disturbing and truly sickening ways, I feel numb. You actually broke me, and I am not even one of your victims. So, if you want to shoot someone, shoot me. Zach let you go because he is just like you. Ted let you beat, molest, and starve his son to the brink of death, because he is just like you. Yet all the lives you ruined, the life you took, wasn't enough for you. So maybe the only thing left in you is to murder in cold blood.

"So do it because I don't want to live in a world where you live. You have ruined so many lives and honestly, I don't think it evens matters who is next for you. But I talked to Ryan and Greg, and their word against yours is you came here on your own. You showed up here to get revenge and no matter how this plays out, that is what the police will know. So, choose your next steps wisely. Oh, and all those pictures of you defiling young boys and girls, and the videos, with your face in them, we have those too. So, no matter how this all plays out, the world will know the truth. So, choose now how you want to go out, because you will go down for all the shit you escaped years ago," I said sternly.

My voice never broke. It never trembled. I needed to say it

and I needed to see if I could feel anything after the numbness that had encompassed my body. I stood firm, staring into his dark, soulless eyes, never breaking contact. I meant every word I said and if this was the end for me, everyone else could be saved. So, I sat and awaited my fate. I slowly closed my eyes as the look on his face said he was going to take my advice, and as my eyelids closed together, I heard a thunderous noise in front of me, then movement all around. My eyes shot open, feeling around my body for a gunshot wound, but I wasn't shot. I wasn't bleeding. When my eyes steadied, I saw standing in front of me Bruce and Cliff. They stormed in our front door and tackled Bailey to the ground. The gun went off, but the bullet didn't hit anyone. The gun slid across the floor and Dad ran to pick it up. Bruce kneeled down on the back of Bailey's neck, while Greg and Tate ran over to help hold him down. Adam grabbed some zip ties from the kitchen and tied them around his wrists. They sat him up and the three of them just stared at him. Sam walked over to Tate and stood holding onto his leg, and Tate began to cry. Bruce looked over at Ryan and then at Greg and said, "Yeah, I saw him come into town on his own. I knew he was looking for all of us to keep us quiet. I got your back."

Sirens were getting closer and closer until there were lights and sirens in our driveway. The police ran into the house and grabbed minister Bailey. Dad looked at all of us and just put a finger over his mouth for us all to stay quiet. He went into the dining room with Tate, Greg, and Bruce to speak with the officers.

Mom called Jack and Edna to come and get the twins and Sam to stay the night, which they immediately obliged. Eve went to Olivia's as soon as the police dismissed her. I sat there with Adam and Ryan looking relieved, but knowing Zach and Ted were still out there. This wasn't over yet.

Cliff walked over to us while sitting in the living room to see if we were okay. He pulled a seat up and looked at Ryan and said, "Your dad was arrested just as we were coming this way. Zach paged him and he asked to use our phone and I could hear Zach frantic through the phone. He said he let Bailey go, and said he took Greg by gunpoint. Ted was trying to leave as soon as the call ended, but I motioned to Bruce to keep him there just a little longer if he could. I left the living room and called the police from our bedroom. I told them I was reporting a disturbance and trespasser in my home and gave his name. They said they already had an alert out for him, and that he was considered armed and dangerous, because someone had just taken a girl into the hospital and said he was one of the parties that hurt her. You did that, didn't you?" Cliff asked.

We all nodded. Cliff leaned forward and hugged me. I felt safe. I felt like this was all over. But then I realized Zach was still out there and I immediately came out of my brief feeling of calm. I leaned away from Cliff and looked at Ryan and said, "But Zach is still out there, this isn't over."

"Monty, Zach is not out to harm you or any of us, and he is out of resources. The police will find him, and we can just relax. We will have Mom and Dad change the locks and we will tell the police what we know and let them find him and deal with all of it," Adam said while rubbing my arm, trying to console me.

I looked up at our broken front door to see the seven police cars parked in the yard. The police officer's radios were going off every few seconds in the kitchen, while mom and Aunt Janet stood near the hallway talking quietly. Everything felt surreal. That numbness was leaving me, and even though there was so much to unfold here, it did feel like we had put the entire puzzle together. It was not the ending I had thought of or wanted, but it was closure.

It hit me while I thought about the previous week, that I said Zach was like Bailey in front of the entire family. I needed to talk to Mom and Dad and just fill them in, so they were not floored by the news. I stood up from the couch and walked over to Aunt Janet and Mom, standing quietly by the hallway. I was more nervous to talk to them than I was to stand up to Bailey. As I walked over, Aunt Janet hugged me tightly while kissing the side of my head. As I pulled away, I looked at them both, nervous to tell them about Zach, when Aunt Janet said, "Monty, you were so brave, I cannot believe you were able to say all of that to that horrible man. I am so proud of you."

"Thanks, umm, I think I need to fill you in on some of it, sorry I blurted it all out in front of the twins and you all, umm, I just had to be honest," I said.

Mom just placed her hand over my mouth and then pulled me in for a hug. She squeezed me tighter than I can ever remember being hugged before. The hug told me she knew. I don't know how she knew or how much she knew, but she knew. Her hug didn't release for the longest time and every second that passed made me feel the hurt she was feeling. Her son betrayed her, his family and purposely hurt others and the pain she was feeling would never subside.

I knew I had to talk to the police and give a statement with my dad present, so he was going to learn it all. But with my mom, I think it would take time for her to take it all in. The way I was feeling, well, I was completely gutted. My world was upside down, so I expected my mom to feel ten times worse. I walked back over to the couch to wait my turn when I saw Aunt Janet look at her pager and then walk downstairs. As she left the living room, so did my mom. She went into her room and even with the sirens, radios and flashing lights, the room felt quiet and empty.

Cliff was being questioned in the kitchen now, and Tate and Greg agreed to go down to the police station. They had evidence to share, and much longer stories. Bruce completed his statement at our house but offered to help in any additional way he could. I saw Cliff standing up and he looked at me; it was my turn.

I wearily walked into the kitchen and sat down. My dad held my hand and told me to simply tell the truth, offer any specifics and details that I could and not to cover for anyone. So, I did. I explained every detail down to the smells in the spaces, the things I learned from the letters, the situation in the field, absolutely everything. I even exposed my parents and the situation with Sam. I had to be fully honest and let them work to find the appropriate justice. I couldn't leave that weight on me any longer. I must have talked for close to two hours, as by time I was done, there were only the two officers left and their one police car.

The police officers commended my assistance and said that my future should be focused on becoming a detective, as my work was more thorough and efficient than many on the police force. We all smiled, and the female police officer gave me a light hug before leaving. She was incredibly supportive, and I felt like she understood why I did all that I did, risk and all, and she would have done the same.

By the time the house was empty, I was ready for bed. It was after midnight before everyone left and I was exhausted. Adam had boarded up the front door with Ryan's help and dad said he would get a new one ordered tomorrow. We were all getting ready for bed when there was a knock on the back door. Everyone looked at each other with alarm as my dad told us all to stand back. As he attempted to heroically open the door, Aunt Janet pushed him out of the way and said it was for her. As she opened the door, there stood Angie. Angie walked into the house, and no one really knew what to say. My mom came out of her room and just stopped and looked at her, confused as to why she was there. Aunt Janet sat her down and told us to listen up.

She called Angie earlier in the evening and filled her in on what was going on. She told her that Bailey was in custody and several victims were here to tell their story, including her son. She said they had ample evidence, were all pressing charges and that Bailey was going to jail and this time, he wasn't getting out. Aunt Janet got our attention to let us know why she invited Angie here. "Angie knows the truth with Bailey and was as scared of him as everyone else. I told her that I would talk with the police and pay for her attorney in exchange for the truth. She could not run from it any more and it was time for her to come clean. She knows that she will probably do time as well, but I will work on getting her a lesser charge for her compliance and testimony on everything. When we were talking, she said that she too has a box of evidence against Bailey. He kept his *trophies* in a box located in their basement inside an empty breaker box. When he went away, she found the box, and has been sitting with it for a few years now. Inside that box has evidence against most to all of his instances of abuse, molestation, rape, but most importantly... murder. Angie agreed to come here in pursuit of justice, but not just for her son, Greg, and others. But for Grace. She has a picture of Bailey with Grace's deceased body and his son after he killed her, as well as a piece of cloth that looks like it was torn from her shirt in the picture. We are going to meet with the police tomorrow and get this process started. For now, she will sleep here, and we will close this chapter of our lives."

Aunt Janet held the box in her hands, while Angie sat next

335

to her quietly. She didn't say much at all, and she looked ashamed. She knew that she could have done more sooner, but didn't. We should hate her for that, but all I could think was at least she was doing the right thing now.

Everyone dispersed to their rooms while Ryan slept in Eve's room. I was so tired, but my body couldn't shut down. I felt wired. I also felt scared. With Zach still out there, I just didn't know what could come next. As I closed my eyes, a million different visions passed through. I didn't have just one emotion about what this meant for me and my family, I had all the emotions. As I drifted off to sleep, I kept looking out the window. Every shadow I saw I thought was Zach, which made me shudder. I finally pulled the blanket over my eyes until exhaustion completely took over.

Six Months Later...

The Bailey trial was shorter this time around, with none of his past supporters. The evidence against him was paramount and with the testimonies given by Tate, Bruce, Greg and Angie, the jury took less than an hour to deliberate. This time he was sentenced to eighty years without the possibility of parole.

When the news was announced, there was some rejoicing, but more of the feeling of closure.

Jason was sentenced to three months in juvenile detention and two years' probation. He was found guilty of several small crimes, but he swore that he never acted on any of the girls sexually when they were under the influence. His actions in helping Maggie along with Katie's testimony aided in his quick release.

Sunny's sentencing was different, as no one would come forward to verify they bought any drugs from him, or he acted in any way seditiously. He was given one year probation and one hundred hours of community service. He said he did supply drugs to strangers and stated his uncle did take from an illegal stash he had. He was willing to do whatever needed so Ted would get charged appropriately. It might be too early to tell, but he seems to be turning a leaf. He has been focusing on school, not being a total dick and is already almost finished with his community service. Maybe there is hope.

Uncle Ted's case was hard on the family. At the end he had seven charges against him and faced over fifty years in prison.

He took an Alford plea on the charges for rape on Maggie and was found guilty on all other charges. He faces forty years in prison with the possibility of parole.

Aunt Lisa sold the house earlier this month and plans on traveling. She never accepted everything that happened, but she said that staying here was simply not an option for her. Mom says she will file for divorce soon, but just hasn't yet. Still taking it all in.

Ryan works for my dad again and has been an exceptional employee. Dad runs a much tighter ship these days, but Ryan works to prove his worth. He has been clean for several months and has no intention of ever turning back. He convinced Dad to let him keep the truck and he spends his weekends doing all he can to make it look and run better. He is with us a lot these days, and he truly appreciates having a family. We love having him around.

Greg still works for Jack and Edna and plans on taking over the farm completely when they decide to retire if they ever do. He goes to therapy now and has had contact with his mother. The relationship is at a distance, and he doesn't want to see her, but they write letters and have spoken a few times. Small steps, but he is trying to move on with his life, and not let his past control his future. His full statement to the police is appalling. He explains how minister Bailey left him chained up in the basement and fed him dog food and he slept without blankets or pillows on the floor. He was repeatedly raped, beaten with a metal pipe and when minister Bailey had a bad day, he would cut marks on parts of his body. He was sometimes left in the basement without lights, food, or water for days at a time and in order to get food of any sort, he was made to videotape and photograph minister Bailey with victims.

I never read all of his statement. The details made me sick. I don't know how he is as normal as he is, but he has come so far. Adam is beginning to apply to colleges and none of them are withing three hundred miles of this place, which I totally get. He and I have gotten closer since all of this, but he has changed. Losing a brother made him different. He is colder and more closed off to anyone new, and he is more protective of the rest of the kids now. He feels he has to be the big brother Zach used to be. He treats girls like queens now, but dates very little. He is focused on family and school for now.

Tate took over the church and is in the initial steps to get full, legal custody of Sam and the attorneys are hopeful he will be able to adopt him within the next year. He told his story and is working on a tell-all book. Tracey is actually working with him on writing it so that it might save other kids from ever enduring what he and the others went through. Tate has to answer a lot of questions the town has of him, but he doesn't mind. He has grown so much in his role for the church and as a dad to Sam and he seems to be doing well. He is talking to a woman the next town up; it is very casual, but he says it is actually the first time he has ever dated. Maybe she is the one – excited to find out.

Aunt Janet helped, as she said she would, to get a lighter sentencing for Angie, which worked. Angie is in a minimal security prison for the next thirty months for her hiding evidence and obstruction of justice. Her testimony and evidence sealed the fate for Bailey and although she should have done it sooner, she did the right thing. Tate, Greg, and Bruce did explain in her favor that she was in the dark about most to all of it and they felt he mentally abused her too. She was not innocent in it all, but they didn't want her to do hard, long time, since she did come forward and help their cases.

Aunt Janet sold her home in Illinois and bought the farmhouse. Although it had so much bad happen there, she said that she was there to give it light again. Dad is renovating it and she is staying with us until it is done. He hopes to have her in by summer. She only had one caveat; the cellar had to go. So, he removed the interior door and had it filled in. The cost was insane, but she said it was a nonstarter, so he did it.

Dad did say Aunt Janet has been easy to work with, as she knows exactly what she wants and never changes her mind. She has good taste, and he will be happy to put his name on the project when done. He is even fixing up the cow barn and helping her space plan for a pool. She said if he wasn't going to build one for the twins, she would, which is so her style.

Eve took all the family attention to build a platform at school for awareness. She is student class president and currently speaks at other schools on staying aware, keeping a safe word with your friends and has been working on an antidrug campaign with the town mayor. She never talks about Zach, but I know her heart aches. She hasn't processed any of it, but she at least is trying to help in her own way.

The twins still don't fully grasp everything that happened, but they miss their brother. Mom and Dad have them meet with a school counselor monthly and write down their feelings. It appears to help, but the brunt of what occurred will take years to fully resonate with them.

Cliff and Bruce came out to the entire town and although it took some time, everyone has welcomed them. They decided to commit to each other and have a ceremony in the spring. Doesn't legally change anything, but shows their commitment to each other. They asked me to stand with them, which I am ecstatic to do. I have dinner with them a few times a month, inside their beautiful home. I always bring a candle when I visit, the scent, Honeysuckle. My imagery of the house was pretty accurate surprisingly, but my scent was off. So, I fixed that. They think it is crazy that I always bring the same thing, but it gives me a little bit of nostalgia from before everything changed. I need that and Cliff understands me.

To no surprise, Mandy and Hunter are now a couple. As my family and I worked through the trials and various life altering changes, I was not able to be around very much. They got closer and with no third wheel, were able to be honest with their feelings. We are all very close still, just different now. That is okay; it's a change I can handle in my life.

Then there is me. It's my birthday today, and I woke up to a small box on my bed. When I opened it, as promised, were the keys to Aunt Janet's Bronco. I don't believe it is really mine. I don't get my license for another month, but Dad said I could drive it into the field and back, so that is what I am doing.

I drove up to the Elm tree this evening where Jack and Greg added a bench, just for me. I brought with me a cupcake, candle and the Ichthys necklace of Zach's. I forgot to mention it months back when I gave my statement to the police, so I just kept it. I put the charm back on and fixed the clasp. I do not wear it, but I hold it occasionally at night. When I wake up, sometimes I forget the nightmare that exists, but then I see it wrapped around my hand, and it all comes flooding back to me.

No one has seen or heard from Zach, but he is wanted. His picture is plastered up places and several women came forward with their experience with him after the news broke. He had been teamed up with Uncle Ted for only a short while but had acted alone for over a year prior. He prayed on women at school and would drug them, rape them, leave a scar on them as his mark rather than take a trophy item or picture, then leave them for dead. Some women came forward with similar stories going back years. They didn't know Zach, but their experiences were at places he had been and the details of their experienced matched others. They just didn't have the mark he began to leave later. A razor blade etching of an Ichthys on their inner thigh. Maggie Gray had the mark which helped tie other victims together. There were over twenty victims so far, but police expect to hear from more.

I think I see him from time to time standing outside of school or the library. Sometimes I feel like he is in the room with me, just watching me. I don't say anything, as people will think I am nuts, but part of me thinks he never ran, and he is somewhere right here, hiding in plain sight. The police said there have been similar victims in surrounding states and think he is long gone. But something tells me he is always close by.

My birthday was always special with Zach. He always made me write down my wish and place it inside my pillowcase to sleep on it, in order to make it come true. When I woke up, the paper was always gone. I knew he took it, but sometimes he really did try to make it come true. Today is an extra difficult day, because it's my first birthday without him, and I am not ready to let that part of my life with him go yet. I wish he was the Zach I knew growing up. Not the Zach of reality.

So, tonight, on my birthday, I told everyone I want to be alone, but we can celebrate tomorrow. Because tonight, I want to make a single wish with my cupcake in my favorite spot, under the Elm tree and begin my own, new tradition here, where I am most at peace.

I sat on the bench, lit a single candle, closed my eyes, with Zach's necklace wrapped around my hand, and made my wish out loud. It was the first time I wasn't going to write it down and place it in my pillowcase, so I just said it out loud to put it out there into the universe. As I opened my eyes and blew out the candle, I knew it couldn't come true, but it was the only wish I had.

I sat on the bench after my wish for a while, just staring off in the distance imagining life if my wish came true. I looked down at my cupcake, took one bite and sighed; reality is that the wish can't happen, and this new life is here to stay.

The sun was collapsing behind the trees, and the sky was beginning to darken, so I stood up under the Elm tree to get ready to head home. Unable to shake the want for things to be better. For my wish to come true. I looked at the bench and the elm tree one last time, then I turned around to walk back to the Bronco. As I looked up, there was Zach standing a few feet from me with a gun in hand.

I gasped. My stomach sank. My heart ached. I felt fear all over.

I closed my eyes tight and dropped the cupcake from my hand. A single tear ran down my face as he said the words, "Happy birthday, Monty… sorry your wish isn't coming true this year."

I began to reopen my eyes to respond but the noise of a gun going off stopped me…